# Spellbinder

MELANIE RAWN

# Spellbinder

*A Love Story with Magical Interruptions*

A TOM DOHERTY ASSOCIATES BOOK

*New York*

This is a work of fiction. All the characters and events portrayed in this
novel are either fictitious or are used fictitiously.

SPELLBINDER

This book is printed on acid-free paper.

A Tor Book
Published by Tom Doherty Associates, LLC
175 Fifth Avenue
New York, NY 10010

www.tor.com

Tor® is a registered trademark of Tom Doherty Associates, LLC.

Library of Congress Cataloging-in-Publication Data

Rawn, Melanie.
Spellbinder : a love story with magical interruptions /
Melanie Rawn.—1st ed.
p. cm.
"A Tom Doherty Associates book."
ISBN-13: 978-0-765-31532-8
ISBN-10: 0-765-31532-7 (acid-free paper)
1. Witches—Fiction. 2. Court marshals—Fiction.
3. Crime—Fiction. 4. Magic—Fiction.
5. New York (N.Y.)—Fiction I. Title.
PS3568.A8553S64    2006
813'.54—dc22                2006005732

First Edition: October 2006

Printed in the United States of America

0  9  8  7  6  5  4  3  2  1

*In memory of my mother,*

*Alma Lucile Fisk*

*August 24, 1928–June 19, 2002*


*and in memory of our ancestor,*

*Mary Bliss*

*1625–1712*

*accused of witchcraft*

*(two trials, no convictions)*

# Spellbinder

# Prologue

*December 2001*

SHRUGGING OUT OF HER OVERCOAT, Denise quickly stripped off the heavy black velvet skirt and tunic—making a face as the embroidered designs of silver moons and golden stars caught the shadows in her bedroom. The things she did to please the masses . . . some of whom had seen *Eyes Wide Shut* a few too many times. Cloaks and carnival masks, indeed. If only one of them had looked even a little like Tom Cruise . . . but his movies had been spoiled for her by the film they'd made of that damned vampire book. How she loathed that dreadful woman back home in New Orleans—that amateur, that fake, that smirking fraud with all her worshipping sycophants—

Well, one did have to play to the mundanes, after all. Although what they considered appropriate to the occasion still had the power to appall her. They expected some sort of show, some nod to traditions they didn't even begin to understand. She drew the line at conical black hats and brooms.

The face reflected in her bathroom mirror was anything but haggish. Of warts and wrinkles there were none. Instead: bright green eyes flecked with golden brown, cheekbones to kill for, a full red mouth that smiled as the tongue came out to lick the last tastes from the lips. Shaking out her hair, she saw the smile fade as she surveyed the tangles wrought by a night of phenomenal sex. It took her four seconds to decide she was too tired to wash the long golden mass of it.

Naked, she settled onto her bed with a cup of hot tea to refresh herself and a laptop to record the night's events. But she was only halfway through her narrative when her eyelids began to droop—not surprising, considering it had been a long day and a vigorous night. Still, she didn't want to sleep until she got everything down while it was still fresh in her mind.

*. . . draped over the lushly padded platform, billowing like a black silk parachute. One by one they came to me, and one by one I made my mark on them*

No, "upon" sounded classier. She backspaced and retyped.

*mark upon them. The masks stayed on*

"Upon" again? No, too close together in the paragraph.

*their faces, and in the anonymity they found pure release of purest passion. They thought they knew me, my face and my nature—and they thought they also knew my body—but I did not know them. Or so they thought. Wrapped in their black masks, rapt in their passion,*

Ooh, that was nice. Interior rhyme.

*they believed themselves ghosts without identity. Yet one day when they least expect it—*

Oh shit, the opening line from *Candid Camera.* She really was tired. Backspace.

*Yet one morning, one evening*

No, that was bad, too.

*one morning, one midnight* (alliteration was always good), *I will see any or all of them again, and know them by my mark upon them—by the scent of their blood that I have tasted—*

Better stop now. She was using too many dashes and her thoughts were getting disorganized. Hitting SAVE, she shut down the laptop and placed it beneath the bed. She was yawning prodigiously by the time she crawled naked beneath silk sheets.

*Let's see how Ms. Goddess-Almighty likes this one,* she thought with a smile. *Too chickenshit to do any honest research . . . thinks she knows everything about everything . . . her and that dreadful woman back home . . . damn, I'm tired . . . I must remember that Chinese guy's name . . . he was something else . . . those black eyes, practically ovulating with lust—ooh, I like that, have to remember that one . . . that moonshine-and-magnolias bitch wouldn't last three minutes with him . . . there's a good reason my sales are through the roof. . . .*

On this happy thought, she fell asleep.

WAKING TO THE SOFT FRAGRANCE of sage, she purred as gentle hands straightened out her limbs. Sated though she was, she still smiled and stretched, ready for more.

"Shh," whispered a man's deep voice. "I want you to lie very still, exactly as I position you. And keep your eyes closed. Can you do that for me, Denise?"

Flat on her back, arms a little out from her sides; surely her legs should be spread wider if he intended—

As a sudden slither of cold silken cord brushed her left side, parallel to her heart, she knew horror for the first time in her life. The cord warmed as it touched her body, and she broke out in a sweat. She tried to move, to speak. But with that first whisper of silk she was effectively paralyzed. Helpless, she could only lie there as the cord traced its fiery way around the outlines of her body. Ribs to hip, hip to knee, knee to toes. Back up the left leg, then down the right, up again to delineate curves and hollows. Each finger and the precise angle of her elbow carefully limned. Her hair twisted aside while the burning cord measured her skull. Down neck and shoulder and arm, finally meeting its beginning near her heart. And then there was the faint metallic scent of blood, an instant's hiss, and a white heat where the cord met and sealed itself.

"That should do it," said a voice—not the man's, but a woman's. "Thanks for holding her steady. You're a good Come-Hither—and I know one of the best."

"Don't mention it. We battled pretty hard over who got to help you tonight."

"Why, sugah-plum, Ah didn't know y'all cared," the woman drawled in an exaggerated Southern accent—no, not just Southern, *Virginian*. Denise thought her heart would burst her chest. *You!* her mind screamed. *You bitch! How dare you!*

"Oh, Blue-eyes," the man replied, a grin in his voice, "the pair of us sigh and tremble whene'er you speak. We worship at your feet, we kiss your ring, we—"

"—are gay right down to your darling, dimpled toes. Do shut up, won't you?"

And the cord was taken away by cool, steady fingers. Denise wanted to shriek, to rip out eyes, to wash her hands in blood.

The man seemed to sense it; his was a truly gifted mind. "Behave yourself, Denise. We have your Measure now, and we won't be reluctant to use it if you make it necessary."

"Such as staging a repeat of your little exhibition tonight," the woman added. "You're not responsible for other people's fetishes, but how you use them for your own purposes is very much an issue. The girl nearly bled to death tonight in the emergency room, you know. And I doubt even plastic surgery will minimize the scar on her throat."

"It's no use," the man said quietly. "Even if she knew, she wouldn't care."

"She gets a chance. Everybody gets a chance."

"She'll blow it."

"Probably." There was an audible sniff of a suddenly stuffy nose. "But we have to make the effort."

With the removal of the cord a portion of control returned; Denise opened her eyes and pushed herself sluggishly up on her elbows. The pair wore black hooded cloaks—ridiculously theatrical, not even worth sneering at—to hide their faces.

"I—know—who you—are," Denise ground out, her tongue like a fat treacherous slug in her mouth.

"Imagine my chagrin," the man said. "Your point being—?"

"Won't—forget—"

"See that you don't." He brushed at the heavy wool of his robe. "Nor am I likely to forget the stink in here. Really, Denise—musk *and* patchouli? And on a red Baphomet candle, no less. Overdoing the lust spells a bit, aren't you?"

"It's no worse than the rest of her décor," the woman observed. "I thought that French Gothic sideboard was going to grow tentacles and attack us." All at once she sneezed, and a hand came up to rub her nose. On one finger was a milky moonstone set in silver. "Damn! Come on, we're finished here." She turned briskly for the door, and the man followed, and with a snick of the lock they were gone.

THE CIRCLE MET IN A top-floor room of an elegant little Manhattan town house. One of the men was elderly to look at but youthful in his movements as he swirled onto his shoulders a robe of deep green silk. The youngest of the women, not yet thirty, was less flamboyant in donning yellow that made her long black hair into a river of shadow. Another woman, blonde and elegant in blue, sat by the hearth sorting a lapful of herbs. The garnets in her many rings shone by firelight like sun through fine cabernet sauvignon.

"They're late," said another man, who entered the room shrugging out of a suit jacket. For all its expensive tailoring, the wool was rumpled and a button was coming loose. He reached for the black robe that hung with two remaining others on a wooden garment rack, saying, "What's that dreadful smell?"

"I'm afraid it's me, Elias," said a young African-American man wearing a dark maroon cassock. "Kate's got me reeking of gardenias, of all things."

"Martin!" The woman by the fire glanced up, brows arching mildly. "If you can't experiment on your friends, who *can* you experiment on? I'm thinking of marketing it under the name 'Victorian Whorehouse.'"

"It'll be interesting when Ian gets here, stinking of garlic as usual," commented the old man in green.

Kate grinned. "'*Italian* Victorian Whorehouse,'" she amended.

Slipping into his black robe, Elias gave in to amusement—but only for a moment—by saying, "'*Gay* Italian Victorian Whorehouse.'"

"Now, there's a concept." The old man shook his head as Elias began to pace. "Stop fretting, Eli. Lulah tells me that Holly's always late, and we all know that Ian's almost as bad."

"As Simon says," came a new voice from the doorway, breezy and warm, like a golden summery day, "I just love arriving in time to hear my character impugned."

"Just stating the facts, son."

Ian went to the garment rack and pulled his red robe from its hanger. Martin helped him on with it, making a face when Ian sniffed ostentatiously. "Not a word," Martin warned.

"If you think you're going to foul the hot tub trying to wash that off— Kate, what in the world were you thinking?"

"Purity—of action and purpose, at any rate," she retorted. "The rest of him I leave to you."

"You smell fairly disgusting, yourself," Martin told his lover.

Ian winced. "Denise had this lurid little candle going—a seated Goat all oiled up with this incredible stink. Nothing subtle about our Southern cousins—no offense, Holly."

"None taken, y'all," replied the tall freckled redhead who was the final entrant into the room. She nodded her thanks to Elias for his help in donning her robe: silvery gray and smelling of rosemary. Her moonstone ring glowed subtly in the candlelight.

"Any trouble?" Elias asked quietly.

"None. Ian's good. I'm sorry to be so late—she didn't get home until three."

"And she's not at all happy," Ian contributed. "Marty, what happened to my candle?"

"Right where you left it, along with your ratty old wand. One of these days we're going to have to cut you a new one." His partner opened an ancient brass-studded leather chest and gathered a few things to distribute among the group.

As the others readied themselves, Elias stayed beside Holly. He didn't wish to be too obvious about it, but checking was necessary and he knew that she knew it. She was still a novice at all this, at least where *his* Workings were concerned. What she had or had not done while in California or Virginia or Washington, D.C., was of little interest to him except for any annoying habits she may have picked up. Nothing serious had arisen so far, but this was only their third Working together.

So he made his inventory. Silvery robe for stability; rosemary for purification, clarity of thought, and, of course, remembrance; a willow wand for healing; a white candle for spiritual strength; moonstone for calm and balance; an ibis feather for wisdom and, most appropriately considering her profession, words. All were either spelled for or inherently possessed powers of protection. He could not risk her in any way. No one could ever, ever put her at risk.

He gave her the chalice himself, allowing a smile as her brows arched. "Waterford?" she asked, and he nodded. "Just for the *colleen*, or is this usual?"

Kate responded to the question with, "He ordered it this summer when he heard you'd be joining us. Mine are always Orrefors in honor of my Swedish grandmother."

"*Et le mien*," added Simon, "*c'est Baccarat*." He held out an exquisite bowl that fit into one palm.

Holly cradled cut crystal in both hands, weighing it. "This is gorgeous. But somebody better've worked something on it to protect it—I'm a terrible klutz."

Elias noted her nervousness, aware that it had nothing to do with the expensive chalice. "Shall we get started? It's nearly daylight, and this has to be done the same night as the Measuring." As Ian opened his mouth to comment, Elias went on, "And no debate about when a day officially starts or ends, either. It's dawn to dawn when you're working with me."

The solemn young woman wearing yellow smiled a little and said, "Dusk to dusk, Elias."

"Celebrate the Hebrew Shabbas whenever you like, Lydia," he replied. "For Witches—"

"Yes, Elias," Martin said patiently. "No, Elias. Whatever you say, Elias. Can we get going with this? Even if you say it's still Thursday, tomorrow—whenever it comes—is inevitably Friday, and I have to be in the office at ten."

"Past your bedtime, lambie?" Kate cooed innocently.

It was the work of a few moments to renew and replenish the Circle on the floor of this room. Kate drew the boundaries with salt, mixed with a few herbs of her own choosing. The faintest fragrance of verbena warmed Elias's senses as she passed. A subtle woman who could use the fewest herbs or scents to the greatest effect, Kate was teasing Martin with that overwhelming gardenia, Elias felt sure. She loved to play with her craftings—indeed took more joy from her talent than anyone he had ever known.

Lydia went to Ian for fire to light the incense within her silver thurible. The fragrance of the smoke thus released was Kate's work, as well: jasmine spiced with cinnamon, exotic and intriguing to the nose. For just an instant he thought about how wonderful Susannah's skin would smell with either scent rubbed gently into it. Elias himself smelled of cypress and rue. Of death and repentance.

Neither were attributable to Kate's sense of humor.

Lydia's movements became as light and flowing as the gray mist emanating from the thurible: inner centering manifested in outward grace. Elias watched her with satisfaction. *Magic is within; everything else is just props.* The maxim was true enough, at least in his experience, but he had to admit that the grounding and readying rituals, with their jewels and scents and wands and candles, seemed more potent since Holly's arrival. It wasn't exactly that he *needed* her special ability; she just made his Work a lot easier.

Earth, Air, Fire, Water called and honored; Circle renewed; compass points guarded by Kate, Simon, Martin, and Lydia with candles on the floor in front of them; time to begin. Elias, Ian, and Holly took different points of the pentacle laid out in golden oak on the parqueted hardwood floor, candles at their feet.

"Have you the Measure of the woman Denise Claudine Josèphe?" Eli asked.

"This is her Measure, attested true," Ian said, withdrawing the sealed cord from his pocket, letting it hang full-length from his blackthorn wand.

"And by me, attested," Holly said.

"Her breath and sweat and the touch of her skin are upon it," Ian went on.

"Also by me, attested. And the spell bound."

Elias nodded, accepting the cord onto the hilt of his dagger. Air, Water, Earth—he had only to add Fire and she would know agonies whenever she attempted magic, until and unless he canceled the spell. But that was for her next offense—and offense there would be, he was sure of it. Denise was a thrill-seeker, an adrenaline junkie, and a fool. She wouldn't be within a thousand miles of his jurisdiction if he hadn't owed Jean-Michel for helping with the renegade Seax Wiccans last spring. Being a Magistrate was work enough, and they all helped each other out when needed, but presiding over New York and environs could be especially bothersome at times.

Elias examined the seamless golden cord looped nine times around his athame. If cut slightly, so as to fray just a bit, Denise would do no more magic, ever. If it was severed, she would die. But Denise was merely an idiot, not a criminal. He had seen that death done once—the slow slicing of twisted rope so that each faculty, each Talent, each sense, down to the smallest particle of self-hood, unraveled and vanished.

"This is her Measure," he said, shaking off the memory, "to be kept safe by me until such time as judgment is required. Agreed?"

"So mote it be," came the responses.

Stepping around the Circle, he held out the cord to the four guardians. Each murmured a brief wish that their wands encouraged. Simon's ancient apple-wood coaxed the healing of Denise's spirit; Martin's polished blackthorn would enjoin her obedience; Kate's hazel awakened hidden wisdom (which Elias sincerely doubted Denise would recognize if it bit her in the ass, but he supposed they had to go through the motions).

When he got to Lydia, whose elmwood wand was useful for Work with the shadowy side of a psyche, he saw that her gentle brown eyes were unfocused, staring at the nothingness beyond the Circle. He approached cautiously, scowling his worry.

Lydia touched her wand to the cord—and suddenly screamed. Trembling as if her slight bones would shatter, she gasped for breaths that left her lungs in high-pitched keenings of terror. Her thurible gushed smoke and her candle flared wildly at her feet, sparking rainbow fire from the opal on her hand as she pointed into the shadows.

"*Swastika!*" she cried. "*Swastika!*"

Kate dug into her robes for something to calm her. Martin raised his black-handled athame in instinctive defense, looking in vain for something to defend against. Simon passed his hand over his chalice, muttering swiftly. Elias let dagger and cord drop and grasped Lydia's shoulders.

"What is it?" he demanded. "What else do you see?"

"Swastika and cross—flames—" Sobbing and shivering, she looked beyond him, beyond everything that was real to him. What she saw was more than real to her. "The chalice and the spear—ravens—and th-the *fire—Sgë! Tsûtû'neli'ga!*" Her eyes rolled up into her skull and with a final shudder she collapsed into Elias's arms.

He swung her up, away from the candle, and snapped an order for the Circle to be opened. Kate did the Work after tossing a packet of herbs to Simon, who mixed them swiftly in clean water. By the time Elias had placed Lydia on the chaise in the corner, she was struggling back to consciousness. Simon placed the chalice against her lips and told her to drink.

"You can tell us about it later," the old man said, casting a warning glance at Elias. "Just rest now, my dear."

A minute or so later she lay limp with sleep. Simon covered her with his own robe and stood there in shirtsleeves and suspenders, shaking his head worriedly.

"What the hell just happened?" Ian demanded.

"She had a glimpse of the past, I should think," Elias said.

Ian gestured impatiently. "Have you ever known her to see the past in any Work we've ever done?"

"But the swastika—"

"With a cross, both in flames."

Elias shrugged. "The Nazis were nominally Christians."

"What else was it she said? It sounded nothing like French or Hebrew, which as far as I know are the only languages she speaks besides English."

"Ian," murmured Elias, "you're my friend and my colleague, and I value you tremendously. But at times your curiosity drives me utterly mad."

"Short trip," Kate retorted, bending over Lydia, smoothing back her sweat-dampened hair. "Let her sleep it off. I'll stay with her—you too, Simon. Elias, see to Holly. The rest of you, go home and get some rest."

There was some murmuring as they hung up their robes and put away implements and doused candles. Someone picked up Lydia's thurible and extinguished it. Elias ignored everything but Holly—who still stood on her point of the inlaid oak pentagram, arms wrapped protectively around the Waterford chalice.

"You can give it back now," he said, gently prying her fingers loose.

She looked at him as if she had never seen him before.

"You know what she is," he reminded her as he took the crystal.

She nodded. "Sciomancer. Diviner of shadows." Shaking herself visibly, she shrugged out of her silver robe as if the action would rid her of magic, too. "Why the swastika?"

"Her grandmother was a Holocaust survivor."

"Diviner of the *future* in shadows," Holly corrected grimly.

"With occasional echoes of the past." He wasn't about to say what he really wanted to say, which was, *How the hell should I know why she saw what she saw and said what she said?*

"The swastika wasn't originally a Nazi symbol, you know."

And now, he told himself, he would be privileged to hear a lecture from one of the greatest collectors of pretty much useless information he had ever met.

"It's found from Ireland, where it was the Cross of St. Bridget, to India, which is where the Sanskrit word 'swastika' comes from. The Hopi, the Plains Indians, and the Maya used it in the Americas. About the only place it's never been found, in fact, is central Africa."

"Fascinating," he said quellingly.

Holly was relentless. "The Sun Wheel, fertility, life, good fortune—it shows up on the feet of the Buddha, as a sign of Artemis, and it's even been found in Jewish temples many thousands of years old." There was an instant's pause for breath. "What direction was it turning?"

He gave a start, surprised at being asked a question. He'd found that usually when she got going, not much slowed her down.

"Right or left?" Holly gestured impatiently. "Deosil or widdershins? Right is the sun and the god; left is the moon and the goddess."

"I don't have the vaguest idea," Elias said caustically. "I didn't think to ask."

"Find out when you can. And those words at the end—what was that? And what about the ravens, and a spear? Those sound like Norse mythology—"

He ground his teeth. "Let's wait until Lydia can tell us exactly what she saw before we speculate on what it means."

"Oh, of course, Your Honor," Holly snapped. "Objection—calls for speculation. Inadmissible as evidence." She flung her robe onto a chair. "I'm going home. Good night—what's left of it." And with that she stormed out of the room.

Simon ambled over. "Don't tell me—photographic memory?"

"No—just eidetic." Or, as Susannah usually put it, *idiotic*.

"And a redheaded Irish temper, too," Simon remarked.

Elias rubbed wearily at his forehead. "It seems to be her default attitude setting. How's Lydia?"

"Resting. Go to bed, Eli."

"Simon—what *about* the ravens?"

"Go to bed, Eli."

DENISE BLUSTERED HER WAY INTO the judge's chambers on Friday afternoon, ignoring the secretary's bark of "You can't go in there!" and the fact that His Honor was on the phone. She could not, however, ignore the basketball on the floor; she nearly tripped over it, and in her fury gave it a vicious kick. It slammed into the desk and then into a pile of case folders, which erupted in a gush of flying paper.

Elias Sutton Bradshaw hung up his phone. "And a good day to you too, Denise. To what do I owe—?"

Glaring down into dark eyes whose tilt and amusement should have reminded her of an elf, she spat, "Lay off, you bastard. You have no right—"

"Your Honor—"

Denise whirled at the sound of another voice—feminine, worried, and belonging to a blonde who should have been on the cover of *Vogue*, not trussed up in a power suit in service to a judge of the United States District Court.

"It's all right, Susannah," Bradshaw replied.

"Shall I find the marshal on duty?"

"Don't bother." It was a Friday, and Pete Wasserman was his assigned protection today; no point in troubling the man. If it had been Thursday, and Evan Lachlan's watch, Elias might have been tempted—just to see the fireworks. "She only bites when she's hungry—and she dined well last night, I'm told. Close the door on your way out."

Frowning, Susannah did so—obviously unhappy about it but also unwilling to argue with her boss. Denise, furious at the interruption, stalked over to the desk to glare more effectively down at her quarry.

"I mean it. You have no authority and no right to—"

"You're in my jurisdiction," he replied mildly, addressing her as if she were a particularly dim-witted six-year-old. "That gives me the authority *and* the right. Just count yourself lucky I'm not using the authority of this office instead."

"You don't dare!"

"Make another mistake, and you'll find out just how much I dare."

"I won't stand for this."

"Denise, you make an excellent living writing clichés, but must you also speak in them?"

"Cliché *this*!" she snarled, and with a muttered word and a complex gesture of her fingers, the spilled stack of file folders burst into flames.

Bradshaw sighed, leaned back in his chair, and with a glance and a nod extinguished the little blaze.

"Play with fire on your own time," he said. "I have more important things to do."

"You can't scare me!"

"Shall I send you back to your own? New York isn't New Orleans, Denise.

Whatever Jean-Michel tolerated in Voodoo Land isn't kosher here. You'd be better off back in the bayou."

"I'm not going back and you can't make me."

"No?" He smiled, but his eyes were bleak. "It's true, Jean-Michel has done me a favor or three. Sending you back wouldn't earn me his undying devotion."

"Whatever he told you was a lie."

"No, it wasn't—and we both know it. Just stay out of trouble, Denise. You know what I mean—and what I won't stand for in my city."

"Fuck you," she responded, and turned on her heel and marched out.

The furrows that forty-nine years had carved into Elias's brow deepened, as if someone had suddenly drawn his face in blacker ink. He sat very still for a few moments, then roused himself and took a can of air freshener from a desk drawer. The fire hadn't burned anything—Denise wasn't that good, and he'd been very quick—but there was a slightly scorched smell in the air.

With a quick spritz of aerosol, a corporate concoction of cinnamon-and-apple filled the office. Elias's nose twitched. Perhaps Holly could brew him up something sultry and Southern, magnolias maybe—scratch that, she was a lousy cook. A pity she had only a minor Talent, one requiring no education at all. She'd done the basics back home in Virginia, of course, but at an age when others manifested their special gifts, she had been found to have nothing special at all. Except the one. Except that strange, dangerous, damned-near unique *one*.

Reminding himself to ask Kate to raid her stillroom for something soothing, he punched the intercom switch and said, "Mrs. Osbourne, can you bring me the Castello case file, please?"

ONE STEP AHEAD OF 'EM, *always one step ahead,* Swinnerton sang to himself as he opened the door of his hotel room.

It was only when he saw a big grin above a shiny five-pointed star of the United States Marshals Service that he realized the door had already been unlocked.

"Hiya, Harry," said the grin. Handcuffs dangled from the fingers of the man's left hand; the right one was dead-steady around a Glock. "You're gonna be a good boy, right?"

*One step ahead—except when I'm one step behind.* Harry Swinnerton sighed, calculating his chances of taking the big guy.

Lousy.

He held out both hands, wrists together. "Do it, Lachlan."

"Now, that's what I like to hear. Philosophical."

Swinnerton was cuffed and Mirandized—the latter technically unnecessary, for as a fugitive convicted felon he had never *not* been under arrest, but Lachlan had begun his career in the NYPD and the right-to-an-attorney speech was hard-wired by now. Harry heard it all out, then turned mournful eyes on his captor. "Where'd I go wrong?"

"Besides offing that guard while you were stealing way too many pretty little figurines, you mean?" The deputy exchanged gun for cell phone and punched a button. "Well, Harry, you've just got to learn to stay off the Internet."

That bitch at the cybercafe. Had to be. She'd come on to him, he'd told her to take a hike, and—

"Or at least if you *do* go surfing, don't browse every antiques dealer on the East Coast who's interested in Etruscan bronzes." He paused long enough to say into the phone, "Got him," before perp-marching Harry out of the hotel room.

In the elevator, Swinnerton looked up at six feet four inches of Deputy U.S. Marshal on the hoof. "Y'know, Lachlan, you're a real asshole."

"So my girlfriend tells me. Into the car, and let's get you back to jail. C'mon, Harry, cheer up. I hear Friday is meatloaf night."

# One

AS HE SET HIS THIRD Corona down after taking a long swallow, Evan Lachlan felt Elias Bradshaw looking at him across the table. When he glanced over, there was a quizzical smile on the judge's face. Lachlan arched a brow in query.

"You really don't know, do you?" Bradshaw asked.

"Know what?" He returned his gaze to the fascinating sight of Holly Mc-Clure dancing with Susannah Wingfield—yeah, two women, like this was a dyke bar or something. A Bonnie Raitt CD was thundering from the sound system while the band took a break at what Holly swore was the only halfway decent blues bar in New York. And whoever would've thought they'd run into Bradshaw and Wingfield at a place like this? An upscale restaurant or exclusive club was more their style—or so Lachlan would have said before getting a good look at Susannah.

The prim attorney was surely a sight to behold, a Friday night fantasy (the last thing he'd ever admit to Holly) in black miniskirt, black stiletto heels, and crimson silk shirt with three—count 'em, *three*—buttons undone. As for the black leather biker-chick jacket that draped the back of her chair . . . incredible. He'd seen her legs before, of course, but never this much of them, or in black silk hosiery. And they were well worth looking at.

Susannah Wingfield, off-duty. Lachlan shook his head in amazement. He would've bet good money that this blonde carbon copy of Audrey Hepburn could never laugh and toss her long hair and sing and shake it like—well, better not go there. He had to work with the lady, after all.

Besides, he preferred watching his own lady. Holly was dancing with as much abandon as Susannah, but her moves were sinuous as a cat's. Above boots with three-inch heels and tight faded Levi's she wore the blue-and-white baseball jersey that had been Evan's congratulatory gift on publication of her *Village*

*Voice* article, "Property of U.S. Marshals Service." Three inches taller than Susannah's five-seven, and outweighing her by at least twenty-five pounds, Holly looked chunky by comparison. Then again, anybody but Gwyneth Paltrow would look chunky next to Susannah—who was, to Evan's discerning eye, too skinny. He liked a woman he wasn't likely to pulverize in bed if he shifted wrong in his sleep. On the Evan Liam Lachlan Scale, Holly McClure rated an eight in most departments. Plus a ten for the eyes.

"You have no idea who she is," Bradshaw's voice said.

"Why, who is she?" Evan asked. *Besides the slinkiest thing in this bar.*

"I'm surprised the subject never came up. I thought you'd been seeing her for several weeks." Bradshaw drank Scotch and leaned back, watching Susannah.

"So?" Lachlan prompted.

"What? Oh. We had quite a chat about it when she came to the office regarding her research."

The judge was enjoying this. The marshal was not. But Lachlan's voice was silken smooth as he said, "Holly went to that ritzy college with Susannah. You saying that puts her out of my league, Your Honor?"

"Not at all," Bradshaw assured him, taking another swallow of Scotch. He looked amused. Lachlan hated that expression on anybody, but especially on Elias Bradshaw.

This was not the couple he would have chosen to double-date with. As a U.S. Marshal assigned to judicial protection, Bradshaw was Lachlan's duty—and sometimes his cross to bear—three days a week. It was Lachlan's Irish luck that the judge's clerk was a woman well worth looking at who, moreover, had interesting friends. The weird part was that from a couple of hints Holly had dropped, Susannah and Elias had become an item about the same time he and Holly had. Lachlan knew how the women had met: Susannah the pre-law and Holly the history major were sopranos who had stood right next to each other in the Women's Chorale.

*"Susannah can sing?"*

*"Like an angel with a solid gold halo," Holly affirmed, digging her hands into the pockets of her coat. Cold wind off the Hudson ruffled her hair and burned bright color into her skin, emphasizing the freckles across nose and cheekbones.*

*He shook his head in disbelief, then eyed her. "What about you?"*

*"Me? A halo?" She grinned.*

*"God forbid! C'mon. Prove you can sing."*

*"Right here in the middle of Central Park?"*

*He stood back from her, arms folded. "I dare ya."*

*"That, my dear Marshal, was a mistake."*

*And right there in the middle of a frosty Sunday afternoon stroll she ran through the scale up to a note that hit the bare treetops—and then soared on into the sky.*

*Lachlan, aware that people were looking curiously at them, made a grab for her. "Exhibitionist," he growled, and she broke off to laugh as he whirled her around, catching her back against his chest. She leaned her head onto his shoulder, chortling. Wrapping his arms around her, lips buried in russet hair, he hefted her a few inches off the ground. "McClure, behave yourself!"*

*"Oh, do I have to?"*

He smiled to himself as he drank beer and watched the two women. They shared the same taste in music—and maybe in men, too. Though Lachlan couldn't see it himself, women *did* appreciate Bradshaw: the frank appraisal he gave them, the honest enjoyment he took in watching them, the intent way he listened to them. Susannah had certainly fallen for it. She was directing a genuinely fiendish shimmy at her boss right now, laughing.

"Okay," Lachlan said, dragging his attention away from the women. "Who *is* Holly, anyway? Homicidal wacko? Notorious embezzler? Convicted felon?" He spoke with no little amount of sarcasm, knowing none of these was true. Bradshaw's amused little smirk was really beginning to annoy him.

"No, as you're doubtless aware. I mean you don't know what her work is, do you?"

"She writes." He paused for a swig of beer. "Articles for magazines." Like the ones she'd been doing when she walked into the federal courthouse and his life.

Susannah had brought her into chambers about a month ago and introduced her around. The implication was that every cooperation should be given her college friend, who was researching two articles—one on the U.S. Marshals Service (*How original*, he'd thought—until he read it in the *Village Voice*) and one on Irish Gaelic (linguistic holdovers from the Old Country, slang and the like). Lachlan had taken Susannah's hint, and was even willing to be nice about it—Holly McClure was a good-looking woman, after all. But he'd been last on her list.

The day Susannah brought her in happened to be Lachlan's birthday—there were cards and gag gifts all over his desk—and he'd thought this would earn him first interview. But Ms. McClure went to lunch with Sophia Osbourne, Bradshaw's secretary. On Tuesday she lunched with Bradshaw's other marshal, Pete Wasserman (who preened like a peacock when he left the office and grinned like an idiot when he got back, flatly refusing to reveal what—or whom—they had discussed). Susannah and Judge Bradshaw had also been interviewed, presumably over lengthy meals at pricey restaurants.

Lachlan's venue had been a hot dog stand at about four on a snowy afternoon. Somehow they got to talking about a thousand other topics besides being Irish and being a cop, and moved on to a little cafe for dinner. And then to his apartment.

Not that he got anywhere. At 10:30 she fell asleep on his couch while he was in the kitchen brewing up a pot of coffee. He spent a couple of minutes deciding whether or not to be insulted, then shrugged, covered her with Granna Maureen's afghan, and went to bed alone. The next morning she was gone before his alarm went off. As he showered and shaved, he wondered if he'd have to chalk her up as One That Got Away. Then his doorbell rang. Not Holly: a delivery boy from the bakery down the street. Bemused, Lachlan accepted a bag of cinnamon-raisin bagels, a gigantic coffee, and a note: *Sorry I faded out, but it was a long day and you must be the only person in New York with a comfortable couch! Will you meet me for dinner tonight so we can finish our interview? You pick the restaurant—my expense account is buying.*

Tired though she'd been that night, she'd been paying attention to what he said; he'd read the manuscript of the Irish article, and a lot of it had come from him (or, more accurately, Granna Maureen, born in County Meath). By the time Holly showed him the article, they'd been seeing each other for two weeks and sleeping together for one.

Not that this had been easy to accomplish.

He'd canceled his Friday night date that week even though it was a sure thing, finding himself more interested in a redheaded writer than a blonde graphics designer (even though their last session had been pretty damned graphic). He had every faith he could charm Holly McClure into a sure thing anyway. But when they parted outside O'Kelley's at one in the morning, he didn't even rate a good-night kiss. This irked the hell out of him.

On Sunday he used the cell-phone number Holly had given him and asked her out dancing for the next evening. First kiss—but nothing else. Not even a *second* kiss. He signaled his displeasure by not calling her on Tuesday. Wednesday she showed up at Judge Bradshaw's chambers around quitting time and took him to dinner and a jazz club—a night that ended outside the club at 1:30 a.m. with two discoveries. First, she had a fantastic mouth and incredible hands and knew how to use them. Second, he'd been right—she didn't wear a bra and didn't need one. But the fantasies this conjured up went unfulfilled. So did he. And it was really beginning to piss him off. A case of the best-planned lays, he supposed.

That Thursday was Thanksgiving at his sister's house, a yearly event that reminded him why he hated this time of year: his birthday, then Thanksgiving, then Pop's birthday, then Maggie's birthday, all featuring too much food, too much booze, and way too much family togetherness. Or what passed for it with Clan Lachlan.

Friday he and Holly were just finishing salads at Da Marino's when his pager went off, damn it to hell. Holly insisted on coming with him. He'd let her take a look, then sent her home in a cab, thinking glumly that the scene of a triple homicide at a Protected Witness location was a hell of a way to end a date. But when he'd phoned her late that night (or early the following morning, depending on point of view), she'd been wide awake and waiting for his call. No tap-dancing, no *Oh-you-poor-baby*, no *How-do-you-cope-with-your-horrible-job*, no *You-still-owe-me-a-decent-meal*. She listened, asked a few questions, and told him she'd pick him up at 7:00, her turn to buy.

And Saturday night, just as he was starting to think he'd *never* get anywhere, he nailed her. Or maybe she nailed him. Because he wasn't quite sure about this, he decided it had been mutual.

Sunday she took him to brunch. After some gorgeous food there arrived a tarte tatin with a lighted candle in it. A belated happy birthday, she told him, producing a brace of cigars to go with their coffee. Like him, she'd quit smoking years ago; like him, she still enjoyed a fine cigar.

Jesus, Mary, and Joseph—did she *ever* enjoy it. Watching her smoke the thing damned near gave him a coronary. Her eyes were wickedly blue above moist satiny lips that caressed the cigar and freckled velvety cheeks that hollowed as she inhaled. His conversation—fluent and wide-ranging during brunch—became somewhat constricted. So did the fit of his slacks.

Lachlan hadn't done more than glance at any other woman since.

Bradshaw had pulled a folded paper out of his overcoat pocket. "She writes a lot more than newspaper articles." He laid the newsprint on the table: *The New York Times Review of Books*.

"One of her pieces is in here? Great! She made the *Times*!"

Bradshaw smiled. Lachlan was peripherally aware that he didn't like this particular variation on the usual smile, but he was too intent on searching for Holly's article.

"I was going to leave this at the office for you, but I might as well show it to you now. Page four."

Evan found it—not a bad photo of her, but she had the kind of face that always looked best when in motion. No still picture could ever capture the quick play of wit and humor across her features. The photographer had caught the sharp intelligence but none of the laughter—or the lascivious turn of mind hiding behind those big blue eyes.

But why would a writer of articles rate a photo?

He began to read.

### *DRAGON SHIPS*: NEW MCCLURE NOVEL ENCHANTS

After a three-year absence, H. Elizabeth McClure has returned—not to the artistic community of Renaissance Italy, scene of her previous bestseller, but to the considerably less civilized yet no less fascinating environs of ninth-century France and a tale of Norse invaders.

McClure's previous work—scholarly biographies and historical fiction—has earned her a loyal following and critical acclaim. *Dragon Ships* delights again with vivid characters, lively action—

He felt his guts roil and stopped reading. He looked back over at the dance floor, where Holly and Susannah were gleefully bumping hips in time to the backbeat. This was definitely not the same Susannah—and all at once it wasn't the same Holly, either.

"Don't kill the messenger," Bradshaw said suddenly, and Evan realized his emotions were scrawled all over his face. Hastily he smoothed his expression as Bradshaw went on, sincerely puzzled: "I thought you'd be pleased. She's quite a catch, Marshal."

The deejay didn't give the dancers any breather—another song came up, slower but with a driving drumbeat. Holly and Susannah went on dancing, the rhythm of hips and shoulders and flying hair provocatively emphasizing the drums.

From somewhere Lachlan dragged up a crooked smile and the words, "Yeah, Ma always told me not to bring a girl home unless she was brainy, beautiful, and rich." Which happened to be true, which was why he'd never even tried to do it. Pleasing the late, unlamented Patricia Lachlan had never been high on his list of priorities—more like down with scrubbing the mildew from the grout in his shower. He leaned back and drained the Corona down his throat before signaling the waitress for a fourth. He wasn't yet numb—and he wanted to be.

"So tell me, Your Honor, before I reel her in—she any good? You read any of her books?"

"A biography of Christine de Pisan—a medieval poet. Yes, she's very talented. And, in certain circles, quite well-known."

*Holy shit.* "Gee, I'll have to run out and get a copy. And a dictionary to go along with it, for all the words of more than one syllable."

Bradshaw's dark brows arched. "Are you about to make a fool of yourself?"

*She's already done a pretty good job of it.* He gave the judge stare for stare and said nothing. His Corona came; he put a five on the table and squeezed the lime wedge into the bottle. As he took a large mouthful of ice-cold beer, he had the feeling he wouldn't be able to drink this one fast enough.

"Do yourself a favor and think first," Bradshaw continued. "She comes from where *all* of us come from. Susannah, me, you, Holly—we all worked our way through college and fought to establish careers. No free rides from rich parents. The town she's from in Virginia is smaller than the one Susannah was born in— and that's saying something. So if difference in social status is your problem—"

"Problem? I got no problems."

Lachlan drained the bottle in four long swallows and stood, threading through the sparse crowd to where Holly was laughing with Susannah. The look those blue eyes gave him went straight to his chest. And then lower.

"Have this dance?" he asked, appropriating Holly's hand, spinning her once under his arm before drawing her possessively close. It wasn't exactly a slow song, but he had no trouble easing her into a swaying, clasping, intimate dance.

"Oooh — smooth, Lachlan, very smooth," Holly commended, eyes full of laughter and promises. Dancing wasn't quite vertical sex, but it was definitely public foreplay.

Her head bent to rest comfortably on his shoulder, and he indulged himself with the feel of her in his arms. So sweet, and so sensual, the way they moved together, as attuned in this as in bed. From their first night together she had sensed his every move telegraphed through his muscles, following his lead so perfectly they might as well have been one person. He gritted his teeth. Goddammit, she smelled so good, and her dark russet hair was soft against his cheek, and her fingertips did their own delicate dance on the nape of his neck. He could feel the warmth of her slowly turn feverish as his arm involuntarily tightened around her back and his hand slid south down her hip. At least her body had never lied to him.

"When were you gonna tell me?"

"Tell you what?" She tilted her head back to look at him, shoulder-length hair glinting gold and copper along every loose, lazy curl.

" 'New McClure Novel Enchants,' " he quoted acidly.

Her quick, expressive face went blank for a moment. Then she tossed her hair back and said, "I never believe my reviews."

"I got one for you now. Headline goes 'Rich Writer Makes Jerk of Mick Cop.' Like it so far?"

Scowling, she began, "Evan, don't be an asshole — "

He dipped her seductively, making it look good for Susannah and Bradshaw. He tried not to react as her thigh slid between his; he tried not to see the line of her throat or the tender hollow at its base. He lost his battle against his own body as her thigh nudged deliberately higher, taunting him. Her head came back up, her body tense and cold in his arms. Angry eyes blazed at him, one hand taloning into his shoulder and the other rigid within his palm. *She* was mad at *him*? What the hell right did she have to get pissed off? He was the one who'd been lied to.

He righted her again and pulled her close. "Now I know why we never go to your place. Why I never even get to pick you up at your place. Almost a month of this musta been a kick for you, slumming with the big dumb Mick who can barely read, let alone read anything *literary*."

The song ended and she yanked herself out of his arms. He tried to hang on, but she was tall and strong—and furious. "You *are* a big dumb Mick if that's what you think!" she snarled. "And if it is—well, fuck you, Marshal, and the horse you rode in on!"

Holly stalked right past Susannah, who was returning to their table from the ladies' room. Snatching up her coat and scarf, Holly flung a furious glare at Bradshaw. "Any more little revelations tonight, Your Honor?"

"Holly," Susannah exclaimed, "what's—?"

"Read all about it in my next *enchanting* novel!" After casting one scathing backward glance at Lachlan, she pushed her way out of the bar.

Susannah turned to him with a disgusted expression. "Nice work, Lachlan."

"Never occurred to you to tell me, did it?"

She didn't pretend not to know what he meant. "She asked me not to."

"Yeah, I guess the joke was too good. You were havin' too many laughs—"

Green eyes ignited. "We weren't laughing at you and you know it!"

"Why the hell not? Seems pretty funny to me." He tried to hang on to his temper. This was no time to feel like a ten-year-old from the wrong side of town who took the same French classes and wore the same St. Thomas Aquinas blazer and played on the same softball team as the rich kids—who never let him forget where he came from.

Susannah latched on to his arm, nails digging in. "Don't be stupid. Do you know what kind of man she usually meets? They're interested in her money, her connections—"

"But I'm the perfect toy boy. I get your drift, Counselor."

"Oh, for Christ's sake, Evan!"

He grabbed his leather coat from the back of his chair just as Susannah was turning on Bradshaw to demand, "Goddammit, Eli, what the *hell* did you say?"

It was piercingly cold outside on the street, and raining. Holly was gone, of course—long gone. *Probably in a limo,* he thought bitterly. Oh, but she was slumming, remember—hiding the Rolls and the platinum credit cards and the diamonds and the penthouse—

It hurt much more than he thought it should.

It was just that he'd let himself begin to think there might be something to this one besides a good time in bed and out. A few rousing arguments about life, politics, religion, whatever. Sharing popcorn at the movies, trading off paying for lunches and dinners—and making breakfasts at his place, which was his task because the woman couldn't cook worth a good goddamn.

He *liked* her. She was smart, sassy, sexy, and let him get away with no bullshit whatsoever. His particular brand of bullshit had gotten him just about every woman he'd ever bothered to want. So why did he have to want some lying rich bitch who probably lived in one of those huge high-rises off the Park, or a three-story brownstone, or a Gramercy Park place, or—

She didn't act it. Not really. Okay, she dressed it right enough. When he met her for dinner last Friday she'd been incredible in sapphire silk and pearls. Her mother's, she'd told him, necklace and earrings and bracelet; it might even have been true. The jewelry was one thing; the clothes were another. In a month of seeing her four times a week, she'd never worn the same outfit twice. The labels he'd noticed as he helped her on with coat or jacket were DKNY, Ralph Lauren, Armani, and others of that expensive ilk. All he'd thought was that, like many another woman, she spent way too much on clothes, and he was glad he didn't have to foot the bills. Which she probably had her accountant pay, never even seeing them.

Fuck it. He didn't need her. There were plenty of other women, dozens of 'em, ones who'd fall all over themselves to get into his bed the first date, not make him wait, the way Holly had. Ones who wouldn't lie to him, the way Holly had.

Ones who, within a couple of days or a couple of weeks, would bore him witless—the way Holly never had.

Fundamental fairness compelled the admission that she'd never actually lied to him. Not directly. But she always had some excuse not to go to her place. The living room was being painted; the heat was off; she was near the courthouse so why didn't she meet him for dinner if his desk permitted—

He could have found out a lot from the prefix of her home phone, but she hadn't given it to him. Clever girl. *"Feel privileged, Lachlan—only the people I want to talk to get my cell-phone number."* As for her work—she'd downplayed it, just saying that she'd had some stuff published, and was working on a novel. *". . . loyal following and critical acclaim. . . ."*

"Fuck!" he snarled to the streetlights.

Uptown girl, slumming around with a Lower East Side Mick cop. He hoped she'd gotten her jollies.

He dug his hands into his pockets, heading for the subway and home.

two

"HOLLY?" THE VOICE ON THE phone was despicably awake.

"Morning, Suze." Holly started the coffee, sparing a disgusted glance out the kitchen windows at bleak gray rain. "I hope your evening ended more agreeably than mine."

"After I cussed Eli out for an hour, yeah. Look, I'm sorry about—"

"It wasn't his fault. I'm sure he thought Evan would be glad to know." She rubbed her aching eyes, cradling the phone receiver on her shoulder. She supposed she was lucky His Honor hadn't told Evan the rest of it. But what happened in the Circle stayed in the Circle; it was as if their Work was done by an aspect of themselves that did not enter the world of their everyday lives. Besides, one *never* admitted to the Craft if possible. In all the years she'd known Susannah, her friend had never even suspected.

"Well, sometimes it's hard to tell with Eli—but you're probably right." Susannah paused. "I think he's a little amazed that you're going out with Evan. They aren't exactly best buddies."

"They're two studs sniffing the mares," Holly said crudely. "Neither can believe the other is even remotely attractive to women."

"Eli told me to apologize for him. I told him that the next time you come into the office, he can damned well apologize for himself."

"It's not necessary. Really. Let's not talk about them, okay?"

"Fine with me," Susannah told her. "But you do have to talk to Evan."

"What you mean is I should've said something to him long before this. It's all my fault, Susannah." She paused, then went on more vigorously, "No, it's not. Am I supposed to apologize for being successful?"

"Of course not. But maybe for lying to him."

"I didn't lie to him!" Not about that, anyway. Not about *anything*.

"Prevaricated a bit, maybe?" Susannah suggested. "Oh, get the fire out of your eyes, Holly, I'm getting scorched all the way from Brooklyn Heights! Look, Evan will come around. It's just that filthy Irish temper of his." There was a smile in her voice now. "The one he shares with you and half the rest of this city. It's a miracle you didn't all annihilate each other back in Ireland."

Holly rummaged in the breadbox for muffins. "We were too busy annihilating you bloody British."

"Give Evan a couple of days to think it over. He's one of the good guys."

"Huh! If he's so great, why didn't *you* go after him?"

"*Me?*" Susannah gasped, and Holly had to grin at the mock horror in her voice. "With that six-foot-four 240-pound lug? He'd crush poor little size-two me if he rolled over wrong in his sleep! All they'd find would be a pancake with pink toenails."

"Hey—he ain't skinny, but he ain't an ounce over 225 either."

"Mmm," Susannah purred. "And just exactly how'd you find *that* out, girlfriend?"

"Why, I looked at his driver's license, of course," Holly replied innocently. "Susannah Dolcebella Wingfield, what *can* you be suggesting?"

"Holly Elizabeth McClure, you'd be a lousy lawyer. You can't lie worth shit."

"I *beg* your pardon. When I'm being a novelist, I'm a *professional* liar—I tell lies for a living, on paper. Maybe we're in the same racket after all, hmm?"

"Stop trying to distract me from the subject."

"Which is?" The fridge was bare of butter, margarine, and jam. Not to mention eggs, milk, and cheese. Isabella must have done a search-and-destroy on it again; the housekeeper was way too impressed by expiration dates. Shrugging, Holly went to the pantry for peanut butter.

"Evan Lachlan."

"Well, you have a point. He'd squish you, sure as shootin'. Leave the big brawny guys to the big brawny girls like me. Are we still on for lunch Monday?"

"Holly—"

"Susannah," she said patiently, "just tell me if I have to get dressed in something other than jeans."

"I'll have to let you know. Can't we leave the alumni thing to somebody else?"

She smeared peanut butter on the muffin. "Our number's up, according to Jemima."

"God, fifteen years in June—I'm starting to feel old, Holly!"

"My heart bleedeth not. You're damned near three years younger than the rest of us, you little grade-skipping genius. Look, all we have to do is pick a Friday in April, corral the New York alums into a bar, and get 'em drinking and dancing."

"Do we bring dates?"

"So you can show off your big-shot honey?" Holly teased.

"Just like you want to show off your big hunky marshal!"

"If we're still speaking to each other. Which is up to him. If he wants to be weird about this, fine. There's a lot of other men out there."

"But nobody like Evan Lachlan and you know it. I saw it the minute I introduced you, and I knew long before that. Which is exactly *why* I introduced you—after you fought me on it for months, you stubborn bitch."

"'Introduced'—?" she echoed indignantly. "You practically handed me over as his birthday present!"

"I'm a sweet and thoughtful friend," was the blithe, bland reply. "To both of you. And he hasn't even thanked me yet. Susannah the Yankee Yenta," she laughed. "As if you didn't throw me at Elias on *his* birthday—"

"As if you didn't want to be thrown!" she scoffed. "You were *such* a pain in the ass—I acted out of pure self-preservation. I flatly refuse to supply tequila and sympathy more than five times over any one man in your life. You'd used up your quota, girl."

Susannah snorted. "Holly, you're *too* good to me."

"I'm a sweet and thoughtful friend," she teased. "By the way, I never did get around to asking how Elias liked his birthday present."

"Bet you gave Lachlan pretty much the same thing."

"Susannah!" She pretended shock. "I bought him brunch and a cigar."

"That's *definitely* not what I gave Eli! And I know Evan—for brunch and a cigar, and whatever else went with it—"

"Watch it, Wingfield!"

"—he'll be back," she finished.

"Well, ain't that jes' dandy," she drawled in the broadest possible version of her native Virginian. "Ah can't *wait* t'be the next numbah in his li'l ol' black book—" She dropped the accent and finished acidly, "—which probably runs into quadruple digits."

"Triple, maybe," Susannah retorted, amused.

"Terrific. Just what I lack—Casanova in ostrich-skin cowboy boots. Where did he get those awful things, anyway?"

"Beats me. I've heard five different stories so far."

"Well, if any of 'em ever sound plausible, send me an e-mail. I'm not gonna be around to hear it."

"Nice try, McClure. You can't fool me. I saw you two last night—"

"Before your oh-so-adorable man spilled the beans? Sorry, I didn't mean that. Tell Elias it's okay. Evan had to find out sometime. It's been unsaid too long."

Susannah was silent for a minute. Then, very seriously: "This one's different, Holly."

"I was beginning to think so."

"I *know* so. See you Monday—if I can't make it, I'll e-mail you."

"Okay. Bye."

She sighed and hung up the phone. *Would* he come around? She had no idea. Evan Lachlan was unpredictable—and she hated that in anything, especially a man. She was a writer, which meant she was a control freak who liked things her own way, at her own speed, in her own time. Evan was indeed different. For one thing, he'd gotten her into bed a mere week after their first real dinner date (the night she'd spent on his couch didn't count), when her adamant rule was a month.

The night after the triple homicide she'd taken him to a trendy bistro. He insisted on springing for an expensive merlot to apologize for the previous evening's interruption, and was his usual self during dinner. But by nine he was starting to droop, overwork catching up with him. She asked the waiter for the check and a taxi, and in the cab Evan apologized ruefully—saying he hadn't counted on drifting off to sleep and reversing their roles of the previous week.

*Holly looked him straight in the eye. "If you think I'm spending another night on your couch, Lachlan, think again."*

*Suddenly the cab couldn't move fast enough. Neither could their hands or mouths. By the time the cab finally stopped, she couldn't have formulated a single thought to save her own life.*

*They took the stairs to the fourth floor, frantically undoing buttons and buckles as they climbed, cursing his knotted tie and her tight cuffs, stumbling, feet and ankles and knees tangling so that they nearly fell on a landing. At last his door was behind her back, and she propped herself gratefully against it, needing the support, while he kissed her and fumbled in a pocket for keys with pretty much equal urgency. She arched against him and he growled low in his throat. And dropped the keys.*

*He crouched down to snag them up. When he wasn't kissing her, when his hands weren't all over her, she could think again. And she started to laugh.*

*"What's so goddamned funny?" he demanded, fingers still scrabbling for the keys on the tiled floor.*

*"Us. We're not a couple of teenagers who only have ten minutes until your parents get home."*

*"Ten minutes?" he exclaimed, outraged. "What d'you take me for, lady? Some kinda amateur?"*

*"I'll take you any way I can get you right now, you egotistical swine! And I do mean right now, Lachlan."*

*He laughed up at her through a tousle of dark hair. She buried both hands in its thickness, something she'd wanted to do forever, and his eyes closed and his lips parted as he luxuriated in the caress. Still crouching, he slipped his hands under her tweed jacket and pulled her blouse from her jeans so he could get his fingers onto her skin. His touch scorched her. He leaned forward and pressed his face to her abdomen, hot breath penetrating layers of denim and silk, lower and lower until the heat of his mouth found the matching heat between her thighs. She moaned, legs suddenly boneless, hands braced on his shoulders to hold herself upright.*

*"Éimhín—" Her breathing was ragged as the long, slow exhalations were replaced by gently biting teeth. "Oh, God—"*

*"I could eat you alive—you been drivin' me crazy since the first time I saw you—"*

*She dug her fingers into the hard curves of his biceps, and with strength born of desperate craving she hauled him to his feet.*

*"Get the fucking keys and open the fucking door," she snarled.*

*"And get on with the fucking?" he suggested, grinning like a madman.*

*"Goddammit, get this door open or I'll commit felony sexual assault right here in the hall!"*

*His eyes had turned to molten emeralds. He opened them as wide as they would go and exclaimed, "Damn! You promise?"*

*"Lachlan—!"*

*"Takin' a lot for granted, aren't you? Maybe I'm not that easy."*

*For answer, she lowered her gaze to his inseam, grinning. "I'm betting you know how to use that—and that you've been practicing since you were fifteen."*

*"Fourteen-and-a-half."*

*"Well, then, you ought to be fairly good at it by now."*

Her coffee was cold and her cheeks were burning.

In retrospect, she was amazed that she'd held out for seven whole days.

LACHLAN WENT TO HIS LOCAL Barnes & Noble on Saturday afternoon. The array of Holly's books made his jaw drop. He bought a paperback, a thick biographical novel of a woman artist in Renaissance Italy who got raped by her father's apprentice. Cheery stuff. Declining a bag for his purchase, he stuffed the book into his coat pocket, went down the block for a fistful of good cigars, and took himself home, where he drank decaf French roast and smoked cigars and read all afternoon.

He liked the book. Not a boring word in it, and she had the knack of completely involving the reader in her characters. She made you feel you were there, that you knew the girl and the rapist and the sanctimonious jackasses who said she had it coming. The trial was a travesty, the aftermath a horror. But Artemisia stuck to her guns—good girl!—and got her revenge by becoming a truly great painter. A color reproduction of one of her canvases was on the cover; he walked back to the bookstore to find and buy a book of her work to add to his collection.

As he waited in line to pay for the volume, he suddenly remembered a Sunday afternoon at the Metropolitan, the day he and Holly had walked in the Park and she'd sung to him for the first time. At the museum he'd let show a little too much of his interest in and knowledge of art. Holly had listened attentively, mostly silent, while he went on and on about Turner's instinct for light and Sargent's for capturing the true character of his portrait subject. His face burned with the memory: he could just see himself standing there lecturing about art to a woman who'd written a book about an artist.

A damned good book, too, though he would've enjoyed it even more if it hadn't been Holly's, with *International Bestseller!* screaming across the back cover, right under a picture of her in a dark sweater, holding a big black-masked white cat.

He hadn't even known she had a cat.

How much else didn't he know about her?

How much did writers make, anyway?

He did a fairly rotten thing then. He went home and called a friend and had him run Holly's name through the computer. Unlisted she might be to everyone else, but not to the New York Department of Motor Vehicles.

Ten minutes of pacing his apartment later, the friend rang back. After some razzing about why he'd want information on a classy babe like this, he was given her address. And learned from it that a writer with a "loyal following and critical acclaim" made a shitload of money.


THEY HADN'T BEEN SCHEDULED FOR anything on Sunday, and when he read the book review section of the paper (for the second time in his life) he found out why. She and five other authors were signing books at a Village store to benefit the families of 9/11 victims.

At the door he paid his five-bucks-for-charity to get inside out of the rain. Oh, very chi-chi stuff, this. Brick walls, oak shelves, framed posters of dead white writers, espresso machines going full blast, and a crowd ranging from art mavens to nose-piercers, all with books ready to be signed. Holly sat at a long table next to a mildly balding professorial type—complete with leather elbow patches and battered unlit pipe—who leaned entirely too close and looked down her blouse while saying something witty. *He* obviously thought it was witty, anyway; Holly smiled politely, then turned once more to the girl who stood waiting for her autograph. Evan couldn't hear their conversation from this far back in line, but obviously Holly was much more interested in talking to her readers than to her colleague. He wondered if he would have appreciated this quite as much if the colleague hadn't been a bit reminiscent of Elias Bradshaw (with a lot less hair), one of those rumpled intellectuals that women seemed to like for no particular reason that Lachlan had ever been able to figure. The guy probably fucked in rhymed couplets.

It got to be three o'clock, and the store manager elicited groans when she announced that the signing would be suspended to give the writers a break. Things would resume in ten minutes, at which time there would be small gatherings elsewhere in the store for readings. This brought cheers. A long, lean, poetic type vanished to prepare himself for his performance. The professor went to pee. Holly chatted with the two women writers who were left, then gratefully accepted a fresh cappuccino and made her way through the store. She was good at this, Lachlan thought as he watched her, his cop's analytical eye watching her work the crowd. With some people she was sincere; with others, not very—but he knew they couldn't tell the difference.

She vanished down a side aisle. He pocketed her novel and sauntered along the next aisle over, wanting to hear without being seen.

"Thanks for coming today. I know we're all still pretty much in shock—and nobody's likely to get over that very soon. If ever. But I guess we all have to try to do what we can.

"I'm going to read from a work in progress—and very slow progress, I might add. It doesn't know whether it's going to be a novel or a short story. But that's one of the dubious joys of writing. You can get suckered in by an idea that shows up, flirts with you for a while, and then leaves without so much as a kiss good-bye."

Evan winced. He took off his coat, folded it over his folded arms, and leaned against the bookshelves between Psychology/Freud and Psychology/Jung to listen. Her voice changed: more formal, the cadences deeper, the sexy throatiness and all traces of Virginia gone.

*They were so fair and fine a splendor, the young knights riding by. From her tower window she gazed down at their proud, unhelmed heads, their faces pure with devotion to God and dedication to Holy Crusade. Crimson crosses on unsullied white silk tabards burned like sacred fire, the same fire that lit their eyes. She saw all this, and wished fiercely that she was a man so that she might join them. Surely their efforts here on Earth would be rewarded and their paths to Heaven would be smooth. They were so beautiful, each with God's Hand on his shoulder and Christ's Finger pointing the way.*

*Each, but for one man who rode alone, apart from all the rest. He too wore the Cross, but there was nothing sacred about him. Tall, powerfully made, he sat his black destrier with the trained suppleness of a warrior and the easy grace of a born horseman. The wind rippled his dark hair, sunlight sparking red glints from its thickness as if flames lingered there still after a journey through Hell. That same fire burned golden in his eyes that were neither brown nor green, eyes that glowed with a light neither splendid nor holy.*

*His gaze caught and held hers. Fire scorched her, and power such as she had never known existed. She averted her eyes. Though she knew nothing of him, not his name or rank or lineage, instinct stronger than reason told her to be wary. He was beautiful, yes — but not with the fervent grandeur of faith. His beauty of proud nose and strong bones and fine, fierce eyes unsettled her. She was young yet, but not so young that she could not recognize danger.*

Holly stopped reading, and there came the sound of pages rustling. Then she said in her usual voice, "This man is based on someone I know. My problem here has been to transfer a twenty-first-century New Yorker into a twelfth-century Crusader. Why, you might very well ask, would I even try? Well, the man I know is a cop."

Lachlan blinked. He'd figured, what with the hair (*"journey through Hell"?*) and the nose (*I guess "proud" is a polite way of describing it*) and the eyes (*I always put down "hazel" on forms — do they really turn gold?*), but to hear her say it out loud like this —

*"Beautiful"?*

A man's voice asked, "So you're saying that a cop's attitude is the same as a knight's — and the legal system is like a Holy War?"

"First, that's not what I'm saying at all. Second, I don't mean to be rude, but if that's *your* attitude toward law enforcement, you may want to reconsider."

*That's my girl!*

"Ponder this," Holly said, the edge gone from her voice now that she'd delivered the rebuke. "The knights are young and full of religious fervor, and have no suspicion how badly they're going to be injured — physically, psychologically. Like a young cop, who wants to help people and catch the bad guys, all idealism and bright illusions. But he's going to get hurt."

"And this guy knows it." This from another man, whose voice was younger and properly respectful.

"He surely does. He looks much like the rest — only of course he's taller, handsomer, sexier, all the usual attributes of the romantic hero —" She laughed with her listeners, and Lachlan rolled his eyes. " — but there's no holy fire of devotion about him. He's seen too much. He knows too much. There's a sequence later on where the girl confronts him, asks why he's doing it, and what he answers is more or less what I think my cop friend would say. That he *does* believe, but not the way these kids do. They think they're seeing clearly, but between them and reality are their illusions. He had those kicked out of him a long time ago."

*Is that how she sees me?*

"He knows that when you finally look reality in the face, your instincts kick in, the most basic parts of what and who you are. And if you're honorable and honest, you can trust those instincts — not only with your own life, but with the lives in your care. Once the illusions are gone, and you see reality for what it is, then and only then can you do the work right."

"I never looked at it that way," a woman mused. "But I bet this goes over real well with the girl."

"She's very young, remember — just sixteen, and deplorably virginal. She wants him to be her White Knight, and he won't oblige. But she comes to realize that she doesn't *want* a White Knight. What would she do with him, anyway? Her sole function in his life would be to keep his armor polished. No, she wants a real man—"

"Don't we all," sighed the questioner, and everyone laughed.

"Tell me about it," Holly agreed, and Lachlan could almost see her wry grin. "You think you've found one, and you're willing to put up with his faults because he's smart and strong and quick and confident, not to mention gorgeous—"

He chuckled silently. From "beautiful" to "gorgeous" in under ten minutes—not bad. But—*what* faults?

"You go, girl!"

"I'm definitely not introducing him to *you*!" Holly laughed, then admonished teasingly, "Back to the book. These two people have a lot to teach each other. For instance, one thing she learns from him is that sex doesn't have to be complicated. He's had about a zillion women—"

*Aw, c'mon—what the hell has Susannah been sayin' about me, anyway?*

"—and sex is the one thing he takes unmitigated pleasure in. For her, it's something to be wary of, because all the men she knows are after something besides her body, and they certainly don't want her love. They want her money, her title, her lands, the power that goes with all that. So she resists this man until she can't hold out any more. When she does give in, it's like falling down a well in the dark. She's terribly afraid that it'll feel like all the other times she's been in love—she'll climb out feeling like she's covered in mud."

*Jesus, Holly—is that you talking, or you talking about the girl?* With her next sentence, he had the answer.

"But with him, it's perfect—cool, clear water, washing her clean. No regret, no betrayal. All the same, she teaches him that he's never really made love before. Had sex, yes. Made love—very different."

A woman asked, "I was about to ask how she changes him."

"If they truly fall in love, she'll open his heart and rekindle his belief—not in the illusion of love, but in the reality of passion and tenderness. Because he does need to believe. He's far too sensitive to live without faith in *something*."

"And if you don't have them fall in love?" someone else asked.

"Where *I* want them to go is irrelevant. Characters in novels do what they're going to do. Remind me to tell you about the guy for whom I had great plans—who got himself killed in a knife-fight without my permission! As for this pair—I'm not sure about them. They don't even have names yet. She might become a symbol—and here's the medieval troubadour tradition of courtly love coming into play—of something he can never have. He might prefer it that way. Love can be hideously cruel. If she's only a symbol, she's easier to deal with, either to accept as his lady fair on a marble pedestal—and nothing more—or to reject outright."

"As if he'd love to love her," a young male voice said eagerly, "but he's scared to—and blames *her* for it."

"Pretty much," Holly agreed.

*Hey, wait a minute—*

"Is this a kind of autobiographical piece set in the past? You and your policeman friend?"

"God, no!" Holly laughed again. "For one thing, I ain't no sixteen-year-old virgin! And he's no knight in shining armor, believe me."

*So much for the romantic hero,* Lachlan mused. *If not a White Knight, how about a "real man"? Still—if I'm him and she's her, and she's sayin' what I think she's sayin'—*

"You can't translate directly that way," she continued more seriously, as if she'd heard his thought. "You can use templates for physical description or character traits, but a twelfth-century French knight has an entirely different mind-set than a twenty-first-century Irish cop." She paused, then said dryly, "Of course, my real problem is I can't keep the guy from *sounding* like a twenty-first-century Irish cop!"

They laughed with her, and went on discussing how to construct character. Evan tuned out, replaying her words in his mind.

*Beautiful* he now dismissed with a complacent little shrug. She'd already let him know she liked the way he looked. But the way she described him—or was she describing the knight?—yeah, that threw him. Was he really like that?

She was the professional. She made a damned good living at this. She must know. Or else she'd just taken his physical description and put somebody else's personality inside. But she'd said the knight was based on him. Had he just been convenient when she needed somebody for a book she was already doing? Or had he truly inspired her to create this character?

And then he thought about what she'd said at the beginning, about an idea flirting with you and then leaving without even a good-bye kiss.

He supposed he really *had* had the illusions kicked out of him. During his few years as a street cop, he'd seen enough to harden him. But everything had avalanched down on him one rainy night when a drug summit gone wrong had ended up in a Lower East Side street cluttered with corpses, two of them fellow cops. It wasn't until the ballistics report arrived that he learned he'd shot and killed four people—him, son of a beat cop who'd never even unholstered his weapon during twenty years on the job. The expression in his old man's eyes that night didn't bear remembering. And the expression that just wouldn't leave his own had scared him. Digging himself out of the wreckage of his rookie idealism hadn't been a painless process, and there'd been some pretty harsh blows to his ego along the way, but the end result was that he had no illusions left at all.

Which had left him with instinct, just like she'd said.

It was hard to remind himself that this was a *story*. Fiction. Not him, not her.

What had she said—something about the characters doing what *they* wanted to do, not what she told them to do?

Just a story. But her speculations about its possible directions shook him. Falling for her—or trying very hard *not* to fall for her, resenting her for his own fear—

She didn't scare him. But maybe what he was feeling for her did. And the outcome—story-wise, personal-wise, and otherwise—was up to him.

Silently, he walked around the bookcases. She was lecturing about plot flowing from character, and the thirty or so people crowded around her were listening and even taking notes. Then she glanced up and saw him.

She kept talking. Even though her eyes widened and her right hand fisted around her pen and a flush burned her cheeks, she kept right on talking. Lachlan stood there, arms folded over his coat, watching her without a single flicker of expression on his face. He had to admire the lady's aplomb.

Now that he knew, he saw the signs—and wondered how he'd been so blind to them. Her hair might be casual, but it was the work of an accomplished stylist. Same with the makeup: the less it looked like a woman used, the more it cost. The clothes were low-key, professional, sophisticated: cinnamon wool skirt, matching cardigan, ivory shirt. The jewelry was a diamond solitaire necklace and matching earrings, not gaudy but very expensive. He'd worked cases in the diamond mart and learned how to tell one carat from two. Or three.

The store manager called for another autograph session, and Lachlan duly got in line. The girl just ahead of him had been at the reading; she said to Holly, "I really liked what you read us. When will the book be coming out?"

"I don't know. As I said, it might be nothing more than a short story."

Evan felt his lips twist wryly.

"Or it might turn into a novel. Who knows?" She held up her hands in a what-the-hell gesture, smiling. "I could want to write about this guy for a long, long time."

Oh, yeah—this was definitely meant for him.

The girl left, arms full of books. Evan stepped up to the table and dug the paperback out of his pocket. "You said the characters don't have names yet," he remarked as he handed her the book. "Have you got any in mind?"

She looked straight up at him, calm and unblinking. "I was considering 'Elisabeth' for the girl and 'Guillaume' for the knight, but I'm not sure yet. I still have reservations."

Evan Liam Lachlan smiled at Holly Elizabeth McClure. "So do I—for two, tonight at La Pasta Vita." He didn't, but that could be quickly remedied. "I was hoping you'd join me."

He knew everyone else in line was gaping. Holly was aware of them, too— and played to them, the vindictive bitch. He stifled a snort of laughter as she tilted her head slightly to one side, her cool blue gaze running down his gray sweater and faded workshirt and battered jeans—lingering at his inseam. She couldn't have been more obvious if she'd ordered him to strip and asked for a ruler. Revenge, he supposed, forbidding himself to be embarrassed by her scrutiny. Or the scrutiny of others—who were looking at his height, his nose, his hair, and his eyes with more than a little curiosity.

At last she arched a brow. "What time?" He'd passed inspection.

"7:30." He kept the grin from his face. "I'm honored, Ms. McClure."

"I'm flattered, Mr.—?" She looked expectantly at him, as if truly not knowing who he was.

"Lachlan."

She nodded, as if storing the unfamiliar name in memory. She scribbled something on the title page of the book, closed it, and handed it back to him with a bright professional smile. "Thanks so much for being here today."

He winked at her and left the store. A phone call later, the reservations were real. He went home and puttered around until 6:30, then changed into stiff new Levi's, soft white shirt, brown pullover that brought out the green in his eyes, and his beloved cowboy boots. Wallet, keys, jacket—he was ready. Then he took a last look at himself in the mirror on the back of the bathroom door. Nope, no knight in shining armor.

Just as well.

" 'Dangerous,' huh?" he asked his reflection, and laughed.

# Three

TO SPEND AN HOUR DRESSING for a date with a man for whom she wasn't going to be undressing was ridiculous, and Holly was disgusted with herself. It wasn't as if anything would come of this dinner. She could've scripted the whole thing. He'd make a few remarks about her using him as a character (Christ on the cross, what she wouldn't give to have chosen *anything* else to read), and she'd shrug as if it didn't matter, and he'd tell her he hadn't been put on this Earth to provide her with material for a short story, let alone a novel. She'd cut to the chase and say *Fine, I do what I do and you do what you do, and you don't like it that I make more money at my job than you do at yours. Personally, I think what they pay me in relation to what they pay you is obscene—but I'm not going to give it back, either.* They'd snipe some more and she'd walk out—leaving a hundred-dollar bill at the front desk to pay for dinner, her last little insult.

She dressed in one outfit, then another, then a third, and a fourth, and finally stood naked in the huge closet, analyzing the situation.

Skirt? Too short and he'd think she was giving him a look at her legs to remind him of what he wasn't going to get later. Always assuming he still wanted it. Besides, he'd already taken a good look this afternoon at the signing. But if she wore a skirt that was too long, he'd get no look at all at what he wasn't going to get.

Trousers. The gray wool would make her look like she was late to a business meeting. Denim was too casual. It was too chilly for silk or linen. Maybe the black velvet jeans. And heels to make her nearer his height. She hated it when men looked down on her. At five-nine and change, she found there weren't many who could. Lachlan was six-four in his socks. She pawed through her shirt collection, telling herself she really ought to get rid of some of this stuff, rejecting all until she came to a teal-blue satin. She hauled on the clothes, brushed her hair, and made up her face while wondering if there was enough powder in the world to minimize her goddamned freckles. Then she went to explore her jewelry cases.

She was tempted to put on something really, really expensive, like the sapphires and diamonds she'd treated herself to when she turned thirty-five. But she stayed with the solitaire diamond that had been her gift to herself on publication of the Christine de Pisan book, and the matching earrings that similarly commemorated Artemisia Gentileschi. Yes, she did have money, and the hell with him if he didn't like it. She bought what she wanted, wore what she wanted, and—and the hell with him anyway. Shouldering into a coat, she went out the door before she could change her mind again.

And stopped at the elevator and went back to her apartment to abandon the jeans for a short black skirt and black hose and a pair of four-inch stilettos—cursing him and herself to kingdom come. By then it was past seven and she didn't have time to dither anymore.

They got to the restaurant at the same time—he walking from one direction, she from the other. He wore a leather jacket that further broadened his shoulders and gave some taper to his waist, making him look slimmer than he really was. His height and heft always hit her like a fist in the stomach—a strength that could be bulky and threatening but for her was always solid, supple, masculine—a *presence*. Powerful; she'd picked the right word for him. And he was so aware of it, so perfectly capable of using it to his precisely calculated advantage.

His sexuality, on the other hand, he simply flaunted. He was casually dressed tonight, but he wore all his clothes the same way: bathrobe or jeans or suit (and those awful ostrich-leather cowboy boots), he gave the feeling that he inhabited fabric only because society required it. The smug bastard knew that his best clothing was his own skin. She thought about that skin for a moment, and the long strong bones and hard curving muscles it covered, and steeled her jaw.

"Nice," he commented as they met outside the door, his gaze running over her legs.

"Thanks. You, too." And then some, the miserable son of a bitch. What that sweater did to those great big hazel-green eyes—

He smiled. She blushed as if she'd spoken her thoughts aloud. He opened the door for her, and they went inside. Ten minutes later, wine and pasta selected, they waited for salads in total silence.

All at once Evan said, "That book you signed for me—I read it, y'know. Yesterday."

"Did you?" She glanced up in surprise.

"Yeah." He sipped Chianti. "I liked it. Not my thing, but I did like it."

"Thanks." She paused. "Did you read what I wrote in your copy?"

He shook his head. "The way you were looking at me, I didn't think it'd be anything I wanted to read."

"You were wrong," she replied calmly.

"So what'd it say?"

"Go home and see for yourself."

Salads came. They ate. Salads were removed. They drank wine and dipped bread in rosemary-flavored olive oil.

"Why didn't you want to read what's in your copy?" Holly asked. "What did you think I'd write?"

"Something about what an asshole I am."

She choked on wine and laughter. Napkin at her mouth, she looked at his twinkling eyes and the impossible grin on his face.

"Well, that's what you were thinking, wasn't it?" he prompted.

She nodded. After a sip of water, she said, "I can't help what I do, Evan. I wouldn't even if I could. I love my work as much as you love yours. I know I should've told you—"

"Susannah says men hit on you because of who you are." He eyed her over the rim of his wineglass. "I guess you're lookin' for somebody who's just after your body, right?"

"You *are* an asshole, Lachlan." But she grinned back. "Look, I really am sorry I didn't say anything. It's just so good to be with a man who doesn't want me to read his Great American Novel, or get his hands on my bank account or my agent, or meet the people who hang around literary events in New York. You don't care about any of that. Do you have any idea what a relief that is?"

"I wouldn't say I don't care about the bank account."

*Here it comes,* she thought. "All right, let's talk money. What's wrong with it?"

"Nothin'—if you earn it."

"Now you wait just a goddamned minute—"

"Which I never said you didn't," he interrupted. "Christ, lady, throttle it back, willya? Red hair, freckles, and an Irish temper—what a cliché."

"Explain yourself," she said tightly.

"I just have to be sure you aren't slumming," he said, trying to sound offhand and failing. "That you haven't lied to me about everything else."

"I never lied to you about this or anything, and you know it."

"You just kinda forgot to mention it."

"Goddammit, I told you—"

"But what really pisses me off," he continued as if she hadn't spoken, "is what's really going on here. You punished *me* for what other men've done. If I fuck up, kick me in the ass, I'll deserve it. But I won't be lied to so you can make up for all the lies other men told you." He sat back, studying her shocked face. At last he asked, "You gonna walk out on me now in a huff, or stay and have dinner?"

"You *bastard*," she hissed.

They were distracted—fortunately—by the waiter's arrival with pasta. They started eating, and after a while both had calmed down.

"All right," Holly said suddenly. "Maybe I *was* punishing you for things that aren't your fault. It's been years since my profession wasn't an issue. Every relationship I've had since I started getting paid good money has been pretty much the same. Lousy taste in men, right?"

"Present company excepted." He swallowed wine and leaned back in his chair again.

"Suze was the one who thought we should meet. It wasn't my idea." She couldn't stop a little smile from touching her mouth. *"Thirty seconds, Holly—I bet it's not more than thirty seconds before you want to rip his clothes off!"* Banishing the memory, she went on lightly, "And I was the one who told her to go for it with Elias. Looks like we're better at picking men for each other than for ourselves."

"Looks like," he agreed laconically.

Holly took a deep breath. "Evan, I'm sorry. I didn't mean to lie to you. I've told you why I didn't say anything." And she'd apologized for this three times now, which was twice more than her iron-clad limit.

He stayed silent for a minute, drank more wine, then shrugged. "Holly, I'm not sayin' I'm exactly thrilled with all this. But I'm not a Neanderthal, either."

He *would* have to be the one man not an anthropology major who actually pronounced it without the *h*. Just her luck.

"I've gone out with women who make more money than I do."

He was trying. He really was. She appreciated that, and understood what it cost him. But it didn't change things in the long run.

"Just not *this* much more," she murmured to her wineglass. "It's okay, Evan. Say good-bye nicely now, and bow out. I understand."

"You understand jack shit. I got news for you, lady." He reached across the tablecloth and circled her wrist with his fingers. "I'm not a *total* asshole. Just don't throw the money in my face, don't rub my nose in it, and I can handle it. Okay?"

She searched his eyes for a long moment, then sighed and turned her palm to fit into his. "You truly are a dangerous man, you know. You make me want to believe you so damned much."

"I've never lied to you. Not once."

She swallowed the implied rebuke—and it went down with surprising ease when he looked at her this way. Then his gaze dropped to their clasped hands, and for a moment she was lost in how his lashes lay thick and sooty on his cheeks. He had a trick of looking quickly away before briefly closing his eyes — and then opening them to transfix his victim with a long, level, direct stare. Like a dragon was supposed to be able to do, she thought distractedly, as a tiny smile teased his lips before his gaze lifted and she was treated to the full power of those eyes. Yes, a dragon would have eyes like his: brilliant, inexorable. . . .

"So do the brave knight and the beautiful virgin ever get in the sack?"

This was so unexpected that she couldn't help laughing. "You *would* ask that! It's the way I said—I don't know if this will be anything more than a short story."

"Make it a novel," he advised. "A long one. With sequels." The dragon's eyes suddenly kindled with golden glints that could mean anger or amusement but right now meant forthright lust. "I can help with the research."

Holly arched her brows. "I'm guessing you heard what I told the group today, but it's worth repeating. I'm no sixteen-year-old virgin, and you're no White Knight, *a chuisle*."

The Irish endearment threw him. It showed in his startled eyes. She'd been saving it for a tender moment, the sweet and slurring *ah-koush-lah*, but tonight it just slipped out. Not exactly the most romantic timing. . . . Still, what he said next surprised her completely, as did the dark, faraway look in his eyes.

"I haven't heard that since—Granna Maureen used to call Granddad that." He shook his head as if trying to shake off a memory. "I told you about her— she was born in the Old Country, kept the accent and even spoke Gaelic sometimes. Granddad married her when she was seventeen, a year off the boat."

"Were they happy?"

"For sixty-three years." He hesitated, his hand suddenly rigid and cold in hers. His eyes were lightless, his mouth thin, his voice sharp and bitter. "If I'd never known them, I'd never've known that not all husbands hit their wives, and not all wives drank themselves comatose by four in the afternoon—"

"*Éimhín*—!" He'd never said a word about it, never hinted—

"Long time ago. Doesn't matter."

Ah, but it did. And she understood all at once why the danger in him was so tightly leashed. Abuse cycled from generation to generation, and this man was terrified of becoming his parents. She held his hand until it warmed in hers. He managed a rueful smile and poured more wine for them both.

They talked of other things, enjoying each other as they always did. At last, over espresso and biscotti, she said, "Evan, I promise I won't throw the money in your face. But you have to promise me something, too."

"Yeah?" he asked warily.

"Please, pretty please—" She folded her hands together in fervent prayer. "Let me buy you just *one* pair of shoes that aren't those damned cowboy boots!"

———

AT HIS FIRST SIGHT OF her apartment, his heart sank to his ankles. It wasn't just one floor in the corner of the building but two, with a graceful half-circle staircase rising from a marble-tiled foyer. The banister was warm red oak, the carpet white Berber, both recognized from lab samples—and couldn't he shut off being a cop for just ten minutes, and look at her place without what he knew damned well were defense mechanisms? But she was nervous, too—she couldn't even look at him. Her cheeks were bright red, and not from the cold outside.

"Living room," she began, leading him from the foyer into a darkened space illumined an instant later by automatic sensors. He blinked a little; the room was bigger than his whole apartment. Beyond the windows, each hung with a small swirly glass sphere to catch the sunshine, were the fairy-castle lights of buildings on the other side of the Park. He glanced at the view, then around the room. Dark green leather furniture, big coffee table of wood and wrought iron, paintings—he recognized the Grand Canyon, Yosemite Valley, Il Duomo in Florence, and a ramshackle cottage amid hills so green, they had to be in Ireland, but the other landscapes were unknown to him. An unmirrored wet bar over in the far corner sparkled with crystal stemware and liquor bottles in glass-fronted cabinets. His shoes sank soundlessly into a superb dark crimson Persian rug as he followed her across the room to the bar.

"What can I pour you? Scotch? Brandy?"

"Brandy."

She selected big balloon snifters and a decanter of amber liquid that was probably twice as old as he was. He swirled it in his glass, inhaling, before taking a sip. "This is good. No balcony?"

"I'm terrified of heights," she explained with a self-deprecating shrug. "This is the only apartment of this size in the building that doesn't have one. Do you want to see the rest, or just sit and talk for a while?"

"Might as well get it over with," he said, and could have kicked himself for the flinch that crossed her face.

Her reply was grim. "Come on, then."

She took him on the grand tour. Elegant white-and-silver powder room off the foyer. Kitchen with lots of copper and Italian plates; formal dining room with a suite of old mahogany furniture and a display of chipped, mismatched milk pitchers. Comfy and homey as it was, he was willing to bet that she rarely used this room, eating instead at the kitchen table or in front of the TV.

Back to the hall, and thence to her office—the Show Office, she termed it—with framed book covers, photos of her with people he didn't know, her undergraduate and graduate degrees, awards ("My ego wall," she said dismissively);

two walls of books and one of windows; carved wooden desk; big brown suede sofa in front of the wide-screen TV and stereo system.

Where she actually worked was a small room next door—and he tried not to stare. Nothing was dirty, but everything was a mess. Papers, books, magazines, letters, folders, manila envelopes, empty coffee mugs, tins of chocolate-covered espresso beans for caffeine fixes. A massive partners desk took up most of the space, its scarred wooden top cluttered with computer, laptop, disks, CDs, manuscripts, printer—

"My housekeeper is forbidden even to enter this room. If Isabella cleaned it up, I'd never find anything."

How she found her own nose in this chaos was beyond his comprehension. He was compulsively neat, a habit pounded into him by his mother. Whatever else Patricia Lachlan had been, whatever else could be said of her, she had kept a spotless house. Nobody could ever believe that such a meticulous homemaker was a drunk.

Lachlan dismissed his memories as not belonging here any more than his work did, and followed Holly into the bedroom. Not the way he might have planned it—she stalked ahead of him, her movements still stiff with tension, and he tagged along feeling distinctly unwelcome.

"Isabella's day off," she said, picking up a sweater from the floor. She looked around for somewhere to put it—but chaise, ottoman, bed, and dressing table were all covered in clothes and more books. She shrugged and dropped the sweater back where it had been.

It had taken her a single day without a housekeeper to create this havoc? As she slid off her heels and lobbed them in the general direction of the huge walk-in closet, he found it easy to believe it had taken her a single hour.

Tidied up, it would be a nice room. A little countrified for his tastes, but nice. Wrought-iron bedstead, oak furniture, colorful handmade quilt, incredible cityscape view. The chaise—what he could see of it beneath clothes, an afghan, and yet more books—was a dark green that matched the brocade drapes. The hardwood floor was partly covered by a braided rag rug. Photos decorated one wall—her parents' wedding picture, obviously, and other people from much earlier times.

"That's quite a collection," Lachlan said, just for something to say. "Your mother's beautiful."

"Yes, she was. I don't remember my parents. They were killed when I was two years old."

"I'm sorry," he said, meaning it.

"Aunt Lulah raised me—my father's sister and Mama's best friend. Papa edited and published the local paper. Mama wrote articles and sold ad space—a real two-mule farm operation, and guess who the mules were."

"The partners desk was theirs, right?"

She glanced at him in surprise. "Yes."

"What happened?"

Square shoulders lifted in a little shrug. "He wrote one too many editorials, and she wrote one too many articles, and they both were in one too many marches, in support of the Civil Rights Movement. At least, that's how we understand it. Nobody ever proved anything. They were in Alabama for an NAACP conference and their car went off a bridge. When word came, our local Klan threw a party."

She spoke matter-of-factly, but he could hear the hurt in her voice. He wanted to touch her, just to let her know he was there. But she was gesturing to the rest of the photos.

"Meet four generations of McClures, Flynns, Kirbys, McNichols, Coxes, Bellews, and Sherers."

"Sure, and nary a *sassenach* somewhere in t'family tree?" he teased in his grandmother's Irish accent. "Get on w'ye!"

Her chuckle was unwilling, but she replied easily enough, "Well . . . a few French and Welsh, plus an early Virginia cattle rancher named Domingo Madeiras, who was probably a Portuguese Jew forced to convert by the Inquisition. Even a Cherokee lady—but they lied up hill and down dale about that, of course, or it would've been a one-way ticket to Oklahoma on the Trail of Tears." She paused, as if having caught herself responding to him, and resumed more formally, "Nobody knows why our McClures left Ireland so early, but there are rumors of everything from murdered landlords to horse-thieving." She traced a fingertip over the small brass heraldic crest on one of the frames. "We're a sept of Clan MacLeod, from the Isle of Skye. Our branch imported itself to Ireland long ago, when Scotland and Ireland were still politically united."

Evidently when she felt threatened, she went into lecture mode. An interesting defense, and wholly appropriate to someone who lived by words. But he also understood that she was trying to reestablish common ground, back to their very first conversations.

"The two kingdoms of Dalriada," he said quietly. "I know my Irish history." He inspected the MacLeod crest, which featured a bull's head and the motto *Hold Fast*. Resisting the impulse to point at it and say, *"Gee, ya think?"*, he remarked, "The MacLaughlins are nobody's sept."

"Why do you use the Scots spelling, by the way?"

"Smart immigrant. After two weeks in Boston she made her husband change 'O'Laughlin' to 'Lachlan.' She wanted to raise the kids Presbyterian, but he drew the line and we stayed Catholic."

"I wondered how somebody named Evan Lachlan could have a map of County Donegal on his face." After a second's hesitation, she said, "Did you know that the last Witch to be hanged in Scotland was Elspeth MacEwan of Clan MacLachlan?"

"You do your research, lady."

"It's my job." And with mention of that point of contention, her smile died. He wasn't surprised when she sought refuge again in words. "That's Richard McClure at age ninety-three," she said, pointing to a photo of a silver-haired man whose nose had been broken more than once, judging by its bumps and turns. His eyes were beautiful, though—like Holly's eyes, large and luminous, and even though it was a sepia-toned photograph Evan knew the deep blue had blazed like sapphires in sunlight. "There wasn't anything for him to inherit, so he made his way through the South as a prizefighter. He must've been pretty good at it, too, because he ended up with quite a plantation before the Civil War. After was a different story, but—"

Lachlan decided that as interesting as all this might be, he was tired of being lectured to. "So the McClures came over on the *Mayflower*, huh?" As she threw him an annoyed scowl, he pretended to remember. "Oh, that's right—that was the Puritans. No Irish Need Apply."

Through gritted teeth she said, "If you *must* know, the McClures got to Virginia in 1623, and the Flynns in 1625."

"Over two hundred years before the Lachlans and Coyles got to New York."

"When did this turn into a dick contest to see who's more Irish?"

"Take it easy. It was just a comment." But he couldn't shut his mouth over the next words: "Betcha you can trace your line all the way back to Brian Boru."

Holly glared up at him, having to tilt her head back now that she was without shoes. "As a matter of fact, yes. So can half Ireland. So fucking what?"

Before he could reply, she stalked out of the bedroom and into the hallway. He followed her upstairs to the second floor. Without the heels, she was half a foot shorter than he—and he discovered he rather liked it when she was smaller, somehow less formidable. On the other hand, he also liked being with a woman who could damned near stare him straight in the eye, and was strong enough to give him a rousing tussle in bed when they both felt like it.

It was very confusing. He had learned recently that a lot about her confused him. She could fascinate him with wry stories or serious conversation; she could bed him in any mood from laughing greed to shy sweetness; she could wake up growly and curt or cuddly and playful; she could look like a little girl with her hair in pigtails, or incite him to near-rape with a silk dress and pearls.

She could live in a place like this, and be as rich and well-known as she was, and probably have twenty men beating down her door—and still want *him*. Insecurity was not one of his failings, and he knew it, and the reason he was feeling it wasn't her fault—he was fair enough to admit that. All the same. . . .

Upstairs, one room contained filing cabinets and the overflow books. Another was supposed to be a family room, with fireplace; two bedrooms and shared bath were for guests; a second powder room was at the end of the hall. Counting the baths, she had fourteen rooms here—six of which it appeared she didn't visit very often. "You don't use the upstairs at all?" he asked.

"Just for storage and guests."

She took him back down to the living room, and after building a fire in the hearth she curled into the corner of a couch with her brandy in hand.

"So. That's it, Evan. The whole show."

He doubted it. There were things she hadn't said about the furniture, things he recognized from cases having to do with the upper crust, or with antiques dealers. But he let that go. He ambled about the room, sipping brandy, glancing at the display of antique brass candlesticks on the mantelpiece, the glass-fronted cabinet full of porcelain this and pewter that, the books on art and travel and castles piled on the end tables.

"Where's the cat?"

"How did you know I have a cat?"

"Book cover."

"Oh. Mugger's probably hiding someplace. I imagine once he heard another voice besides mine, he made a run for it. He'll make an appearance eventually." She finished her brandy and set the glass down. "You still haven't said what you think of the place."

"It's nice."

"*That's* lame."

He turned from examining a lovely plein aire oil painting of a flower-strewn meadow. "So whaddya want me to say? At least it's not *decorated*." He waved a hand to indicate his disgust with homes where couches were designed to make the pillows comfortable, not the people.

"Oh, thank you," she snapped. "I'm *so* glad I took off all the plastic slipcovers before you arrived."

"Look, lady, what do you want? I say I like it, you slap me down. I say the reason I like it is because it doesn't scream money, and you get insulted. Make up your mind."

"Oh, shit." Holly bent her head, dark red hair falling forward to hide her face.

He sat next to her on the couch, placing his brandy glass on the table. "Hey."

"I'm sorry, *Éimhín*." The slurring Irish version of his name—Ay-*veen*—trembled a little. "I just—I wasn't prepared for this. For you being here."

Brushing aside her hair, framing her face with his hands, he gently coaxed her to look at him. Insecurity? It was all over her, from the bitten lip to the apprehensive eyes to the defensive tension tightening her square jaw. It hit him out of nowhere then, and with all the subtlety of a freight train: she didn't know whether or not he still wanted her, and she wanted him to—because *she* wanted *him*.

So he kissed her, gently at first, then with more urgency. She needed persuading tonight; she was still nervous. Worried about his reaction. Maybe she was right. Not that he'd been afraid to find solid-gold faucets and Louis Quinze furniture—not her style—but it was a big place with a lot of expensive stuff in it. And the rocks in her earlobes weren't rhinestones, either.

*So I've caught myself a rich one,* he mused as he unbuttoned her shirt. *The old lady would be so fucking proud of me. Good thing she's dead so she can't gloat.*

He'd never be able to give Holly diamonds like these, he thought distractedly, parting her satin shirt. The scent of her perfume in the warm hollow between her breasts usually drove all other thought from his mind. But that damned insecurity still nagged at him. He couldn't give her what she was used to. What if she wanted more than he could—

"Hey. Lachlan."

He lifted his head. "Mmm?"

"If you're going to be here with me, be *here* with me, okay?"

Now, how had she done that—sensed that his mind was wandering?

"Kiss me like you mean it," she whispered, "or get your coat and go."

"And don't come back?"

She nodded slowly.

He pulled away from her, reaching for the brandy. Draining it down his throat, he set the glass aside and got to his feet. When he looked down at her, the hurt on her face was more than he could bear. Swiftly he bent, one arm going beneath her knees, the other around her back. He lifted her up—unable to prevent a grunt of effort from escaping his lips. She was no anorexic, this one.

Holly was laughing at him. "Nice gesture, Lachlan—now put me down before you get a hernia!"

Growling, he hiked her up more firmly in his arms. In four long steps he was at the fireplace, and knelt, setting her down. The gold-patterned hearth rug was scarred here and there by scorching, and he liked what that said about her: nothing about this place was perfect, and she kept things she loved even if they were a little worn. He stripped off his sweater and shirt while she reclined on her elbows, watching him with firelight dancing in her eyes.

He would never know quite how it happened, but all at once she had pulled him down, shoved him onto his back, and was undoing the buttons of his jeans. The heat of the fire caressed him all along one side—and she was on the other, her hands and lips and tongue everywhere, starting at his forehead and covering every inch down to his groin. Following her fingers and tongue was the tantalizing silken caress of her hair.

"Holly—take your clothes off—come on, babe, I want to see you—"

She shook her head and coaxed snug denim down his hips and thighs. "It'd interfere with your concentration. No distractions, lover-man. This is all for you."

Kneeling, she hooked his legs around her back, the position damned near precisely the one *he* should have been in, and the reversal of roles was doubly arousing. Sometimes a woman asked if he wanted her to be the aggressor; sometimes a woman did so without asking, and didn't much care about his satisfaction as long as she got her precious multiple orgasms. Which he was always happy to provide, being more or less a gentleman, though he did get a little weary sometimes of feeling like nothing more than a convenient, anonymous cock.

But when Holly was in a mood to ravish him—her word, damned writer's vocabulary—she took unrepentant control. He was hers to play with, hers to drive insane slowly or swiftly as whimsy took her. A nameless convenience was the very last thing he felt like when she did this to him. Looking up at her dreamy eyes and sultry smile, he realized that tonight was going to be one of the slow ones. He gave an involuntary shiver of mingled anticipation and impatience. He *knew* she was about to drive him totally, thoroughly, absolutely berserk, and leave him a wrecked, ruined husk; she'd done it before, though not quite this way. He'd felt her lips before, but only as a prelude to his entering her. Tonight would be different.

"Close your eyes," she whispered. "Just feel, *a chuisle*. Don't do anything but *feel*."

He couldn't have done anything else if his life depended on it, not after hearing that endearment again; it seemed to melt every bone in his body.

A long time later he felt her snuggle down with her head on his chest. "Back among the living yet?" she teased.

"You—" He cleared his throat and tried again. "You been savin' that?"

"Your reward for being a sweetheart. Mostly a sweetheart, anyway."

"Wasn't exactly fair," he murmured.

"Very considerate of you, *a chuisle*, but don't worry about it. Making you crazy is my idea of a great time. Sort of an early Christmas present to myself."

"Sadistic bitch," he accused amiably, and sighed down to the bottom of his lungs. "Christ, Holly, I won't be able to get it back up for a week."

"I can wait."

"I can't."

She chuckled silently. "Stake your claim?"

"You got it. Besides, I'm startin' to think it'll only come up for *you*." He knew he sounded bewildered. He hadn't meant to admit that.

"Precisely what I had in mind. That's why I staked *my* claim just now."

He thought that over—*Hold Fast*—and grunted.

Sliding off him, she stretched luxuriously and dragged a well-worn brown afghan from a chair. Quite matter-of-factly she stripped, tossing skirt and shirt and hose and silk underwear wherever, then threw another log onto the fire. At last she draped the afghan around them both and cuddled her cheek to his shoulder.

"We're sleeping here?" he asked fuzzily.

"I like looking at you in firelight. And I promise I'll wake you up before Isabella comes in tomorrow."

"I might wake up first." He grinned, leaving no doubt as to his meaning.

"I thought you'd decided you're incapacitated for the next week."

"Darlin' Holly," he smiled, "never underestimate an Irishman in love."

It went right through her, every muscle flinching, every nerve jumping. "What did you say?"

"I said I'm in love with you. Why shouldn't I be?"

"And when did you realize this?"

"When I found out how rich you are."

She nipped at his lower lip. "Cute, Lachlan. Damned cute. You'll pay for that. Now tell me for real."

"I'm in love with you. For real." And then, as her head lowered once more: "Christ, Holly, don't bite me again—"

But this time she kissed him, soft and sweet, until he was sighing in her arms. "Sleep, *a chuisle mo chroí*," she whispered against his lips, and put her head back where it belonged on his shoulder. He held her as tight as he possibly could for a moment, then relaxed his arms into a comfortable embrace.

HOLLY WAS RUDELY AWAKENED WHEN Evan yelped and jerked his knee into her thigh. "Huh? Evan—?"

He sat up, half the afghan going with him. "What the hell was that?"

She was spared having to answer by the arrival of a warm mass of long white fur that wriggled into the space between her and Evan. She grinned into amber eyes shining from the black mask covering most of his face; the cat responded by trilling softly. "Hi, Mugger. Meet Evan—whose toes I bet you just tried to have for a snack."

"Does he do that all the time?" Lachlan demanded.

"Just to me. He probably spent a while padding around, sniffing at you. And because you smell of me, and I smell of you, Mugs decided you were okay."

"Imagine my relief."

"C'mon, scratch his ears. Yeah, right there. See? He does like you."

"Jesus," he muttered. "What woulda happened if he didn't? Or don't I want to know?"

"Oh, he's not vicious. He didn't actually bite, did he? Just nibbled. If he didn't approve, he'd just ignore you until I took the hint and got rid of you. Cats have ways of letting you know what they think."

Mugger levitated from a half-crouch to settle himself across Evan's broad bare shoulders, and proceeded to purr like a Porsche. Evan froze, eyes wide.

"He's never done *that* before," Holly remarked.

"Great," he replied sourly. He reached up a hand to scratch white-tufted black ears. "So he likes me enough to let me stay?"

She stifled laughter, knowing he was imagining the possible timings of Mugger's feasts. "Relax. He sleeps in his own bed in my office. But don't move too suddenly. He isn't declawed." She doubled over laughing as his eyes went wider than ever with apprehension.

"Holly—get him off me, willya? C'mon—"

Five minutes later, with Mugger duly ensconced in his pillowed basket, Holly crawled back under the afghan and huddled against Evan to warm up. Why was it, she mused, that when you put any two people together, one of them always slept warm and the other always slept cold? The warm one—and Evan was a furnace—always kicked the covers off, and screamed bloody murder about cold hands and frozen feet, and—

But there was nary a complaint from him. There never had been. He simply tucked himself along her back from neck to knees and took her chilled hands between his big warm ones while his feet rubbed hers. *Heaven in ostrich-hide cowboy boots,* she told herself happily, and snuggled back against him.

"So how long you gonna be away for Christmas?" he asked, lips moving on her nape, deep voice rumbling through her chest.

"I'm not. Every airport between Maine and Atlanta will be snowed in by tomorrow afternoon. First in a series of storms all the way to Christmas Eve, or so they say. Aunt Lulah called yesterday and told me to stay here. So—no Christmas in Virginia. But that's okay. I already got my present." She brought one of his hands to her lips and pressed a kiss in the hollow. "A big Mick cop who says he's madly in love with me."

"Huh. Don't recall saying 'madly.'"

"It was implied. I hope. What about you—are you going to your father's? Your sister's?"

"Neither. I work Christmas so the other guys can be with their families."

"How very sweet and noble of you."

"Nobility has nothin' to do with it. It saves me from my sister's cooking. I take New Year's to compensate—otherwise everybody'd think I have no life," he finished wryly.

"Want some company at the office? Just point me to an empty desk. I'll bring my laptop and work on letters or something."

"Holly, you must have friends you'd rather be with—"

"Nope." She paused. "I know a lot of people, but I don't have many friends. Not real ones, like Susannah. In my business you kind of become a collectible, you know? I can usually tell when somebody wants to know Holly McClure the person or H. Elizabeth McClure the commodity. However it plays out, I spend a lot of time by myself. A writer's life is only spasmodically social, anyway. And even then it's mainly schmoozing."

"You're good at it. I was watching you today in the store."

"Years of unwilling practice." She gave a little shrug. "I don't get out much, when it comes to it. Besides, there's too many people out on those mean streets."

"New York scares a country girl like you?" He snorted. "I don't believe it."

Holly gave another uneasy shrug. "So—can I spend Christmas with you? You wouldn't be taking me away from anything. There's nobody I'd rather be with."

He was quiet for a time. Then: "So I guess you're in love with me, too."

"Didn't I say so?"

"No."

Extricating herself from his arms, she turned and propped herself on her elbows and looked down at him. "I'm sorry, *Éimhín*. I thought you knew. You must've known practically since the first minute I set eyes on you. I've been obvious enough about it—haven't I?"

He shook his head slowly.

"I'm sorry," she repeated. "I would've bet the farm that you're the type of man who never says it first. And I'm one of the few people you'll ever know who actually has a farm to bet!"

"Are you trying to distract me from the main issue?" But he was smiling.

"If I wanted to do that, I'd kiss you here—and here—and—"

"Holly. Say it."

"Say what?" she asked from behind his left ear.

"You know damned well what! C'mon—you're madly in love with me. Say it!"

She took his face between her hands, gazing into his eyes. They changed from hazel to forest green to darkest brown depending on his mood, what he wore, how much sleep he'd had—and sometimes, she could swear, even the weather. But the one constant was the brilliant golden sparkle that came into his eyes when he looked at her. A fire that wasn't holy—not him!—but certainly splendid.

"I love you, *Éimhín Liam Lochlainn*. I love your eyes and your smile and your amazing body—" She nipped an earlobe. "Stop smirking, you conceited pig, I'm not finished! I love talking with you, and listening to you, and making you laugh, and I even love how goddamned mule-headed you are—no, I do!" she insisted as he shook with silent laughter. "I love everything about you—I've fallen madly, passionately, hopelessly in love with you."

"Mmm . . ." He gave her one of those impossible, irresistible grins. "I can see there's definite advantages to getting a writer-lady in bed. You do know how to sweet-talk a man, Ms. McClure." He smoothed her hair back. "I gotta tell you, though — 'madly' and 'passionately' I like — but 'hopelessly'? That sounds pretty grim, lady love."

"Far from it. Trust me, *a chuisle*, it's wonderful. It means all I can do is relax and enjoy the ride. That's never happened to me before, and it's kind of fun."

"Even if I'm dangerous?" He looked up from under a thick screen of black lashes.

She laughed, felt herself blush. He'd heard all of it this afternoon, right enough. "Dangerous? Lachlan, you're a menace." Lips teasing his earlobe. "A threat to decent women everywhere." Tongue tickling his long throat. "Ruinous to a lady's self-control." Fingers stealing down his belly — she smiled as muscles tightened involuntarily. "Definitely a lethal weapon —"

She gasped as she was flipped onto her back. He loomed over her, grinning. "Fully loaded, darlin'," he purred wickedly.

She wrapped her arms around his shoulders, gazing up at him. It wasn't a beautiful face, strictly speaking — the nose was too big and the mouth not quite wide enough. But any less nose and his face would be nothing but eyes, and any difference in the mouth would forfeit the tender, vulnerable curve of the lower lip.

He took his time — and took her over the edge again and again and again. Softly at first, with exquisite care, so subtle that she whimpered and sighed with the silken pleasure of it.

"Sing for me," he murmured against her mouth. "I love to feel your body sing for me —"

"Oh, *a chuisle*, you're the only song I know —"

He chuckled low in his throat. "Nice line, writer-lady. You gonna use it in the book?"

"*Line* — ! Lachlan, you miserable —"

He smiled at her and she caught her breath. His eyes had become dragon's eyes. He reached down with one arm, hooking the elbow under her knee, opening her to him completely — and began to make love in earnest. His endurance maddened her; his control infuriated her. She clawed his back like a crazy thing, cursing him, begging him, using everything she knew about him to hurry him on. When she swore at him, he laughed. When she pleaded, he kissed her and said, "Shh — easy, now, lady love. I'll give you what you want — don't I always?" With him, she got more than she'd ever learned to want. And he knew it, the smug son of a bitch.

When she finally came back to herself, with very little memory of where she'd been except that it had been glorious, he was smiling an insolent little smile that somehow managed to be incredibly sweet. It was, in fact, the most beautiful face she'd ever seen.

"Were *you* saving *that*?" she murmured.

"Your present for saying you're in love with me."

Holly thought this over. At last she said, "If that's your idea of a present, Christmas will be the death of me."

"If you don't freeze first. Fire's almost gone —"

Yawning, she made a thoughtless gesture. In an instant, flames flared up from the logs, sparks snapping against the brass firescreen.

"— out."

"Oh, damn," she whispered, and turned away from him. *Idiot! Moron!*

It took several minutes for him to get his voice back. When he did, his words were very soft, very controlled. "*That* was interesting."

Holly covered her face with her hands.

"Is there a reason, or does spontaneous combustion just come naturally?"

"There's a reason," she muttered miserably.

"Good," Evan said. "Just so long as you're not something out of a Stephen King novel, I'm okay with it."

Unpredictable? He was absolutely unfathomable. Taking a deep breath, she sat up, faced him, and announced, "I'm a Witch."

He arched a brow, his expression mildly curious.

"No, I mean it. A piss-poor one, but I really am a Witch." Holly gestured to the fire once again, and once again the blaze leaped higher. "See?"

All he did was smile a little, as if she'd done nothing more peculiar than flick away some stray lint.

Glaring, she huddled into herself, wrapping her arms around her shins. "What d'you expect me to do — wiggle my nose like Samantha? Stand over a boiling cauldron stirring eye of newt into the pot? Sorry, honey, my broomstick's in the shop for repairs —"

"I just want an explanation. That too much to ask?"

"I told you. I'm a Witch. From a long line of Witches. But I don't cast spells, I don't work hexes, and I don't mix up potions. All I ever do is bleed."

"You *what*?"

"I can't believe I'm telling you this." Raking her hair back from her forehead, she took a steadying breath and went on, "I'm not a Witch in the popular sense — those silly TV shows and fantasy novels, that's mostly drivel. I don't have much magic at all. What I am is a Spellbinder. Other people use me. Or, more specifically, my blood."

"Blood," he echoed impassively.

"Yeah. I'm the rarest kind of Witch there is. I'm like an alchemist, except I don't turn base metal into gold, I turn a genuinely gifted Witch's maybe-it'll-work into stone-cold-guaranteed. Love potion? A drop of me—" She snapped her fingers. "—and it's instant helpless devotion for life. Or until somebody works an opposing spell with another drop of my blood."

"Sounds like a fairly valuable thing to be," he noted.

"No shit, Sherlock!" She knew she was telling him too much, but she couldn't stop herself—she was too damned mad. And anger demanded that she go on telling him things until something eventually obliterated his expression of genial interest—as if she had revealed that she collected bottle caps or had a salacious tattoo.

"See those pretty glass globes in my windows? They're not suncatchers. They're *spell*catchers. They get filled up with nasty Workings directed at me, and then they have to be destroyed—by an expert. There are spells of protection in the rugs, on the walls—even my goddamned front doorknob!"

"Holly—"

But she was off and running now. "This apartment used to belong to other Witches. When they rented it to me, all the protective spells were reWorked to focus on me. We do that for each other, in the community. No, it's not called a coven, not in polite society. We don't have a school, like Hogwarts in the *Harry Potter* books—I wish we did, because then maybe people who spend their lives wondering what's weird about themselves could learn they aren't really freaks—"

"Holly! Slow down. I'm still back at people wanting your blood—"

"Yeah, I'm popular as all hell," she said bitterly. "When I was little, a vampire came after me—that's how I met Uncle Nicky and Uncle Alec—"

"Who?" He shook his head as if to clear it, then said with a resigned sigh that further infuriated her, "Yeah, sounds as if this is gonna take a while. Why don't we go to bed and get comfortable?"

All she could do was stare at him.

"Bed," he repeated patiently. "Comfortable, y'know? Warm? Blankets, pillows, all like that?"

"You're kidding! You don't want to leave?"

"Over a little thing like you bein' a Witch?" he asked, the smile playing around his mouth again.

"Don't patronize me!" she snapped. "You obviously don't believe—"

"Don't tell me what I believe, lady. I'm trying to understand whatever it is you're trying to tell me. And I'd really like to be in bed with you while we do it."

"I'm trying to tell you I'm a Witch!"

"You said that."

Completely frustrated, she jumped to her feet and, taking the afghan with her, strode over to the bar to grab the spare vodka bottle from a lower cabinet and a shot glass from the shelves. "Watch and learn," she snarled. Bottle in one hand, glass in the other, she returned and sank down, tangled in the afghan. "Here—feel. Both at room temperature, right? Neither was in the fridge. Now pour."

He did so, and she smiled grim satisfaction when the hand holding the shot glass jerked a bit in response. "A trifling sample of Uncle Alec's magic. He knows I like my vodka ice-cold."

Evan looked at the bottle. He looked at the glass. Then he looked at her. And the look he'd worn earlier was finally and completely gone. "You're really not kidding, are you?"

She shook her head slowly. When he said nothing more, she took the vodka from him and gulped it. The glacial burn down her throat made her eyes water. And that, by damn, was the *only* reason his face became a little blurry.

"Holly? I thought Witches couldn't cry."

A snort met a sniffle and she ended up coughing. "Oh, for the love of— Do I have to go through every single cliché and tell you why it's wrong?"

"Well, I know right off there's *one* that's not true." He coaxed her close to him, one palm cupping her right breast. "Nice and warm—not cold at all."

# Four

ON TUESDAYS AND THURSDAYS, Evan Lachlan was assigned to protect Elias Bradshaw. Which meant that unless the judge went someplace other than his chambers or his courtroom, paperwork was the order of the day. Once upon a time, back when he'd been with the NYPD, Evan had looked on deskbound law enforcement as oxymoronic—emphasis on the "moronic." But that had been before he'd figured out computers and discovered that legwork was much easier when you let your fingers do the walking.

On Mondays, Wednesdays, and Fridays, Lachlan worked various and sundry cases assigned him by the United States Marshals Service. The arrangement was highly experimental, but it got past the head office on Pearl Street because for him and Pete Wasserman, it worked out just fine. Pete was a twenty-two-year veteran who had done more than his share of time on protection duty at the Supreme Court in D.C.; when Bradshaw started attracting serious threats, Wasserman had been only too happy to move home to New York. And, in the way of things within any profession, he had been even happier to request the son of an old friend as his backup. Like Evan, Pete had started as a beat cop. His partner for a year or so had been Evan's father.

Wasserman was, in fact, part of the reason Evan switched to the Marshals Service. Watching his father move sideways, never up, taught him that he wanted more for himself. With a stint in the NYPD, a hard-won college degree, and one hell of a lucky collar (taking down a burglar who happened to be a Federal fugitive), Lachlan had found himself on the fast track. Good work since, and good friends in the right places, had allowed him to put together the unusual arrangement that kept Elias Bradshaw protected and still gave Evan three days a week to pursue other cases.

This particular Monday morning, however, he was in pursuit of something else.

Telling the switchboard that he was deeply busy and to hold all calls, he closed his office door and sat down at his computer. Three hours later he had found out everything he ever wanted to know about Witches.

He also found out exactly nothing.

Magic came in white and black varieties—anybody who'd ever given it a second thought could figure that out. But according to various Internet sites, it also could be red, yellow, purple, green, blue, brown—and probably puce, vermilion, and burnt sienna, Evan told himself with a snort. And if he saw "magic" cutely spelled with a *k* one more time, he was going to throw up.

Gardnerian, Alexandrian, Dianic, Eclectic, Celtic, Welsh, Arcadian, Isian, Shamanic, Seax Wiccan. *Neo*Gardnerian, for Chrissakes. And all of them with different emphases. It was enough to make a person glad to be Catholic. Most of them ascribed to the same basic idea, expressed as "An ye harm none, do as thou wilt." Which he supposed was another way of saying "Do unto others." Sort of.

Eventually he realized what he was really accomplishing: avoidance of the issue. Not that he'd believed the Witch thing until the trick with the shot glass. He could still feel the raw cold of it on his fingertips.

Someone knocked on his door. "Evan?" Susannah called. "Come on, open up."

He wondered suddenly if she knew about Holly. If she, too, was a Witch. Rising, he unlocked his door and motioned her in.

She was back in a power suit—dark blue, with a severe white blouse and pearl earrings, her long blond hair confined in a French twist. He spared a sigh for the black leather of last Friday night.

"For me?" he asked, nodding to the huge basket of flowers in her arms. "You shouldn't have."

"I didn't. Holly's forgiven you," she told him, setting the arrangement on his desk. "I guess that means *I* should forgive His Honor, too, right?"

Lachlan arched a brow at her. "Up to you. Who do *I* get to forgive?"

"Well—me, I suppose." She perched a hip on the credenza near the door. "Open the card."

He did, and read, *Find out anything interesting lately?*, and shook his head in amazement. Holly couldn't possibly know what he'd been doing all morning. Or, then again, maybe she did. She *was* a Witch.

With very little magic except her blood, or so she'd said.

He looked more carefully at the flowers, finding their color scheme odd, to say the least. Purple hyacinths, red and pink roses, white chrysanthemums, and a lone white violet. The usual ferns, but no baby's breath or eucalyptus.

"None of your business what the card says," he replied to Susannah's questioning look, adding pointedly, "Don't you have work to do, Counselor?"

"Time for lunch," she retorted. "You up for Chinese?"

On the way out of the office he glimpsed the judge, who gave him a look he didn't particularly like. That wasn't unusual; he and Bradshaw didn't get along all that well. But it wasn't Evan's job to like his assignment, just to make sure a long list of crazies with a longer list of grudges didn't use Bradshaw for target practice. So far in their year's acquaintance he'd confiscated twenty-three revolvers and eighteen knives ranging from switchblades to plastic shivs, and intercepted nine accused felons or their surrogates outside Bradshaw's home. At first he'd wondered what the guy did to earn such devotion. Then he sat in on His Honor's trials and sentencings, and discovered that Bradshaw shared an "object all sublime" with *The Mikado*'s Lord High Executioner. The punishments indisputably fit the crimes.

Over kung pao chicken, Susannah filled him in on the details of Holly's career. Lachlan got the impression she'd been dying to do so for months. He listened, nodded, filed the information in his brain, and wondered idly why he'd been so upset about how much Holly made. And why he hadn't been—and wasn't—more upset that she was a self-confessed Witch.

"—enough money that she could quit teaching," Susannah was saying, "and write full-time. That summer we took off together for Europe—England, Ireland, Italy, Greece—" She sighed wistfully. "Glorious."

"And expensive." The *money* was real, tangible. Comprehensible. The Witch thing wasn't. Unless he thought about that shot glass.

"It's the planes that cost big bucks—well, and Italy, of course. But we got some great deals through some friends of hers. Alec Singleton and Nick Orlov. Have you met them?"

"Heard about them," he allowed.

"Alec used to work for Eli's uncle's firm, Fairleigh and Bradshaw. Nick owned a bookstore in the Village. They both retired last spring, which is when Holly moved into their old apartment." She finished her rice and leaned back in her chair. "And that brings you pretty much up to date, except that *Dragon Ships* got published this month. So. What do you think, Evan?"

"I think it's my turn to pay for lunch," he replied, taking out his wallet.

"Thanks. Fortune cookie first." She cracked hers open, read the slip of paper, and made a face. "'Open your eyes; magic will find you.' Don't you love how generic these things are?"

Evan kept a straight face and duly read his own aloud. "'Know yourself before judging others.' I think this one was meant for the boss. Shall we go?"

Back at the office, Evan looked at the list of his morning's downloads and was tempted to relegate all of it to the recycle bin. He supposed he could simply ask Holly to fill him in on what she believed, what she did, how she viewed being a Witch. He wasn't entirely certain why he didn't do just that. It would be rude, of course, and she'd probably feel she had to explain and justify herself—not something either of them would enjoy. Or maybe he was just reluctant to find out. Belief, after all, was a tricky thing.

They'd established their mutual Catholicism early on, and their mutual lip-service to it. Evan hadn't lost his faith, exactly, but it had undergone a radical transformation since his childhood. He supposed this was fairly typical. But how could Holly be a nominal Catholic *and* a practicing Witch?

And what constituted a "practicing Witch," anyway?

The basics were straightforward enough. The wand was expected—after all, what was a Witch without a magic wand? He'd read Harry Potter. (He'd had to, or there'd be nothing to talk to his niece and nephews about.) But the variety of wood that could be used was amazing. Alder, apple, birch, blackthorn, elder, hawthorn, hazel, myrtle, oak, pine, poplar, rowan, spruce, willow—Evan was a city boy and half these trees he'd never even heard of.

Sometimes crystals were set into the wand's tip. A smoky quartz to amplify earth magic, a garnet for courage and energy; a black onyx to repel dark magic, an amethyst for protection. That was just for starters, of course, in the crystal magic department, but he took one look at the huge list of stones (more than half of which he'd never heard of) and went back to looking at the tools.

Specifications for a cauldron were definite: black cast-iron, three-legged, with a handle, in which potions were brewed. The cauldron was distinct from the chalice, which held wine—just like Holy Communion. In fact, he was running across several things that corresponded to Catholic ritual. The thurible was used to burn incense, swung back and forth on its chain to spread the smoke around, purifying the air. Witches used candles, too, in more colors and scents and attendant meanings than he really wanted to explore. Fire, Air, Water—he suddenly recalled his mother's funeral, when the priest had thrown clods of Earth on the coffin.

Were Catholics more pagan than they knew? He knew enough Irish folklore to know that Brighid had been revered on the Emerald Isle long before Patrick arrived to make a Saint out of her. Clever, really, the way the Church had co-opted local deities, aligning the new religion with the old by turning pagan gods and goddesses into Blesseds and Beatifieds and Canonizeds.

Shelving that concept for later—right beside so much else he'd discovered this day—he went on through the list. Robe; cingulum (they even used the Latin word for the "cord around the waist"); something called a bolline, used for cutting herbs and inscribing candles and so forth. The major thing, though, seemed to be the athame: a double-bladed dagger with a black handle. It was never used to cut anything in the physical world—bread or herbs or whatever—but only for magical purposes. The twin edges symbolized that power cut both ways. As far as he could tell, all Witches had an athame. They just couldn't agree on how to pronounce it.

Evan learned about casting a Circle, about the broom used to sweep the Circle metaphorically clean, about the Book of Shadows that recorded spells and charms and incantations, about the bell of brass or crystal that some traditions used (and there was his own religion again)—

Bell, Book, and Candle?

And then he ran across something that made him laugh for the first time. It was a simple acronym: IRAB. It stood for *I Read A Book*—a satirical term for "Witches" who presented themselves as authorities after having done just that.

Well, at least some of these people had a sense of humor.

Changing positions to ease his stiffening back brought the basket of flowers into his line of sight again. He stared at them thoughtfully. Not the usual orchids or carnations or calla lilies—not Holly. Something about the flowers was peculiar enough to evoke his curiosity anew—as if he hadn't already been inundated in information today. Something he'd read this morning came back to him, and after some searching, the Internet yielded its trove of pictures, descriptions, and Victorian flower symbolism.

Three purple hyacinths: *forgive me*. Three red roses: *I love you*. Three pink roses: *believe me*. Three white chrysanthemums: *truth*. And a single white violet for *take a chance on happiness*. All thirteen flowers nestled in ferns, for magic.

TO HIS SURPRISE, THE DOORMAN at Holly's building—a tall black man with muscles on top of his muscles—greeted him by name before he could even open his mouth to ask if Ms. McClure was at home.

"No mystery about it, Marshal," Mr. Hunnicutt said with a grin. "Ms. McClure phoned down at noon to have you put on the list. She gave us the time of your arrival in her company last night, we pulled the tape, made a print of your picture, and started a file. And if whoever's on duty doesn't recognize you at once whenever you arrive, heads will definitely roll."

Evan approved of security, but this was . . . excessive? Then he considered who Holly was—or, rather, *what* she was. And wondered if Mr. Hunnicutt and his relief security guard were Witches, too.

And what about the other people who lived in the building? There were eight separate luxury apartments here. Were all of them inhabited by Witches?

From now on he'd be thinking about that wherever they went, whomever she spoke to. He couldn't decide whether such musings were paranoid or not. Well, hell; he was in law enforcement—paranoid was in his job description.

"Thanks," he said to Mr. Hunnicutt. "What sort of file?"

"Name, photo, address, phone, occupation, physical description, and which resident pays up if you make long-distance calls from the hall phones."

He had to laugh a bit at that. "As bad as the IRS."

"Worse, I hope. Mr. Singleton pays us better."

Then Uncle Alec must own the building. Nodding, Evan asked, "How long were you on the job?"

Mr. Hunnicutt didn't ask how he'd guessed. "Did fifteen in the Richmond, Virginia, PD. The man who had this post before me retired about six years ago, and I came in through the friend of a friend. Shall I announce you, or do you want to surprise her?" He nodded to the wine bottle in Lachlan's hand.

"Whatever the drill usually is. Thanks again."

"A pleasure, Marshal."

*My God, another of 'em—has to be,* Evan thought as he went to the elevator. *Virginia, friend of a friend—*

On his way down the hall to her door, he passed a pair of middle-aged gentlemen. One was slight and well-dressed, with hair the color of old amber; the other was tall, dark, and *very* well-dressed. They smiled at him and nodded, but did not speak. Wondering if they too were Witches—or was it Warlocks?—he rang Holly's doorbell.

She opened it so quickly that he was certain the two men had just left. "Hi! Come on in. Did you get the flowers?"

"I not only got them, I looked them all up." He leaned down for a kiss, then handed her the bottle of wine. "Who were those two guys?"

"My uncles. I mean, not really my uncles, just honorary. They're in town from their place in Connecticut, and stopped by for a couple of minutes." Shutting the door, she started for the kitchen to open the merlot.

Following, he spent a moment appreciating the fit of her Levis, and spared an interior grin for her pigtails. "'Their place'?"

"Yep. They've been together thirty years or so. Where's the damned corkscrew? I know I put it—aha!"

"So they're—"

She turned, arched a brow, and interrupted, "Gay? Yes, but only with each other. Married? Better believe it. It's probably the best marriage I've ever seen, actually. Witches? Absolutely."

Mildly, he said, "All I was gonna ask was, 'So they're not going to stay for dinner?'"

Holly laughed. "Sweet of you, *a chuisle,* but you were curious, admit it!"

Whatever he might have replied was forgotten when the phone rang. Holly snatched the phone off the kitchen counter. "Hello?" After a moment she grinned. "Whaddya mean, 'nice'? It's the best in all five boroughs—at least since you two moved out of town." A slight pause, and then she actually blushed. "Uncle Nicky, I'm going to tell Aunt Lulah on you. She still thinks you're such a sweet—what? No, he just wanted to know if you were staying to dinner. Next time, okay? I don't think I'm quite ready for him to meet the troops." She winked at Evan. "And what were you two doin' lookin' at my man's ass, anyway?"

Lachlan made a face at her and started opening the wine.

"Oh, of course," she laughed into the phone. "Nothing but the best for Our Holly. I understand completely. You trust my taste, but you just had to check him out for yourselves. Well, next time give me some warning, okay? I'll get Isabella to make her Caribbean goulash. Drive carefully."

She hung up, and Lachlan said, "How many 'troops' are there?"

"Blood relatives, about ninety. None closer than fourth cousins, though, except for Aunt Lulah."

"You keep track of fourth cousins?" He barely knew his first cousins.

"*Éimhín* darlin', we keep track of *everybody*. It's very Southern, to know which ancestors you have in common with whom. And with the other stuff that shows up in the family, we keep special note of who's descended from whom and what they're likely to be."

"What kind of Witch, you mean."

"Yeah." She eyed him. "You're taking this a lot better than I thought you might."

"So that was the famous Alec and Nicky. Tell me about them."

"Like I said. When I was a little girl, they saved me from a vampire."

"And now I'm supposed to laugh, right?"

"You rarely do what you're supposed to, in my experience," she retorted. "Evidently I didn't explain as much as I should have last night, so let's go have a drink while the wine breathes and you can ask me whatever you want."

At the bar he poured Scotch and vodka into Waterford crystal tumblers— the Scotch stayed at room temperature, but the vodka chilled instantly—then sat beside her on the couch. "Start with Alec and Nicky," he suggested.

"They're retired—Nicky from his bookstore, The Recommended Sentence—"

"Mysteries?"

"Got it in one," she approved. "Alec was a lawyer, but don't hate him for it. He did corporate stuff, not criminal defense. I'm not their only honorary relation. They've got 'em all over the country—all over the world, for all I know."

"All Witches?"

"Some—maybe most, I'm not sure. I've never met any of the rest, but the hall gallery in that farmhouse is something to see." She laughed and sipped her drink. "All of us in our college graduation photos, everyplace from Caltech to

Oxford—the Oxford guy is with the FBI. Muldoon or Mulroy, something like that, with a foxy little redheaded partner whose name completely escapes me. But Alec and Nicky are very careful that we don't any of us run into each other."

"Why?"

"You know, I'm not entirely sure. Probably a case of the right hand and the left—we only know what others are doing if it becomes necessary."

"Such as?"

"Well . . . there used to be what Alec calls a Better Business Bureau for Witches. He and Nicky worked for it, making sure people didn't do what they weren't supposed to, and dealing with them if they did. Nowadays there's regions, and a Magistrate for each, and instead of sending people like Alec and Nicky all over the world, things are dealt with locally."

"Oh."

When no further comment was forthcoming, she shifted uneasily and said, "Isabella made pot roast for us tonight. When do you want to eat?"

"I want something else first."

A grin lit her face. "*Not* before dinner. Or for twenty minutes after, either."

"That's swimming, not sex. Besides, I had something else in mind." He smiled and reached over to curl a lock of russet hair around his finger. "Work me a spell, Witch-lady."

She frowned. "I've already told you, I strengthen other people's magic. I don't have hardly any of my own."

"I just want to see how it's done. C'mon, where's your Book of Shadows?" When she favored him with an *Are you kidding?* look, he added, "I thought all Witches—"

"First, there's no such thing as 'all Witches.' Everybody's different, even within the same Circle. Second, I don't have a Book of Shadows."

"And third?" Knowing there was more; with Holly, there was *always* more.

"Where the hell did you pick up all this stuff, anyhow?"

"Well, I could say IRAB, but actually it's more like IRIOTI," he told her, making words out of the acronyms.

"'Irioti'?" she echoed.

"I Read It On The Internet."

"Wonderful. Just exquisite. Okay, let's see." She thought for a minute, then smiled. "There's one for sweetening a romance—you write your names on a piece of parchment and put it in a jar with honey, then seal the jar and put it under the bed. But it has to be done on a Friday of a waxing moon."

"Is that stuff really important? Days and moons and all that?"

"How should I know? It's what I was taught when I was little. Nowadays I just show up when I get told to and bring alcohol to swab my thumbs."

She was getting annoyed, but he persisted. "What about words, then? Aren't there supposed to be magic chants and incantations and all like that?"

Another long-suffering sigh. "You know when the priest holds up the Host? Or when you say a Hail Mary? That's all spoken spells are, really. Mnemonic devices to help you concentrate. As a man I know is fond of saying, 'Magic is within—everything else is just props.'" She eyed him. "You're disappointed."

"Only by your attitude. All day I've been thinking that here I've got this Witch-lady who knows all this cool stuff about magic, and you're a writer to boot so you must've composed some interesting spells—and now you're telling me you can't do hardly anything and you don't know very much, and the words aren't really important. And you don't seem to take it seriously."

"Other people's magic, yeah, that I *do* take seriously," she replied thoughtfully. "Theirs really works." After tossing back the rest of the vodka, she set the glass down and got to her feet. "I've got most of the props, for what they're worth. You might as well take a look."

She took him into the bedroom, where Isabella had obviously been at work. He'd been right: cleaned up, it was a beautiful room. Clothes hung up, bed made, books neatly stacked, chaise properly pillowed and draped with a chenille throw. Over in the far corner was a small triangular table. It was to this that she led him.

Evan looked first at the chalice. It was a strange white porcelain thing with a slightly uneven base and tendrils swirling up to cradle a bottom-heavy basin. It looked organic, as if it had been grown, not made.

"There's a formal one I use in the Circle," Holly said casually, "made of Waterford crystal. But this one I found at a crafts sale in college. Ever look at something and know it's yours without even thinking about it?"

He might have told her he'd known she would be his from the instant their eyes met, but he kept his mouth shut.

"I hope you weren't expecting anything spectacular by way of a wand," she said, again with that same studied nonchalance. "It's just a willow switch."

"'Witch' comes from an old word for 'willow,'" he said.

"Meaning 'to bend,' yes. You *have* done your homework, Marshal," she said lightly, and picked up a silver bell about four inches high. It tinged a sweet note before she set it down again. "This belonged to the Kirby side of the family, used for nothing more esoteric than letting the servants know it was time to bring in the next course at dinner. Aunt Lulah thinks it was probably a wedding present, because of the ivy pattern—Victorian flower symbology for married happiness."

"The cauldron's not what I was expecting." He pointed to the little iron pot; it looked like a child's toy. "I guess you really can't cook, even magically, huh?"

"It's for incense," she told him, making a face at the insult. "It doesn't have to be very big." Next she picked up a pendant on a silver chain. "Alec gave me this when I got my master's. In English, I might add, not magic."

"Pretty," he said. The outline of a pentacle was tripled in white, yellow, and rose gold. "Where's the athame?"

She opened the table's shallow drawer. "In alphabetical order—athame, bolline, besom—it's just symbolic, a little cinnamon broom, but it makes everything else smell good—cingulum, dagdyne—"

"What?"

She picked up a scrap of blue velvet, in which was a golden needle. "For sewing. Aunt Lulah spelled this one for me a long time ago, when I was helping with Alec and Nick's wedding quilt. That was my first real magic. I was so proud of myself! Silk and velvet and satin, with flowers embroidered onto it and used as the quilting patterns—" She smiled. "Other people Worked the spells, but I got to put in little sachets for fragrance, and bits of various stones. Nicky knows a lot about herbs, and Alec's pretty good at lithomancy."

"Uh—'litho' like 'neolithic,' for stones?"

"Yep. Nick gave me the bolline. It's one of a set of three from his childhood with the Rom—Gypsies—and very old. The athame looks kind of like a hunting knife, doesn't it? I found the deer antler myself when I was about fifteen, and Cousin Jesse made it for me."

"Cousin Jesse," he repeated.

"He's the sheriff down home. His specialty is metal working. You should see the cauldron he did for Aunt Lulah's fiftieth birthday—gorgeous." Holly slanted a glance at him. "All these things—other people had to Work whatever magic is in them. They used my blood to make it binding, but . . ." She finished with a shrug.

"This isn't long enough to use as a belt," he said, touching what he'd assumed was the cingulum.

"Actually, it's a source cord. Nine feet of gold cording, knotted and netted around different rocks of my choosing. I take it with me when I travel."

He recognized tiger eye, moonstone, golden topaz, garnet, lapis lazuli, onyx, amethyst— "What're the pink and orange ones? And the green?"

"Rose quartz, carnelian, and malachite." She rubbed her finger over the striations of the flat green oval, smiling a little. Before he could ask, she said, "I hate to fly. Some people use worry beads on airplanes—I use this. They all have meanings, of course. The onyx and amethyst protect against nasty magic and manipulation, for instance."

"Get a lot of that, do you?" He tried to sound as casual as she, but all at once the idea of anyone's using her, her blood, for their own ends was like something fanged gnawing at his guts.

"If people find out what I am, yes. I'm pretty much incognita even within the

Circles. Only the people I Work with regularly know what I am. The others—"
Holly shrugged. "Let's just say I have clever friends who make it seem as if I'm
actually doing something, instead of just standing there looking silly."

"I bet you could do a spell on me and it'd work," he teased.

"Oh, very funny, Lachlan."

"You want me to believe you're a Witch? Work me a spell."

"You just won't let this go, will you?"

"Nope."

Five minutes later they were seated before the fire. Holly had collected a few
items and now spread them on the hearth rug.

"I swear, Lachlan, if you laugh at me—," she warned.

"I won't." He hesitated, then asked innocently, "But aren't we supposed to
be naked? I mean, 'skyclad'?"

"One-track mind. Later, Marshal. This particular spell is probably from a
time when cinnamon was incredibly expensive and to sacrifice a couple of
sticks meant you were serious." She tied the sticks together with purple thread,
saying:

> *"One to seek, one to find,*
> *One to bring, one to bind,*
> *Heart to heart, me to thee:*
> *So say I, so mote it be."*

She wrapped the cinnamon in a square swatch of black velvet, then took up
the golden dagdyne.

"No," he said suddenly, catching her hand. "You don't have to bleed on it.
That's not what I meant."

A perplexed quirk of her eyebrows was there and gone before he could react
to it. "*Go raibh maith agat, Éimhín,*" she murmured. "Thank you." And she
stitched the velvet closed with the needle and thread. "Now we hide it where it
won't be found—meaning out of reach of Isabella's vacuum and Mugger's
paws!"

"And that's it?"

"That's all most Witchcraft is, Evan—household stuff, a rhyme, and a wish."

"Hmm." He waited a few calculated moments, then gave a gasp. "Holly!"

"What is it? What's wrong?"

"I think—I don't know—" He clutched his heart, wondering if he was overdoing it a bit. "I feel strange—it might be—" Without warning he tackled her
back onto the rug and grinned down into her startled face. "It worked! I'm in
love!"

Five

"ELIAS," SAID KATE, "I HAVE a small problem."

The Circle had gathered for their January meeting at Elias's town house to discuss Denise, who had been a surprisingly good girl so far in the new year. Other matters had also been dealt with—among them a stockbroker Ian suspected of not leaving his magic at his office door; a promising student in Kate's brewing-and-stewing class; and rumors about a group of excruciatingly rich wannabe occultists with neo-Nazi inclinations. That was when Kate mentioned her problem.

"Do you need us here, Kate?" Lydia asked softly.

"No, dear. The neo-Nazi group isn't the one I'm worried about. The one I've observed is a Satanist gathering on Long Island."

"Excellenter and excellenter, said Alice," Martin observed, both inaccurately and ungrammatically. "C'mon, let's motor. Need a ride, Lydia?"

She eyed him sidelong, a smile playing around her lips. "Angling for cheesecake? Or did you have in mind a dozen crullers to go?"

"Well, you didn't have to marry the best baker in Brooklyn, sweetie." Martin took Ian by the elbow and Lydia by the hand, and they left the town house for the snowy city outside, negotiating doughnuts and chocolate cake all the way.

Simon, too, donned coat and gloves. "I'm off, children. It's a long drive, and Silence won't be if I'm late." He smiled, wound a purple cashmere scarf around his neck, and departed.

"Silence—?" Holly echoed.

"His wife," Elias explained.

"I didn't know Simon was married," she remarked. "Or Lydia, either. And I thought people stopped naming their kids things like Patience and Mindwell and Thank Ye The Lord a long time ago."

"Not in her corner of Rhode Island," Kate said. "Could you stay awhile, please? I don't need your blood, just your advice."

Holly sank back into the overstuffed corduroy chair, hugged a sage-scented pillow to her stomach. "If I can help, sure."

"Well, it's not a problem yet, but it could become one."

"Say on, say on," Elias sighed, pouring more coffee and dosing it with cream.

"It's a bit intimidating, you know—trying to tell a coherent story in front of a novelist," Kate chuckled. "My narrative powers are sadly lacking. The night of the Solstice last month, I was awakened quite suddenly—" Here she grinned irrepressibly. "—by a disturbance in the Force."

Elias groaned. Holly shushed him.

"No, really," Kate insisted. "It was the oddest feeling. So I did some checking, and it turns out that a group of kids had met on that hill in back of my house and were messing around with magic."

"For you to feel it," Elias commented, "at least one of them must be Talented."

"Exactly. One of my apprentices is a senior at the local high school, and he did some nosing around. The boy's name is William Scott Hungerford Fleming."

"Junior?" Elias sat up a little straighter. "Can't be."

Holly frowned. "What am I missing?"

"Flaming Fleming," Kate said, "is a fundamentalist reverend with a thing about pagans."

"That's one way of putting it." Elias set down his coffee. "Kate, what's his kid doing fooling around with magic?"

"The boy doesn't know enough to call up anything really vicious, but there were some nasty little phantoms hovering around. Evidently he's gotten a Pylon together and they're going to try something spectacular on Imbolc. Now, my problem is, do I let them try, and maybe call up things I don't even want to think about, which will scare the crap out of them, or—"

"—or intercede," Elias finished succinctly. "This isn't a problem, Kate. It's a no-brainer. Where are they meeting, and what time?"

Thus it was on the night of February the second—Imbolc, the Feast of St. Brighid, Candlemas, or Groundhog Day, depending on one's orientation—Holly picked up Elias in her black BMW for the drive out to Long Island.

"I always liked Imbolc," Holly said. "Right turn or left?"

"Left."

"Aunt Lulah and I always got our candles from Cousin Clary Sage. Beeswax from her own hives. One in each window—was it six lights to Kate's street?"

"Seven."

"Okay. We'd draw sun circles in the snow around the house and barn."

"Any more pastoral lore you'd like to share?"

"C'mon, Your Honor. I'm trying to make nice here with the man who's sleeping with my best friend."

"All right," he replied genially. "I'll make nice with the woman who's sleeping with one of my marshals."

"How do you get away with this, by the way? Sneaking around sans escort? I thought you were supposed to have an armed guard at all times."

"Only in court and chambers."

"These days there are quite a few otherwise law-abiding citizens who think all you judge-types should be horsewhipped at the very least."

Reluctantly, Elias pulled up the hem of his fisherman-knit sweater to reveal the tidy little pistol tucked into his belt. Holly whistled under her breath.

"I really hope that's not a MacGuffin."

"No," he said mildly, "it's a Beretta nine-millimeter. What's a MacGuffin?"

"Hitchcock. You show it, you have to use it by the end of the movie."

"I've never had to use it yet." Settling back in his seat, Elias changed the subject. "How many of you country cousins are there down in Virginia?"

"About ninety, when we all get together from three states and the District of Columbia. Not all Witches, but all Catholic." Holly laughed. "Clary calls Imbolc her St. Brighid's Day clan reunion, which makes it acceptable to the ones who haven't inherited the magic."

"Turn here. The last house on the cul-de-sac. Careful—they don't plow this road." Reaching into the backseat for the two black hooded robes he'd brought along, he mused, "I wonder if we'll ever be able to celebrate the Sabbats without cloaking them in 'acceptability.'"

"Ain't gonna hold my breath." She used the gears to slow the car to about five miles an hour. "Besides, to become official we'd need rules and regs just like every other belief system on the planet. Part of what's kept us safe for thousands of years is that no six of us believe exactly the same thing."

"Would it have to be that way?" he mused. "Believe this, do that, spread the faith, march in lockstep or get excommunicated?"

"Even the possibility of it horrifies me," Holly confessed. "And it would kill what we are."

"Ah, but there's the real question, isn't it?" he asked, smiling a little. "What exactly *are* we?"

She shrugged. "The pallid remnant of an ancient religion, according to some. The vanguard of the new millennium to others. No, Elias, if we became a codified religion, with a scripture and a hierarchy and so forth, we'd become visible enough to celebrate whatever and however we chose, just like any other faith— but then people like *us* would become visible, too."

"Not a happy thought."

A few minutes later, Kate welcomed them into a very modern ranch house that she shared with five cheerfully disreputable mutts, three identical Burmese cats, a brace of guinea pigs, a housebroken lop-eared rabbit, and a tame squirrel. The hearth-warmed air smelled of diverse herbs and spices and perfumes; Elias saw Holly scratch at her nose, and smiled.

"Tea?" Kate offered. "I know you prefer to Work on an empty stomach, Eli, but just a little something to take the chill away? I've got soup for later."

"No, nothing right now, thanks. Have the kids arrived out back?"

"In about half an hour, maybe less." Plucking the squirrel off a brass baker's rack, Kate stroked its luxuriant tail. "Sorry, Percival, you're for the cage tonight."

"Percival?" Holly asked, bemused.

Kate shrugged. "He answered to it. All my companions are Arthurian."

"Really? All our cats are criminals — Bandit, Mugger, Ruffian, Swindler —"

Elias shifted impatiently. "Fascinating, ladies, but can we get this show on the road?"

"And a fine show it will be," Holly replied, unfurling the cloak Elias gave her. "Is this theatrical enough, Kate, or should we have brought our wands?"

With Percival the squirrel and Ban the bunny safely caged from mischief, and the dogs and cats shut inside the house for their own good, lights were extinguished and three figures in hooded cloaks left the house through the back door. A low fence was climbed, a quarter mile of snowy hill was traversed, and a convenient stand of trees was found for shelter. Though exercise had warmed Elias's muscles, it was very cold and very dark, heavy cloud cover hiding the moon.

"I'm freezing," Holly whispered.

"Bonfire soon," Kate promised. "They're here."

Ten, eleven, twelve — finally the thirteenth arrived, stumbling in shin-deep snow. There was a brief confusion while the Pylon arranged itself around a small wooden table one of them had lugged up the hill.

Holly leaned close to Elias and breathed in his ear, "What's in the sack?"

One of the black-robed figures — it was impossible to tell male from female — had carried a squirming burlap bag up the hill, and now set it on the ground near the altar. Elias shrugged. "Whatever it is, it's alive."

"Oh, swell — the whole show, complete with blood sacrifice."

In the center of the circle of hooded black figures was a pile of wood and kindling, presumably to be lit by the candles each person held. All these were black, except for one slim white taper placed on the right side of the makeshift altar.

Elias focused his attention on that — the flame that in this ritual symbolized the path held in contempt. The right-hand path. His path. This was the fire he would use tonight if necessary. And when he heard the opening of this ritual, chanted as some sort of thick, heavy incense was ignited in a ceramic altar bowl, he was depressingly certain that it would indeed be necessary.

*"Gloria Deo Domino Inferi, et in terra vita hominibus fortibus. Laudamus Te, benedicamus Te, adoramus Te, glorificamus Te, gratias agimus tibi propter magnam potentiam Tuam: Domine Satanus, Rex Inferus, Imperator omnipotens."*

The young man's Latin was almost priestly—something his fundamentalist Protestant preacher of a father would doubtless find horrifying. Elias had heard it all before, the adulteration of the Catholic Mass to suit other purposes.

*Glory to God the Infernal Lord, and on earth light and strength to man. We praise Thee, we bless Thee, we adore Thee, we glorify Thee, we give thanks to Thee for Thy great power, Lord Satan, Infernal King, Almighty Emperor.*

Beside him, he felt Holly shiver, and not with the cold. For a moment he wondered how someone raised Roman Catholic would react to this deviant Mass—and then nearly got lost in speculating how one could be a Roman Catholic Witch.

Shaking himself mentally, he watched the boy who was acting as high priest. Very tall, all leg, and lanky in the way of young men who've grown too fast for their reflexes to catch up with, his only visible identifying feature was his hands. These were long-fingered and bony, scarred with cuts and burns—not souvenirs of attempts at ritual, but from his hobbies of woodworking and stained glass. Bradshaw had done a little research this week, and learned that Flaming Fleming's namesake was nineteen years old, artistic, rebellious, his mother's much-indulged darling and his father's much-reprimanded despair. Watching him now, Elias saw the restless intensity common to that age—he could just about recall that same seeking uncertainty in himself during his college years—but, more significantly, he sensed a real talent about the boy.

The choice of Imbolc was an odd one for a ritual of this kind. A Sabbat of Light, not darkness; perhaps young Fleming was testing himself, trying out his power by challenging the fire. Or perhaps he knew, consciously or instinctively, that dark wraiths banished by life-affirming light would be attracted to a place where fire celebrated destruction.

The ceremony progressed, with Fleming in charge. A bell was rung nine times while he turned counterclockwise; a silver goblet was charged and filled—with wine, mercifully, not with other fluids Elias had witnessed on occasion. The four quarters were ceremoniously sprinkled with an aspergillum in the shape of a nine-inch ceramic phallus. Satan was called at the South, Lucifer at the East, Belial at the North, and Leviathan at the West. A sword that could have starred in a *Conan the Barbarian* movie was waved about rather amateurishly before it was touched to the bent hooded head of each participant. A gong was rung to herald every "dubbing" by the high priest, right after he called the name of an archdemon.

"Adramaleck, Prince of Fire! Meririm, Prince of Air! Rahab, Prince of Oceans! Rimmon, Prince of Lightning and Storms! Mammon, Prince of Greed! Agratbatmahlaht, Princess of Whores!"

"Whoever *she* is," Holly whispered. "I'm impressed that he even tried to pronounce it." Elias elbowed her, wanting to hear the remaining names Fleming called, but she was relentless. "That gong is giving me a headache. Let's do it, huh, and get the hell out of here?"

So casual—hiding nervousness? No, he decided, glancing at her. She didn't sense what this boy had called. Hell was indeed hovering around this hillside. And it was up to him to get it out of here.

He fixed his gaze on the white candle that trembled all alone in the darkness. *We are strong enough, you and I,* he thought. *Tonight is Imbolc, when Light returns.*

Willing the slight flame to grow and brighten, he began to chant very softly.

*"Brighid of the hearthfire, Brighid of the braided hair,*
*Brighid of the fair sweet face, Brighid of the women's wisdom,*
*Brighid of the healing hands, Brighid of the sacred fire —"*

By now he was walking from behind the sheltering trees, his voice ringing, the poetry of three thousand years shaping his words. *This* was power; this was magic, living inside him, awakening the flame to confront the chill that fire challenged and defeated. His will and his gift became one.

Fleming stood with the sword held limply in his left hand, gaping at this hooded apparition that had appeared out of nowhere in the trees—to be joined by another figure just as anonymous around which fresh pure fragrances whirled, banishing the cloying odor of the altar incense. And then another cloaked shape, standing at the edge of the darkness and singing, singing the Latin words in a high, clear soprano, calling and lauding the Lady:

*"Salve, Regina, mater misericordiae,*
*Vita, dulcedo, et spes nostra,*
*Salve, salve Regina!"*

Elias strode into the very circle itself, breaking its outline with Light, drawing the necessary Fire from the white candle that he took into his hand as he kicked the altar table over into the snow.

*"Brighid of the triple flame, Brighid of the kindling,*
*Brighid of the waters, Brighid of the power of shaping,*
*I call on the Gracious Lady of tender blessing —*

*That all might be healed, that all might be transformed,*
*That darkness shall flee and Light shall reign."*

Very suddenly, in the circle's center, the bonfire flared to sudden brilliant life. Elias flinched. The fire wasn't his.

Some of the Pylon simply screamed, broke, and ran. Others held their ground for a moment, perhaps three—and then fled down the hill, slipping in the snow, too frightened even to cry out. The sword fell to the ground. The ceramic phallus, the goblet from which none had drunk, the bell, the gong, the black candles—all lay abandoned in the cold snow.

The high priest remained, and two of his Pylon. Elias stared at the boy from the concealing shadows of his hood, seeing Fleming's pallor and defiance—and his outraged knowledge that whatever malevolence had been attracted to this place had given up and fled. Dilettante, novice, dabbler—these things the boy was. But given years and learning, he would become powerful. Perhaps dangerous.

Kate's herbs, thrown onto the bonfire, fragranced the air. Gently she took the last three black candles from the boys' hands, extinguishing them with three soft breaths and a few whispered words of banishing, leaving only Elias's white Light shining off the snow, and the roaring flames behind him. The trio of would-be Satanists clung together, two not much more than panicky boys, one still dark-eyed with rebellion.

"You don't know what you were playing with here," Elias said.

"We weren't playing!"

"No?" He kicked at the goblet with casual contempt. "Wine stolen from your parents' cellar, right? Go for the Château Margaux, forget all that stuff about drinking piss."

"The piss," said the Reverend's son, "was in the clay dick."

Holly approached to stand at Elias's right hand. "Do you have any idea what you tried to do tonight? There's no such thing as the Devil, despite what they teach you in Sunday school. But there *are* some repellent little entities just itching for a chance to make mischief in this world. You're lucky a Witch or three came along to protect you."

William Scott Hungerford Fleming straightened to his full six feet five inches. "I don't need protection from anybody—or any*thing*!"

"You're Witches?" one of the other boys asked.

"If you are," said Fleming, "why didn't you join our ritual?"

Holly shook her head within her hood. "You're so wrong about what a Witch truly is and what a Witch truly does that it beggars even *my* celebrated imagination."

Elias made a grab for control of the situation. "Clean this mess up, please, while these gentlemen and I have a little talk." He gritted his teeth, grateful for the concealing cloak as Holly gave him a purposely overdone bow, her hands folded inside wide sleeves, and joined Kate by the toppled table that had served as an altar.

A five-minute lecture later, the pair of acolytes had departed, expressing such sentiments as, "Never again—this is *too* bizarre!" and "If that's power, I don't want anything to do with it!" As Bradshaw expected, Fleming was harder to convince. It followed; he was the only one among them who had any gift. And he knew it.

"My preceptor says I can be a major power—and he's right. I *feel* things— and it would've been awesome tonight if you hadn't ruined it!"

"'Preceptor,'" Elias echoed distastefully. "Did he happen to mention that you can choose what you feel, and which path you follow?"

"We don't choose our path. It chooses us."

"Parrot," Holly chided on her way past with an armful of black candles. "Speak—and above all *think*—for yourself!"

"What I *think* is that you're all full of shit."

"Yeah?" But whatever else she might have said was interrupted by a gasp as she slipped in someone else's icy footprint and landed on her ass. The candles went flying. And so did the hood of her cloak, revealing her face and her freckles and her dark red hair. Elias took firm hold of his temper and bent to help her up. She waved him off, pushed herself to her knees, and started grabbing black tapers.

Fleming stood back, arms folded, and regarded them with the vastly tolerant gaze given only by the young to their elders. "You're a Witch, you know about the powers of Satan."

Elias sighed. "Is that your father talking, or your 'preceptor'?"

For the first time there was a flinch of reaction. "How do you—what do you know about my father?"

"It seems to me that you're caught between your father's Bible and your preceptor's—well, whatever version of that twaddle he subscribes to. Both affirm the power of the Devil from opposite directions. But did it ever occur to you that there are more than two paths?"

"These feelings you talk about having—" Holly had finished stuffing candles in her pockets, and rose gracelessly to her feet. "Ask yourself what the best use of those feelings would be."

The boy turned to her. "You're a Witch."

"Yep."

"And you don't worship Satan."

"Nope."

"You were singing in Latin," he accused.

"Sure was," she drawled. "From the original version of the Mass. Much nicer, if you ask me."

"Then—you're Catholic? But how can you, like, be that and be a Witch, too?"

Holly shrugged. "It'd take too long to explain. Look, kid, follow my friend's excellent advice and think this through. Make your own decisions. You've courted the Darkness, and tonight you saw a bit of the Light. It all depends on what you want to see in the mirror every morning."

"Go home," Bradshaw told the boy. When he saw hesitation in the dark eyes, he summoned his own magic and commanded, "Now!"

Snow spewed up as Fleming ran down the hill. Elias paused for a deep, calming breath, then turned a scowl on Holly. But all at once he was too tired and cold to reprimand her as she deserved for her multiple interruptions—and for stupidly allowing the boy to see her face.

"Oh, the poor little thing!" Kate suddenly exclaimed.

He turned in time to see her freeing a scrawny lamb from the burlap sack. Its jaws had been taped shut and its eyes were dazed from its struggles. Kate carefully peeled the tape loose, and it bleated piteously before trying to hide in her cloak.

"The Lamb of God," Holly murmured. "I don't like this boy, Elias. I don't like him at all."

"It's all right now," Kate crooned to the exhausted animal. "I'll take you home and you can play with Percival."

"We're done here, Kate," Elias said. "Leave the cleansing for tomorrow in the daylight. And put out your fire before you burn down half of Long Island."

"It isn't her fire," said Holly. "It's mine."


HOT FOOD AND HOTTER COFFEE were the work of a few minutes in Kate's kitchen. Elias did the honors; Kate was busy settling the lamb in the spare bedroom. Holly banished herself from the preparations to go wash the stink from her hands and remove the robe. Her sinuses were still twitching unhappily as she left the bathroom, but three deep inhalations of the brewing Kenyan Blue Mountain cleared her head.

"Caffeine, I beg of you," she told Elias.

He handed over a filled cup. "Want a kicker in it?"

"I'd love some brandy, but I'm driving. God, that's good!" She drank, burning her tongue and not caring. "You think the Fleming kid will take the hint?"

His reply was a shrug. She watched as he set bowls of soup and a plate of fresh bread on the kitchen table, ducking around hanging bouquets of drying herbs as he passed from the stove to the table to the refrigerator for butter.

"I have to tell you, Elias, I didn't think you had that kind of poetry in you. And *don't* tell me it was just another prop. Who taught you those lines?"

"My mother," he answered reluctantly. "Her grandmother came from the Old Country. County Kerry, to be precise." He eyed her. "How many points do I get?"

"I'm not sure," she teased back. "The pollution of all that New England Puritan blood—"

"Almost four hundred years of it in Connecticut and Massachusetts."

"And probably with half the Bradshaws wanting to burn the other half." She buttered bread for them both. "Speaking of blood, I think this is the first time I've ever been part of a Working and nobody wanted mine."

"Is it also the first time you've ever meddled in a Magistrate's work?"

Kate arrived, all smiles, saying, "I've tucked Guinevere up with Galahad, nice and snug. You'd never know he's part sheepdog."

"Guinevere?"

"She was almost burned as a sacrifice, too, remember? Oh, lovely, you found the bread. Can I get anybody anything else?"

"No, we're fine," said the Magistrate. "One thing, though—find out who this 'preceptor' person is. Someone may have to have a little chat with him."

"I'll see what I can do. No more talk. Eat."

Perfectly willing to obey, Holly kept her gaze from brushing Elias's for the next half hour. But with soup and bread finished, and the coffeepot empty, it was time for the drive back to Manhattan. Holly knew very well that along the way the Magistrate would rip her a new one—and her ass was already sore after that tumble into the snow. Kate as well was cognizant of Elias's mood; as she walked them out to the BMW, she whispered in Holly's ear, "I wouldn't be you for the next hour for anything in this world—or the next."

Sure enough, after five minutes of lethal quiet, when Holly stopped the car at a red light Elias spoke.

"Almost four hundred years in this country," he said as if their earlier conversation had not been interrupted, "and in all that time I don't think anyone has ever done to another Bradshaw what you did to me tonight."

"All I did was—" She broke off as he made a gesture, and she realized two things with infuriating abruptness: that she couldn't speak, and that for the very first time he'd used magic on *her*.

Into the enforced silence he spoke five words.

"Don't. You. Ever. Interfere. Again."

He released her. She dragged in a breath that filled her lungs to bursting.

"Light's green," he announced calmly.

Horns sounded behind her. She concentrated on driving, gained the expressway without breaking too many traffic laws, and settled into the calming rhythm of the engine.

"What, exactly, got up your nose?" she asked, her voice dangerously controlled. "Did I spoil the effect when you stormed in to kick that altar over like Jesus in the temple with the moneylenders? I timed the bonfire perfectly, I said what needed to be said to that kid—"

"You opened your mouth. That was enough. You let him see your face. The only thing you missed was calling me or Kate by name."

"What's *that* got to do with anything?" she exclaimed. "No—wait a minute, I see now. We're anonymous, we Work in secret, it's all part of the mystique—or is it that you're ashamed of what we are? We hide our faces and our names—"

"—for damned good reason! What would happen if what we are became common knowledge? A writer and a judge—we're public commodities. Though, granted, you're for sale and I'm not—"

"Go fuck yourself, Magistrate!"

As if realizing he'd gone too far, he moderated his tone: "It's not shame, Holly. It's self-preservation."

It was as close as he'd ever come to an apology. She knew that. She also knew that one day he *would* tell her he was sorry for something he'd said or done, and he'd damned well mean it. Deciding she could wait, and succumbing to a certain rudimentary honesty within herself, she said, "I know what you mean." Then, because she was still angry: "It's why neither of us has ever told Susannah."

"Leave her out of this."

*Good,* she thought. *That got to him. One more, and I'm done for the night.*

"And why neither of us ever will."

One lean, manicured hand lifted—but the gesture was aborted before it truly began. In spite of herself, Holly held her breath until his hand returned to his lap.

"That's enough, Spellbinder."

"Whatever you say, Magistrate."

Six

CHRISTMAS TO GROUNDHOG DAY CAME and went—or, as Evan was learning, Yule to Imbolc. Not that he gleaned much information from Holly. She would neither take him to a Sabbat nor perform ritual magic for him, and while she answered his questions readily enough he knew the subject of Witchery bothered her.

Well, it bothered him, too. Some. He'd forget about it for days at a time, but then she'd tell him she couldn't see him that night because she had to Work. Her voice supplied the capital letter.

Her other work, the writing stuff, was lowercase. He met her agent, her editor, and her publisher at various dinners. Everyone, including the various literati at these gatherings, tried not to act surprised, curious, and/or bewildered, from which he gathered that he was the only man ever to accompany her on such occasions. Lachlan was polite, used the right forks and spoons, tried not to eat or drink too much even though somebody else was picking up the tab, and battled boredom by counting Holly's freckles.

He was never introduced to any of her fellow Witches. Taking his cue from her determinedly offhand attitude, he never asked for such introductions.

One evening in February—the fourteenth, to be precise, which was both Valentine's Day and her birthday—they were dining late when she looked up from her veal and nearly choked. "What the hell are *they* doing here?"

"Who?" Turning in his chair, he saw a vaguely familiar pair—of course, the two men from the hallway last year. One blond, one dark, both bundled against the cold, they made straight for Holly and Evan's table. Lachlan got to his feet, folded his napkin beside his plate, and gestured to the waiter for two more chairs. Holly set down her fork and looked unhappy.

"Holly Elizabeth," said the tall dark one, in an accent redolent of Boston's

Beacon Hill, "you are a difficult woman to locate." He bent, kissed her cheek, and started removing layers of expensive wool.

"Don't blame Isabella," the blond one added with a smile. "She didn't want to tell us."

"Let me guess," Holly said. "You tortured her by reciting Alec's recipe book."

"Puritan gruel with molasses muffins does it every time." Holding out a hand to Lachlan, the blond one said, "Nicholas Orlov—Holly's Uncle Nicky. This is Alexander Singleton."

"Evan Lachlan. Pleased to meet you."

"At last," Orlov appended wryly. "Sorry to interrupt your dinner." His accent was more difficult to place—the name was about as Russian as one could get, but the cadences of his voice were an odd combination of upper-class Brit, a touch of New York, and something that definitely wasn't the Russian heard in Brooklyn.

Holly looked sour as all three men sat down. "I take it I can't prevent you gentlemen from joining us."

"How very gracious of you to ask." Singleton grinned. "Caesar salad," he told the waiter. "I'm watching what's left of my figure."

Orlov opened a menu and zeroed in on the pasta selections. "Alfredo," he said blissfully.

"The only figure he watches is Uncle Alec's," Holly explained. "So why are you two here? What couldn't wait?"

Singleton gave her a cloyingly sweet smile, dark eyes dancing. "We only wanted to wish you a happy birthday, my precious."

"Right." She attacked her veal again with a fork. "So where's my present?"

"Patience," she was counseled; Singleton paused as plates, silverware, and napkins were provided, and when the waiter departed, continued, "We stopped by the store today."

"If you're not doing anything tomorrow," Orlov suggested, "why don't you go take a look?"

"What am I looking for?"

Lachlan eyed Holly over his wineglass. She was sulky in tone and expression, a complete departure from her cheerful mood of ten minutes ago—well, admittedly his gift of her favorite perfume had mellowed her out very nicely.

Orlov appeared unperturbed by her annoyance. "You'll know it when you see it. Alyosha, pass the butter."

Holly folded her arms and leaned back in her chair. "I hope you have a better reason than that for spoiling our evening."

"It's not spoiled," Evan said. "I've been looking forward to meeting—"

"So have they," Holly interrupted. "This has nothing to do with the bookstore at all."

"Ah, but it does." Singleton paused again while a fumé blanc was presented, opened, poured, tasted, and approved. When glasses had been filled, he and his partner toasted each other silently with, it seemed to Lachlan, a gesture half their lifetimes old. "Obsessed as we have been with conjecture about Deputy Marshal Lachlan, and rude as you have been, my darling girl, about not inviting us to dinner—still, the bookstore has everything to do with it."

She sighed, picked up her fork, and plunged into her dinner once more. "Okay, okay. Regale me."

Orlov shook his head. "After I eat. It's been a long time since lunch."

So, as food was brought and then consumed, Evan found himself making small talk with Holly's honorary uncles. It turned out that they, too, were Knicks fans, and this topic occupied them during the whole of Alec's salad. Holly didn't bother to conceal boredom. As Nick polished off the last of his Alfredo, the men were agreeing to go to at least one game together this season.

"I don't suppose," Evan said finally, "you've ever considered giving them a little help now and then?"

Nick's brows shot up. "He knows?" he directed at Holly.

"He knows."

"Ah."

"As for the Knicks," Alec said, "it's a matter of ethics. If Holly's told you about us, then she's also mentioned the rules."

"It was just a thought." Lachlan sighed wistfully.

"Don't think I haven't been tempted! End of the fourth quarter, down by two, one shot from outside the key to win—"

"Enough, already," Holly chuckled. "Besides, it's common knowledge about the '69 Mets."

"That wasn't me," Alec protested. "I'm a Yankees fan."

"Don't pay any attention to her," Lachlan advised. "She not only kissed the Blarney Stone, she bit off a chunk and swallowed it whole."

"Noticed that, did you?" Alec turned to his partner. "Nicholas, old son, are you finally finished stuffing your face? If so, I suggest you tell the tale."

"Dessert first," replied his partner, beckoning the waiter.

"Hollow to the ankles." The older man shook his head. "I've been waiting thirty years for him to get fat. I'll wait another thirty if necessary."

"Superior European genes," the blond chuckled.

"I've been meaning to ask," Evan ventured, "if your name is Russian."

"Very. But in actuality I'm mostly Hungarian, somewhat German, and a quarter Gypsy. Long story," he said in a fashion that indicated Evan wouldn't be hearing it anytime soon. The waiter hovered; Orlov ordered something opulently chocolate, plus espressos all around. At last, replete and relaxed, he began.

"When we decided to retire—Alec from lawyering, me from books—I sold

The Recommended Sentence. Which wasn't easy. Suffice to say, my advertisements didn't bring in the sort of person I was looking for. So I changed the manner of the listing." Here he smiled a little at Holly.

"Uncle Nicky," she said to Lachlan, "is what Aunt Lulah calls a Come-Hither, and other folks call a Summoner, and still others call a Coercer."

Digesting this with a swallow of wine, Evan nodded. "Be useful in my line of work," he remarked mildly.

The other two men blinked. For the first time since the pair had come into the restaurant, Holly gave a genuine smile. "Now you know why I adore him."

"Peculiar you may be on occasion," Alec retorted, "but stupid, never. Keep going, Nick."

"Hmm? Oh—of course. My sign and doorway, properly prepared, brought in only qualified and interested candidates looking for a rewarding life with books. People who treasured the printed word, the smell of leather bindings, the luxury of fine paper—"

His partner interrupted. "—the stink of mold, the crumbling of ancient dog-eared pages—and the art of the literary murder. Get on with it, will you?"

"Philistine," Nick sniffed. "I had scant luck to begin with. The spell required some fine-tuning. For instance, there was the gentleman with masses of money and an abiding fascination with ritualized S and M."

"And that mousy little guy who wanted to turn the place into a gay bookstore in the vain hope that he might get laid." Alec reached over to scrape leftover chocolate from his partner's plate.

"I've worked assiduously to blot him from my memory." Nick grinned.

"And the gorgeous little leather blonde with the nose-ring who hit on you."

"Most especially have I worked to forget *her*."

Amused, Lachlan poured more wine and said, "I gotta say, you people sure have interesting problems."

"He's just finicky," Alec said.

Haughtily, Nick replied, "I spent half my life building up the business, the clientele, and the collection—damned if I'd let it be taken over by some idiot."

"So who'd you end up selling it to?"

Alec snorted. "A six-foot-six blue-eyed beanpole. Stick him at one end of my granny's garden, run a clothesline out from the house, and hang the laundry."

"A beanpole with a Ph.D. in Literature," Nick retorted, "erudite, charming, more than a little gifted, although unaware of it—"

"You only liked him because he recognized that Wilkie Collins first edition," Alec put in. "Pushover for anyone who fawns over ancient pages. I can't tell you how glad I continue to be that Holly had contributed to our Handfasting."

"Moron. He isn't my type. I like things older than I am," Nick said with poisonous sweetness.

Holly laughed. "Get a room, you two. So you sold this guy the store?"

"I'm carrying the paper, and his payments are perfectly on time. That was that. Or so I thought." The clear blue eyes darkened below a frown. "I visited the shop last autumn, that day we almost met in the hallway, Evan. Not much had changed. A new sofa in the reading area, some artwork, a little rearranging of the shelves. Not much new stock."

"We were there again today," Alec interrupted. "Me for the first time since the sale. I knew he should've had me scope this guy out in the first place—"

"The point!" Holly exclaimed, thoroughly out of patience.

"He's turned it into an occult bookshop," Nick announced in disgust. "All the other stock is gone. Conan Doyle, Sayers, Christie, Peters—Ellis *and* Elizabeth—Chandler, Hammett, Lindsay Davis, Laurie King, Steven Saylor— all my lovely mysteries and thrillers and historical whodunnits, all the critical studies and biographies and anthologies—gone."

Holly sipped wine, then said, "He has a right to run the store the way he wants. He pays the mortgage. Esoterica is very chic, you know. Well, of course you know—you've dealt with enough wannabe Witches."

"That's just the point. He's no amateur. I don't like what he's up to. Alec and I would like you to go to the store and give us your opinion."

She regarded them for a time in silence. Then: "What you mean is that you're considering a Working, and want my cooperation—which means my blood." Her voice changed, and Evan blinked in surprise at the manifestation of an icily controlled anger he had never seen from her before.

Her honorary uncles were unimpressed. Alec said, "Your opinion is what we're after. Then, if necessary, we'll consult the Magistrate."

"The what?" Lachlan couldn't help it.

"There are rules and formalities in what we do," Nick told him. "Difficulties are taken to a Magistrate for investigation. If the Circle agrees, and the subject is unwilling to modify his or her behavior—" He finished with an eloquent shrug.

Lachlan was further intrigued, but even more certain he wasn't going to get any concrete answers. Still, he had to try. "Holly said they used to send you two out to deal with people like that."

Alec consulted his wristwatch in a purposely ostentatious gesture. "Another long story, and one we have no time for tonight." Rising, he leaned over to kiss Holly again. "Think about it, would you?"

"Yes, just think about it," Nick seconded as he beckoned the waiter for their coats. "We're at the Plaza tonight, but we'll be going home tomorrow. Call us at the farmhouse, okay?"

Holly said nothing.

The men shook hands with Evan, skipping the usual *Nice to meet you, let's have dinner again sometime* pleasantries, and started for the door. Halfway there, Nick turned, came back, and placed a small, square box wrapped in silver paper on the table by Holly's wineglass.

"Think about it," he repeated. "Happy birthday, sweet."

"Aren't you going to open it?" Evan asked when Orlov was gone.

"Later."

Catching her eye, he said bluntly, "I've never seen you rude before."

"I don't like it when that life intrudes on real life."

"From what I understand, 'that life' is anything but unreal."

"*You* are real life for me. Can you see that, Evan? The other thing—that's just something accidental, something I was born with. You, and my books—" She gestured helplessly. "It's the difference between what I was born and who I am."

"Like I was born Irish and can't do anything about it, but my career is my own choice?"

She nodded. "It has to do with other people's definitions of who you are, as opposed to how you define yourself."

He considered that for a moment. "But aren't Alec and Nick just asking you to be what you are?"

The waiter interrupted politely to inform them that the bill had already been paid. Lachlan made a mental note to come up with really good seats for that promised Knicks game, and escorted Holly outside into the February cold. They walked for a bit at her suggestion, which let him know she wanted to tell him something private and couldn't wait until they got back to her place.

Without preamble, she said, "When I was little I knew there was something special about me. We took it for granted, yet we didn't—you know? Like being good at sports or music. It was just something that was *there* for Aunt Lulah and me and some of our kin. Something we could do that was out of the ordinary. But at some point I started feeling that it wasn't just not ordinary, but downright not *normal*. And I spent a lot of energy wanting to *be* normal, have a life like everyone else's. Home, husband, family—"

He tucked her gloved hand into the crook of his elbow. "One person's genius is another person's freak. But it's like that with everyone who can do something *not* ordinary, Holly. Whose definition of your talents are you willing to accept?"

She gave a little shrug and leaned into his shoulder, hunching a little in her coat. "I wanted being special to come from something I could *do*, not just something I happened to *be*."

"I got news for you, lady love. You could never be 'ordinary'—and it's got nothing to do with the magic."

———

THE NEXT AFTERNOON, TELLING HERSELF she was at a sticky point in *Jerusalem Found* and didn't feel like working—it was raining in New York, and not conducive to writing about sunny Medieval Palestine (that was her excuse, anyway)—Holly went to The Recommended Sentence as requested. And was, more than anything else, annoyed by what she found.

Before, the shop had been a discriminating haven of first editions, autographed copies, and an impressive collection of framed letters from famed authors thanking Nicholas Orlov for his friendship and support. He'd taken the letters with him when he retired, of course, and a new coat of paint had obliterated the dark unfaded rectangles where the souvenirs had been. That alone was enough to irritate her—the letters had always felt like the welcoming smiles of friends. What made it worse was that the new owner had chosen to smear the walls with a deep grayed maroon rather like the color of dusty, half-dried blood.

And it smelled strange in here. Nicky's shop had smelled of old leather and old paper and good coffee; now there was something heavy and musky in the air that made her nose sting.

The new owner was indeed a beanpole. Long-limbed, lanky, pale of skin and eye, she had to admit he would be attractive if one appreciated the type. His thick, straight hair was reddish brown, swept back from a high forehead to cascade over his shirt collar. He moved with the curious grace of a too-large bird: the long arms and legs awkward in stillness, but revealing an elegance in motion and hinting at an unexpected strength. All in all, an odd character.

Busy with a customer at the front desk, he barely glanced up as Holly entered the shop. After a few moments of observing him, she wandered the once-familiar shelves, taking in the embellishments of his decorating scheme. There was a suite of twenty-six small woodcuts depicting a Devil's Alphabet: *A* for Asmodeus, *B* for Baphomet, and so on. Just the thing for teaching a Satanist's child the ABCs. One huge frame, alarmingly curlicued and gilded, surrounded a displayed tarot deck, each card's illustration skewed to the demonic. Holly wondered who would want to read a future told by cards featuring Lovers who had stabbed each other in the back.

In the middle of the store, where Nicky had kept cozy chairs and handy tables, there now resided a stone basin on a stone plinth that looked for all the world like a Druidic pedestal sink. Holly wasn't surprised to see scorch-marks inside the basin, and wondered what the fire marshal would make of this. She walked toward the coffee bar, sparing a glance for the assortment of cookies in the glass case. Skulls, pentagrams, and phalluses, all iced in Day-Glo colors.

Turning her attention to the books, Holly picked a row at random, and was unable to credit that there could be so many volumes written on demons, let alone on specific categories of them. At least three vertical feet of books about incubi, a similar number on succubi, and twice that about the hierarchies of Hell. A quick flip through one of the latter volumes told her that someone—or something—named Kobal was Entertainment Liaison, Paymon was Master of Infernal Ceremonies, and Nysrogh was Palace Chief of Staff. Sternly forbidding herself to speculate on their duties, she rubbed absently at her nose, replaced that book, and pulled out another. This one revealed an unexpectedly feminist slant, being an encyclopedia of goddesses, demonesses, evil spirits, and princesses of Hell.

Resisting the impulse to shake her head in amazement, she turned a corner to peruse another aisle. Vampires, Devils, Ancients, Goth, Voudon, Santería, Temple of Satan, History, Languages (including Runes and Magical Alphabets), Modern Religions, Witches—

She winced, and decided she didn't want to know.

All at once it occurred to her that this must have been how Evan felt when initially investigating the Craft. Not that he didn't want to know, exactly, but that he worried about what he might find. Well, if he wouldn't give in to intellectual cowardice, neither would she. Reaching the fiction shelves, she pulled out a book titled *Witchtales Retold* and opened it to the table of contents.

*Someday My Prince of Darkness Will Come; Bring Me the Heads of the Seven Dwarfs; Hansel and Gretel—Gluttons for Punishment; Cruella's Coup d'Evil; Why Is My Sister under that House, and Where Are Her Ruby Slippers?*

Suddenly it all seemed very silly and harmless. This was nothing more than a playground for dilettantes, amateurs, dabblers, and nitwitches. Holly regretted the demise of Nicky's wonderful bookshop, but no doubt some other dealer had purchased his stock and it resided in a mystery-lover's sanctuary waiting for buyers.

Convinced now that her adoptive uncles were simply pissed off by the changes, she started back for the front desk, taking with her the volume of reworked children's stories to read on her trip to Europe next month. As she waited for the owner to finish with another customer, who was having trouble deciding which earrings to buy (inverted pentacles in silver, copper, or what purported to be bone of goat), she opened the book again to smile over a few more story titles.

"You find our religion amusing?"

He had a deep musical voice and a hint of a Boston accent—probably one more reason Nicky had liked him to begin with, for Alec had the same remnants of pahk-the-cah-in-Hahvahd-Yahd.

"No more so than my own," Holly replied easily. "Interesting shop you've got here. Used to be mysteries, right?"

"It did. You knew the store then?"

"I was in once or twice," she lied. "Why'd you keep the name, if you don't mind my asking? 'The Recommended Sentence' was a fair-to-middling pun for a mystery bookstore, but it doesn't quite fit this merchandise, does it?"

The earrings girl (who had chosen the goat-bone set) looked up from rummaging in her capacious handbag. "Oh, but it's perfectly appropriate. The Master's judgments on life and death—"

"Serenity." The owner shrugged and smiled a little, taking the sting out of his mild warning. "See you next week?"

"Absolutely, Noel." With a toss of maroon-streaked hair and a swirl of black wool, she was gone.

"Some people get a little . . . enthusiastic," Noel said ruefully.

"Evangelicals—if that's the appropriate term," Holly couldn't help but reply, and saw the man's pale blue eyes glint with humor. She paid for the book with a credit card, after adding a greeting card from the rack near the counter—a lovely photo of Stonehenge by moonlight, blank inside—and while her purchases were being processed inspected a tall glass display case of candles. Fairly disgusting, some of them; she wondered that he didn't have an Adults Only area sectioned off, then decided his relations with the authorities weren't her problem. After accepting the bag Noel handed her, she smiled and wished him a good afternoon.

Back at home, she used the Stonehenge card to write Nicky and Alec a note saying thank you for the cloisonné brooch, she missed the old shop but the new owner and his merchandise seemed pretty harmless, and stop worrying like a couple of old maiden uncles. She appended an invitation to dinner and/or the next ritual sacrifice on Salisbury Plain, whichever they preferred, signed the card, sealed and stamped the envelope, and put it in the correspondence pile.

And then she sneezed. Even a brisk walk through the Village before taking a taxi home hadn't blown the store's scent from her clothing, and her nose had finally had enough. Rummaging around the office for tissues (none—she used toilet paper from the bathroom instead), she sneezed again. And cursed. She hadn't had allergies like this since first moving to L.A. for grad school, and back then it had been the smog, not a flower or plant.

No, that was wrong. After leaving Denise's apartment that night last autumn she'd sniffled until the next morning. *"Musk* and *patchouli?"* she heard Ian say in memory. On a red Baphomet candle just like the ones she'd seen in the store.

Was Denise getting her supplies there? Ridiculous to suspect that she was. There must be half a hundred occult shops in the five boroughs where one could procure candles and essential oils and implements. Yet when she considered the slant of Noel's store, which seemed to be just Denise's style . . .

Damn. She would have to report it to the Magistrate, as anything that might concern Denise must be reported to the Magistrate.

———

HOLLY LIFTED HER HAIR FROM her nape so Evan could fasten her mother's pearl necklace. "It may be my imagination, but it seems as if all you people in law enforcement know each other."

"Turn a little, I can't see—yeah," he said, snapping the clasp before leaving a kiss behind her ear. "Same as all you Witches know each other, I guess. Different religions—" He grinned at her in the mirror. "—but the same craft union."

"Then there must be the same kind of hierarchy as well."

"Turf," he corrected with a shrug. "With a lot of overlap. NYPD Narcotics and the DEA are always in each other's faces, for instance. The FBI wants a piece of everything. And of course there's Homeland Security, the new kids on the block."

"But the Marshals are the oldest service in the country." She turned and straightened his tie. "You guys have the coolest badges, too," she added with a wink. "So if you all engage in pissing contests, why are we going to a retirement party for a Secret Service suit?"

"Because Frank Sbarra worked liaison for twenty years with the police and the Marshals on VIP protection, for one thing. And for another, he's a good friend of Pete Wasserman's, which means he also hangs with my dad every so often."

"You didn't tell me I'd be meeting your father tonight," she said, frowning.

"You won't. He's up in Boston with the aunts." Eyeing her, he went on, "Usually women *want* to meet the folks."

"I do. I'd just like a little warning beforehand, that's all."

"When do I get to meet Aunt Lulah?"

"One of these days."

He considered this evasion for a while as they gathered up coats and keys. Then: "Oh. The commitment thing."

"What?"

"Getting introduced to the relatives. It's kind of *definite*."

"So is my intense need to knock you into the middle of next week."

"Why don't you just turn me into a toad?"

"If only I could. Keep laughing, Lachlan, I have several very gifted friends who'd just love to try out new spells on you."

In the elevator, she tossed him her car keys. He was deeply in lust with her black BMW, and she knew it, and taunted him with it whenever they drove instead of taking a taxi. "Here—I like you better as a chauffeur than as a toad."

Settling into leather luxury, he fired up the engine and sighed his content-ment.

"Daayaamn," she drawled, "but y'all look cute behind the wheel of this here car!"

"I know," he shot back. "But you'll have to adjust the mirrors back before you drive it again. And the seat and steering wheel."

"When we stop, I'll show you the buttons that control the memory. Different drivers," she explained. "I'm One—this *is* my car!—and you can be Two."

"Aw, gee—first I get a drawer, then some hangers in the closet, and now I get programmed into your car? I guess you must kinda like me, huh?"

"I know, I'm too good to you," she said breezily. "So tell me about Frank."

He smiled as he drove out of the garage onto the street, calling up a mental image of the beefy Italian and his tiny Brazilian wife. "He and Maria are married thirty-two years, with four daughters, five grandkids—so far—and a big house in the Jersey burbs. They met when her father was doing business in Washington, and she never went back to Rio. Frank wore an earplug on the Presidential detail until somebody cycled feedback by accident and damned near fried his eardrum. That's when he started being a social director."

She laughed softly. "So that's what they call it when you have to make sure nobody tries to assassinate a VIP?"

"That's what Frank calls it. You'll like him. He smokes cigars even stinkier than mine."

Two hours later, replete with martinis and canapés, Lachlan and Frank Sbarra were doing just that—out on the back porch, by Maria's command, so the cigars didn't malodorize the whole house. Inside the living room, friends and colleagues and daughters and husbands and grandkids milled about, drinking and laughing. It was the kind of gathering Lachlan wished his family could have. Just once. Just to see what it felt like.

"Where've you been keeping this girl, Evan?"

"Away from you, Franco," he retorted fondly. "I know you. One pat on the ass and she'd be head over heels—and seeing as how Maria's had you on a choke chain for over thirty years, you'd only break Holly's heart."

"*Madonn'*, but it's such a nice ass," Sbarra chuckled. "I can look, though, can't I?"

"All you like," Evan replied breezily. "So what're you gonna do with yourself now that you're an old retired fogy?"

"Start a security business, what else? It's all I know how to do, and I'm pretty good at it." Flicking ash from his cigar, he gazed out at the backyard, all hung with fairy lights from the fences and apple trees. Though it was thirty-five degrees outside, there were a few couples strolling Maria's tidy flower beds and herb garden. The best salsa Lachlan had ever tasted started life in this yard every spring. "You ever get tired of playing Wyatt Earp, you come join me, Evan."

Adopting a cowboy slouch and an exaggerated Texas twang, Lachlan said,

"Nah, gotta stick around and catch all them gol-durned cattle rustlers, clean up Dodge City." It was an old joke, part of the pissing contest among officers of differing agencies. He was about to tease in his turn when he caught sight of a pair of new arrivals taking off their coats. "What the hell is *he* doing here?"

Sbarra squinted. "Get enough of Judge Bradshaw at the office, do you? Didn't Pete ever tell you about the time he and I worked security for an up-and-coming D.A. who had half the Klan gunning for him?"

"Some of 'em still are," Lachlan muttered. "How come Bradshaw's so popular, Franco? I get bulletins every other week about the Klan, the Aryans, the Mafia—the Chianti kind *and* the vodka kind—"

"—and the slivovitz and rice wine and sake kinds, too, I bet. The thing of it is that Bradshaw doesn't scare, Evan. He can be reckless. I used to think it was because he had something to prove about himself. But it's not his own *pisello* he's screwing them with, it's the law's."

The last thing on Elias Bradshaw's mind at that moment was anybody's *pisello*, even his own. Maria Sbarra, scorning a caterer, had made all manner of gorgeous Brazilian food for her husband's retirement party, and Bradshaw was happily loading a plate with delicacies.

He had just accepted a glass of red wine when a familiar voice said at his shoulder, "There's a store in the Village you ought to check out."

"Good evening to you, too, Ms. McClure," he retorted.

"I'll make small talk when Suze gets back from the bathroom." Holly poured herself a glass of wine and went on, "Anyway, this store—"

"Shopping isn't a guy thing."

"I'd noticed," she said, giving his suit a once-over. "I mean an occult shop. It used to be a mystery bookstore, but the new owner has turned it into—well, go see for yourself. Personally, I think it's pretty much nothing, but Alec and Nicky asked me to check it out. And I have a feeling Denise shops there for some of her toys."

"And this concerns me how?"

Her mouth thinned. "Just reporting in, Magistrate, like it says in the rule book," she snapped, and walked off.

A few minutes later, making the rounds, Elias approached Susannah. "Is there something wrong with my clothes?"

She looked at him as if he had lost his mind, then made one of those mental jumps he could never predict, and grinned. "Well, you have to admit that Evan Lachlan's wardrobe has improved exponentially since he started dating Holly."

"Gee, and here I thought he'd had a *Queer Eye for the Straight Guy* makeover."

"Oh, hilarious," Susannah growled. "At least let me buy you a few new ties."

"No."

"A shirt or two? Those white button-downs are really boring, Eli."

"Double no."

"How about a sweater? Argyle socks? Suspenders with cute little gavels on them?"

Two glasses of wine and another heaping plate of food made Bradshaw's evening complete—until Maria brought out the desserts. He pounced, and got his hand slapped away from the chocolate-rolled *brigadieros* for his trouble.

"Only on condition that you perform for my skeptical grandchildren," Maria scolded. "They've heard from their mothers for years and do not believe a word."

"Oh, God," Elias moaned.

"Heard about what?" Susannah asked.

"*Laranja.*" Maria folded her arms and grinned.

Two daughters and a grandson standing nearby had regrettably sharp ears, and the clamor began. Maria vanished into the kitchen and returned a moment later to toss Elias a navel orange the size of a softball. He caught it one-handed; the children recognized this as tacit agreement to *Laranja*, and cheered. With great ceremony Maria then presented a long-handled fork and a paring knife, which Bradshaw accepted with a courtly bow.

After sticking the fork into the orange, he held knife and fruit aloft as some-one dimmed the lights so only the tabletop candles glowed. "Thank you, thank you," he intoned. "Here we have a common, everyday, completely ordinary or-ange. Nothing special, nothing extraordinary. Just an orange." He paused. "Or is it?"

Holly's Virginia drawl: "Really workin' it, ain't he?"

Susannah's laughter: "You should see him in a courtroom."

"Out of order!" Bradshaw thundered.

Frank Sbarra called out, "He'll see you in chambers later, Counselor!"

"I'm counting on it!" Susannah retorted, and everyone laughed.

"Where was I?" Elias complained. "Oh, yes—a common, ordinary orange." With an artistic flourish he brought knife and fruit together. An impressively narrow spiral of peel began to droop lower and lower. Maria produced a copper saucepan and set it on the floor at his feet. Longer, longer, until the peel nearly reached the lip of the pan and there was only a small circle of untouched orange left at the top. Then the knife was tossed onto the table, and he closed a fist around the orange, squeezing gently so juice ran in delicate rivulets down the peel.

"Now, if my lovely assistant would assist?" he asked, and as he held the or-ange out on the fork Maria extended a silver candlestick, flame flickering in the darkness—and sudden fire spiraled down the peel to the gasps and applause of the crowd.

*Laranja* completed, lights and music were restored and Elias happily gorged himself on *brigadieros* and the nastily named but utterly delicious confection of coconut, prune, vanilla, and clove, *olhos de sogra*—"mother-in-law's eyes."

An hour or so later he was upstairs getting his and Susannah's coats when the bedroom door slammed behind him. Turning, he beheld Holly McClure.

"I assume you know how incredibly stupid that was."

"You assume wrongly." He shrugged into his overcoat, slinging Susannah's over his elbow.

"Goddammit, Evan's primed to see Witches wherever he goes with me— never mind that this was a party for one of *his* friends—no, you had to show up and do your little magic act—"

"It wasn't magic."

"—and to think you had the *gall* to yell at me after that Imbolc thing! How could you be so stupid?"

"It wasn't magic," he said again.

That stopped her. At last. "It wasn't?"

"No. Maria injected liquor into the orange—it takes about a pint to saturate it enough, so I hope she used the cheap vodka. I learned how to do *Laranja* back in law school. Now, if you're finished being paranoid, I'm going home."

"Paranoid!"

"You're the writer with the million-dollar vocabulary—what would you call it? It's not explanations you're into; it's excuses. Your magic is like a stash of pornography that you shove into a corner when somebody visits. Which reminds me—how *do* you excuse all the protections on your home to the uninitiated? Quaint old Virginia folk art?" he jeered.

"Back off, Magistrate!"

"What the hell is your problem anyway? That bookstore you mentioned tonight—if you'd used just a little of what you've got, you could have discovered all kinds of things, but there's no doubt that you went in there as an ordinary customer. Too much effort, Holly? Would it put you out to investigate a little for a couple of men you claim to respect and value? Or would that be too close to actually thinking like a Witch?"

"And just how compartmentalized is *your* life, Your Honor? Doesn't your Craft get checked at the courtroom door? And what sort of *excuses* do you make to Susannah?"

"Probably the same ones you've made for almost twenty years."

"At least Evan knows what I am."

"How'd that happen, by the way? 'Welcome home, Marshal, pass me the bat's wings'?"

"At least," she repeated with vicious sweetness, "he *knows*."

Bradshaw stared at the slammed door for a full minute after she left. Susannah did not know—and if he had any powers at all, she never would.

# Seven

DENISE CLAUDINE JOSÈPHE WAS SERIOUSLY pissed off.

Her editor—an annoying little man with a beard that clung to his face like a frightened animal—had questioned her latest chapters for the most ridiculous reasons. "It's too violent—all that blood! That sort of thing is on the way out. And not even your most faithful readers would believe that this kind of sex goes on, even at heathen rituals."

After pointing out to him that a "heathen" was a person who lived on a "heath," she'd fumed her way out of the office for a long walk.

It was her own fault. She'd forgotten to bring the gris-gris bag, present from a friend in New Orleans, that guaranteed cooperation and approval. Oddly enough, she'd been forgetting a lot of things lately, all of them to do with magic.

At Yule her special recipe for corn cakes had produced none of the usual raves; it wasn't until a few days later that she realized she'd left out certain essential ingredients. In March there'd been a man she'd wanted and hadn't gotten, because although she'd brought the right scents, candles, and herbal sachet, she'd forgotten the words of the right spell. Only last week she'd been shopping for a new carpet for her living room, and the gallery owner had politely but firmly refused to lower the price for her—though he'd done so on other occasions. When she got home she found her luck-and-money amulet still hanging over her bedroom altar.

Or maybe it wasn't so odd after all.

She still shivered when she recalled the night her Measure had been taken. Who knew what Elias Bradshaw had done with it? Her absentmindedness could be the result of his Work. It would be just like him, too—some puny little spell of overlooking, nothing with any real jizz to it.

The more she considered it, the more certain she was. That self-righteous interfering bastard, with his patronizing New England morality and his useless ethics—how dared he?

She walked faster along the busy noontime street, newly furious, but with a worthier object now than her editor. Anger gave her purpose, and fifteen minutes later she pushed through the double doors of a shop she'd used only once before. Back in November it had barely yielded her needs; now she spent a satisfying half hour gathering information and supplies from a much improved stock.

The owner was helpful, if sketchily educated in the techniques of Voudon. Tall and thin, with a surprisingly lovely voice, he listened to her oblique explanation of her problem with his pale blue eyes fixed intensely on her face. She was used to being looked at, but not with such cool probing.

"Somebody's hexed you," he said at last. "Do you have any idea who?"

"Some," she said, then heard herself continue, "Two people in particular. And they're protected up one side and down the other."

"I see."

She had the most grotesque sensation that he did indeed see. Far too much, with those eyes of chill silvery blue.

"Let me think about it for a while," he continued, "and you browse the store, see if anything occurs to you." A slight pause. "You've been in here before, right?"

"Last year, for oils and candles. You've made some changes."

"A few," he agreed, a glitter of amusement in his eyes now. "Some of the new stock took time. Try the display case in the back—there's some interesting stuff."

There was. Denise knew with a happy smile that her mail-order days were over. This shop could supply everything she could possibly need, now that it was fully equipped. Her earlier anger vanished as she roamed shelves of books and candles, implements and incense, jewelry and oils and semiprecious stones. True, the more arcane items must still be had from New Orleans, but this store contained quite a bit more than just the basics of spellcraft.

She was contemplating with amusement the effects of bloodstone, black pepper oil, and a seven-knob wishing candle when the owner appeared beside her, so suddenly that she gave a start.

"You need to turn the hex back on the maker and fix it so no more hexes can be sent against you, right? Well, let's start with a black candle for banishing, a brown for neutralizing, and a silver for protection. As for the scents—"

"Pepper, jasmine, and pine," she snapped. "Do you think I'm an amateur?"

"I think you've probably never run into anyone who's got it in for you, so you're not as familiar with this kind of spellcasting. For instance, what phase of the moon would be best?"

The spells she worked were always of her own initiation for her own purposes, not to respond or counteract someone else's. Which was something else to be angry at Bradshaw for. "Okay, so you know your stuff," she told him. "How much is this going to cost me?"

"Not as much as you'd think—" All at once he grinned, and became markedly more attractive. "—because you manufacture the main ingredient personally."

When he'd finished writing down the basics of his recommendations, she understood what he meant. It was drolly appropriate—she'd just as soon piss on Bradshaw as look at him. And as for Ms. Holly-Holy-Goddess McClure . . .

"Sounds like fun," she said, chuckling.

"Magic should always be enjoyable," he replied. "Whatever the intent, we should all take pleasure in our Craft."

"Some spells are more pleasurable than others."

"Granted. But those without real gifts, real power, have to take our pleasures where we can find them." His head tilted slightly to one side. "You're going for some pretty powerful stuff here. Are your targets believers?"

"Yes," she replied reluctantly. "I wish it were otherwise."

"I know what you mean. This kind of thing works better on somebody who doesn't believe." His voice lowered to confidential, almost caressing tones. "It's the so-called 'enlightened' person who scoffs at what he sees as superstition who's easiest to curse. His instinctive fear is deliberately pushed to the back of his mind. It lurks in his subconscious, links up with the curse, and makes it more powerful. But someone who believes will worry about what might be happening, even if he's not aware of the actual, specific threat. His inner defenses are alerted and he can counteract a spell without even knowing it."

"I think what we've put together here will suffice."

"Do you want it known that it's you?"

Denise considered. Then she smiled. When they finally realized what was happening, she wanted them to know who had authored their predicament.

"I thought so," the man said, comprehending and returning her smile. "It's a poor excuse for a practitioner who hides the Work. You don't seem that type at all. And anyway, I don't think you could even try to hide it in this case, because one of the ingredients is too—um—*personal*, as it were."

"So to speak," she agreed. "Wrap it up and tell me the damages."

"To your targets?" His smile widened to a grin. "Severe. My name's Noel, by the way. Yes, like Christmas."

"Heard it a thousand times, right? I'm Denise."

His frown puzzled her, until his eyes lit and he exclaimed, "Now I know who you are! It's been nagging at me since you walked in. You're Denise Josephs!"

"Josèphe," she corrected, but not as coldly as she might have done. He had, after all, provided a very interesting new spell.

"It's an honor to meet you—and I hope I'll see you in here often."

"Perhaps."

Noel bagged her purchases and wished her a good afternoon. On her way out the door she nearly ran into a tall, muscular, windblown man with the most astonishing hazel eyes she'd ever seen. She'd seen them before, she knew it—

"Sorry," he said with a smile, standing to one side so she could leave.

Denise nodded distractedly, trying to remember where she remembered him from. She was halfway to the Starbucks down the block when she had it.

Holy *merde*! A launch party for a novel she hadn't read and didn't intend to—Holly McClure with a tall, hunky piece of eye-candy on her arm—they'd left early and Denise had heard someone say that he never thought he'd see the Virginia Virgin with some guy who looked like sex on a stick.

At Starbucks, she found a table and sorted through her purchases, mind racing as she adjusted and adapted for a new and different intent. She'd heard that Holly McClure was out of town for a couple of weeks. Perfect. Sipping slowly at her coffee, she held certain items caressingly in her palm, murmuring gently under her breath, and waited for him with perfect confidence that he would come.

"YOU HAVEN'T BEEN IN HERE before," said the skinny, long-haired proprietor.

"No," Lachlan replied, getting his first look at the man who'd annoyed Nicholas Orlov so thoroughly. The promised Knicks game had occurred two nights ago—with Lachlan winking at Alec Singleton when a three-point jump shot came up short and the Knicks won—and spending time with the two men had reminded him that he'd wanted to visit the bookstore and see what the fuss was about. Running down an address on a Federal warrant had taken him to the Village this afternoon. So here he was, spending his lunch hour in a sorcerer's lair.

Which was exactly what the place looked like. His reading had taught him quite a bit; still, the minute he stepped around the blonde and got a good look at the place, he agreed with Nick: this was excessive. Atmosphere was fine, and helped sell product. But he could have done without the incense smoldering in what looked like a stone birdbath, the mysterious nuances of lighting and paint that made some sections of the walls look as if they were bleeding, the downright spooky array of framed tarot cards, and the featured exhibit of demonic jewelry, including an inverted pentagram necklace on a chain of tiny silver skulls.

"Interesting place," he commented, fingering an iron candleholder.

"May I help you find anything? Books, candles, incense—?"

"Just browsing, thanks."

He wandered around the shop, liking it less and less. This was the epitome of public misconceptions about Witchcraft: Satanism, sex, and surgically sharp "ritual" knives. It was as if someone had stocked a Christian shop with flagellation whips, hair shirts, saints' fingerbone relics, and all the persuasive contraptions of the Spanish Inquisition. Holly had merely been amused by the place: "Kind of creepy, but essentially harmless." Evan had a different feeling from it altogether. Creepy, yes; harmless—maybe not.

A cluster of high-schoolers sat on the floor near the back door, Goth from their black clothing to their ashen faces. Witchcraft as fashion statement. He stepped around them, noticing a dozen brightly colored flyers taped to the door. The papers advertised piercing and tattoos ("It's not *self*-mutilation—*we* do it *for* you!"), various covens, tarot readers, Voudon gatherings, classes in Elementary Spellcasting, Advanced Aphrodisiacs, Infernal Hierarchies, and the Annual Beltane Ball.

"Need a date?"

Glancing down at the girl who'd spoken, he felt his brows arch involuntarily. He'd never seen anyone so young with so little of her original equipment unaltered. It wasn't just the piercings in odd places or the tattoos in even odder ones. The stark black-and-maroon of her hair was as unreal as the startling dimensions of her breasts.

"Beltane," she added, giving him a once-over and liking what she saw. "It's always a great party."

"Uh—no thanks," he replied. "I have other plans."

"Serenity," one of the boys warned. She turned, making a face as he went on, "No outsiders."

"He wouldn't be an outsider, Scott, once he's been inside," Serenity retorted. Scott made an annoyed gesture with oddly singed and scarred hands. Nobody had to ask *Inside what?*

Lachlan retreated back up the aisle of shelves, wondering if he ought to rethink his desire to have children. Nah, he'd see to it that they toed whatever lines he and Holly cared to draw—redheaded Irish tempers or no redheaded Irish tempers.

A smile at the thought of a couple of smart and feisty offspring carried him out the store and into the brisk April wind. Then his stomach rumbled, reminding him he hadn't yet eaten lunch. Fine dining at restaurants, and even finer dining on Isabella's creations, had put ten pounds on him since Christmas. There was a box of nutrition bars waiting for him in his desk, but he needed something to wash down the taste of shrink-wrapped sawdust. So he stopped at Starbucks—and bumped into the blonde from the bookstore.

"We meet again," she said brightly, smiling up at him.

"So we do." He gave her his habitual once-over, liking the curves of her cheekbones and breasts, not so crazy about the odd green of her eyes, speckled with brownish flecks like a spring apple going bad. Besides, he'd developed an appreciation for peaches-and-cream complexions, and roses didn't do it for him anymore. Neither did the just–shy–of–Sir Mick Jagger dimensions of her lips.

"Twice in twenty minutes," she went on. "Maybe it's fate."

The accent was Southern, but not the right kind. Damn it, did Holly already have a ring through his nose and her initials tattooed on his ass? First the girl in the store, and now here was another good-looking female obviously attracted to him, and all he could think about was—

"What do you think?" she asked more pointedly.

"Who was it who said there are no accidents?" he asked, smiling.

"Get some coffee and we'll discuss it."

He wasn't sure if the bleat of his pager was a welcomed interruption or a damned nuisance. Whichever, he had to answer the thing. A flip of a switch and a glance down at his belt—and he nearly yelped with delight.

WYATT YOU'VE GOT MAIL

"Well?" the blonde asked, invitation and more in her eyes.

"Wish I could. Duty calls."

"Does it? How loudly?"

"Very. But maybe I'll trip over you again sometime," he said by way of soothing her ego.

"I'm sure you will," she told him, winking.

He watched her go, wondering how many different kinds of fool he could possibly be. Two weeks now that Holly had been in Europe, and two unmistakably interested women had flirted with him, and six months ago he would have blown off work for the afternoon and nailed the blonde to the mattress.

It irked him that Holly could have that strong a hold on his body. And his mind. And especially his heart, he admitted at last.

Bidding a reluctant farewell to his caffeine fix, he left the store. Now—where to find an online computer? It was too far back to the office, and he didn't see any cybercafés in the area. Hadn't there been a computer behind the counter at the bookshop?

There had. As he pushed through the door once again into the wizard's den, he held a brief debate with himself about secure lines and public places, but decided if this was the e-mail he thought it was, he didn't have time to waste. Messages for "Wyatt" were few and far between. His other aliases—"McCloud" and "Dillon" among them—received many more hits.

"You're back," the proprietor said, startled.

"You have e-mail on that computer, right?"

"Yes, but—"

"Can I borrow it?"

"I don't let customers—"

Lachlan flashed his badge. "Federal officer." Swinging around the counter, he punched buttons, wielded the mouse, and within two minutes was on his own Internet service. A few moments later, there it was: the message "Wyatt" had been anticipating for several weeks.

GODZILLA TODAY ONE THIRTY

"Yee-haw," he muttered, glancing at his watch. He had just enough time to get to Koronet Pizza in Morningside Heights, where the famous twenty-eight-inch Godzilla was created for worshipping fanatics. Logging off after deleting his tracks, he thanked the store owner and left a five on the counter. "That's for your trouble."

One of the more enjoyable features of Lachlan's job was helping to manage forfeited assets—everything from boats and cars and houses to jewelry, whole libraries of books, and fine art. The U.S. Marshals Service handled property forfeitures for the FBI, INS, DEA, and half the rest of the alphabet agencies. The fun part was that sometimes, if one read one's target right, such items could be used to lure an otherwise canny criminal out of hiding and back into the tender arms of the law.

In brief, "Wyatt" ran his own personal eBay.

A couple of years ago, for instance, he'd located a fugitive arms dealer through the woman's passion for Degas pastels. Through delicate and roundabout negotiations, "Wyatt" offered and she accepted a gorgeous suite of drawings. Of course, Lachlan had had to promise the property guys an arm, a leg, and the left lobe of his liver if anything happened to the art during the capture. But for a day and a night, the Degas drawings had resided in his apartment as if he'd truly owned them—almost as satisfying an experience as driving to another lure-and-lasso in the '32 Duesenberg that a Venezuelan drug trafficker just *had* to own.

Lachlan checked his watch again and slowed his stride a bit, not wanting to be early to Koronet Pizza. As he dodged lunchtime pedestrians, he thanked Whoever and Whatever that people let their greed get the better of their sense. He'd seen some otherwise sharp and ruthless felons turn into raving imbeciles over the prospect of possessing a particular jewel, a special sculpture, a mint-condition car. He supposed greed was one of the main reasons for crime to begin with—*I want more, and I want it now.* But when was enough enough?

Contempt had a lot to do with it, too, he reflected as he stopped half a block from Koronet to watch for his contact. Contempt for authority, for other people's intelligence and rights and property and lives—as if the world existed for the gratification of one person and one alone, and be damned to everyone else. Lachlan enjoyed demonstrating otherwise.

While he waited, he used his cell phone to call the office, where Mrs. Osbourne gave him about half the usual grief over the mess in his filing cabinets before condescending to sort through it for the warrant he needed. It didn't actually have to be in his hand when he made the collar; it just had to be excavated from his files. Because Judge Bradshaw wasn't due back from a luncheon at Gracie Mansion until three, Pete Wasserman was available to run the warrant over to wherever Lachlan ended up—if, that was, he ended up in the presence of his real quarry.

The woman he hoped would be his ticket there finally arrived: greed, contempt, and arrogance personified in one long, lean, nasty piece of work. She emerged from a black Cadillac limo, all leg, and glanced around the crowd of flawed humanity with active dislike. Lachlan smiled with pleasurable anticipation. Felicia Holton had a mane of well-kept brown hair, a stable of Andalusians, a ski-bum nonentity of a husband, and a grandpa whose birthday was coming up. Grandpa, known to his chemical company's board of directors as Edward Reynolds Phippen IV, had been indicted on RICO violations and hadn't been seen in public for the six weeks since the warrant had been issued. The FBI was convinced he had skipped the country to live on his gazillions somewhere in Europe.

Lachlan had arranged that Mrs. Holton would know him by his beloved and much-maligned cowboy boots. It tickled him mightily to see her squinting down at the feet of every man she neared. He watched for a while, grinning, then smoothed his expression and ambled toward her, pretending he was looking for someone, too.

Big brown eyes narrowed as she looked down, did not widen as she looked up. "Mr. Wyatt?"

"Who wants to know?"

A frown tainted her elegant face. "I have no time for games. Let's go where we can talk."

"Suits me, honey." He took her arm; she reclaimed it as if he were infected with several loathsome contagious diseases.

She preceded him into the limo, careful of the swirl of tailored silk skirt—presumably to prevent giving the unwashed masses a look at a pair of truly aristocratic legs. Lachlan sat, stretching out his legs to rest his bootheels on the opposite seat, and hoped he was scarring the leather upholstery.

A block later, he said, "So you want a little something from my collection."

"As we discussed in e-mail, the 1922 Roullet cognac."

"Fine. When do you want me to deliver?"

"Now."

He spread his arms a bit—not enough to part his jacket and reveal his holster. "Does it look like I've got it on me?"

"Then fetch it."

As if he were a dog ordered to retrieve the morning paper. Oh, yeah, this was going to be fun. "Why don't *you* do it?" he suggested, taking a key ring from his breast pocket and sliding one off—key to a bike lock he hadn't seen since college. "This goes to a P.O. box. There's another key in that. Leave the money there and take the key to the Greyhound station on—"

"A *bus* station?"

Had he invited her to get down and get funky with Serenity, Scott, and the Goths at the Annual Beltane Ball, she could not have been more shocked.

"You might want to lose the limo first. The second key goes to a locker. That's where the bottles are."

"Meanwhile you have the money and I could have nothing more than the key to an empty locker."

"Okay, leave the money in the locker when you're sure you have what you want," he replied with a shrug. "But I'll be watching, so don't try to stiff me."

She made a bored face. "Doubtless your next line is that you have powerful friends. We'll go to my home. Then I'll go to this post office box and so on."

He eyed her with no little amusement. "Doubtless *your* next line is that there'll be a couple of guys with guns to watch me."

"Only one. If you're playing fair with me, you have nothing to worry about."

"Oh, I'm just all kinds of okay with this."

And he was. One guy with a gun he could handle; probably even two. Any more than that and he would have modified his plan a bit. But she was taking him right where he wanted to go: her home, where Grandpa might be hanging out in avoidance of his civic responsibility to appear in Federal Court. Even if Lachlan didn't get that lucky, he felt sure he could find something that would indicate where Phippen was holed up.

He regarded his hostile hostess, who sat as far from him as possible in the limo. Charming girl. No wonder her husband absented himself to whichever part of the world had the best skiing in any given season. The arctic circle would be balmy compared to this bitch.

"Y'know," he said casually, "if you like what you buy this time, I have a few more cases you might be interested in."

She didn't even glance at him.

"There's a '22 Baron de Lustrac I can give you a great deal on."

"Mr. Wyatt. Close your mouth."

As they drove uptown in glacial silence, Lachlan rehearsed the charges: Racketeer Influenced and Corrupt Organization Act violations involving the clandestine dumping of toxic chemicals into six different rivers. Pity he couldn't deliver that case of twelve-hundred-buck bottles laced with a liberal sampling of Phippen's industrial cocktail.

He watched the city slide by and reflected that he liked being a deputy marshal much better than being a cop. The justice system had already decided that so-and-so was bad news, and all he had to do was serve the warrant and haul in the perp. No long drawn-out detective work to build a case, no weighing this evidence against that alibi, no hassling with the D.A.'s office over probable cause for a warrant. No crimes to investigate, no puzzles to solve—or, more likely, get an ulcer over because they were insoluble. Lachlan was content to leave the Sherlock Holmes stuff to people who got off on it; he much preferred exercising his analytical talents on ferreting out bad guys who had already been identified as bad guys.

Of course, it all would have been much easier if he'd had Nicholas Orlov's "come-hither" talent. Still, he didn't do too badly.

At last they arrived at a co-op building not far from Holly's place. Not far in distance, anyway; in price, halfway to the moon. A private elevator from the garage floated skyward, finally decanting them into a grim gilded foyer. The promised big-beefy-with-gun materialized, listened to his employer's instructions, and nodded—all without taking his eyes off Lachlan.

The marshal considered. He could probably take the guy without breaking too much of a sweat. All the same, the muscles beneath this man's brown silk suit made Lachlan glad he was carrying the Glock. Sloppy of them not to pat him down, but after all he was just a dealer in rare wines of shady provenance. And he wasn't disposed to point out their carelessness.

After Lachlan told Mrs. Holton the location and number of the post office box, she departed. He found a side chair that looked as if it wouldn't swallow him whole—he had his doubts about the vast orange sofa over in the corner—and sat himself down to wait.

After about five minutes, he looked over at the muscles and offered, "Nice place."

No response. Just that flat, constant stare.

"You with a personal protection agency, or freelance?"

He might as well have been speaking to the gold-veined marble walls.

After another few minutes, Lachlan stood up. "I gotta pee."

The hulk moved, one thick finger pointing to a door. Lachlan sauntered toward it, and glanced over his shoulder to find himself escorted as soundlessly as his own shadow.

"You gonna help me hold it?" he asked genially, and pulled open the door.

It was slammed shut behind him. No sense of humor, he told himself, ignoring the bathroom's lavish appointments—more gilt and way too many mirrors—in favor of biting back a whoop of delight.

There was a connecting door.

Locked, of course.

Not for nothing had he run with Mike de Corona and his crowd in the fourth grade. There wasn't a lock on the Lower East Side that Mike couldn't open, and Lachlan had been his star pupil. The guys at the Police Academy and the Marshals Academy had been suitably impressed. Out came the little leather case of tools, and a few seconds later the door was open.

He jammed the other door lock with a wad of tissues, flushed the toilet, and left the water running in the sink. The connecting door led into a blue country French living room so overdecorated that his teeth hurt. Padding softly across a rug three inches thick, he listened at another door.

Someone was taking Italian lessons. *"—a table, please? Potremmo avere un tavolo, per favore?"* said a woman's taped voice. After a brief pause for the student to repeat the phrase, the tape went on, *"By the window—Potremmo avere un tavolo vicina alla finestra?"*

Lachlan hooked the leather case of his badge onto his jacket breast pocket so the shiny five-pointed star was clearly visible, shifted his body slightly to confirm the presence of the Glock at his side, and opened the door.

*". . . sulla terrazza?"*

The sitting room was painted a vile shade of green. It had been fitted out with a hospital bed and various medical equipment, including an Amazon of a nurse currently absorbed in a thick paperback novel. Hunched over a desk, working with a magnifying glass under a mini-klieg light, was a small, skinny woman Lachlan was delighted to recognize as Samantha Knightly—Sam the Sham, inevitably, to her customers—forger of everything from birth certificates to stock certificates. And lounging on a brown leather sofa, wearing a crimson brocade dressing gown while listening to his taped Italian lesson on a boom box, was a man whose face, half-wrapped like an unfinished mummy, sported a magnificent crag of a nose between two black eyes.

*"É compreso il servizio?"*

Lachlan had heard of several felons who'd had substantially more than a nip-and-tuck done for reasons of disguise, and had once arranged a new nose and chin for a protected witness, but he'd never actually seen somebody in the throes of recovery before. He decided on the instant that whenever his own face started to sag, he'd let it. Gladly.

*"I'd like a spinach omelet. Vorrei una frittata di spinaci."*

"Edward Reynolds Phippen—," Lachlan began.

The man glanced up, scowling with majestic white eyebrows. There wasn't a line on his black-and-blue face or a wrinkle around his bruised eyes, for all that he was pushing eighty.

The nurse lifted her gaze from her book, and screamed. Startled, Samantha looked around myopically and dropped her pen.

Lachlan smiled pleasantly. "Hiya, Sam. Put your glasses back on and stand

up, away from the desk. Good girl. Mr. Phippen, you're under arrest. You have
the right to remain—"

"*What kind of seafood do you have? Che genere di frutti di mare avete?*"

"Who the hell let you in?" Phippen roared, the effect slightly spoiled by the
muffling bandages.

"—silent," Lachlan finished, shaking his head.

"*—do you recommend? Cosa consiglia?*"

"Sam, you and Nurse Ratchett get over here beside Mr. Phippen." He got
out his cell phone and punched the speed-dial. "If you choose to give up this
right, anything you say—"

"*Please bring me another glass. Per favore, mi porti un—*"

"And turn that damned thing off!"

"I got nothin' to do with this, honest," Sam babbled, inching toward the second door. "You gotta believe me, Marshal, I'm innocent—"

"Yeah, yeah, heard it all before." When the nurse drew in a long breath, he
added, "If she screams again, you're gonna get deputized to stuff her support
hose down her throat."

"*Are there any local specialties? Avete—*"

Lachlan drew the Glock. "Shut that fucking tape off before I shoot it!"

In the abrupt silence, Pete Wasserman's voice came through loud and clear.
"Evan? What the hell's going on?"

"I need the NYPD and an ambulance at Felicia Holton's place—"

"Somebody wounded? Besides the tape player, I mean."

"Funny. No, Grandpa Phippen bought himself a new face, and he's not done
healing yet. You might want to call the prison ward at the hospital, too—"

The foyer guard and his musculature surged through the door; Lachlan had
been wondering when he'd show up. As Holly might say, the guy was not exactly the sharpest tool in the shed.

"Shoot him!" Phippen demanded.

"Don't tempt me," Lachlan retorted.

The man hesitated, then became statuary again. Wise choice—though probably not the best career move.

"Just get here, huh, Pete?" When acknowledgment came back, he snapped
the phone shut. "Where was I? Oh, yeah—anything you say may be taken
down and used as evidence against you in a court of law. You have the right to
an attorney. If you cannot afford one—that's a laugh—counsel will be appointed to you at no charge. Do you understand your rights?"

"Stewart!" Phippen yelled at the guard. "Do something!"

"Yeah, Stewart," Lachlan agreed. "Get on the phone and call the lawyers."

"Marshal," Sam whined, "let me outta here, this is nothin' to do with me—"

"I knew it," said Felicia Holton's voice. "It was just too easy."

Evidently Lachlan had made a mistake in calculating how much time it would take her to get to the post office and discover the key didn't fit.

"Mr. Wyatt, or whatever your name is—"

"Deputy Marshal Evan Lachlan," he introduced himself pleasantly. "Mrs. Holton, you're about to interfere with a Federal arrest. Please don't."

"Who are you trying to arrest?"

"Your grandfather."

"You're mistaken," she replied, cool as a cloud. "This is my uncle George, who as you can see is recovering from surgery. I don't know where my grandfather is." She crossed the room to stand beside the old man. "How are you, Uncle George? I hope this hasn't upset you too much."

"Lady, you just pissed me off," Lachlan said.

The sweet song of sirens wafted up from far below, proving once again that however much you paid for a place to live in New York, you never escaped the noise. Lachlan figured a couple of minutes to get past the doorman, another couple for the elevator, and then he'd have backup.

Which didn't come soon enough to prevent Felicia Holton from heaving a free-form lump of marble knickknack at him. Or the nurse from charging with a loaded hypodermic. Or Stewart from drawing his pistol. Or Sam from bolting through a side door.

Lachlan shot Stewart in the shoulder. At the same time he dodged the marble chunk and rammed a knee into the nurse. She and Stewart both collapsed. The marble crashed to the hardwood floor, landing at just the right angle to shatter it. Lachlan gritted his teeth and hoped the bones of his left forearm hadn't shattered as well; he hadn't been quite fast enough in dodging.

A minute late, four NYPD patrolmen stormed in, weapons drawn, followed closely by am EMT crew with a stretcher. By the time everyone had been sorted out and arrested (including Sam, who was discovered cowering in the master bedroom closet), they'd run out of handcuffs.

Lachlan spent the night with an icepack and a six-pack.


MIDNIGHT OF A WANING MOON.

Denise's cauldron was that rarest of antiques, a *nganga*. Her grandmother's grandmother had made it long ago in Cuba according to an age-old rite involving, among other things, rum, ashes, cinnamon, garlic, lizards, ants, bats, termites, worms, a tarantula, a scorpion, and certain bones from the corpse of a criminal. Denise used the *nganga* rarely, but when she did, she charged it the same way her ancestors had done: with rum, pepper, dry wine, and her own fresh blood.

She held the black cauldron between her hands for a few moments, calling on the spirits of those long-dead women who had been feared and respected throughout the bayous. Then she began her ritual of banishing and cursing.

A tall black candle was affixed to the bottom of the cauldron, extending a few inches over the rim. A pint of salt, a pint of cornmeal, and a pint of her own urine went into the cauldron, nearly filling it. With the candle lit and a fire kindled under the *nganga*, she sat in silent contemplation of what she wanted to do to Elias Bradshaw and Holly McClure.

Such lovely things. Impotence for him and frigidity for her, to begin with— Ms. Goddess Almighty didn't deserve that big hazel-eyed hunk, and Denise had her own plans for him. Add a little anxiety, a touch of unease, an abrasion or two for the temper, a nightmare or three for the hell of it—subtle, luscious annoyances.

That she was able to Work at all was proof of the Magistrate's deficiencies. By pitting her will against his, Denise had overcome the contemptible little *geas* he'd placed on her. The forgetfulness would end tonight—and be directed back at him and at Holly. During the next waning Moon, and the next, and the next, until she was satisfied, she would target more and stronger banes using the *nganga*. And include lures meant just for Holly's lover.

# Eight

PETE WASSERMAN, WATCHING LACHLAN WAVE off the kid with the snack cart, heaved a long, long sigh. "Look, Evan, have a bagel. A doughnut. Anything — just do something with your mouth besides talk, okay?"

"You're just jealous," Lachlan replied haughtily, rubbing a hand over his stomach.

"Anybody ever tell you what a pain in the ass you are when you're being healthy? Christ, am I gonna be glad when Holly gets home. Maybe she'll give you something else to think about besides lettuce and the gym."

"'Maybe'? I'm countin' on it."

Over the last fifteen days there'd been postcards and letters, funny and informative and gossipy, and on occasion so steamy that he understood why there were laws about sending salacious material through the mail. At least she'd put the postcard of a certain statue's vital parts in an envelope — with a note reading, *If Michelangelo had seen you, this would've been just the rough draft.*

But Monday she'd phoned, lonely and homesick and abruptly tearful as exhaustion caught up with her. He'd ordered her to take the next day off from research and schmoozing, bullied her into agreeing, and yesterday had received a FedEx package at work: a box containing a silver medal from the Vatican. The small oval featured St. Michael the Archangel, patron of law enforcement officers. The note read: *So you turned out to be my White Knight after all. In token thereof: the enclosed, with my love. (Don't scold — just shut up and wear the thing!) Yours, and you know it, Holly.*

He'd put the medal around his neck, and the note with the letters and cards in a compartment of Granddad Lachlan's mahogany cigar box. And had taken them out time after time, trying to be with her in some way, *any* way, when the grim stuff went down, that thing that had sent him to the gym to punish his body with muscle strain and blank out his mind with fatigue. He shied away from thinking about it and returned to the topic upon which he'd been rhapsodizing for a good ten minutes now, a topic that had finally made the redoubtable Pete Wasserman crack.

"It's the perfume that does it to me every time," he mourned. "It's the same all over her, but everywhere it's different, you know?"

Pete sighed deeply and glanced up from paperwork, gray eyes suddenly dancing in his likably homely face. "Would you define 'all over' and 'everywhere'?"

Evan grinned. "In your dreams."

Pete eyed him, pulled a face, and said, "The sooner she's not just in *your* dreams, the happier I'm gonna be." Then his gaze shifted, and a smile broke across his face—the smile reserved for seriously lovely ladies arriving unannounced in Judge Bradshaw's chambers.

All at once Lachlan was breathing that perfume. The next instant he was enwrapped by long arms around his shoulders, and heard a throaty voice whisper in his ear, "I've been wanting to kiss this exact place on your neck for weeks." The place was duly kissed: warm, lingering, with a delicate flicker of her tongue.

His immediate reaction was to damned-near fall out of his chair.

She steadied him, hands on his chest, laughing softly. "Careful, big guy. Don't injure anything important. I have plans for it tonight. Hi, Pete. Miss me?"

"Welcome home, Holly," Pete said warmly. "Lookin' good. You better believe I missed you—he's been impossible."

"Then he *was* a good boy! Bless your philandering little heart, Lachlan—hey!"

Evan grabbed her by the waist and pulled her onto his lap for a long, thorough kiss. "So," he said when he finally let her up for air, "you missed me so much you flew home three days early?"

She didn't wriggle to get comfortable; she always fit him whatever position they were in. Thinking about some of those positions made his heart lurch. She wrapped her arms around his shoulders and laughed at him—she was sitting on his response to her, after all—and tossed the mane of russet hair from her face.

"Pete, tell me truthfully—has he really been behaving himself? Don't bother to lie, you don't have the eyes for it."

"He's been so good it's nauseating. Go on, take him outta here before he embarrasses us."

If she got off his lap anytime soon, he'd definitely be embarrassed. Evan held her tighter and looked into her eyes. "And have *you* been a good girl?"

Her brows arched wickedly. "Would I tell you if I hadn't?" Then, leaning close to his ear and whispering in a lilting brogue, "Mar to t'point, me boyo, would I be wantin' t'strip ye bare-ass naked, t'row ye acrosst yer very desk here, and proceed t'foock ye senseless?"

With Herculean effort he managed to dismiss the image of being consensually raped on his own desk. Touching her nose with a finger, he said, "You've been in the sun—you've got new freckles."

"And *you've* been working out—you've got new muscles." Her fingers stroked over his shoulder and arm. "I figured you'd gain another ten pounds guzzling beer."

In his own thickest brogue, with a plaintive sigh that would do credit to a martyred saint, he replied, "Ah, I drowned me sorrows every night in *uisque-baugh*, darlin', so I did."

Again her whisper was just for him, warm breath caressing his ear. "Liar. And your stomach isn't the only thing that's hard, in case you hadn't noticed."

The only thing that saved him—but not from a blush—were the clipped New England tones of Mrs. Sophia (with a long *i*—literally and figuratively speaking) Osbourne, Judge Bradshaw's secretary and undisputed empress of suite 710. "Ms. McClure, would you kindly unhand my deputy?"

Holly leaped from Evan's lap, smoothed her skirt, and apologized.

"Nice trip?" Mrs. Osbourne went on, settling her five-foot-five and two hundred pounds against the credenza. "Thanks for the postcards, by the way. I loved the one of Michelangelo's *David*."

Lachlan choked.

"Wonderful trip, thanks," Holly said, rummaging in the flight bag she'd left on the floor. "I brought back a whole slew of guidebooks and stuff for your grandsons—I thought they might get some use of them in school, and I never met a kid yet who didn't love castles—damn it, I know I put them in here somewhere—"

"That was very thoughtful," Sophia said. "Don't go looking for them now— I can tell you'd like to take Evan home early." And, incredibly, she winked.

Holly grinned back. "If it's all right, yes."

"You'll be doing us all a favor by getting him out of here," Mrs. Osbourne added. "He's been hell in cowboy boots ever since you left."

"And," Pete added, "he made up a new story about where he got the stupid things—"

"—just as bogus as all the rest," Mrs. Osbourne finished. Stabbing a finger in his direction, she warned, "Someday, Marshal, I'll get the truth out of you."

He made his eyes wide and innocent. She snorted.

"Don't you already have plans for the evening, Evan?" Wasserman asked with an eager helpfulness belied by the glint in his eyes.

"Such as?" Holly inquired.

Lachlan gestured to the newspapers on his desk. "Apartment hunting. My building's going co-op and I gotta find another place."

"Oh, the heartbreak," Holly mourned. "No more listening to the neighbors fight. Can you put off the shopping until tomorrow? I want to go home. I've got a ride waiting and presents to unpack —"

"What did you bring me?" Pete demanded.

"As a matter of fact, I have a little something right here." Again she hunted through the bag, and came up with two small gold boxes. "I had some extra lira to get rid of, so I got these in the Rome duty-free. But there's more in my luggage."

She handed one box of chocolates to Mrs. Osbourne and the other to Pete, who caressed it tenderly and announced, "I worship this woman. Dump Lachlan and become the third Mrs. Wasserman, Holly. We'll honeymoon in Hershey, Pennsylvania."

"Third time's the charm?" Mrs. Osbourne asked, dark eyes dancing.

"Who needs charm when you've got chocolate?"

"So true," she agreed. "Thanks, Holly. Now get him out of here."

After a show of reluctance that nobody believed for an instant, Evan stood up and shrugged into his suit jacket. "Aw, geez," he moaned, "what're you gonna do when they got eyes like that?"

"'Eyes'?" Pete asked incredulously. "What're you gonna do when they got *legs* like that?"

"Say yes, Lachlan," Mrs. Osbourne advised, pointing to the door. "I'll make it an order."

"I hear you, ma'am." He flipped her a casual salute.

As the pair left, Wasserman observed, "He'll be lucky if she doesn't rip his clothes off in the taxi."

Mrs. Osbourne's brows arched. "I'd say he'll be luckier if she *does*."

IT WASN'T A TAXI. It was a limousine — a long white Caddy, fully equipped with blackout windows. Evan whistled as the chauffeur opened the door for Holly.

"Thanks, Jacob," she said, and the young man smiled and tipped his hat to Lachlan. "My publisher sent it," Holly went on as Evan got in. "So shut up."

"Yes, ma'am."

"My oh my, ain't we just the sweetest, most obedient li'l ol' thang today?"

Lachlan batted his eyelashes. "You promised me a present." He'd asked for a couple of art books; he figured she'd come up with a whole library. Relaxing into the leather seat, he unbuttoned his suit jacket and turned to look at her. Just look at her. Inventorying freckles, blue eyes, windblown red hair, and linen suit the exact color of lime sherbet. "Missed you."

Her eyes softened, and her fingertips brushed his mouth. Then she leaned forward and said to the chauffeur, "Put something good on the stereo, please, Jacob? Thanks." A toggle raised the blackout window between the driver's seat

and the passenger compartment, sealing them in privacy. Then Holly rubbed a
hand over Lachlan's stomach. "When did *this* happen?"

"Like you said—I been workin' out."

"But I *liked* your belly," she complained as she loosened his tie and began on
his shirt buttons. "And nothing should ever be perfect."

"Wait a minute—what're you—?"

"Why waste a perfectly good limo ride? Didn't you ever see *No Way Out*?"

"Huh?" He wasn't tracking too well—not with her fingers busy at his zipper.

"Kevin Costner and Sean Young in the backseat of—"

"Holly Elizabeth McClure—!"

"Can I get a little cooperation here, Lachlan?"

"You're crazy! There's eight million people out there—"

"—half of 'em women who'd purely love to get their hands on you, and not
one of 'em can see us or hear us." She gave him a cheerfully lascivious smile.
"Oh, come on. You wouldn't care if the windows were wide open. You're an exhibitionist and you know it. The way you walk, the way you grin, the way you
flaunt it—"

"I do *not*—"

"Evan, me darlin' man, ye're *such* a liar! But I love you anyway, *a chuisle*."

Holly undressed him as quickly as possible considering the confined space,
the length of his legs, and her own eagerness. When she had him sprawled sideways across the seat, stunned by kisses and hazy-eyed with desire, she drew
back to look at him. Just look at him.

"Are you gonna get on with it, or just sit there starin' at me?" he growled.

An unknown amount of time later, when he finally got his breath back, he
chided, "Naughty, naughty. You're not wearing any underwear." He pushed her
back far enough so he could unbutton her jacket. "No blouse or bra, either. And
you on a plane with two hundred people all the way from Rome!"

"I *missed* you," she defended.

He laughed at her. "Nothin' better to do with three extra days, so you come
home to fuck me senseless. What'm I gonna do with you?"

Laughing, unrepentant, she teased, "Do it again before we get home!"

"With the windows down this time?"


THEY ARRIVED AT HER APARTMENT to find dinner in the oven and the kitchen
table already set; all they had to do was light candles and open wine. Lachlan
cheerfully stuffed himself with Isabella's enchiladas.

"Have I told Isabella lately that I love her?"

"Y'all go right on ahead, boy—if you're prepared to deal with her six-foot-
five former linebacker husband and her six-foot-six right tackle son."

He winced. "Sounds like I'd better keep my mouth shut."

"You haven't closed it except to chew for the last forty-five minutes." She eyed him thoughtfully. "You really were a good boy, weren't you?"

He nodded, making his face and eyes the very portrait of virtue. "Like Pete said—nauseating."

"I have to say I'm surprised."

He polished off the last enchilada and set his fork down. "It kinda surprised me, too, if you want to know. But it's not like I didn't try."

"You *what?*" Her back became a ramrod and sparks shot from her eyes.

"I told myself I had to. But I just couldn't get interested. Pissed me off, too."

"I'll just bet it did," she said through her teeth. "Who was she?"

"Just some bottle-blonde at Starbucks. But that was it. Honest, Holly," he insisted as her eyes ignited to full fury. "I didn't *want* to. She wasn't you."

She chewed her lip for a moment, eyes narrowed, then gave an annoyed snort. "Oh, stop trying to look like a scolded puppy. I believe you. As if the way you reacted in the car wasn't proof enough."

"I didn't notice you lagging behind." He grinned.

"When do I ever, with you? Marshal, you're *too* good."

"But not too good to be true," he said as he poured more wine.

"That was absolutely foul. People have been shot for less. What's all this about your apartment?"

"Like I said—goin' co-op. I can't afford it. So . . ." He shrugged.

Taking a large swallow of wine, she set the glass down and regarded him with squared jaw and determined eyes. "You could afford to live here, you know. Half my rent is about what you pay per month on your place, right?" Suddenly she was looking anywhere but at him. "I'm a very reasonable land-lady. You'll be paying your full share of rent—don't think you won't!—but I won't make you take out the trash or clean the catbox—"

Evan sat back. "What're you talking about?" he asked carefully.

"What do you think I'm talking about?" she countered. "There's a whole floor I don't even use, and it's ridiculous to have it sit there with nobody living in it. Half your clothes are here, anyway. You'd have your own bedroom and bath, and—"

He felt his lips curve in a smile. "Hold on." Rising, he took her shoulders and drew her up to stand before him. "Holly, are you asking me to live with you?"

"In the same apartment, yes, but not in the way that you're thinking—unless you want to," she added, looking down. "Would it be that awful?"

He would never understand how she could change from confident woman to insecure teenager in two seconds flat. But as dizzying as the change was, he was totally unprepared for what came next. She looked up at him, eyes bright with mischief, and slipped her arms around him, hands fitted to his ass.

"I want this long, lean, luscious Irish carcass where I can get my hands on it whenever I like."

"I don't know why you think I'd move in without letting you make an honest man of me. My good Catholic ancestors would do cartwheels in their graves." He pulled out of her arms, went down on one knee, took her hand, and gazed up into her thunderstruck face. "Holly Elizabeth McClure, will you do me the honor of marrying me?"

She stared. Then she sat down. Hard.

"I love you, Holly," he said gently. "I want to be your husband, and I want you to be my wife."

Still she said nothing. Her face was so white that the freckles stood out like splotches of sepia ink.

"I want to come home to you every evening, and sleep beside you every night, and wake up to you every morning, and—"

"Evan—*a chuisle*, are you sure?"

"Yes. I love you, Holly. Marry me."

Tears filled her eyes. She nodded wordlessly.

"And for Christ's sake, don't cry," he admonished, rising from his knee to pull her up into his arms again. "Whenever I make you cry, I go all to pieces and want to shoot myself or something."

"You never make me cry," she sniffled. "Besides, a woman is supposed to cry when the man she adores asks her to marry him. My God, I'm such a cliché. How depressing." She hesitated, then looked at him without a trace of a smile. "And the man's supposed to say they'll live off *his* salary. Are you going to say that, Evan?"

He bit his lip. This was something he'd thought about more than once. His pride had gotten in the way before—he still cringed whenever he thought about the weekend he'd found out who she was, and what she did for a living, and how tidily that living added up in her bank accounts. Time to put up or shut up. He could be prideful and stupid, or stomp on his *machismo* and be happy. And make *her* happy.

That was what decided him—after all, as her husband, her happiness would be his responsibility every hour of every day. Might as well start here and now.

"I'm not gonna punish you for makin' more than I do. I'm still not nuts about it, but I'm not stupid, either."

The delight that shone in her eyes embarrassed him; he hadn't known she'd be so worried, which told him she'd expected him to be an asshole about it.

"Don't get any big ideas," he warned. "No expensive presents or vacations—"

"Not even the honeymoon?"

"Well . . ." Thoughts of nude sunbathing on a private Jamaican beach danced in his head. Lolling in a hot tub at a mountain resort somewhere, just him and Holly and a gazillion stars. Watching the Arno flow by from the hills above Florence—

"I promised you before, Evan—I won't throw the money around. Just don't yell at me too often for breaking my promise, okay? Like now. I brought you something from Dublin."

Before he could say another word, she vanished from the kitchen. He sat down, a little breathless now that he'd asked and she'd said *Yes*.

He glanced around the room, wondering why it looked different. Well, of course: it wasn't just her kitchen anymore, it was going to be *their* kitchen. All the things his sister Maggie had told him he could have—an Army wife traveled light—would find places here. Grandma Coyle's copper pots; the Staffordshire bowls sent from England by Grandpa in 1944, just before he was killed in the invasion of Normandy; Granna Maureen's handmade lace tablecloths; great-grandmother Lachlan's sterling flatware with the ornate *L* engraved on every piece. The rest of his clothes; his basketball and softball trophies; CDs, DVDs, books—oh, Christ, all *his* added to all *hers?*—and the big leather armchair he'd splurged on with his first paycheck as a U.S. Marshal—his stuff would join her stuff in what he was morally certain would be total chaos.

*Married.*

In retrospect, he could have done a little better by her than to propose in the kitchen over the wreckage of dinner. Not exactly romantic—and he didn't even have Granna Maureen's ring to give her. Well, hell—how was he to know Holly would come home early because she missed him? At least he'd remembered to go down on one knee. He'd do the rest of it up right when he got the chance.

On the other hand, there was something homey and comforting about this. Maybe not the ambiance of daydreams, but it was *real*.

Suddenly she stood before him, blushing and apprehensive, holding a small green velvet box. Inside was a ring. The only one he'd ever worn was his Marshal's Academy ring—on his left hand, and he realized suddenly he'd have to change that when she put a wedding ring on his finger. This was a gold *claddagh*: hands clasping a crowned heart. Masculine but not massive, beautifully wrought, with something written inside. As he peered at it, she finally spoke.

"It's Irish Gaelic."

And so it was. *Éimhín Liam Lochlainn.*

"It's perfect," he murmured. Then he looked up at her. "It's my wedding ring, isn't it." Not a question.

"I didn't buy it to be, but—" She looked down at her hands. "I was just hoping you'd wear it sometimes. . . ."

"I will. I'll wear it always. But we'll save it," he said, putting the ring carefully back in its nest. And to his surprise, for the first time in his memory—for the first time in all the years he'd been alive—the whole world was truly *right*.

To his greater surprise, every candle in every holder in the kitchen sprang into flame. Holly gave a start, eyes wide.

"Now, stop that," Evan scolded gently, and kissed her.

THE NEXT MORNING HOLLY WAS in the tub when Evan stumbled into the bathroom, groggy and unfocused, hair sticking up in twelve different directions, one side of his face red where he'd scrunched into the pillow for too many hours.

"Great day in the mornin'," she marveled, "it walks just as if it's awake." When he yawned wide enough to crack his jaw, she scowled at him. "Lachlan? Are you going to pull a 'God, was I drunk last night' on me?" she asked suspiciously.

"Hmm?" He scrubbed both hands through his hair, creating an even worse disorder, and blinked owlishly.

"You *do* remember last night?"

"Uh . . . yeah, sure."

Most unconvincing. "What you said? What you asked me? What I said?"

"Yes, yes, and yes." He stood beside the tub, grinning down at her, adding, "Mrs. Lachlan." Then he began to sing "That's Just Love Sneakin' up on You."

He had a scrumptious speaking voice, deep and caressing and seductive. His singing voice was also baritone—and that was all that could be said for it.

He sounded, in brief, remarkably like a constipated rhino.

Holly pressed her hands over her ears. "Mercy! I'll do anything—just *stop!*"

"Anything?" he leered.

"Oh, shut up and get in the bath." When he had settled in behind her, she leaned back comfortably and asked, "So did you finally get Ramirez?"

"Not yet, dammit—but I collared Phippen." He filled her in on recent events—although she knew the recital was truncated. He didn't like describing the sordid parts of his work: protecting her, and the place they had together, as if the first week she'd known him she hadn't seen pretty much the worst of his world's viciousness.

*The corpse of the not-so-Protected Witness was two days old. Whatever blood had been in the body had drained hours ago from countless stab wounds. Holly wasn't sick and she didn't faint—but she did sway a little as she watched Evan prowl the site. A few minutes later an NYPD officer found the second corpse. And the third. Each had been carved up as hideously as the first.*

*"Officer Stradling, take Ms. McClure home."*

*"I'm all right, Evan, I—"*

*"Take her home."*

*Direct order. No arguments allowed. He hadn't even spoken to her—merely commanded a subordinate from the NYPD. She felt her temper begin to ignite, then saw the expression in his hazel eyes. His was a powerful personality, he was as arrogant as the day was long, and he could dominate just about anyone he chose to—but his command to the officer had nothing to do with that. He wanted to keep her out of this. She was unconnected to his work, untouched by all the blood and greed and rage and evil. And that was how he wanted it. Suddenly she understood something very important about him. He was a man in search of a haven from the tense darkness that sometimes haunted this work.*

*"Ms. McClure?" A tentative voice, but one that obeyed. She couldn't imagine anyone disobeying Evan when his eyes were dark and hard and cold like this. Not even she would dare. "Ms. McClure." More insistently; he had to follow orders. By extension, so did she. Well, they'd see about that—but not here, not now.*

*"It's all right, Officer. Please don't trouble yourself. I can take a cab." She waited another moment, but Evan didn't look at her. She spoke his name, and he half-turned, and she said, "Call me tonight when you get home." A command of her own, and he knew it. The heavy brows descended, and his lips compressed for an instant—a look that snapped,* Shut up and do as you're told, woman. *But then he studied her, speculating, evaluating. As he ran his fingers back through his hair she realized exactly what it was she was offering him.*

*Anything he wanted. Anything he needed. Anything.*

*Her own helplessness scared her. It was as sudden as lightning, the change he wrought in her—sudden, natural, a force of nature. And she felt herself falling for him, right then and there at the grisly scene of a triple homicide.*

*"Okay," he said at last, nodding slowly, a tiny smile touching the corners of his mouth. An I'll-get-you-into-bed-yet-lady smile, but with something more in his eyes. Gratitude, perhaps; curiosity; hope. She wasn't the only one falling. He just didn't know it yet.*

It had been her first experience of his work, though not her last. He still tended to shelter her from it, but his instincts required a sounding board, just as his emotions demanded a release and his heart and mind needed a refuge. She was never any real help—her genres were biography and historical novel, and she couldn't have written a mystery or police procedural to save her own life—but he never expected any suggestions. The most she ever contributed were questions that sometimes clarified things for him.

So she lazed in the tub with him, hot scented water moving gently in time with their breathing, and listened while he talked about the cases on his desk—pissed off about some, pleased with the progress of others.

"There's one other thing," he said at last—slowly, reluctantly. "I have to go talk to my old man today. Yeah, I know, rotten timing. But I have to go."

"Want me to come with?"

"No. I mean, yes, but—"

"But no. It's okay. I still have to unpack, and get poor old Mugger out of hock at my neighbor's."

"It's just—I have to tell him about some stuff."

She heard something in his voice now that made her sit up and turn around, wanting to see his face. There was something haunted and hollow about his eyes that she hadn't expected.

"Not us," he went on, trying to smile. "I want you there with me when I tell him and Maggie. I'm not goin' through *that* by myself!"

What *had* he gone through by himself that had put this look into his eyes? "Evan, what happened?"

His reluctance was almost palpable. "There was this trial. Did I tell you anything about that priest, Father Matthew?"

Before she'd left for Europe he'd canceled on her signing weekend in D.C. to concentrate on a current trial. "Kidnapping and rape, wasn't it? A young girl?"

"Bradshaw granted a plea bargain yesterday." A brief, bitter laugh. "'Bargain' is right. I guess I better start at the beginning. I wasn't quite thirteen when Father Matthew came to the parish. Wednesday afternoons the altar boys did cleanup around the church—washing the floor, gardening, sorting robes for the laundry. That sort of stuff. I remember that day I was polishing this silver crosier—really beautiful, about six foot high—I was wondering when I'd be as tall as it was. Everybody else had left, but I wanted to finish even though it was getting late. I finally lugged it back to the sacristy—the thing weighed a ton.

"And there was Father Matthew over in the corner, goin' at it with some woman. She's bent over the linen chest and he's doin' her from behind. He was one of those priests who liked the attention he got wearin' a cassock, like he was always just off the plane from Rome or somethin', and it's hiked up over his ass just like the woman's skirt was hiked up over hers. It was a white dress, with purple flowers—

"I dropped the crosier—I just sort of went numb all over. They didn't even hear it. But Father Matthew must've found it later, and figured out somebody'd seen. At Sunday Mass he kept lookin' at all of us altar boys. I gave it away, of course. So that next Wednesday he calls me into his office. There was a lot of crap about a counseling session gettin' out of hand, even priests are human, he'd confess and repent and be forgiven, that was the beauty of our faith. And if I ever said a word, who would people believe—a kid or a priest of the Holy Roman Catholic Church?

"I never told anybody," Evan went on. "He was right—who'd believe it? But it was drivin' me crazy—the signs were all over the place, now that I knew what to look for. Afternoons out on parish business—yeah, right, takin' care of business with women whose husbands weren't home. The next year he transferred to another parish, someplace upstate, I think. I guess he'd run through all the local women and wanted fresh meat. And that was the last I heard of him until this year.

"He finally picked somebody who wouldn't lie down—a fifteen-year-old girl.

Plenty of women fall in love with their priests for one reason or another, and he was clever at playing on that. But he's a lot older now. What used to be easy for him—well, the girl told him to leave her alone or she'd take it all the way to the Pope, but he was obsessed, and he snapped—at least that's what his lawyers said."

"What happened to the girl?" Holly asked quietly.

"He took her across the border to Canada, to some cabin a hundred miles from nowhere. In the middle of fuckin' February. She got away after a couple of weeks, and damned near died of exposure before a trucker saw her by the side of the road.

"Anyway, Bradshaw drew the case. I usually don't pay much attention to the particulars, as long as the research shows me there's nobody involved who's likely to take a shot at him, but when I saw the name I almost threw up." He was silent for a few moments. Then: "If I'd said something twenty-five years ago, that girl wouldn't've gotten raped for twelve days."

"Evan—"

"Let me finish. I told Bradshaw what I knew. But there wasn't any way to work around the plea bargain. He lawyered up pretty expensive. And the girl's parents don't want her put through any more. So they pled him out.

"Dad called me the other day—wants me to explain in person. All the shit he heard on the news—" Again he shrugged. "I wanted to get it all out of the way before you came home, so I told Dad I'd be over this afternoon. I could cancel—"

"No, you can't. Go. I'll be here when you get back."

"Now, that's gotta be the nicest thing I've heard in three weeks."

Taking her cue from his deliberately lighter tone, she said, "Of course, I'll probably be in no mood to pay attention to you. I haven't watched *Gladiator* in forever and I need my Russell Crowe fix."

He pulled a face. "What do women *see* in that guy?"

Oh, yeah—she'd picked just the right thing to say. As she got out of the tub and reached for a towel, she replied, "Not much. He's just the dictionary definition of 'gorgeous,' is all."

"And I'm not?" he demanded, pretending to be hurt.

She left off rubbing her hair dry long enough to peer at him from under the towel. "Hey, do I complain when you ogle those *Baywatch* girls?"

With great and injured dignity he announced, "I. Do. Not. Ogle."

"You positively drool when that Pamela person bounces across the screen."

"I don't 'drool,' either. Anyway, it's different," he said with that air of genetic masculine superiority that punched every button she possessed. "Guys look at girls. We can't help it."

"No shit, Sherlock! I got news for you—girls look at guys, too. And we can't help it any more than you can."

"Yeah, but there's a difference," he insisted stubbornly. "There's babes, and chicks, and girls, and women—and then there's *ladies*."

"Aw, gee, let me guess—in descending order of breast size." Holly reached down and rumpled his hair. "What do you want for dinner when you get home?"

"Anything, as long as you don't cook it."

AFTER HE WAS GONE—taking with him the wool scarf in the Lachlan set she'd picked up in Dublin for his father (she wanted to soften him up)—she unpacked. Then she sorted presents, among them three huge books on the collections of the Uffizi, the Pitti, and the Vatican for Evan, just as he'd asked. One of these days, she mused, she'd take him to every major museum in Europe. She could just see him wandering in a wide-eyed, glutted daze around the Prado, the Louvre. . . .

Eventually she sought the deeply soothing anarchy of her office. She sat at the computer, intending to read e-mail—but somehow couldn't make her fingers type the password. Instead, she picked up the phone and punched in a number.

A half-hour later, shaken and furious and sickened, she called up a manuscript template on the computer and started writing.

It was nearly three in the afternoon before she finished. She could barely shift her shoulders, her feet were almost numb, and the small of her back ached ferociously. Experience told her not to move too suddenly or too soon; circulation had to be restored first. So she leaned slowly back in her chair, flexed her neck warily, and tried to tell herself she'd dumped all her anger into the story.

Not quite all.

How could a man who probed other people's lives and analyzed—anticipated—their actions know so little about his own heart? But was it any wonder he'd been scared to look? Abused children were shrewdly observant from an early age. For Evan, a child's terror of examining a revered father's failings had transmuted into a man's fear of turning those instinctive skills of analysis on himself. Afraid, without even knowing it, of what he might find inside.

Holly's own past held no darknesses even remotely comparable. She'd been too young when her parents died to remember them; grief was something learned as she grew older and understood what had happened. For the rest—Aunt Lulah had raised her in the old farmhouse in the foothills of the Blue Ridge, ten miles outside a town where whole years could go by without Cousin Jesse—Sheriff McNichol—dealing with anything more serious than weekend rowdies and Old Man McCraw's deer hunting off-season.

Evan's life should have seemed utterly alien to her. And yet she understood.

Perhaps because it *was* him; probably because she had spent her childhood imagining, and her adulthood creating, worlds and people and events completely removed from rural Virginia. Imagining was her job—though she would have given much to be unable to imagine this.

It should have ripped him apart long ago.

You were supposed to *love* your mother. Even if you were scared of her, even if she was a drunk who spread her legs for any man who'd have her, including the parish priest—you weren't supposed to hate her. It was forbidden. Evil.

And your father—you could worship him, you *had* to worship him, because if he wasn't one-step-from-God-perfect, then it meant that he cared so little about his own kids (about *you*) that he wouldn't do anything—

Holly shook her head, regretting it as neck muscles twinged. She needed to distance herself from an acute need to vent her rage on the only object left alive who deserved it: Daniel Patrick Lachlan. She knew she'd have to meet him soon. Before then, she'd have to bury her anger deep and forget where she put the shovel. Evan would scarcely appreciate it if his fiancée belted his father a good one in the jaw.

# Nine

EVAN GOT BACK TO HOLLY'S at five, sodden with exhaustion. Although visits to his father's house usually did that to him, this had been almost as bad as the night his mother died. Using his key, he let himself into the foyer and yelled for Holly.

No answer.

She wasn't in the living room, Show Office, or real office. She was sprawled across the bed, sound asleep. He leaned over, kissed her forehead lightly, and settled onto the chaise where he could watch over her.

After a while, during which he dozed a bit, she became aware that she was looking him over. "Everything's right where you left it," he said.

"It better be. How's your father? Everything all right?"

"Yeah. He still drinks too much, but the doctors say he's got a cast-iron liver." He paused. "Y'know, it's been ten years, but he still misses Mom. I guess they loved each other in their way. It's just not any way I ever understood."

"You're a completely different person."

"I'm a combination of them both. That's DNA, babe."

She was quiet for a moment, then leaned over and switched on the bedside lamp. "My father didn't look anything like his own father, but the minute I saw that photo of great-grandfather McClure, it was Papa down to the cleft chin. Things skip generations, Evan. Character traits as well as looks."

"Let's hope our kids skip my parents' generation completely."

"Umm . . . speaking of kids. . . ." Holly pulled in a deep breath. "Okay, here's the deal. I'm thirty-six. I can't give you a dozen children. If you want more than a couple, you'll have to find yourself some twenty-three-year-old."

"Did I say I wanted a dozen kids? Or a twenty-three-year-old? One boy, one girl—that's my idea of a perfect family."

She exhaled in relief. "Not that I really thought you'd keep me barefoot and pregnant until my ovaries give out, but you never can tell with people sometimes. Are we going to decide their names now, too?"

"You name the girl, I'll name the boy."

"Fair enough. Speaking of names—I hope you don't mind too much, but professionally I have to keep McClure."

"I know. It's okay. That's just good business." He shot her a sideways smile. "God forbid your books should stop selling because nobody can find 'em."

"I have to stay McClure in legal matters, too. Everybody can call me 'Mrs. Lachlan'—I just won't be Holly Lachlan officially—I mean, I'll *be* Holly McClure Lachlan, but—oh, damn, this isn't coming out right."

"You bet it ain't," he said through his teeth. "My wife will have my name. And so will my kids. I don't care what you call yourself on your book covers, but you damned well better sign your name 'Lachlan' everywhere else or—"

"Or what? Evan, be reasonable. Everything is in my name. I get paid in my name. I get *taxed* in my name. Changing it all over to 'Lachlan'—"

"—is exactly what you're gonna do. Don't you have a lawyer for that kind of stuff? Make him earn his retainer."

"He's a she, and that's not the point. My agent also has legal things to deal with. And he said long ago that unless there's a pre-nup, he'll fire me as a client."

"You want me to sign some goddamned paper that says I won't rip you off if we get divorced?"

"I'm perfectly aware that you'd rather have some waitress or secretary who makes half what you do, but that's not the way things are."

"You sayin' I should be grateful you don't need me for a meal ticket?"

"I'm saying shut up while I explain. I have stocks. I have property. I have a literary estate that'll go on earning money for my heirs for seventy-five years after I'm dead. All the pre-nup says is that what's mine is my kids'."

He frowned, still suspicious. "Nothin' about payin' me off, or if we stay married for at least five years and then get divorced I get more money?"

"Hell, no!" she said indignantly. "You make a good living—you can damned well support yourself, Lachlan. I'm not paying you a goddamned dime in alimony."

"Just so it's clear I don't want your fucking money."

"My hero," she snapped. "Don't do me any favors."

They glared at each other for a few more seconds—until Holly gave an unladylike snort. "This is perfect. We're not even married yet and we're arguing about the divorce."

Grudgingly he admitted, "I just didn't think getting married would be so complicated. And that reminds me—how big is this shindig gonna be? Are you gonna go all formal on me? Big gown, a hundred yards of train, all like that?"

"You're just scared I'll make you dress up in a morning coat."

"Careful, lady, or I'll show up in a ruffled purple shirt and a Lachlan hunting-plaid jacket."

"Don't be silly. You're much too vain not to want to look shatteringly gorgeous on your wedding day."

Rising, she grabbed clothes, and he grinned at the hip-twist it took her to get into tight jeans. "Now I know where all that Italian food went."

"It's only three pounds—okay, five. And stop acting so damned superior—we've both got big Irish butts. You do this same thing, I've watched you."

"Yeah, but it's cuter when you do it." He rose, crossed lazily to her, and placed his hands around her ass, pulling her against him. "And I happen to like your Irish butt."

"We could go psychotically ethnic with the wedding, y'know," she laughed. "Harp, shamrocks, green beer and soda bread at the reception—"

"Dress up a few cousins as leprechauns instead of flower girls—"

"I draw the line at corned beef for three hundred of our nearest and dearest."

"I thought you wanted small," he began, then realized what she was really saying. "You're—Holly, you're *not* payin' for this."

"Bride's side always does. I'm the bride." She gave a start. "I'm the *bride*. Tell you what—you buy the honeymoon."

"Ireland? Hawaii?" He grinned. "Hershey, Pennsylvania?"

"I tell you here and now, Lachlan, you want a Hawaiian honeymoon, you'll spend it alone. After one day I'd be burned to a crisp—"

"Hey, I think you'd look cute with freckles all over your ass."

"O light of my eyes and pulse of my heart, what part of 'I'm not going to Hawaii' are you not understanding?"

"Okay, okay. No Hawaii." He sighed, as if regretting the thousands it would've cost him. "Maybe we should go someplace you've never been. Someplace just for us." When she nodded, he asked, "So where haven't you been?"

She thought for a while. "Antarctica."

"Oh, terrific. Just you and me and the penguins, freezin' our asses off."

"I didn't say I want to *go* there, just that I've never been."

With vast patience, he asked, "So where d'you want to go?" Praying it wouldn't be someplace outrageously expensive. It hit him then, for the first time, that he didn't have to worry about it. Ever again. He was marrying Money.

No, he told himself firmly, he was marrying *Holly*. Who happened to *have* money. And who evidently believed in *What's mine is yours and what's yours is mine*. Which was nice, but would have been better if what was his didn't fall so far short of what was hers—

"Charleston," she said suddenly. "It's close, it's beautiful, it's romantic—all those big old antebellum mansions—and the food's fantastic. Ah'm a Suthanah, honey-lamb," she drawled with a grin. "Even though Ah *am* marryin' a Yankee."

"Mansions," he said, and shook his head. "You want to go on a honeymoon to look at *mansions*?"

"Some of them are bed-and-breakfasts now."

"That's more like it. Tell me about the 'bed' part."

"How about a four-poster, the kind you need a stepladder to climb into? No, really, Evan, the houses are gorgeous. Miles of lawn, Spanish moss dripping from the oaks, us guzzling mint juleps on the balcony—" She stopped, seeing his expression. "You've never had a julep? That's immoral! And you fixin' to marry a Virginian! That settles it. We absolutely *have* to go South on our honeymoon."

"Because you want to play Scarlett O'Hara. Okay, Charleston it is." He paused for effect. "But—frankly, my dear, I don't give a damn."

Holly buried her face in her hands and groaned. Shamelessly satisfied with himself, he ambled into the kitchen to see what there might be to eat. He was just putting eggs back in the fridge when Holly spoke behind him.

"Are you going to tell me why visiting your father upset you so much?"

He swung around, nearly dropping the carton. His instinctive reaction was to snarl that it was none of her damned business. The part of him that already felt married made him bite his tongue. After a moment he shrugged.

"Happens whenever I go over there. Every so often I see my old man in the mirror. And sometimes it scares the crap out of me. Mostly I don't mind. He was a good cop. An honest cop. I think what defeated him was the heart attack, when he couldn't work anymore. His job was his whole life. Even with a wife and kids to come home to—but we didn't see much of him. We weren't even half his life."

"We all only have so much to give to anything," she said thoughtfully. "There've been times when I gave it all to my work—for years at a stretch, in fact." She tapped a finger on his wrist. "But in case you need reminding, you've got *me* to come home to. I stake my claim to half your life."

"'Hold Fast'?" He smiled whimsically.

"You got it, lover-man."

Gratitude stung his eyes, the back of his throat. He turned his face from her before she could see his expression. "Anybody call while I was out?"

"Pete. Very apologetic, but Elias needs your notes on the Croft case Monday morning."

"That son of a bitch! Croft, not Elias—no, Elias, too."

"Sometimes I'm not especially fond of His Honor, either," she admitted. "But I'd like to invite him and Susannah over to dinner one of these days. It'd be nice if we could all hold a polite, civilized conversation over Isabella's pot roast."

"I'm always perfectly polite."

"Yeah, and Elvis is gonna sing at our wedding. Come on, Evan."

"Okay, okay," he groused. "Jesus, Holly, you're already starting to sound like a wife."

She made a face at him. "Who's Croft?"

"Insider trading. He thinks he's gonna get three years in Club Fed to work on his tennis game. The only time I really like Bradshaw is when he's handing down a sentence."

Holly's lips twisted wryly. "I've heard he's good at that."

After dinner, he worked for an hour, formalizing his scribbled notes, then sat back, gazing idly at the icons on her desktop. Schedules, tax records, calendar, research, rough drafts of books, short stories, articles—he and she were alike in that they simultaneously juggled seven or eight projects in the normal course of things. There were a couple of unfamiliar icons that must be new projects— including one titled *Evan*. He opened it, thinking it was a note—she did that sometimes, wrote him letters which she then e-mailed to the office or his apartment. The ones that arrived at work were invariably erotic—Holly's idea of fun, the sadistic bitch.

*Evan* was not a letter. It was a short story. He couldn't help but read, and with the first sentence his heart started thudding with sick dread.

*It was between Hallowe'en and his birthday that the photographs changed.*

*Twelve-year-old boy pretending to be a pirate: bootblack for a beard, his mother's gold hoop earring screwed precariously to one lobe, rubber knife in his belt, blue bandanna wrapping the mop of thick dark hair. His pose was comically fierce, laughing, excited, a party coming up tonight with girls—his first real party, though strictly chaperoned. He was very young, and trying to be older; the last of boyhood was soft in his face, with hints in his eyes of the man he would become. And a worthy manhood it would be: the face held a promise of great strength and greater tenderness that lacked only the learning years of adolescence to become self-knowledge and perhaps even wisdom.*

*But at thirteen, mere weeks later, he didn't have to try to look older. His face was thinner, his jaw longer, the round softness of childhood gone—and too quickly, much too quickly for the days separating that Hallowe'en from his birthday. All the laughter had vanished, though the tenderness of the mouth lingered—but it was a wounded tenderness now. He was older than those scant weeks should account for, but without wisdom, without real knowledge of self. Those required time, and the years that should have separated this grim boy from the grinning pirate had been denied him. He had been forced into growing older.*

*Defiance and shame and guilt in equal, self-bewildering measure squared his bony shoulders, and his face was solemn and constrained as he stood beside the priest after confirmation of his faith.*

*The faith he no longer had.*
*The faith this very priest had shattered.*

AT AROUND TEN SHE CAME into the office, dressed in a white nightgown that went from her throat to the floor and would've made her look like a nun if the material hadn't been so flimsy. Over it she had thrown a blue crocheted shawl. His gaze ran over her, taking inventory from clean-scrubbed face to bare feet and pale pink toenail polish. He had done this from the first minute he set eyes on her: catalog what she wore, appreciate how good it looked, and estimate how quickly he could get it off her. But as instinctive as the once-over was, it seemed removed from reality.

He'd finished reading the story long since, shut down the machine, and had been staring at the swirls of the amber Witch sphere in the window. Now he stared at her instead, without an idea in the world of what he could say.

What was past was past. The only reality that could stand between him and it was standing right in front of him.

"How did you know?" he demanded suddenly. "How'd you know what it was like—when I saw them—" He bit back the rest, revulsion roiling in his belly just as it had then.

"I didn't know," she replied, so calmly that his temper flashed. "I phoned Susannah and she told me the basics. It's my job to imagine—"

He glared, a spark away from full fury. "My *life* just became part of your job?"

"I was angry. When I get that way, I write. It's how I work things out."

"You're not publishing this," he warned.

"Of course not!" she exclaimed. "What do you take me for?"

"Okay, then." He relaxed a little.

"Don't you want to know why I was so angry?" she asked softly.

He knew. "I didn't tell you about it because—"

"If you say it wasn't important, I'll shove the words right back down your throat." She was looking at him as if he was lower on the evolutionary scale than something that deserved to go *splat* on the windshield of her BMW.

"So I didn't tell you," he said, shrugging. "So fuckin' what?"

"And to think you nearly dumped me for not telling you what I do for a living."

"This is different."

"Educate me."

With ice to match hers, he said, "I'm *not* sorry I didn't tell you. You weren't even here to talk to—" He shoved aside the memory of wanting her beside him so bad, he could hardly think. She had her work, it wasn't fair for him to interfere in it because he couldn't handle what was going on with *his* work— But he heard himself repeat the accusation: "You weren't even *here*."

"For which I *am* sorry," she said, her voice softening a little. "I just need to understand how you hid it from me so well. Why you felt you had to hide it." Only then did he see pain in her eyes. "I need to know," she finished in a whisper, "how I can love you this much and not know this was going on inside you."

He wanted to get angry. Yell at her. Demand to know why the hell she'd been gone when he—when he needed her? *Needed* her?

No, that wasn't it. What he wanted was to stop talking about this and walk out. But he couldn't. Lachlan drew in a deep breath and spoke to his hands. "Everything you wrote in that story—I still don't see how you could know so much. Right after it happened I worked so damned hard *not* to think about it—to forget what I saw—just like you wrote. I got real good at keepin' it from myself. Doesn't surprise me that I could hide it from you." He shrugged that off. "Every time she wore the dress she'd been wearin' that day I wanted to throw up. Maggie and I picked it out for her birthday that April. It had purple flowers, and green leaves and stems—I never saw her face that day, but I knew that dress. She was still wearing it that evening when my dad came home from work."

"He never knew."

"Never. My mother was a saint, y'know," he continued acidly. "Mass three times a week, six parish committees—the perfect wife and mother. How could I tell my dad? He had enough to carry, without that added to it."

"So you carried it for him. All these years."

"She's dead. What does it matter?" Then: "And what if I hadn't found the story? Would you have told *me* what you know?"

"No," she answered bluntly. "And that's not right, Evan. Telling you what I am—that was an accident. I've kept it to myself for so long—but I guess that deep down I trusted you, so I made the slip. Accidentally on purpose. If we're going to have any kind of life with each other, the trust has to be out in the open."

He nodded slowly. "Yeah. I see what you mean. But I still don't understand how you could *know* so much. It's almost as if you'd been there, watched it all happen—"

She pursed her lips, head tilting slightly to one side. "I never knew the boy you were, but I know the man you've become. I traced things back. And I've seen the pictures, remember. I've always seen things in that boy's eyes. How he changed. That's why I used the device of the photographs to structure the story."

"It's good work," he admitted, "even if it's about me. Why can't I find the words, like you do? Talkin' to my old man today—nothing came out right, I couldn't explain so he'd believe me—not that I said anything about Mom—but he just kept shakin' his head—" He snorted. "You'd think that after all that child abuse all over the goddamned country, he'd get the idea that a halo doesn't automatically come with the collar. But he kept sayin' that no priest of the Holy Roman Catholic Church—" He choked on it, but made himself go on. "He wanted to know why I didn't say anything back then. As if he woulda believed me! Not then, and not now—"

"I know, love," she said softly. "There was no one, then."

"What could he have done? Nothin'." He heard himself make the old excuse, and for the first time *knew* it was an excuse. "Oh, God, why didn't I tell somebody? *Anybody*—all the women after my mother, and that girl chained up in that cabin—none of it would've happened—"

Holly wrapped him in her arms, and he hid his face between her breasts and held on for all he was worth. Real. She was *real*—

"There was no one, Evan. You were a child. All the power was on the priest's side."

He felt the cobwebby fineness of the shawl against his face, and the warmth of Holly beneath, and the strong steady beating of her heart. He managed a couple of unshaken breaths. She was here. She was real. He'd been wrong not to come to her with this—but he was so used to there being no one. He couldn't remember ever having sat like this, with loving arms around him and gentle hands soothing him, surrounded by warmth and tenderness and the scents of clean skin and subtle perfume. Patricia Lachlan had smelled of cheap gin and stale cigarette smoke, and when she held on to him it had only been to get a better grip that left bruises—

He shied back, for those memories had no right to exist here, not in this place that Holly had somehow created for him.

"Tell me the rest, love," Holly murmured.

He didn't question how she knew there was more. But it seemed her gift for words had rubbed off a little. He found some of the right ones, anyway, to explain what Patricia Lachlan had done to her children. Holly made no sound, didn't move at all—she was barely breathing that he could tell. It was as if he'd put her into an iron box with his words, and he hated that what he said imprisoned her like this—but he had to say it.

"I was firstborn. She spent years tryin' to make me into her idea of perfection and it wasn't working—obviously—not even when she put me into private school. They put a regulation blazer on me and taught me French verbs, but they couldn't change a damned thing about who I really am. The mistake sittin' at the dinner table. I was, y'know. I'm the reason she and Dad had to get married.

"One day—I musta been about twelve—I got back from softball and Mom was passed out on the couch. Maggie was hiding in the hall closet. She stank of gin—Mom had thrown a bottle at her and it broke—I told Dad when he got home, and he drove us over to Granna Maureen's for the weekend. She never knew—Mom didn't like her, thought she was low-class with her Irish accent—and they lived in Jersey, so we never saw them much when I was little. It wasn't until I was old enough to take the train by myself that I could go visit as much as I wanted.

"Anyway, when he came to take us home he said it was an accident, and that was that." He paused, shaking his head. "She knew I'd told on her and first chance she had, she took it out of my hide." He felt Holly flinch, and hurriedly said, "It only happened that once. I was growin' real fast, and before long I was taller than she was. Skinny, though—" He gave a little shrug and tried to smile. "If you can believe it."

She brushed the hair from his forehead. Her voice was soft, even, calm. "I've seen the pictures—all big eyes and raw bones. Who would've guessed you'd grow up beautiful?"

"Not too long after, she raised her hand to Maggie and I grabbed her arm and told her that if she even *looked* like she was gonna hit her again, I'd show her what it felt like." He stopped, staring into Holly's eyes as if he'd suddenly glimpsed an answer there. "She never hit us again. We both got out as soon as we could."

"And it was over," Holly murmured. "Except it wasn't over."

"No. My dad—he about fell apart when she died. He always believed her—how could he *not* believe her? But how could he not have *seen?*" It burst out of him for the first time, without warning—everything that had been festering for years, the horror and the betrayal and the hatred. And the ugliness inside him, the cowardice. He raised his head, and she looked down into his eyes. "I missed you," he said, his voice raw, trembling a little. "You'll never know how much."

One finger stroked his brows. "I'm here now, *a chuisle*. I always will be."

He couldn't talk any more then, not for a long time. Holly held him, giving him a place to rest. There was comfort in trusting her; peace in knowing she loved him; safety in the sureness that she would be here whenever he needed her.

It was her fault that all the old poison had welled up. Those words in the story were hers. Yet as she'd taken him through the story of himself, yet not completely himself, it was like reading her other work: she got you inside a person's skin, made you feel and understand and come out the other side along with the character. Separate from that person, no matter how similar your lives were; but connected to that person, too, no matter how different your lives were.

At last Holly spoke again, very softly. "Your father didn't want to see. Nobody could force him to open his eyes. You couldn't—you were so young—Evan, what if you'd told him and he hadn't done anything to stop it? You would've lost him, too, the love you felt for him. You couldn't risk it."

"Coward—," he managed, and tried to pull away, but she held him fast.

"*Never.* You can't blame yourself. It wasn't your fault, not any of it. Do you see that?"

He nodded slowly, too exhausted to speak. He waited for his heartbeats to calm down before drawing back a little. This time she let him go.

"Holly, I know I gotta stop blamin' myself—" He clamped his jaw shut around the rest of the words, things he'd learned to say when anyone got too close to his truths. Holly didn't deserve the kind of glib lies he told other people.

"You don't believe that. You never have and I doubt you ever will." Her fingers touched his face, stroking away tears he hadn't known were there.

And then he saw it. "My God—when I stood up to her—it was only a few days after I saw her with Father Matthew—I thought I shouted her down because I was scared—that I just couldn't take any more—"

"Evan, look back at that boy. He told her no, and stared her down, and—look at yourself! See who you are, the man you've become. There's not a cowardly bone in your body—not then, not now. Not ever."

In her eyes was everything he'd ever wanted to see in a woman's eyes—and even more, things he'd never known how to want. Most astonishing of all was her fierce willingness to do battle with any demons that might threaten him. No one had ever fought for him before.

She hesitated, then told him, "This ring you're giving me—it had better not be your mother's."

He didn't know why, but somehow it was the perfect thing to say. He felt a smile touch a corner of his mouth—it felt like forever since he'd smiled. "Granna Maureen's."

Holly nodded. Then: "Evan, would you do something for me?"

"Sure. What?"

He followed her into her bedroom. From the little corner table she brought out a gold cord and nine small votive candles, and a vial of fragrant oil. This she used to anoint the candles, one drop on each. A long fireplace match was lit and handed to him. He knelt beside her.

"Cousin Jesse taught me this when I was about twelve," she said. "Light one of the candles after I make each knot."

*First begins, Second proclaims;*
*Third casts, Fourth tames;*
*Fifth refines, Sixth strengthens;*
*Seventh anneals, Eighth lengthens;*
*Ninth seals.*

Holly coiled the cord around the grouped candles, which now gave off a scent of apples. "Magic," she murmured.

"For me," he said softly.

"Only for you."

# Ten

LACHLAN CAUGHT UP WITH HOLLY in the foyer just as she was reaching to open the front door. "Showtime," he told her, then winked.

The doorbell sounded again just as she turned the knob. A moment later an overabundance of yellow roses appeared above two pairs of legs in Levi's.

"I never sing for my supper," said Bradshaw from somewhere behind the roses.

"For which we are all profoundly grateful," Susannah added at his side.

"They're beautiful!" Holly wrapped both arms around the bouquet and buried her face in the flowers. "Thank you!"

"I told him white are your favorites," Susannah said. "But he insisted on yellow."

"My grandfather had a credo," he explained. "Yellow for redheads, white for blondes, pink for brunettes. Red only for *extremely* special occasions."

Susannah blushed becomingly. Holly grinned. Lachlan wondered what the joke was, then shrugged it off.

"My father," Bradshaw went on, "had another excellent piece of advice when it came to women. Whenever you give her something, tell her you chose it because it would look good on her. *Never* that she would look good in it. Always imply that the item is singularly improved by being in her possession." He smiled at Holly. "So—yellow for redheads, but *this* shade of yellow because it looks great on you."

Lachlan tipped him a salute. "I'll remember that, Your Honor," he said, thinking that a dozen roses would've been a polite guest-gift, but two dozen could be considered excessive. *I've never given her flowers, even on her birthday. Didn't even know she likes white roses. Okay, another note for the engagement dinner: great restaurant, candlelight, romance, ring, white roses. The whole formal thing.*

Tonight was casual. Thank God. It was his first time playing host, and he'd told Holly that the dress code had better be Levi's or else. Susannah had topped her jeans with a short-sleeved pink print blouse; Elias wore a Harvard baseball jersey; Holly had chosen a green tank top. Lachlan was actually the most formal of them all in a crisp blue shirt—though open at the neck and with the sleeves rolled up.

"We have something for the host, too, Evan," Susannah said, presenting him with a plain blue bag exuding silver tissue paper.

He gave a start, then frowned at her. "It bites, right?"

"Just open it."

Gingerly he stuck a hand into the bag, and pulled out something made of heavy cloth. Unfolded, it proved to be a spotless white chef's apron with words on it in bright red:

> Women want me
> Martha Stewart fears me

"And you don't even work for the SEC," Susannah drawled.

"Whatever happened to 'Kiss the Chef'?" Lachlan complained.

"Oh, I can do that, too," Susannah told him, and brushed his cheek with her lips.

"Down, girl," Bradshaw admonished. "He's took."

"Shows, huh?" Lachlan asked ruefully.

"Four-color neon, right across your forehead."

Holly snorted. "If it was about three feet lower down, it might do some good. Evan, pour us something to drink while I put these in water." And she vanished down the hall into the kitchen.

He kicked himself mentally. Some host. As they went into the living room, he tried not to act as nervous as he felt and asked, "Scotch and tequila, right?"

"Thanks, Evan." Susannah perched on a bar stool and beamed at him. For a minute, as he poured liquor and added ice—these weren't Alec's special glasses—he wondered if she knew. But Holly had told no one, not even Aunt Lulah. Neither had Lachlan. He was stubborn about wanting to wait until he'd given her the ring.

"I like the apron," he told Susannah. "Really."

"Uh-huh."

"Beautiful place," Bradshaw remarked, wandering around the living room. "But I thought all these co-ops had balconies."

Susannah shook her head. "Holly's afraid of heights. She can't even climb a ladder."

"I can't even stand on a stepstool," Holly added, coming into the room with a huge crystal vase overflowing with roses. She set it on the coffee table, came to sit beside Susannah at the bar, and smiled at Lachlan. "Where's my Stoli, bartender?"

"Comin' right up." He poured, and Bradshaw joined them, and they lifted their glasses in a silent toast.

Silent—until Susannah said, "So have you set a date yet?"

Evan traded a startled glance with his intended. "How the hell—?"

"I don't know!" Holly wailed. "I didn't tell her, honest!"

Susannah smiled like a cat who'd gotten the canary, a can of salmon, and a bowl of cream for dessert.

"Date?" Bradshaw asked, then tumbled to it. A grin spread across his face and he raised his glass. "*Mazel tov!*"

"How'd you know?" Holly demanded of her friend.

"If you insist on keeping secrets from someone who's known you almost twenty years," Susannah replied serenely, "you shouldn't have the May issue of *Bride* magazine in your briefcase when you meet that person for lunch." She downed her tequila and held out her glass for more. "So what am I wearing?"

" 'Wearing'?" Holly echoed blankly.

"I introduced you. I get to be a bridesmaid, don't I?"

"Best Woman," Holly answered.

"I like it," Susannah approved. "So what *am* I wearing?"

"A taffeta hoop skirt in the Clan McLeod tartan."

"Marshal, if they're going to discuss weddings," Bradshaw said firmly, "we're going to go watch the game. Where's the TV?"

"Elias!" Susannah exclaimed.

"Oh, let them go." Holly shrugged. "We'll pretend we're domesticated and go putter in the kitchen like we know what we're doing." With a brief caress to Lachlan's hand, she finished, "We'll yell when dinner's ready."

It was a little strange to be sitting on the big suede sofa drinking Scotch and watching a basketball game with Elias Bradshaw. But if things continued as it looked like they would for Elias and Susannah, there'd be plenty more evenings like this. It felt very . . . *married*: the women in the kitchen and the men watching the game. Truth be told, he liked it. He just wondered if he'd ever like Bradshaw.

"Good call, Marshal," Elias said as a commercial came on. He wasn't talking about the game.

"You called it first, Your Honor. 'Quite a catch,' I think you said."

Bradshaw took a long swallow of Scotch. "If you don't treat her right, Susannah will come after you with a machete."

He tried to picture it. "Wouldn't a pearl-handled switchblade be more her style?"

"Huh. Don't let that delicate little face fool you. She's about as subtle as a hydrogen bomb when she's pissed off."

"No wonder she and Holly get along so good."

"Yeah, they're quite a pair." Bradshaw contemplated his drink. "I'm not sure how it happened, but I think we both got lucky."

"*I* know how it happened," Lachlan retorted. "They planned it."

Two minutes from the final buzzer, Susannah appeared in the doorway. "Evan, Holly says come make yourself useful and open the wine. Personally, I prefer a man who's more decorative than utilitarian, but there's no accounting for taste."

Bradshaw shook his head. "You see what comes of educating women?"

"Uppity," Lachlan agreed. "I'll be there when the game's over."

"That's telling her," Elias approved.

Susannah put her fists on her hips. "You want to eat before midnight?"

"If that's when the game ends, that's when we'll eat," Bradshaw replied.

She gave him a disgusted look. "Don't tell me—it's a guy thing." Turning on her heel, she left the office.

Five minutes later, game over, TV off, and the scents of dinner drawing them inexorably to the kitchen, Lachlan and Bradshaw found the women guzzling vodka and tequila, seated at the breakfast bar gossiping about former classmates. The men found themselves completely ignored.

"—hasn't seen the kid in months and he'll only be home for a week before college starts, but she tells him to go to his dad's because it's Date Night."

"Anybody who needs to get laid that *bad* ain't gettin' laid that *good*," Holly declared.

Lachlan, seeing the blue gift bag on the sink counter, steeled himself. Apron donned, he went to the fridge for the two bottles of wine he'd bought for tonight, found the corkscrew, and performed his hostly duty. Practice, he told himself, for the Friday night in July when they'd take his father, sister, brother-in-law, nieces, and nephew out to dinner, plus three aunts from Boston. Compared to them, Bradshaw and Wingfield were a walk in the park.

"You know, of course," Elias said to Susannah, "that your fellow alumni are still gossiping about you two. After that exhibition you gave them last week—"

"It was a karaoke bar, Elias," Holly reminded him. Rising from the breakfast bar, she took the string beans out of the microwave and dumped them into a serving bowl. "We *had* to sing."

"And you *had* to sing that song, right?"

Susannah smiled sweetly. "Would you have preferred 'Drop-Kick Me, Jesus, through the Goal Posts of Life'?"

"'The Vatican Rag,'" he retorted.

"How about 'Lawyers in Love'?" Holly inquired sweetly.

Lachlan, filling an ice bucket from the freezer, bit his lip against a grin and shot a glance at Holly. She winked at him as she transferred Isabel's stuffed pork loin to a serving platter. "Behave yourself, McClure," he chided.

On her way by with the platter, she bumped her hip into his. "That's not what you said last night at about two in the morning."

He turned an accusing stare on Susannah. "You see what I gotta put up with? And it's all your fault, too."

"Keep complaining, Evan—someday I might even buy into it. Which reminds me, Holly, you haven't thanked me yet for playing matchmaker."

"I don't recall hearing any heartfelt words of gratitude from *you*, either." She took dinner in, calling back over her shoulder, "After all, Lachlan was easy. With you and Elias, I accomplished the impossible!"

That this was news to Evan must have been clear on his face. Bradshaw grimaced and took himself and his empty glass back to the living room bar.

Susannah made a face at his retreating back, then turned to Lachlan. "She never told you?" He shook his head. As Holly came back in, Susannah turned an accusing stare on her. "You never told him?"

"So I took you and Elias out to dinner. So sue me."

"Jesus Christ, woman, what's wrong with you?" Lachlan exclaimed. "Never say that to a lawyer!"

Susannah leaned across the counter and rapped her knuckles on his forehead. "Do you want to hear this or not? Last October third. She knows it's Elias's birthday. *I* know it's Elias's birthday. Even *Elias* knows it's Elias's birthday! She insists on taking us to dinner at Chanterelle—"

"You didn't even *say* Happy Birthday to me," he complained. The first bottle gave up its cork; he started in on the second, telling Susannah, "And it doesn't sound like you've got anything to bitch about. All I got was a hot dog."

"Didn't want to spoil you too soon," Holly shot back, and left with the salad.

"Anyway," Susannah went on, "there we sit, drinking and waiting for menus, while Holly blithers on and on and *on*, and Elias looks like thunder— and all at once her cell phone rings. It's her publisher." She pretended to be holding a phone to her ear. Evan reflected that to really do the sweet innocence bit right, the eyes had to be blue. "'Walter? What's wrong?' She's quiet for a minute, then gets this horrible frown on her face. 'Calm down. You'll live.' More silence. Then the kicker—'Okay, I'll be there in twenty minutes. Hold the fort, pour your best Scotch, and tell 'em the one about the new rabbi who didn't know what to do with the foreskin after a *bris*.'"

Evan choked. Walter had told him that one, and it was dreadful.

"She stuffs the phone in her purse. Sorry, major crisis, don't worry about the check, have fun—and leaves before Elias or I could get a word in edgewise!"

"Devious," Lachlan observed, then added with a leer, "So did Elias have a nice birthday?"

Susannah batted her eyelashes at him. "Let's just say he got his present *on* his birthday—whereas you had to wait awhile."

"Jesus! Do you two tell each other *everything?*" When she just smiled, he grimaced. Turning in the direction of the dining room, he bellowed, "Holly Elizabeth McClure! Get your ass in here *right now!*"

"Go play with yourself, Lachlan!" she shouted back.

Susannah was whooping. "I love it! Evan Lachlan, Terror of the U.S. Marshals Service—laid low by a mere woman!"

"First of all, she ain't no 'mere' anything. Second of all, I get laid low, high, middle, and sideways, and that's the *only* reason I put up with her."

"Yeah, Evan—I believe you. Thousands wouldn't." Susannah bit her lip, still giggling, then asked, "Low, high, middle, sideways—what about backwards and upside down? Is Holly slowing down? Or aren't you that adventurous?"

"Sometimes," he answered sweetly, "I even get to be on top."

"She must really like you, then."

"There's a rumor to that effect." He crammed the bottles into the ice bucket as Susannah picked up the basket of bread. She slid her free arm around his waist to hug him.

"I knew you two would be great together."

"So I guess this is where I finally get around to sayin' thanks?"

"You just be good to her. That's all the thanks I want."

"Okay, then, fair's fair." He slung an arm around her slender shoulders as they walked into the candlelit dining room. "His Honor ever gives you any trouble, let me know. I carry a bigger gun than he does."

"Wingfield, you sneaky slut," came Holly's stern voice from the other side of a dozen of Elias's roses, "get your mitts off my man."

Susannah jumped away from Evan as if they'd been caught in a guilty embrace. "Don't hurt me," she whimpered woefully, cringing behind the bread basket.

"Eats my food, guzzles my tequila, slinks all over my fiancé—"

Susannah responded with a bluesy song that Holly joined with high harmony. Bradshaw came into the dining room just as they were finishing the chorus, which advised a woman to be wise, keep her mouth shut, and don't advertise her man.

"They do this a lot, huh," Evan said to Bradshaw as he removed the apron and took his seat at the head of the table.

"Individually and as a team," Bradshaw agreed, nodding his thanks as Evan poured him a glass of wine. "Trouble is, you never know when it's gonna happen."

"Tell me about it." He stuck the serving fork into the meat; Bradshaw held out his plate. "The first time it was the middle of Central Park."

"Christ, Lachlan, don't give her any ideas!"

Susannah rounded on him. "You think we just stick to karaoke bars?"

"I only wish you *would*."

THEY WERE BACK IN THE living room with coffee and dessert when it happened. Susannah was at the bar, browsing Holly's collection of single-malt Scotches, her back to the room—for which Elias sincerely thanked all the Deities he could think of—when Holly's cat leaped from the hearth rug and howled. All eyes were on him as he landed, paused for an arching, hissing growl, and streaked from the room.

"What in the world got into Mugger?" Susannah exclaimed.

Bradshaw caught a glint from one corner of his eye. And turned. And saw a spark flash from the window—and another—and another, brighter this time, fierce and angry, an irregular pulse of amber light. Holly almost imitated the cat rising from her chair, the beginnings of panic in her eyes as she stared at the throbbing glass sphere.

"Hey, Susannah," Evan said suddenly, "come help me see what's got Mugger's tail in a fluff, huh? I know some of his hiding places, but not all."

Just as Bradshaw cast a warding in the general vicinity of the window—sloppy work, but it served to hide the witch sphere—Susannah walked from behind the bar to join Lachlan, saying, "Never figured you for a cat person."

He gave her a tiger-growl as he escorted her to the hall—hurrying her without seeming to, Bradshaw noted. "You take upstairs, I'll take downstairs, and if we can't find him we'll borrow that little rat-dog from next door to lure him out. Mugger loves to beat the shit out of him."

Aware that he didn't need the distraction of wondering what Lachlan knew or why he knew it, Bradshaw hauled Holly toward the window. "I need your help."

"It—it shouldn't be doing that," she managed, freckles standing out dark in her white face. "Nicky gave it to me less than a month ago—it should've lasted longer—"

"Well, it hasn't. Come on."

Together they stood before the window, the ward mostly protecting them from the sparking malevolence encysted by the sphere. Within the dark golden glass depths the pulsing continued, maddeningly random, like a heartbeat that had lost all life-giving rhythm. It leaked malice, and evil.

Bradshaw dug into his pockets, wondering if he'd brought anything he could use, searched his mental library for something appropriate. The light intensified as his hasty ward faltered, every beat hammering at his eyes, his brain. Holly wrenched away from him, eluding him when he made a grab for her arm.

But she wasn't running away. Instead, she went to the unlit hearth and delved into the basket of firewood. "Oak or pine?" she demanded of him.

He stared at her.

"Goddammit, Magistrate, which one?" she snapped.

"Pine," he heard himself say, as his fingers closed around his key chain. From fat silver links dangled a lump of polished red jasper—his grandfather's good-luck piece, it had seen the old man through World War One unscathed.

Holly brought him a small log, wincing as she neared the fluctuating ward and the *diablerie* plucked at her again. Elias took her arm and pulled her as close as he dared to the sphere. And, as a hunting dog senses the unattainable presence of its quarry, within the amber glass the sorcery began to whine.

Bradshaw picked at the wood to tease off a good-sized splinter. Words tumbled through his mind, associations learned long ago, Basic Defensive Magic 101: *Red jasper—return negativity to its source—reversing—protective—barrier—* The glass shivered from the inside out, light pounding furiously. *Pine—counter-magic—purification—exorcism—protection against evil—*

Holly stood beside him again, visibly trembling. She held one of the yellow roses he'd brought her, plucked from the vase on the coffee table. A thorn pricked her thumb, conjuring a single thick ruby of blood.

Stone, wood, and blood combined with words that came to him with their usual suppleness. The orb emitted an anguished keening, one side and then the other bulging as light concentrated all its strength into a last attempt to burst free. It was like watching boils rise on shiny dark golden skin.

And then it died.

In the silent, blessed relief from that thrumming malevolence, Bradshaw swayed slightly against Holly. She pulled back from him, reaching to unhook the sphere from its chain, and cradled the cold, dead glass between her hands.

"Who do you think it was?" Her voice was remarkably calm, and if he hadn't glimpsed her eyes at that moment he would have thought her recovered from her terror.

"I don't know. Who hates you enough?"

She gave a little shrug. "Maybe it was you they were after."

"In that case, the line forms on the right." He looked around as Susannah's laughter came from the hall. "Quick—"

Wood back in the basket, rose back in the vase, Witch Sphere consigned to a cabinet drawer, they were waiting with impeccable nonchalance when Susannah and Lachlan came back with Mugger draped across the latter's shoulders, digging in with all twenty claws.

"Holly," he complained, "get this furball off me, willya?"

The next few minutes were spent coaxing the cat into Holly's arms, where he licked her nose several times before curling up tight against her. It was entirely clear that Mugger would not be moving anytime soon. Holly sat in a chair by the hearth, and said, "Would somebody pour me some coffee, please?"

"What spooked him?" Susannah asked.

"Who knows?" Lachlan made himself useful with coffee and brandy. "The air-conditioning probably twitched a curtain or something. He's such a scaredy-cat, it's embarrassing."

Mugger yawned, and Susannah laughed.

Bradshaw made himself comfortable on the couch, Susannah beside him, while the little rituals of serving were performed. Lachlan made an efficient host, he had to admit—but there was something in the marshal's eyes when he glanced Bradshaw's way, something that had suspected, and now knew beyond doubt.

Elias cast about for some harmless topic of conversation. Suddenly Susannah pointed a finger at Holly and demanded, "Why are men like coffee?"

"Great! You got a new one! Okay, why?"

Purring, she replied, "The best ones are smooth, dark, hot, and can keep you up all night long."

Holly groaned. "All right, you deserve this one. Why are men like parking spots?" She waited a moment, then said, "The best ones are taken and the rest are handicapped."

Lachlan grinned. "Why are women like the weather?"

"I know that one," Bradshaw said. "Women are like the weather because you can't do anything to change them."

Susannah threw a pillow at him.

Just as Bradshaw was beginning to think the conversation would be innocuous for the rest of the evening, Lachlan caught his gaze and said, "I've been meaning to ask—where'd you learn your magical *Naranja*?"

"Oh, his parlor trick?" Susannah chuckled. "I'd heard rumors, but I never believed it until I saw it at the Sbarras'."

"College," Elias said. "I don't do card tricks or sleight-of-hand, though."

Lachlan nodded, smiling slightly. Bradshaw wanted to squirm.

"Holly has a thing she does with fire," Susannah said. "Salt, isn't it? Or some kind of herbs. Something folksy and backwoods Virginian, anyway."

"Not at all," Holly assured her. "Anybody can make colors in a fire. Me, I'm more likely to blow up the lab."

Susannah snorted. "I remember, I remember! Professor Harbison banned you from the science building." Leaning gently against Bradshaw's arm, she mused, "I wonder what happened the first time somebody accidentally dropped salt or whatever into a campfire—you know, huddled at night on the savanna, listening to the sabertooths growl, and then colors suddenly spit from the flames—" She laughed. "The first magician!"

"Oh, magic started long before that," Holly said.

Bradshaw fought his misgivings, telling himself that the quickest way to arouse suspicion was to change the subject. Best to brazen it out. Or so Holly obviously thought; she started a lecture.

"The first magicians had to have been singers. Think about it. What must've happened the first time someone grunted a rhythmic chant—probably in time to a heartbeat? Primal. Elemental. Certain organ notes can elicit a feeling of awe. Voices do the same."

"Pavarotti," Elias said, intrigued in spite of himself.

Holly made a sour face. "Susannah's told me that you can't carry a tune with both hands and an SUV, but *must* you equate 'Nessun Dorma' with some grunting Cro-Magnon? And I think it has something to do with the music itself as well. Mozart. Beethoven." She grinned. "The Beatles!"

"Absolutely!" Susannah agreed. "But the first time someone hummed something that caught the emotions of someone else, it probably got him or her offed in a hurry. It'd be terrifying, the first time it happened to you."

Bradshaw nodded. "A voice that touches something inside, creating a response without physical contact."

"Spooky," remarked Lachlan. "But what's it like to be the one doing the singing?"

Holly tilted her head slightly as she looked over at him. "What it feels like to make music . . . the control of air in your lungs, the vibrations in your throat, the buzz in your head, the concentration on getting the notes right—"

"—the look on other people's faces that means you have power," Susannah added. "People who could make music that provoked reaction were perceived as having power—a reaction they recognized and used. They became magicians by mutual consent of singer and audience. Imagine sitting in a cave around the fire, with voices echoing off the stone—"

"It would be religious in a way, don't you think?" Holly sat forward, eyes bright, scratching Mugger absently. "It's called 'singing' a Mass—and in Judaism the cantor sings the words. Ritual requires words—put the words together with the music, and the magic intensifies. And wasn't the universe created by a Word?"

Elias had a sudden vision of what Susannah and Holly must have been like in college—bouncing ideas off each other, the synergy almost electrifying. This was a kind of magic, too.

Holly went on, "The written word has always been magical. During the Middle Ages, about the only people who knew how to read and write were priests—and they had a direct hotline to God."

"Rhythm, music, words," Lachlan murmured. "Sounds like that adds up to you, Holly."

This was getting a little dicey. Bradshaw said quickly, "But what about dancers? Artists? Some people respond to the dance—and the people who do the dancing certainly do. I've watched you two ladies often enough to know that," he added with an attempt at humor.

Holly gave a dismissive shrug. "Any idiot can jump around and wave his arms. The rhythm is internal, not shared."

"Not art, either," Susannah agreed. "It must've been wonderful to be able to take a stick and draw in the dirt and have it look like something—and even better to use pigments and create Lascaux. But that was much later. And it's the response of the audience that really counts. Drawing a map to where the mastodons were herding wouldn't've elicited anything but feelings of hunger!"

"Works for me," Lachlan drawled.

"Feed him and he'll follow you anywhere." Holly grinned.

"Shamans were healers, weren't they?" Susannah asked. "Maybe that's when magicians really got started, when somebody found out that if you ate a certain herb your bellyache went away. I mean, that would be *real*, wouldn't it? Demonstrable. Painting and dancing and singing and so forth provoke emotional reactions that are unquantifiable. But healing someone with herbs—now, *that* would be magical."

"Personally," Lachlan observed, holding up his brandy snifter, "I think the first doctor or magician or whatever you want to call him was the guy who figured out how to brew hooch. And I bet he was Irish."

As they all laughed, and conversation drifted into a comparison of whiskies, Elias relaxed. It wasn't until he and Susannah were leaving that he met Marshal Lachlan's gaze and again saw the *knowing* there.

"So say something," he invited, sotto voce.

"Such as?" Although amused curiosity shaded Lachlan's voice, his eyes were merciless. The two men were almost of a height, Elias an inch or two shorter— but he had the years, the experience, and the magic. None of it felt like much when confronted with the look in those hazel eyes.

He cast a glance at the women, who were busy making plans for lunch that week. Both were scratching Mugger's ears; the cat refused to leave Holly's arms. "It's not something any of us advertises, as Holly will have told you."

"That's not the issue."

"What is?"

"Her." In that one word was a world of warning. "My old man never had anything useful to say about women," Lachlan went on, "but my granddad did. He told me you never know what they're really like until you get caught in the rain. If she screams and tries to protect her hair and makeup, take her home and don't ever call her again. But if she starts to laugh—" He smiled slightly. "—you laugh with her, and then make sure you're always around so nothing less gentle than the rain ever touches her."

Elias regarded him with new respect. "It's my job to take care of her just as much as it is yours," he murmured.

"Not exactly."

"No," he agreed. "Not exactly. But you know what I mean."

"Just as long as we both know." Lachlan paused. "And Susannah doesn't."

"No." Reluctantly, he added, "Thanks for—"

Lachlan shrugged it off. "See you Monday morning, Your Honor."

# Eleven

HOLLY NUDGED THE FRONT DOOR shut with a hip, hoisted Mugger higher in her arms, and turned to face Evan. "Okay, let's have it."

He made wide, startled eyes at her. "Right here in the hall?"

"Very funny. You know what I mean."

"Yeah, but my interpretation woulda been more fun." Sauntering back into the living room, he poured them both another brandy. "Y'know, a couple years ago there was this guy from Mexico on trial in Bradshaw's court. Pete was on duty that first day, and in the wife's purse he found this grimy little bag of rocks and chicken bones and stuff. He let her keep it—said it smelled to high heaven, but she didn't want to give it up. So I knew to look for it the next morning, and he was right—stinkiest thing I ever ran across. After the guy was convicted, I heard her say to her sister that her mojo bag had always worked before, down in Mexico, and she didn't understand why it hadn't worked on this judge." Raising his glass to Holly, he finished, "Now I guess I know why."

"Yeah," she said, seating herself wearily. Mugger resumed his place in her lap, hardly opening an eye. "Now you know why."

"Why didn't you get into medicine?"

Left field? This one hadn't even come from inside the ballpark. "What do you mean?"

"Just what I said. Why not Work with a doctor?"

She countered with, "What happens when we start curing people?"

"They get to live."

"Evan, think about it. *I* have," she added bitterly. "Word spreads that sure-fire cures are available. Investigations start. Witchcraft? Insanity! But it's proved, over and over. The scientific community goes nuts. The Church gets involved—*all* the churches. Just because you accept what I am doesn't mean other people could."

"Even if they let you live, and if the government didn't get you, somebody very rich and powerful would—and keep you in a cage."

"Yeah. And the really fun part is that they bleed me on a regular basis while taking exquisite care of me for the rest of my long, locked-up life. What happens when I finally die? Everything goes back to the way it was before. So what purpose has my life served in the long run?"

"That's not even considering your kids."

Holly gave a start, nearly dropping her brandy snifter. Mugger grumbled at the interruption of his nap. "What?"

"Haven't you ever taken it that far? They'd harvest you, lady love," he said gently, "hoping that at least one egg turned out to have the right genes."

"I never even considered—," she whispered, then gathered herself. "When I was old enough to understand, the technology didn't exist for—for that kind of thing. So we never had to think about it, Alec and Nicky and Aunt Lulah and I." Eyeing him narrowly: "But you obviously have."

"Only to swear that it never happens." He took a swig of liquor. "So tell me about Elias Bradshaw."

She thought about that instant when she and Elias had looked at each other this evening with identical alarm—a look that had shut Evan out; how swiftly he had recognized the need for secrecy; how smoothly he'd gotten Susannah out of the room, despite what must have been a rampaging curiosity.

Holly gave a shrug. "It's a rather luscious irony that he's a judge in public life, because within the Craft he's a judge, too. More formally, a Magistrate."

He seated himself on an ottoman near the empty hearth, gesturing with his glass for her to go on. Forbidding herself to react as if she were on trial, she began.

"After Mr. Scot died—" She interrupted herself irritably. "Sorry, he was this amazing old man, a real Magus, incredibly powerful. I think Aunt Lulah met him once, in D.C. He had a network of people like Alec and Nicky, who went around solving problems and bringing people to him for justice. But he knew he wasn't going to live forever, and before he died he set up a new system. Elias is one of his hand-picked Magistrates. There are others all over the country—I Worked with the one in L.A. when I was in grad school. There are similar systems all over the world, but not connected like when Mr. Scot was alive. Everybody agrees we have to discipline ourselves for our own safety. But things are more piecemeal now, even though individual Magistrates have more power within their regions. Every five years they all meet to review the system, make any necessary adjustments."

"The United Nations of Witchcraft," Evan murmured whimsically.

"Not 'united,' no. It's usually a muddle. Still, at least they make the effort."

"And Bradshaw runs New York."

"He likes to think he does," she answered, chuckling a little. This was going better than she'd expected.

"What do these Magistrates do, trade you around like a first baseman?"

"The fact that they can't is something I owe to Alec and Nicky." As Mugger shifted slightly, she started rubbing between his shoulder blades to hear him purr, wishing it were as easy to sweeten her lover, whose dragon's eyes were watching her narrowly as she said, "Aunt Lulah had her suspicions, but it wasn't until they came along that we knew what I am. They made sure I got to live my life. There are always people watching over me—"

"Mr. Hunnicutt downstairs, for one," Evan remarked.

"Well, yes. How'd you know?"

"It's obvious. Go on."

"Okay. I'm a valuable commodity, so everybody who knows about me protects me. But Alec and Nicky made sure I wasn't stifled. I'm sure a few people had fits when I went to Europe with Susannah that time—if somebody had decided they wanted me to stay there, it's not as if there are any extradition treaties! But I proved I could take care of myself."

"I'll bet somebody was watching you the whole time. You just didn't know it. And I'll also bet that it still happens whenever you leave New York."

She shrugged edgily. "You're probably right. I don't think about it much."

"You said you proved you can take care of yourself. What happened?"

"We were in Greece. Someone tried to run us off the road. Delphi is up in the mountains, and driving those winding roads—I thought we'd plunge over the side. We were both terrified. Susannah didn't know, of course, she just thought it was a bunch of men who saw a couple of American girls on their own and—well, you know. I guess driving the Virginia backwoods and L.A. freeways stood me in good stead, because eventually I lost them. Back in Athens that night we drank ourselves to sleep—with all the lights on and the dresser shoved against the door. The next morning there was a piece in the paper about some Bulgarian tourists who went off the road near Delphi. Their car exploded. They died."

"Jesus," he whispered.

"Nicky checked into it after we got home—he left Europe a long time ago, but he still has connections—and it turned out the Bulgarians were working for the Berlin Magistrate, who also happened to be connected to the East German secret police. Things were pretty nasty in the Warsaw Pact countries then, and this Magistrate wanted a trump card, I guess."

"I hope somebody fried his synapses."

"Next best thing," she told him. "The Greek Magistrate—a wonderful old woman on Santorini—she sent me a case of her best wine to apologize for what had happened within her jurisdiction—anyway, she and the Hungarian and Romanian Magistrates unWorked this man's magic. Which ain't easy, but they did it. It was a punishment, but also a warning." Finishing her brandy, she set the glass aside. "So that's the story. I suppose I didn't really *prove* anything, except that I know how to drive. I was just so goddamned furious that Suze had been put in danger—"

"And she didn't know. Will she ever?"

"It's not something easily admitted, Evan."

"I understand that," he said impatiently. "Don't you trust her?"

"Of course I do!"

"With everything but this."

"It's up to the individual about who to tell and who not to tell. Not everybody is as tolerant about it as you've been." She eyed him considering. "And I keep wondering why."

"Would there be a point to having hysterics?" he asked wryly.

"That's not an answer, Evan."

"Okay, how about, 'I love you no matter what or who you are'?"

"Better." But she smiled again.

"Holly, I wish I knew why it doesn't bother me that much. Maybe because I've never had to see it up close and personal. I believe in it—your thing with fire, and whatever happened here tonight—speaking of which, what the hell *did* happen?"


"ELIAS, WHAT THE HELL HAPPENED?"

"Hmm?" he asked, pretending he was absorbed by traffic.

"Don't play dumb, Your Honor. I know when I'm being hustled out of a room so the people in it can do something they don't want me to witness."

"You think Holly and I made mad, passionate love on the carpet?"

Susannah laughed aloud. "First of all, you barely tolerate each other. Second of all, you may be pushing fifty, but you're good for at least ten minutes and Evan and I were back within five."

Bradshaw turned a glower on her. "'Ten minutes'?"

"At least," she teased. "And third of all, rug burn isn't your style. Come on, what are you hiding? And why?"

*What I am. Because I love you.* And because he loved her, he lied to her. "She was about to read me the riot act over that priest—the history with Lachlan's mother. I didn't want to screw up a pleasant evening, and evidently neither did she—or Lachlan."

"So you did a wink-and-nod at Evan to get me out of the room?"

"Yeah." He wondered if he could get away with changing the subject, and decided it would be too blatant.

Susannah, bless her, did it for him. "I'm glad they're getting married. I always knew they'd be perfect for each other."

"The kids will be interesting," he commented. *And then some.*

"I can't wait to be an auntie. Of course, I'll have to battle Holly's Aunt Lulah over who gets to spoil them the most!"

Miracle of miracles, there was a parking space near his brownstone. He escorted Susannah up the stoop and nearly had a heart attack when a quiet, feminine voice came from the shadows of his doorway.

"Judge Bradshaw, may I have a moment of your time?"

"Lydia. Of course." Cursing lyrically, if silently, he opened the front door and switched on the hall light. "Susannah Wingfield, Lydia Montsorel."

"I'm sorry to interrupt your evening," Lydia said softly.

"Not at all. Shall I make coffee?" Susannah asked.

"Uh—yes, thanks," he replied, feeling a fool.

Susannah vanished down the hall to the kitchen. Bradshaw drew Lydia into the living room, asking low-voiced, "What are you doing here?"

"I couldn't get you on the phone." She glanced around nervously. "I need light, Elias. Please."

He obliged, knowing that his Sciomancer was afraid of shadows. Lydia's was an odd talent, intense and erratic. The only predictable thing about it was that when it hit her, it really hit hard. With the table lamps on, he saw the wildness in her dark eyes, the tumble of her long black hair, the quiver in her delicate fingers.

He guided her to a chair. "Quickly, before Susannah gets back."

"Yes, of course." She fixed her gaze on a lamp, pupils pinpointed, face ashen. Her lips parted slowly, her breath a labored whisper that worried him.

"Lydia."

Startled, she looked up at him. "Elias," she said, as if only now recognizing him. "I had to tell you—I was downstairs in the bakery this evening and I happened to look up and there was something moving in the corner—"

"Shadows."

"Yes. Always shadows. I had to tell you there's a change. What I saw last year—the cross still burns, but the swastika isn't the only other symbol. The inverted pentagram is the only one I recognize. All the shapes and designs— swirls and writhings—I'm not a scholar, Elias, I don't know what they mean!"

"Shh. It's all right. Can you draw them?"

"I think so." She scrubbed her hands across her face. "I hate this. I hate this. I hate seeing what I see."

"Not always," he soothed. "You've seen pleasant things, too, happy things. It isn't always terrible."

"No. Not always."

"You saw David six weeks before you met him, and the wedding a month before he asked you—"

"Yes, there *are* good things. Alec and Nicky always told me to concentrate on the good things—" She looked around as if suddenly becoming aware of her surroundings. "I should go—you have a guest—"

"It's all right."

"I want to go home." Rising on unsteady legs, she attempted a smile. "I'm fine. I'll do the drawings tomorrow. There were numbers, as well. And birds."

"Ravens?" he asked, remembering her vision of last year.

"I think so. But whether they were Teutonic ravens, fugitives from the Tower of London, or just common garden variety crows—"

Elias rose, slipped an arm around her shoulders. "Hush. It's all right. We'll figure it out."

"At least the swastika is gone. That's something, isn't it? I could have been mistaken originally, though, it could have been a much more ancient sun-wheel. The swastika wasn't always a symbol of evil."

"Lydia. Let it go. Let me call David to take you home. It's almost midnight."

If Susannah was bewildered by Lydia's abrupt departure with her husband after ten minutes of coffee and innocuous conversation, she didn't show it. Alone with Elias again, she regarded him with dancing green eyes over the rim of her cup and asked, "Do you get a lot of pretty women arriving distraught on your doorstep?"

"She's the daughter of an old friend." This, at least, was not a lie. "And if you're really interested, I prefer them to arrive on my doorstep in tight jeans, a pink blouse, and a blonde ponytail."

"What happens then?"

"Play your cards right, Counselor, and you just might find out."

THE NEXT MORNING SUSANNAH DROVE to her mother's home in Connecticut. Elias was lingering over the paper, still in his bathrobe, when a messenger arrived. The package was from Lydia, who must have sat up all night transcribing what she remembered. Bradshaw tipped the boy and shut the door, weighing the thick envelope in his hand. So much for a lazy afternoon puttering around the house.

Upstairs, in a small library off the locked Circle room, he spent a few minutes gathering books before seating himself at the desk. Lydia's pages before him, he worked for two hours before deciding he couldn't stomach any more.

His discoveries were, if anything, more sinister even than the swastika. Eleven symbols had been drawn, one to a page, and, of the eight he had identified, all of them were connected to the darkest, most malevolent deities in the world pantheon.

It was somehow obscene even to admit such names existed in this serenely elegant place he had created for himself. No computer here, no telephone, no electronic or mechanical devices at all—not even a typewriter. The most modern technological device within its walls, in fact, was the lock on the door, which wouldn't even yield to its proper key when he muttered a few words that made the place more secure than any lock. He let his gaze wander the oaken shelves, where the gilt-stamped spines of leather-bound books echoed the dark greens and crimsons and indigos of the Persian rug. Susannah might be standing in a similar room in her mother's house right now—similar but for the polished oak and the expensive rug in Elias's library. In the past, the Wingfields had produced any number of wealthy and influential Old and New Englanders, but Susannah's branch had been out of the money for several generations. They had little besides the big old house built in 1796, and the books—thousands of volumes collected by an unbroken succession of rabid bibliophiles. Maybe that was where all the money had gone, he mused, knowing he was avoiding Lydia's list by thinking about Susannah.

*"Judge Bradshaw?"*

*He didn't glance up from the file on his desk. The new candidate for assistant/ associate/gopher had arrived; great résumé, nice voice on the phone, who cared about the rest? She'd last only a few months, anyway. None of them could cope with him longer than that.*

*"Good morning, Ms. —" What the hell was her name again?*

*"Wingfield," she supplied.*

*A very nice voice, he amended, not looking at her. "I don't have time for an interview this morning. See Mrs. Osbourne and reschedule for tomorrow."*

*"Certainly, Your Honor."*

*He would never know how she did it, but the temperature in his chambers dropped thirty degrees. He glanced up. All he saw as she stalked out the door were the outlines of a slender body and an opulence of wheat-gold hair.*

*The door didn't quite slam. He dug up her résumé. By the fifth line he was reaching for his intercom, requesting Mrs. Osbourne to have Ms. Wingfield wait.*

*"Why aren't you still a prosecutor?" he said without preamble as she walked back into his office. "Or in private practice? Or aiming for your own judgeship?"*

*Seating herself in the brown leather chair before his desk, cool as a cloud and just as remote, she replied, "I got frustrated in the prosecutor's office. I got bored in private practice. I don't want to be a judge."*

*"Then what do you want, exactly?"*

"I don't have a clue. My father says I'm unfocused, my sisters think I'm crazy, and my mother wants me to settle down and raise grandchildren."

"Still don't know what you want to be when you grow up?"

"Oh, I knew that when I was eight. I've just never found an aspect of the law that suits me."

"I don't do guidance counseling in my spare time. For one thing, I have no spare time—and neither will you, working for me."

"If I'd wanted a life," she retorted, green eyes crinkling at the corners as she smiled, "I'd've followed my mother's advice a long time ago."

"You start this afternoon," he heard himself say.

"If it's all the same to you, I'd prefer tomorrow morning. A friend is visiting from Virginia and I promised to take her to lunch."

He settled back in his chair and regarded her thoughtfully. "So you keep your promises, do you, no matter what?"

"As a matter of fact, I do."

"Even if your new boss wants you to start this afternoon?"

"I didn't expect to get this job."

"Why not?"

Before she could answer, Mrs. Osbourne appeared in the open doorway and said, "Ms. McClure is here for you, Ms. Wingfield."

Virginia, McClure—couldn't be. He'd heard about her—every Magistrate in North America had heard about her. It just wasn't believable that this would be the same woman—

Elias grimaced, recalling his birthday dinner at Chanterelle, and the note Holly had sent him via the waiter: *Wake up and smell the cappuccino—you'll have a much happier birthday if you do.* His expression resolved into a wry smile. Yellow roses for redheads, white for blondes, pink for brunettes—and red for the morning after your first night together.

Elias pushed his chair back and rubbed his hands over his face. He had spent the day with, among others, Collin de Plancy's *Dictionaire Infernale*, Francis Barrett's *The Magus*, and the *Grimoire* of Pope Honorius. Not exactly cheery company, these pantheons of devils and hierarchies of demons, with guides to their manifestations and powers and filthy little tricks. It was disgusting to think of Susannah in this room.

He generously gave himself the no-brainer choice between the refuge of Susannah and the further research he knew he ought to do this evening, rose from the desk, locked the library door behind him, and went downstairs to make dinner reservations at their favorite restaurant.

# Twelve

"ARE YOU SURE YOU WANT to do this?"

"You went to Easter Mass with me," Evan replied. "The least I can do—"

Holly slouched in a kitchen chair and peered up at him. "I still don't know why we went to church. You didn't confess, you didn't take Communion—"

"I took you to church to see if you'd melt when you touched the holy water."

"What am I, the Wicked Witch of the West?"

"Don't let any houses fall on you today. I got plans for tonight." He leaned down to kiss her nose. "I'll bring the wine—and the food. Don't you go near that stove."

When he was gone, Holly chewed a thumbnail, caught herself at it, and scowled. Why he would want to witness a Sabbat was perfectly understandable; why he would want to participate was completely beyond her.

*Well, of course,* she thought suddenly, and laughed aloud. *It's Beltane. And if we're gonna do this, we might as well do it up right, with all the pagan bells and witchy whistles.*

So she phoned her two favorite authorities—Alexander Singleton and Nicholas Orlov—for advice on planning the perfect Beltane.

DENISE DIDN'T PLAN RITUALS. She starred in them—and Beltane was her truest role. Invitations had been arriving since March; all she need do was select a venue.

After some sorting she had decided on three possible locations: an estate on Long Island, an oceanfront mansion in New Jersey, or an exquisite Manhattan penthouse. Each had drawbacks. The beach property was a dream, and as private as could be wished, but it was owned by the Ken and Barbie of wanna-

be vampires. The penthouse gig would include a predominately gay audience—
entertaining in their way, but inappropriate for the holiday. So Long Island it
was.

A phone call to her host announced her acceptance of his invitation; he was
thrilled, and promised to send a car for her at seven. She made a mental note
not to be ready until seven thirty; half of being a true diva was making them
wait. The other half was giving them even more than they expected when she finally showed up. She had honed both to a fine art.


EVAN ARRIVED AT HOLLY'S PLACE before sunset, juggling grocery bags and a
florist's box while he let himself in and locked the door behind him. Luscious
fragrances were in the air. He wondered about their meaning and purpose—
everything had meaning and purpose in ritual magic. That was the whole reason
for rituals: to make a person think beyond the ordinariness of everyday life.

How ordinary could life be when you were in love with a Witch?

Grinning to himself, he walked through to the kitchen, noting that the living room door was closed, and began unloading the sacks of food. His research had been fun—though he'd been astonished at how many different
foods were considered aphrodisiacs. Bananas, okay, that was obvious—but
pine nuts?

He'd chosen asparagus and celery to dip into salmon mousse and feta pesto,
featuring the puzzling pine nuts. And there was red wine, in which he'd steeped
ginger, cinnamon, and a split vanilla bean according to a recipe. After choosing a
couple of wineglasses and dumping the munchies into serving bowls, he arranged
everything on a silver tray and left it on the kitchen counter. In the same cabinet
as the tray was a cut crystal vase; he filled it with water and the flowers, hoping
Holly would appreciate their symbolism. Three each of red tulips, yellow tulips,
orange roses, crimson roses—all of them having to do with love, desire, and
passion—and a single golden rose for perfection. Standing back from his work,
he nodded satisfaction, and then went looking for Holly.

A note was taped on her bedroom door: *Try the bathroom.* He did. On the
mirror was another note, this one a list of instructions.

1. Light the candles. Fill the tub. Use the bath salts from the green bowl.
2. Choose one stone from each glass bowl on the counter, and place in
   the water.
3. Take a bath.
4. Put on the bathrobe.
5. Get your gorgeous Irish ass into the living room, and bring the stones
   with you.

Fifteen minutes later, clean and relaxed and wearing the thin white silk bathrobe, he went through the Show Office to the living room. And found it transformed.

The furniture had been pushed back against the walls, leaving a cleared space before the hearth. A circular sisal rug about ten feet across had replaced the worn old carpet, and on this was her little triangular table. To one side was the vase of flowers; to the other, the tray of food and wine. Four unlit candles rested in flat silver dishes at what he assumed were the cardinal points of the compass: green, yellow, red, blue. Exactly the colors of the four stones in his hand, he realized. Holly, her hair loose on her shoulders, her body covered by a white robe that matched his, stood by a window. She turned as he entered, and smiled.

"The flowers are gorgeous."

"Y'know, I actually had fun doing the research. What do we do first?"

"You really want the whole thing?" she asked. "Casting the Circle, calling the Quarters?"

"I want the whole thing," he affirmed.

"It's been a while since I did this on my own. I had to read up on it and—"

"Stop blithering and get on with it."

"Yassuh, Marshal Lachlan, suh." Gesturing for him to join her on the sisal rug, she knelt in its center. He sat facing her, cross-legged, glad for the silk that separated his bare ass from the scratchy weave.

"Let's see which rocks you picked," Holly said, and as he handed them over she grinned. "I might've known. The blue one is lapis, Stone of the Pharaohs. Malachite—the green one—is the masculine principle. You don't bother to hide it, do you?"

His only reply was a look of sweet innocence. "What about the others?"

"I'd need Uncle Alec to interpret the more esoteric stuff, but the basics are—" She laughed. "—pretty basic! Just what I'd expect from you. I've seen people pick out rocks that are as accurate about their personalities as any psychological testing. Red jasper is very lucky, very protective—and is said to help maintain passion," she added mischievously. "The golden topaz is the most interesting of the bunch, actually. Mental clarity and personal power, among other things."

"And yours? What do they say about you?"

"Now we're getting into magic," she smiled. "Yours and mine together are something fierce. Garnet, citrine, aventurine, and turquoise—briefly, sex and devotion, confidence and energy, love and healing, happiness and luck. Between us, we've got it all pretty much covered." She rose and placed her four stones beside the four candles, matching color to color. "Set yours on the other side of mine. Good. Now we're ready."

She lit the incense—not with a match, but simply by gazing at it a moment and gesturing very slightly with her right hand. A tang of cinnamon wafted on the smoke. Then the candles, similarly lighted. Next she lifted her small chalice of water, and finally held up a little dish of salt. All the while she chanted:

> *"East is Air, and sweetest scent of lovers' trysting passions spent.*
> *South is Fire of deepest red to warm our souls, our hearts, our bed.*
> *West is Water, sweetly flowing, cleansing, freeing, wisely knowing.*
> *North is Earth that yearns for tilling, rich soft soil, warm and willing.*
> *Sweet Lady, Queen of Earth and Night, Proud Lord, King of Fire and Day.*
> *We our passion and trust do plight; bless us lovers this First of May."*

IT WAS THE MOST INCREDIBLE house Denise had ever seen—not that she would admit it to her hosts. They were dot-com zillionaires who, lacking anything resembling taste, still had the smarts to hire someone to do their shopping for them. Either that, Denise reflected as the limo pulled around the circular gravel drive, or they simply told their minions to buy the absolute unqualified best.

Which this mansion definitely was. A robber baron of the Victorian era had spared none of his questionably acquired fortune to build a Gothic fantasy of turrets and spires, crenellations and pointed arches. Originally the summer residence of a large family, forty-six rooms and who-knew-how-many baths were centered around a courtyard, where the limo purred to a stop.

Denise waited for the driver to open her door. Her host and hostess, dressed in the epitome of tweed country-house taste, emerged from a double oak door to welcome her.

So pleased you could be here, such a delight, read all your books and love them, what can we get you to drink, come meet our other guests. Denise smiled and nodded and was hard put to contain her surprise when she glimpsed an unexpected face at the far end of the living room.

The bookstore owner. What was his name? He saw her, silvery-blue eyes suddenly alight, and made his way through the throng to her side.

He was introduced as Noel, and whereas his gray trousers, casual black shirt, and battered sneakers were nowhere near appropriate, Denise sensed the authority of real power that made everyone else seem not only overdressed but insignificant.

Interesting, she decided, accepting a small glass of very old, very pricey sherry. Reminded of her weeks-ago encounter with him, she was also remembering her first try at snagging Holly McClure's lover. *Bon dieu de merde*, what a night it would be if he were here—

"I think you and I are the only true aficionados present," Noel said softly.

He had followed her over to admire a hearth big enough to roast an ox, a stag, and a couple of small boar, and still have room for the soup cauldron. Denise ran a fingertip along the outline of a flower carved into the stone—hyacinths were prominently featured in all the décor, presumably the original owner's favorite flower—and glanced up at him through her lashes.

"Amateur night," she murmured. "But entertaining nonetheless. I'm surprised to see you here."

"Didn't they tell you? I'm the chief entertainment."

She met his gaze, her brows arching. She hadn't approved him on her host's list of participants.

"Ringmaster only," he added. "I leave the . . . celebrating . . . to others. How did the spell work, by the way?"

"Well enough." She gave a shrug. In fact, her efforts appeared to have had little, if any, effect. But she wasn't about to admit that to Noel.

He required no such admission, evidently. "They must have something on you—something powerful." He paused to sip his drink. "Mojo bag? Poppet? Maybe even your Measure?"

Denise laughed to cover annoyance—and nerves. "The first two are beneath their exalted scholarly notice. As for the third—if they did, and if it really worked, would I be here tonight?"

"Depends," he replied in an infuriatingly casual drawl. "Are we talking the Magistratum here? If so—"

"You're extremely curious," she remarked, looking up at him through her lashes. "One might even say 'nosy.'"

"I like my merchandise to give satisfaction," he countered. "If it doesn't, I like to find out why. What you're up against that's so potent."

She started to reply that it was nothing that need concern him, then abruptly reconsidered. He knew a lot; he had resources at his store; there was a certain power about him. Perhaps he could help her. Galling though it was, she had to acknowledge that maybe she *did* need some help. She wanted Elias Bradshaw and Holly McClure damaged.

So instead of telling Noel to mind his own business, she murmured, "If you run across anything useful against a Spellbinder, let me know."

His shock was everything she could wish. But whatever he might have replied was lost when a young couple, neither of them older than twenty, approached. The boy was even taller and lankier than Noel, wearing doeskin pants, a white silk shirt with unmanageably full sleeves, and so many ear-cuffs with dangling charms that he clinked when he walked. The girl was a study in black and silver Goth with piercings in improbable places.

"I think it's just *wicked* cool that you're here tonight," the girl enthused to Denise. "My parents didn't think you'd come."

"Denise," said Noel, recovering himself, "this is Serenity, daughter of the house. And her friend, Scott."

"Hi," Scott said.

"Good evening," Denise replied, not showing her interest. He didn't much intrigue her personally—too skinny for her tastes, and much too young—but his presence here was a coup. His name on the list had made her laugh for a full ten minutes. The boy's father had spent an entire hour on someone's talk show excoriating her and her books as the Devil's work. Delicious.

"I've never been to a real Black Mass before," Serenity was saying. "But I turned eighteen last month, so I'm finally old enough—according to my parents."

Noel laughed. "Psychodrama, nothing more. Something to shock the children." He fixed his pale blue gaze on Scott. "Are you shocked?" But before he had a chance to answer, a bell rang. "Ah. I think we're about to begin." He held out an arm to escort Denise. "May I have the honor?"

Five minutes later everyone had changed out of whatever they'd worn to impress each other, and wore plain, utilitarian, equalizing black robes. Denise and Noel led the way down an appropriately dark stone staircase, carrying black candles, to the basement room fitted up for the rite.

Like the rest of the house, it was just a breath short of excessive. Outside, just one more turret or tower would have rendered the whole preposterous; inside, especially within this chamber, a single additional yard of dark crimson velvet would have created a parody. As it was, the surroundings were luxurious without opulence, atmospheric without exaggeration. Bare, rough-hewn stone walls with high, opaque transom windows in small alcoves; velvet chaise longue rife with pillows; silver-veined black marble plinth on which rested the ceremonial tools. Denise approved.

As people arranged themselves—the twelve chosen men claiming their places, the other men and women finding vantage points—Denise inspected the accoutrements. The candelabrum was particularly fine: thirteen fat black candles, six to either side of a high central taper, the whole made of silver stems writhing about a beautiful young man with delicate horns. The bell was brass, as were the thurible, incense boat, chalice, and aspergillum—the last in the shape of a phallus of exceptionally heroic dimensions.

When everyone was in place, Noel nodded to their hostess. She rang the little bell nine times. Noel sighed quietly into the ensuing silence.

*"In nomine Magni Dei Nostri Satanus introibo ad altare Domini Inferi."* In the Name of our Great God Satan I will go in to the altar of the Infernal Lord.

Denise gave a sigh of her own. Latin; swell. She supposed the decisions of Vatican II regarding use of the vernacular wouldn't have much influence on this bunch. Noel had an amazing voice: deeply resonant, compellingly sensual. As she stood beside the chaise, bare feet warming the cool stones beneath her, she mused that a voice such as his might almost make her start believing in all this shit.

"*Domine Satanus, Tua est terra. Orbem terrarum et plentitudinem ejus Tu fundasti. Justitia et luxuria praepartia sedis Tuae. Sederunt principes et adversum me loquebantur, et iniqui persecuti sunt me. Adjura me, Domine Satanus meus.*" Thine is the Earth, Lord Satan. Thou hast founded the Earth and the fullness thereof. Justice and luxury are the preparation of Thy Throne. Princes sat and spoke against me, and the wicked persecuted me. Help me, Lord Satan.

Noel spread his arms wide as if to embrace the assembly. "*Dominus Inferus vobiscum.*" The Infernal Lord be with you.

And they responded, "*Et cum tuo.*" And with you also.

The thurible and incense boat were brought forward by their host. Noel reached into a pocket of his robe and sprinkled incense on burning coals once, twice, thrice, saying, "*Incensum istud ascendat ad Te, Dominus Inferus, et descendat super nos beneficium Tuum.*" May this incense rise before Thee, Infernal Lord, and may Thy blessing descend upon us.

She watched him, this long and lanky bookseller who ought to have been awkward but was instead oddly lithe, disturbingly graceful, as he censed the chalice, the candelabrum—and her. But all response within her dissipated when the smell of the incense flowed across her. This was her least favorite part of any rite: the stink. Asphalt from the streets had been specified long ago by some fussy idiot, so asphalt from the streets it was, mixed in with the bitterness of myrrh and the traditional "flying" herbs: henbane, datura, and nightshade. Knowing these to be psychedelic, hallucinogenic, and deleriant if cured in certain ways, Denise closed her eyes and breathed deeply of the smoke. Despite the stench, it would add to the experience.

She kept her eyes shut and listened to the resonant cadences of Noel's voice, gradually recapturing the pinpricking excitement of her own sensuality. South, then East, then North, and finally West, he circled her with scent and power and sound.

"In the name of Satan, I bless thee—in the name of Lucifer, the Morning Star, I bless thee—in the name of Belial, Prince of the Earth and Angel of Destruction, I bless thee—in the name of Leviathan, I bless thee."

"*Ave Satanus,*" responded the congregants.

Hail Satan.


"WHEN DO WE EAT? More importantly, when do we—?"

"You're incorrigible. Just relax and enjoy, okay? This next part is from Aunt

Lulah—she sent me the wood chips." Holly took a little bag from the pocket of her robe and upended its contents into her palm. As she sprinkled the slivers into the cauldron, she half-sang,

*"Birch to honor the Lady of Summer,*
*Oak for the Lord of the Day,*
*Rowan for magic*
*Willow for mourning,*
*and Hawthorns for the fey."*

She paused. "That's faerie folk, just in case there are any hovering about."

"Don't expect me to be skeptical, lady," he told her. "Granna Maureen always said her family had its very own *bean sidhe*, who yelled its head off whenever a man of the clan was in danger."

"Really? You didn't tell me that when we talked about Ireland last fall."

"I was kinda distracted back then," he explained blandly, "tryin' to figure out how to get you in the sack."

"One-track mind," she sighed. "Where was I? Oh, yeah—

*"Hazel for wisdom,*
*Apple for love,*
*Vine for the Earth,*
*and Fir for rebirth."*

The wood chips blazed, a mix of scents that merrily tickled his nose. "One of these days I'm going to have to rework that so it all rhymes.

*"We celebrate the Year's renewal*
*With Flame and Wine, with Scent and Jewel*
*We honor Life and Love this night*
*And with desire our troth do plight."*

A gesture to the wine and glasses invited him to pour for them both. When he had done so, she toasted him and said, "Beltane is the night when our ancestors in Ireland met in the greenwood after the long cold winter, and reaffirmed that they were alive by making love. It is Tana's Day, symbolized by the Sword of Nuada, one of the four magical treasures of the Tuatha, which we in modern times call the athame. Beltane is a night of fire and flowers, of light and energy, of feeling and being. It is the music of the lute and the guitar, all stringed instruments whose notes weave the song of the universe." Smiling, she toasted him once more. "And tonight, *a chuisle*, that song is me and thee."


THEY WERE ALL NAKED NOW, except for Denise. As she gave a shrug of one shoulder and her black silk robe cascaded to the floor—exactly as it had been designed to do—she was gratified to see that every man, even those not among her twelve, instantly responded. She let her body slide sinuously onto the chaise longue, and within seconds their visible response had become imperious need. She saw it glitter in eyes of brown, blue, green, and gray, heard it rasp in quickened breathing, smelled it in their sweat-beaded skin.

Except Noel. He was still wearing his robe, no indicative swelling outlined by the material as he moved toward her. Neither did his eyes flicker, nor his nostrils flare, nor his flesh exude the musk of desire. He approached her, seeming to float, so supple were his movements, and extended his hands, palms downward, over her body.

"*Dominus Inferus, miserere nobis. In spiritu humilitatis, et in animo contrito suscipiamur a Te, Domine Satanus; et sic fiat sacrificium nosterum in conspectu tuo hodie, ut placeat tibi. Veni, Magister Templi. Veni, Magister Mundi. Pleny sunt terra majestatis gloriae tuae.*" Infernal Lord, have mercy upon us. In a humble spirit, and with contrite heart, may we be received by Thee, Lord Satan; and may our sacrifice be so offered as to be pleasing in Thy sight. Come, Lord of the Temple. Come, Lord of the World. Earth is full of the majesty of Thy glory.

Denise shifted slightly, anticipating. But Noel wasn't finished. The bell rang again—the silly thing was beginning to get on her nerves—as he went on, this time in plain English:

"O mighty and terrible Lord of Darkness, we entreat You to accept this rite, which we offer that You may make us prosper under Thy protection, and cause the fulfillment of our desires and the destruction of our enemies."

Then he did something Denise had never seen done before at such rites. He took from his pocket an elaborately carved wooden crucifix, about eight inches tall and touched here and there with gold, and held it high to all assembled.

"Behold the body of Jesus Christ, lord of the humble and king of the slaves. *Jesus*," he sneered, "crafter of hoaxes, swindler, deceiver! Since the day of your birth from the bowels of a false virgin, you have failed. Imposter, Filth of Bethlehem, cursed Nazarene, we drive deeper the nails into your hands, cram the crown of thorns upon your brow, bring blood from the dry wounds of your sides."

Denise was annoyed. And bored. If she'd wanted a sermon, she would've stayed home with the television tuned to an evangelical channel. Why didn't he just get on with it?

"Great Lord Satan, Infernal Majesty, condemn the pretender to suffer in perpetual anguish. O Prince of Darkness, call forth Thy legions and send the Christians to their doom!" Noel spat on the crucifix. "Vanish into nothingness, fool of fools! You are nothing, compared to the majesty of Satan!" He immersed the painted wood in the cauldron and fire leapt a full ten feet high, crackling angrily.

Denise repressed a peevish sigh. Ringmaster, he'd said? Exhibitionist.

"NOW COMES THE 'LET ME count the ways' portion of the evening," said Holly. "We take turns wrapping a ribbon around the candle, and say what we love about each other."

Evan took one end of the red ribbon. The candle smelled of vanilla, and the combination with cinnamon made him think of baking day at Granna Maureen's. "Me first," he said, passing his end of the ribbon to her around the candle. "I love your freckles."

She wrinkled her nose at him, and gave him her end of the ribbon. "I love your dragon's eyes."

"I love your hot Irish temper."

She grinned. "I love your hot Irish ass!"

He winked back. "I love your smarts, writer-lady."

After a moment's pause, she turned serious. "I love your total dedication to everything you do."

"I love your face when you're sleeping."

"I love your power."

"My—? Oops, sorry. I love your voice."

"I love yours—except when you start singing!"

"I love your rasty sense of humor."

"I love it that you can match me quote for quote from *A Hard Day's Night* and *Star Wars*."

"I love your lectures."

"Liar! I love your stupid ostrich-hide cowboy boots."

"*I'm* a liar?" They were running out of ribbon, and he hadn't even gotten started. "I love it when you call me *a chuisle*."

"I love it when you smile."

"I love it that most people have personalities, but you have character."

She looked startled for an instant. Then: "I love your pride."

Last bit of red silk. "I love your magic."

Knotting the ends, she replied, "I love *you*."

She lit the candle with a little flick of her fingers. "Y'know, I'm getting pretty good at that again. I lost the knack of it for a while."

"There's something else you're pretty good at. Do we get to practice now?"

WITHIN A FEW MOMENTS THE wooden crucifix had burned to ashes. Noel sifted them down into the chalice, a tiny smile curving his wide mouth. His eyes were alight now, his brow sheened with sweat, as he used the huge bronze phallus to stir the ashes into the wine. He drank, then presented the chalice to each worshipper. *"Accipe calicem voluptatis carnis in nomine Domini Inferi."* Accept the chalice of voluptuous flesh in the name of the Infernal Lord.

Replacing the chalice on the black marble plinth, he turned to Denise. Now his face was radiant, exultant, and he ran his eyes over her body as he groped for the bronze phallus. He held the thing as if he were holding his own. Suddenly Denise realized that to him, it *was* his own.

*"Ecce sponsa Satanus,"* he proclaimed. *"Domino Inferi in medio ejus est. Qui stitit, veniat; et qui vult, accipiat aquam vitae."* Behold Satan's bride. The Infernal Lord is in the midst of her. He that thirsteth, let him come; and he that will, let him take of the water of life.

With the phallus he pointed to a wonder of Nordic manhood, who came forward and spread Denise's thighs.

*"Fornicemur ad gloria Domine Satanus,"* Noel invited in that rich, burgundy-and-silk voice. Fornicate to the glory of Our Lord Satan.

HOLLY HELD UP HER PALMS to Evan. He laced their fingers together, watching candlelight shimmer in her eyes. Quietly, almost formally, she said, "The Great Rite is ours to celebrate—in Greek, the *Hieros Gamos*, the Sacred Marriage of seed and soil, rain and earth, God and Goddess." She smiled slightly, almost shyly. "Thee and me, *a chuisle mo chroi.*"

It was strange and stunning, how different it felt, making love to her amid the candles and the wine and the scents and the little chunks of brightly colored stones. It was just him, just her, something they'd done a thousand times—but it somehow was more this time. Not only an act of love, an act of—belief?

Or maybe even faith?

The thought snagged in his mind. His Catholic education, in the form of Sister Mary Lazarus, advanced to bring her four-foot-long aluminum pointer down on his knuckles—

Holly seized his face between her hands, laughed up at him, and demanded, "Hey! Pay attention!"

So he let the word *faith* escape him, and chased more pleasurable and much less articulate things, and lost himself in loving her.

Yet at some point, he couldn't have said when, blue eyes darkened to brown—flecked green, russet hair paled to blonde, the sprawl of white silk beneath them transformed to the dark red of blood, and the giving body in his arms began to *take*—predatory, greedy, insatiable.

It lasted only an instant; Holly was Holly again, in a circle of candlelight. And he was in her, and she was around him, and together they rejoiced in an act of true faith in living.


*"PLACEAT TIBI, DOMINE SATANUS, OBSEQUIUM servitutis meae; et praesta ut sacrificuum quod occulis Tuae majestatis obtuli, tibi sit acceptabile, mihique et omnibus pro quibus illud obtuli."* May the homage of my service be pleasing unto Thee, Lord Satan, and grant that the sacrifice I have offered in the sight of Thy majesty may be acceptable to Thee and win forgiveness for me and for all those for whom I have offered it.

Not even halfway through her twelve chosen, Denise was tired of the whole foolish mess. Did they think she was a whore? Only there for them to fuck under the pretense of a ritual offering? Number Three—the Chinese guy from last November—had been a real stallion, and she was starting to enjoy herself when he unexpectedly finished, leaving her far behind. Number Five was occupied now, in full rut. Denise could have been his own right hand for all the attention he paid to her pleasure, and she was monumentally peeved. Despite several such evenings, she hadn't had a truly spectacular night since—

—since Holly McClure had taken her Measure.

Was that it? Or had her own spell been directed back at her? *Merde,* what if it had all gone wrong? Was Holly that powerful? Was Bradshaw? All the little forgettings and irritations—had that been only the beginning?

Grinding her teeth, she seized her current lover's face between her hands and forced him to look at her. His surprise mirrored hers: she hadn't even realized that a new man had come to her. Not even a man—the boy, Scott, son of a Fundamentalist Christian Reverend, the jewelry on his ears bloodily shining by the light of Noel's flaunting fire.

"Fuck me like you mean it," Denise growled. After an instant's frozen shock, he did. His eyes turned wild—incense smoke, she told herself, wishing it would take her as thoroughly. Maybe then she wouldn't have to look at Noel. His silvery-blue gaze was focused, cold, and not quite sane. He loomed over her where she lay on her back amid the silk and sweat and spilled semen. He snaked his long fingers around Scott's throat from behind—delicately at first, then more deeply, and just as the boy gasped and arched and spent himself in Denise, Noel snapped his neck.

"Behold the Sacrifice," he murmured as the boy crumpled to the stones. "Life force, psychic power, arcane energy—all released by death at the supreme moment of existence. All *mine*." He bowed to the altar, then turned to the congregation with his left hand extended *in cornu*, in the shape of horns, saying: *"Fratres et sorores, debitores sumus carni."* Brothers and sisters, we are debtors to the flesh.

Another man started forward for his turn, tottering on drug-addled legs. When the boy did not move, the newcomer blinked several times, then blurted, "Is he—?" Stumbling backward: "He's *dead!*"

"Yes," Noel confirmed with a nod and a secretive smile. "He is. *Ego vos benedictio in Nomine Magni Dei Nostri Satanus, Ite, missa est.*" I bless you all in the Name of our Great God, Satan. Go, you are dismissed.

Shrieks carved through the firelit chamber. The celebrants hurtled, naked and horrified, up the stairs, staggering into each other, and flames fluttered like silk flags in the wind of their flight. Only one person remained behind, the girl Serenity, who knelt beside the boy and begged him to talk to her, to wake up, to be all right.

Denise was as paralyzed as the night her Measure had been taken, unable to flick an eyelash. Noel stuffed his hands in the pockets of his robe, watching with interest as the girl pleaded with the dead boy. The shift of his robe showed Denise that only now was he erect. When he turned pale eyes on her, she had an instant's perfect terror that he was about to use that erection on her.

"Don't worry," he reassured her, his smile curling crookedly. "They all saw it, they all witnessed it, and they all have something to lose if they talk about it."

And so, she realized, did she.

The incense drugs purged by the adrenaline rush of fear, she lurched to her feet, snagging up her black silk robe with one hand. "Stay away from me," she hissed, backing toward the stairs. "You sick, twisted bastard—don't you ever come near me again!"

"But you make such an inspiring altar," he murmured, laughing at her without sound. "I can't wait to read about this in your next novel."

Thirteen

DINNER WITH THE LACHLANS: Evan knew Holly was dreading it. So was he. But there was no way to avoid it and he'd put it off as long as he could—for damned near three months, in fact. Father, sister, brother-in-law, two nieces and a nephew, and three widowed aunts escaping Boston's July inferno. God help her—and him.

On their way out the door, her phone rang. She let the machine pick it up, cursing under her breath when it turned out to be her publisher.

"Holly, my precious sweetness, save my wretched life and check your e-mail the instant you get in—please please please!"

She looked at Evan, who shrugged.

"He sounds pretty desperate," she said. "I'd better go see what he wants."

Five minutes later she was back, fuming. "Are you ready for this?" she demanded. "Walter wants me to go to Kenya! Ben Wolaver—you don't know him and be thankful for it, thinks he's the greatest thing since movable type—he's got pneumonia. Who the hell gets pneumonia in summer?"

"Ben Wolaver, evidently. What's the gig?"

"Two weeks of seminars in Nairobi and Mombassa. Now, there's a climate I really want to experience in the middle of July!"

"They have air-conditioning," he remarked.

"At that fancy hotel they're dangling in front of my nose—you damn betcha they have air-conditioning. Plus a big fat honorarium, all expenses paid, anything I want—yeah, they're making it really sweet."

"Gonna go?"

"Hell, no! There's a wedding to plan, and an engagement party, and—" She frowned at him as they got into the elevator. "Why do you want me to go?"

"Didn't say that," he parried.

"Not in so many words."

"It's your work. And you like teaching. You turned down an artist-in-residence for this summer because of me," he reminded her.

"I wasn't doing you any favors. I hate Chicago." As the elevator doors opened, Holly tossed him the car keys. "Okay, what? Are the jitters setting in?"

"No." He gave her scowl for scowl. "What, you think I'm gonna ask you to marry me, then send you a text message to say it's over from twelve thousand miles away?"

"Well, what am I supposed to think?"

He waited until they were on the street, the BMW purring like a pleased panther, before saying, "Just that you might want to take some time, think it over."

"Are you saying *you* want time to think? Are you having doubts? No bullshit, Evan, I need the truth."

"Holly, I swear I don't have a doubt in the world—except maybe about what kind of husband I'm gonna be to you—"

"You're not your father, I keep telling you. When are you going to listen?" Her voice gentled and she brushed a caress to his hand. "You could just as easily be like your grandfather, the one you're named for, whose wife called him *a chuisle*."

"I hope that's how it'll be. Don't go to Kenya if you don't want to, but don't turn it down on my account, either. That's all I'm sayin'."

"No, it's not. What is it you're not telling me?"

"Like I said. I want you to be sure. I can be pretty irresistible when I'm in the immediate vicinity—" He tried a grin; she wasn't buying. "Holly . . . I don't want to feel like I'm holding you back or holding you down—"

Her temper exploded. "That's the stupidest thing you've ever said! Did it escape your notice that I didn't cancel my European trip? You don't interfere with my work. I'd never allow it."

"I know," he said, not fully successful at keeping the wryness from his voice.

She was silent for a few moments. Then: "Do you remember that first week, when we were at dinner and Pete called you out on a triple homicide?"

"Yeah." He frowned again, bewildered. "So?"

"You didn't want me to come. Once we were there, you ordered a cop to take me home. It wasn't because the scene was horrifying—it was, but you didn't want me there because you wanted to keep me separate from that world."

He thought it over. "I didn't want you touched by all that filth. I was pretty sure you weren't gonna faint or anything—it's just such a shit-hole I deal with sometimes, Holly, you're above all that."

"No, you *want* me to be above all that. You'd do the same thing if I was a waitress or a secretary. When you talk about your cases, you keep things back. Like about the priest. Usually I don't mind—you tell me what you need to, what I need to know so I can understand. But I've never deluded myself that I'm any help to you. Our minds work differently. We both use our training, what we know, what our instincts tell us, but you're in the here-and-now—and I spend my working life centuries in the past. Maybe—maybe there's only one place we both belong: the world we make between us. It's ours, and nobody else gets inside it."

He drove in silence for a while. "Every night I see people goin' home to their families. I want that. I always have. It's expected, part of the life story—you know, what you're supposed to do with yourself. But I do want a home, Holly. I want kids with you. A world that's separate from everything else, where nobody can get at us, nobody can find us—I didn't know how much I wanted it, until you." He smiled ruefully. "Is there anything else about me that you know and I don't?"

"The day we stop surprising ourselves is the day we start to die."

"Did you write that?"

"Not yet—but I will!" She smiled back. "So. Kenya. You want me to go."

"I want you to do what you want to do because *you* want to do it. Not because of me."

She repeated deliberately, "You want me to go."

"I guess maybe I do, some. Mostly I don't, but—"

"But you've got this idea in your head that it will prove you're not holding me back or holding me down. And they accuse women of being irrational!"

As he parked the car and pocketed the keys, he was wondering how he could ever find words to explain that as much as he loved her, his very apprehension of her being gone was what made him want her to go.

It didn't make any sense. Except it did, in a convoluted way. He wasn't used to depending on anyone. Childhood had taught him that relying on someone else for love, for comfort—a safe haven—was dangerous. Yet inside their world, his and Holly's, was his life. He didn't fool himself that he contributed much to that world. *Her* apartment, *her* things inside it; *her* arms wrapping him safe; *her* words making him clear to himself. *Her* eyes, to see himself in.

When she got back from Kenya (he knew she'd go; the opportunity was too good to miss), he'd marry her. After this one last test. Not of her; of himself. To see if he could conquer the dread of being without her.


THEY WALKED INTO THE RESTAURANT at 7:25. Evan's beeper went off at 7:29. He borrowed her cell phone and went outside while she was escorted to their reserved table. When he came back, he looked angry enough to chew the stainless steel bar.

"I'm gonna kill Carlos Hermangildez. He was supposed to cover for me tonight. He broke a finger playin' softball this afternoon. Softball! He couldn't hit a beach ball with a two-by-four."

"Go," she said.

"I can't just leave you here to explain—"

"They're already on their way. Go. I'll make your excuses."

"Holly, let's just leave a note with the—"

"Are you out of your mind? Even if they expect something that rude from you, it'd look terrific for me to stand them up. Evan, *go*. It'll be okay."

He shook his head, smiling slightly. "Did I ever tell you—"

"—that you worship and adore me? That I'm the love of your life? That I—"

Leaning down, he kissed her lips. "That I'll wrap this up as quick as I can and come rescue you. Just don't turn your back on my old man—he likes big Irish butts, too." And with that and a wink he was gone.

IT WAS GETTING ON FOR ten when Lachlan finally returned to the restaurant. Holly was at a booth in the bar with a brandy, a cigar, and an ashtray. Her back was to him, shoulders a little less square than usual, russet hair coming loose from its upsweep. She reached to rub the back of her neck, and he saw her sigh deeply before drinking from her brandy.

*Rough evening, huh? I owe you big-time for this one, lady love.*

He paused to order a drink, and when he turned back toward her table, a tall, trendy man with carefully sun-streaked hair was trying to hit on her. Lachlan took one long, angry step, intending to shove the guy's tie down his throat—and then made himself approach slowly. He'd never watched her react to other men's advances before. This might be interesting.

"So who's the fool who left you here all alone?"

She didn't even look up. "He's six-four, two-fifteen, and standing right behind you."

The man laughed—and half-turned, and saw Evan. Who smiled, all teeth.

"Uh—sorry—"

Lachlan made a shooing gesture with his hand. The man fled.

Holly was regarding him with brows arched above slightly unfocused eyes, and before he could speak, said, "Hi, sailor. New in town?"

"As a matter of fact, yeah. You come here often?"

Blue eyes strafed him head to toe. "I could come just looking at you."

He damned near choked. Rallying, he slid into the booth opposite her. "I thought you were spoken for—you know, six-four, two-fifteen?"

"Oh, him." She contemplated the glowing end of the cigar. "He did leave me here all alone, in point of fact."

"Definitely a fool."

"It could have been worse." She was speaking very precisely, her words almost clipped—which told him she'd had a helluvalot to drink. "If he'd stayed,

he would have wrecked a very nice evening with his sister. She told me all about
him, and I told her all about him, and we agreed that he really is the biggest asshole ever to walk this sweet green Earth."

*Shoulda known,* he thought wryly. "What about the rest of the family?"

"Haven't met them. That's why I'm glad he wasn't here. 'Pissed off' wouldn't
even begin to describe it."

"What the hell happened?"

"Various and sundry for the kids. The father—"

"—was too drunk to go out in public." He rubbed his forehead, trying to
avert an incipient headache. "I'm sorry."

"I'm not. Maggie and I had a good time. I like her. She likes me, too—at
least, she said I wasn't as impossible for you as she thought I'd be."

"After I finish killing Carlos, I'm gonna kill my sister."

"Speaking of homicides, what went on tonight?"

"Gangbangers," he said shortly. "Federal warrant, my name on the file."

"Ah."

Grateful that she didn't push for details, he asked, "How'd you know it was
me just now? You had your back turned."

"Lovah-man," she drawled, "Ah could pick y'all outta a full house at Yankee
Stadium with mah eyes squeezed shut. Ah do believe it's called 'chemistry'?"

"And here I thought you were some kinda Witch or something." He grinned,
finished off his drink in two long swallows, and got to his feet. "Let's go. Unless
you're still waitin' for the other guy."

She looked him down and up, then concentrated her gaze below his belt.
"Looks like 'bout eight inches to me, when it gets all riled up." She stubbed out
her cigar. "Y'all'll do. C'mon, sailor."


THE NEXT MORNING LACHLAN LET Holly sleep in, waking her around noon
with a large cup of coffee. She opened bloodshot eyes on him and croaked out,
"Caffeine!" But before he could hand her the mug she paled, and her freckles
turned green, and she bolted for the bathroom.

He waited a decent interval, wondering how Maggie was feeling today.
Then he called out, "Holly?"

"Go away." She returned to bed and he plumped pillows behind her, trying
not to laugh as she gulped coffee and glowered at him. "I hate you," she announced.

"Wasn't my fault you drank like a fish last night."

"Fish don't drink." She paused, rubbing her temples. "At least, I don't think
they do. You might as well tell me—did I do anything felonious?"

"You don't remember the fight?"

"Nice try, Lachlan. I've never hit anyone in my life." She paused. "Except for a guy in high school who goosed me. I don't know which of us was more astonished when I backhanded him."

"Not you in a fight, me in a fight. With the guy you were trying to pick up. After he and I got into it, you started makin' book on who'd win."

She downed more coffee, then said, "How much did I make when you beat the crap out of him?"

"How d'you know I won?"

"Because there's not a mark on you. Q.E.D." Placing the coffee cup on the night table, she squinted at him. "So? Where're my winnings?"

"You lost."

"Huh?"

"I gotta tell ya my feelings are hurt. You bet the bartender two hundred bucks that I'd lose — and me your fiancé and the love of your life and everything —"

All at once a pillow slammed into his head. "You lying bastard —" With another groan, she collapsed. "Just kill me now, okay? Have mercy."

"Go back to sleep. You'll feel better tomorrow."

"No I won't. I'll be dead tomorrow."

"I ain't into necrophilia, babe."

She raised her head cautiously and squinted at him. "Huh?"

Jeeze, she was articulate today. He'd have to remember that: whenever he wearied of the river of words, a bottle of vodka made a mighty fine dam.

"Dinner?" he reminded her pointedly. "Champagne? Engagement ring? Fucking until dawn to celebrate? Like I said, I ain't doin' it with a corpse."

"If you don't go away and leave me alone, I'll get out my bolline and make sure you never do it again with anybody."

"HEY, BEAUTIFUL," HE MURMURED TO her as the maître d' escorted them to their table. "Did you know every man in the place is lookin' at you?"

She shook her head, smiling slightly. "They were glaring at *you*, Evan. You've got more hair and a better backside than any of them."

"Guys don't think like that."

"You don't, because you don't have to. You're the one with the great backside, after all. And besides that, every woman in here was staring at you. Except for a very few who were looking at me — wondering whether you're with me because I'm rich or because I'm good in bed."

"Both," he replied promptly, and bowed as he held out her chair.

The waiter arrived, unfurled napkins, presented menus, touted the evening's specials, and took their orders for drinks. When he had gone, Holly cocked her head to one side and regarded him meditatively.

"You know, there really ought to be a model or actress or somebody stagger-ingly gorgeous on your arm."

Evan's lips compressed for a moment. "Maggie told you about Donna, didn't she."

"Which one of all the hundreds was that?" Holly parried.

"Knock it off. Maggie told me later that Donna scared the shit out of her. I'd found somebody exactly like our mother—blonde, beautiful, and the center of the universe," he went on bitterly. "You worshipped her—or else."

"I think the way Maggie put it was 'dancing on a razor.'"

"That about sums it up. She was every kind of wrong for me."

"Doesn't make it any less painful that she left you," she murmured, then ventured, "And broke your heart."

"That was just pride," he said dismissively.

"You know what? I think I'm starting to like your stupid cowboy boots, even if you won't tell me the truth about where you got them." She saw his frown return with puzzlement at the non sequitur. Nice to know she could still throw him for a loop every so often. "They make you something less than absolutely perfect."

His lips twisted wryly. "Like when we're at one of your literary parties, with people tellin' me how brilliant you are—but I just spent an hour listenin' to you whine about screwin' up the plot so bad they oughta pay you *not* to write?"

"Just so. I keep asking myself 'Why me?' You think you're not smart enough for me, and I think I'm not pretty enough for you—but I'm the only one who's right."

"Bullshit." He signaled the hovering waiter. "I have a question for you," he said to the young man. "Would you say that this lady here is just average, very pretty, or a total knockout?"

"Does his tip depend on his answer?" Holly asked caustically.

"No, and shut up. Well?"

The waiter considered her. "Knockout," he said, grinning.

"Nice try, kid," Holly growled.

"It's the hair," he explained to Evan. "And the eyes."

"I think so, too. Bring her the escargot appetizer. I'll have lobster ravioli."

"Very good, sir." He turned, paused, turned around again, and said, "And the legs. Honest, ma'am."

When he left, she hissed, "That was *so* humiliating!"

"Why? Does his opinion matter to you?"

Narrowing her eyes at him, she asked silkily, "Do the opinions of the people at those cocktail parties matter to *you?*"

"Touché." He laughed softly, having made his point. "I think you're gor-geous, and you think I'm brilliant. Isn't that all that really matters?" When she shrugged, he sighed his exasperation. "Lady love, I'm about to ante up the engagement ring. Isn't this kind of a weird time to start all this?"

Appetizers, salads, and sourdough bread came and went. Pasta and wine, gelati and biscotti, espresso—knowing what was coming next, she excused herself to go to the ladies' room to get herself together. Sure enough, her mascara was smudged, and she'd left her repair kit in her other purse. Her hair was hopeless. The Italian freckles had faded back in May, but there were plenty left; she looked like Doris Goddamned Day photographed without Vaseline smeared over the lens. Plus she'd spilled sauce on her skirt.

*This* was what he wanted to marry?

She scrubbed at the splattering of red dots, and bits of paper towel rolled soggily into the silk. Why her? It wasn't that she'd taken for granted that he desired her—she'd just avoided thinking about it. Her response to him was so overpowering that even if she had sat down to think it through, it wouldn't have mattered. She'd been helpless from the instant she set eyes on him. She'd gone along for the ride, loving every minute of it—and only in the last few weeks realized that he had truly become what *a chuisle mo chroí* meant: the pulse of her heart.

Chucking the towel into the wastebasket, she glared at her reflected face in the mirror. *Idiot! The man of your dreams is about to make the engagement official, and all you can do is bitch about the spots on your dress—acting like you're still eighteen at the fancy college with the rich blue bloods, and you just know they're gonna smirk at your hillbilly accent and your hick clothes and your freckle-face—*

*—and suddenly in Chorale practice there's this scrawny sixteen-year-old next to you who it turns out is just as scared and nervous as you are, and you wind up eating lunch together and it's as if you'd known each other all your lives—*

Holly smiled, imagining Susannah's exasperation. *"Will you remember tonight because you spilled sauce on your dress? Or because that sweet gorgeous man is about to give you a ring worn by a woman who called her husband a chuisle? Get a grip, McClure!"*

As she returned to their table, Evan smiled and got to his feet. Champagne had been poured. As she sat down, he regarded her with arched brows.

"You want I should do the kneeling part again?"

She shook her head. "Once is enough in any relationship, Lachlan."

He resumed his chair and lifted his champagne flute. "Drink up. This is the good stuff."

She raised her glass to him and sipped. "'Good'? This is bottled sunlight!" As she set the glass down, she heard something rattle. Casting him a suspicious glance, she peered at the bubbles. "You didn't."

"Kinda risky, I know. You coulda swallowed it if you'd been thirsty enough."

She poked a finger into the glass. It was too tall. She had to drink the rest of the champagne and then upend the flute. Onto the tablecloth fell a delicate circle of platinum filigree.

Lacking a diamond.

They stared at the ring. Then, horrified, at each other.

"Oh God—" Holly felt her eyes widen. "You don't think I—"

"Did you?"

"I don't think so—" Frantically she turned the glass over again, shaking it. "Evan, I *couldn't* have swallowed it—"

"Are you sure?"

The glass finally yielded a small square of white-fire diamond. Holly let loose a tiny whimper of gratitude, and then couldn't help but giggle. Evan rolled his eyes and gave in to laughter.

"You want to know why?" he demanded. "*This* is why!"

"Because I make you laugh?"

"Because nothin's ever normal with you! It'd be just like you to've swallowed the goddamn diamond—"

"It's not my fault the stone came loose!"

"—havin' doubts practically at the altar—what am I gonna do with you?"

She grinned into his sparkling eyes. "Marry me." Giddy with relief, she slid off her chair and went down on one knee, primed to pop the question.

She heard silk rip.

"Umm—is there anything wrong, ma'am?"

Oh, splendid; the waiter. Very carefully she stood up, one hand on the jagged tear where the back seam of her dress used to be.

"Nice ass, too, right?" Evan asked the waiter.

"Very."

She glared. "This is *not* funny!"

"Sure it is," her intended said with infuriating sangfroid.

"If the lady has a wrap . . . ," the waiter ventured.

"The lady does *not* have a wrap," she snarled. "Evan, give me your jacket." As he made no move to comply: "Give me your goddamned jacket, Marshal, or I'll shoot you with your own goddamned gun."

"I think she means it, sir."

Shrugging out of his suit coat, Evan replied, "I *know* she means it."


IN DUE COURSE EVAN JOINED Holly in the restaurant's foyer, and in superbly well-mannered silence they waited for her car to be brought around. The merciful quiet lasted eighteen blocks—just long enough for Holly to start chuckling and Evan to start brooding. The pessimist in him was positive the diamond couldn't be reset before she left for Kenya. Being a fundamentally superstitious Irish Catholic, he didn't like the omen.

"Are you sulking?"

"No."

"C'mon, lover-man. We had a great dinner and laughed our asses off. I'd say that's a pretty successful evening. The only thing that got ruined was my dress."

All at once he swung the BMW in a tight U-turn.

"Where are we going?" Holly asked.

He gave her a sidelong smile. Eventually he stopped the car on Fifth Avenue. After hitting the emergency blinkers, he reached into his jacket pocket for the dashboard card that let him park wherever he damned well pleased.

"What are we doing at St. Patrick's?" Holly asked.

"We're goin' to church."

He popped the trunk and got out of the car. Sorting through the mess of jumper cables, CDs, coat, first aid kit, bottled water, snacks, and other effluvia, he located the plastic bag she kept a change of clothes in. The reason for this, she'd told him when asked, was that while at UCLA she'd stocked her car in case The Big One hit. When he pointed out that she lived in New York now and didn't have to worry about earthquakes, she informed him that hurricanes and blizzards weren't much fun to get stuck in, either. Slamming the trunk, he went to the passenger's side and waited for her to roll down the window. She did, giving him a sour look.

"Just get dressed," he said, shoving the clothes at her. "Can't go to church with your butt to the breeze."

She struggled into the jeans, with only a brief glimpse of bare breasts as she rid herself of the silk in favor of a workshirt. She got out of the car, he keyed the alarm system, and they went up the steps of St. Patrick's Cathedral.

"I'm not confessing," she warned as he opened the great doors.

"Neither am I."

"What are we here for?"

He didn't really have an answer.

Cool, soaring, beautiful—he tried to feel God's presence, but something was getting in the way. A few elderly women knelt in prayer; a middle-aged man emerged from a confessional; a priest was polishing the altar candlesticks. Lachlan bypassed the font, but halfway up the nave he paused to genuflect and cross himself. Holly didn't do likewise. He sat in the front pew, eyes on the Presence Lamp. She sat beside him, fidgeting. When he took her hand, she stilled.

"I wanted to give you the ring before you leave for Kenya," he began quietly. "I just wanted there to be something that means you're mine."

"Nothing could make me any more yours than I already am."

"I'd marry you right now, this minute, if I could."

The priest was limping toward them. "Something I can help you with?"

Another omen? After what he'd just said, to have a priest approach as if—

Holly was smiling slightly, shaking her head. "No, but thank you, Father."

"Go in peace." A gnarled hand sketched a cross over them, and he departed.

Holly said very softly, "I won't go to Kenya if you don't want me to. Ask me to stay and I will."

"You can't not go. And like I said, I want you to be sure about me. About us. I want you to have some time away."

"But you also want your ring on my finger." She slipped away from him and padded barefoot to a rank of votive candles flickering in red glass holders. He rose slowly to follow her, watching as she knelt and chose a candle from the box.

*"Salve, Regina, mater misericordiae, vita, dulcedo, et spes nostra, salve, salve Regina,"* she sang softly, lighting the candle—not bothering with the thin, lit taper provided for the purpose—and placing it with the others. Rising, she turned to him. Her expression was slightly defensive, slightly defiant. "I've offered Fire to Her in every church I've ever been in."

He stroked stray curls from her cheeks, smiling a little. "Holly Elizabeth McClure, you really are a pagan."

"Especially on Sundays." She relaxed and winked. "And now, Marshal, I'm about to do something very medieval—cathedrals have that effect on me. Your hand, please." She took his fingers in her own, and—perfectly serious now—said, "Here, on holy ground, I plight thee my troth in true faith and honor—because you are the only man I've ever known who truly understands what faith and honor mean. Now kiss me, *a chuisle*. God won't mind."

# Fourteen

"I DON'T BELIEVE THIS!"

Evan looked up from his computer screen. With Holly in Mombassa as of yesterday, the engagement party was his to organize. On his lunch hours. She'd done this to him with malice aforethought, he was sure of it. Susannah's presence — even breathing fire and waving a blue-backed writ — was a welcome reprieve.

"What damnfool jackass of a prosecutor got a bunch of shit-wits together for a grand jury that could return *this?*"

"I applaud your faith in the legal system. Hand it over."

She slapped it onto his desk, fuming. The high-flown legalese meant that one Denise Claudine Josèphe, along with several as yet unidentified co-conspirators, was hereby indicted on Federal racketeering charges. The name was familiar — he hadn't read her books, but he and Holly had run into her once or twice at parties.

"RICO?" he said. "That's creative."

"That's just the sauce to cover the stink. Read on."

The main course, it seemed, included drugs, sex with minors, kidnapping, and human sacrifice. Lachlan stared wordlessly up at Susannah.

"Want me to slug you so you know you're awake?" she asked. "I'd just love to hit something right now."

"I'll pass. What is all this crap, anyhow?" He read a little further.

At the above-named residence, on May 1st, 2002, the body of Scott William Fleming, aged nineteen, was discovered—

"Fleming?" The penny dropped. "As in the Reverend—"

"Yeah, the Reverend. He's got Congressman Parkhurst in his back pocket and they're both out to get *their* version of God into the White House. Looks like they plan to do it over the corpse of a nineteen-year-old boy."

He sank back into his chair, shaking his head. Not just another penny but a great big shiny silver dollar dropped while Susannah spoke. May first equaled Beltane. He'd read enough to know how some people celebrated it. He also knew he'd be doing a whole lot more reading and researching and requesting personal files before he asked Judge-Magistrate Elias Bradshaw what the hell was going on.


WHEN BRADSHAW READ THE POLICE report and the judicial memo assigning him the case, he wished his ethics permitted him the use of a few esoteric curses.

Denise, Beltane, and the Reverend Fleming's son. Shit.

He had to recuse himself. How the hell could he recuse himself without giving a reason why? Worthless mental gymnastics were interrupted by Susannah's arrival in his office. She was holding a videotape.

"I have a present for you—a tape of Reverend Fleming's latest talk-show appearance. You're gonna love it, guaranteed."

"Can't wait," he replied, in a voice that meant just the opposite. Bradshaw sprawled back in his leather chair and waited while she stuffed the cassette into the VCR, turned on the television, and came to stand behind him with one hand on his shoulder and the other holding the remote control.

"Welcome back to God Forum," said the program's host. "My guest this evening—"

"Pause it," Elias said. When Susannah complied, he craned his neck to look up at her. "What's 'God Forum'?"

"Local cable show in Jersey. This is from a week or so ago. It got picked up by most of the New York news outlets. I'm told the Reverend might be on *60 Minutes* next Sunday."

"Oh, that's just exquisite. Okay, roll it. I might as well get a preview of what I'm going to hear in court."

"—received his Doctorate of Divinity from Yale University, and has ministered to congregations all over the world. Some will remember his appearance here a year ago, after his return from a mission to India. Today he is visiting with us despite his terrible grief—for his nineteen-year-old son, Scott, was killed in May by a Satanic cult. Reverend Fleming, I want to tell you how sorry I am for your loss."

The camera switched to the Reverend—tall, silver-haired, a wedding ring gleaming from his left hand and a gold class ring with a large diamond sparkling from his right. He wore a black suit, somber tie, and a small American flag lapel pin. The perfect dream of a televangelist, he scorned the airwaves and stuck to his pulpit. Bradshaw had to give him credit for that; he probably drove his handlers crazy by not agreeing to a TV show of his own.

"Yale Divinity, huh?" Elias murmured. "Presumably, then, he has a brain. Why is he using it to annoy *me*?"

"Hush up and listen," Susannah admonished.

"—here tonight to beg anyone who has ever thought of looking into such cults to consider the consequences of such action," the Reverend was saying in a deep, velvety voice. "To those already involved, I say to them that with Divine Guidance, they can renounce all involvement with Satan, Satanism, and demon worship, with Witchcraft, White Magic, Black Magic, voodoo, and the Black Mass. For the sake of their immortal souls they must repudiate all kinds of fortune-telling, tea-leaf reading, palm-reading, crystal balls, tarot cards, astrology, spirit guides, pendulum swinging, levitation, and automatic handwriting."

"'Automatic handwriting'?" Elias snorted.

"Oh, he's just getting started."

"—abandon all psychometry, geomancy, cleidomancy, aeromancy, amniomancy, ceromancy, crystallomancy, lithomancy—"

There was a hypnotic rhythm to it, like the relentless clatter of a train as it bore down on where you were tied to the tracks.

"—arithmancy, lychnomancy, necromancy, pyromancy, sciomancy, tasseomancy, rhapsodmancy, and all other auguries that are part of fortune-telling."

"And just what are all these things, Reverend?" the host asked, curiosity warring with bewilderment on his face.

"Wickedness," came the prompt reply. "Evil. Abomination. Surely on the Day of Judgment these horrors will be worthy only of being cast into the lake of everlasting fire. For sinners, there is only pain and suffering, despair and misery awaiting them. As there is for all those who believe in reincarnation, metaphysics and spiritualism, transcendental meditation, yoga, Zen, all Eastern cults and religions, mysticism, idol worship—every cult that denies the blood of Christ and every philosophy that denies the Divinity of the Lord Jesus."

"So much for pluralism and tolerance," Susannah muttered.

"Yeah. When does he start in on Jews, Catholics, Mormons, Muslims, and Zoroastrians?"

"Reverend," said the host, "the Bible teaches us specifically that thou shalt not suffer a witch to live."

"It does, it does," the Reverend agreed, nodding. "Yet killing is not of Jesus Christ. We pray for our enemies that God will be merciful unto them, and bring them to know the truth. So how do we reconcile God's injunction in the Old Testament with the universal love and peace and gentleness preached by His Son?"

The host smiled slightly. "Did God change His mind?"

Reverend Fleming smiled back, flashing an exemplary set of teeth. "Not at all. Remember the commandment: Thou shalt not kill. In the original Hebrew, the sense of the teaching about witches is that the people of God must not allow a witch to live among them. Such persons must be cast out and utterly condemned. Yet even witches may enter into the community of God if they accept Jesus as their personal Savior, if they become true Christians and live Christlike lives."

Susannah remarked, "This is the really good part."

"In Jesus's Holy Name, they must renounce all psychic heredity that they may have, and break any demonic hold or curses over themselves and their family lines back to Adam and Eve through the power of the blood of the Lord Jesus Christ."

She paused the tape again, and Bradshaw glanced away from the frozen image of the Reverend Fleming, eyes ablaze with righteous fury.

"Eli, he actually believes in hereditary witchcraft. Is that incredible, or what?"

"Or what," Bradshaw echoed, trying to sound casual. "Did I have to watch this before lunch, when my blood sugar's low and I'm pissed at the world anyway?"

"Better before lunch than after," she retorted, cueing the tape.

"They must renounce the Prince of Occult Sex and all the sex spirits which enter through occult involvement, participation, transfer, or by inheritance. They must command all demons to forsake their loins, hands, lips, tongues, breasts, masculinity, femininity, and all organs and orifices of their bodies. They must confess and repent of all fixation with sensual desire and appetites, and indulgences of them—all longing for the forbidden—all inordinate affection—all unnatural and unrestrained passions and lusts."

A brief snarl of laughter escaped Bradshaw. "Well, he sure as shit believes in sex! Does this get any racier, or have I heard all his best lines?"

Susannah stopped the tape and walked over to switch off television and VCR. "You'd better take him more seriously, Elias. He's not kidding."

"I never thought he was." Then he asked a question he'd been afraid to ask ever since she'd first walked into his office. "What do *you* think about Witches?"

She gave a shrug of slender shoulders. "I think people have a right to believe whatever gives them comfort and a moral center, as long as it doesn't harm anybody else. I *don't* think that anyone has the right to say that his way is the one and only way—or that anybody has a direct hotline to God. I *don't* like being proselytized. I'm sure they only have my best interests at heart, and what they're trying to do is very noble and generous from their point of view—saving my soul and all. But keep it out of my face!" She smiled fleetingly. "Can't you just see the Rev in India?"

"What do you mean?"

"Let's say somebody in New Delhi started quoting the Vedas, expecting him to accept those scriptures as unassailable truth. Just the way he expects them to accept the Bible." She gave a most unladylike snort. "Fundamentalists are fundamentalists, whatever religion they belong to. For them, a thing is true because the Bible or the Qur'an or the Torah or the whatever says it is, and that's that."

"It's my understanding," he said carefully, "that Witches, as a rule, don't accept Judeo-Christian scriptures as the word of a god—any god. If they did, they'd probably be Jews or Christians, not Witches."

"Exactly my point. Justifying yourself with Bible verses to people who don't believe in the Bible—it's preposterous." She went to the credenza and poured them both glasses of iced tea. As she did, she went on, "As for Witches, who knows? You can see Mozart as a Witch, or Einstein—anybody who can do things other people can only be flummoxed by. People who make things happen that nobody else even dreamed of. It's what we were saying that night at Holly's—one man's genius, incomprehensible to ordinary people, makes another man cry 'Witch.'"

He accepted the tall iced tea and sipped gratefully. His throat had been a little dry with apprehension regarding her answers. "And one man's *religion* can make another cry 'Witch.' But the issue with this case is Satanism."

"I'm surprised at you, Elias Sutton Bradshaw!" she exclaimed, green eyes glinting. "All these questions about Witches, and you were born in Salem!"

"Very funny," he retorted.

"Not actually," Susannah countered. "Reverend Fleming's son did die at some kind of Black Mass. Lots of people play at Goth and vampirism and all that." All at once she grinned. "I was in Virginia a few years ago, visiting Holly's farm, and one evening her Cousin Jesse came over for dinner. We were right in the middle of the most luscious apricot cobbler you ever tasted when the phone rang, and poor Jesse had to leave. Know why? A farmer had found one of his calves dead in the field, all its blood drained, and wanted Jesse—he's the sheriff—to arrest the local vampire."

"Excuse me?"

"That's about what I said, too. Lulah packed up some cobbler and sent Jesse on his way, and then said with an absolutely straight face that she wasn't surprised, the vampire had gotten married and his new wife was probably wearing him out, so he needed a decent meal." Assuming a Virginia drawl, she finished, "'Though why he picked Ephraim Fuller's stock to harvest, I couldn't begin to say—that old bull of his is flat outta jizz an' sires the scrawniest calves I ever did see.'"

Bradshaw choked on laughter. "One day I've *got* to meet Aunt Lulah."

"You'd love her. Most men do, according to Holly," she added with a twinkle. "She could've married a hundred times, but she never could see why she'd want some whiskery ol' crotch-scratcher around messing up Grandma Flynn's carpets with his muddy boots."

Elias rubbed his freshly shaven chin. "What happened about the vampire?"

"I laughed so hard, I forgot to ask!"

Aunt Lulah, he reflected, was one savvy lady.

"Anyway," Susannah went on, "what I was saying was that Satanism and all that is pretty trendy these days. I've yet to figure out why. It seems to me that whatever your faith is, it's pointless unless it awakens the best parts of you."

"I agree," he murmured.

"That's why I could never stomach organized religion—at least, not the way we got it in Connecticut. I suppose that nominally I'm a Christian, but I've never joined a church."

"Why not? I'd think a good Episcopalian upbringing—"

"Baptist!" she corrected. "Great-grandpa Wingfield married a Baptist, got disinherited except for the house he lived in, and we've thumped Bibles to varying degrees ever since."

So that was where the money had gone, he mused. Lost for love and religious differences.

"What I object to is that it's all based on fear," Susannah was saying. "Do this, and God will be pissed off. Do that, and burn forever."

"That's a bizarre attitude for a lawyer," he remarked. "What keeps people on the straight and narrow is fear of the police and the courts. It's comparable to religion, that way."

"You're entirely too cynical, Your Honor. Shouldn't it be instead that right behavior—whatever your faith says it is, which is pretty constant among all the world's great religions—is rewarded, rather than wrong behavior punished? Where's the comfort in a grim old God sitting up there watching, waiting for you to screw up so He can consign you to the Pit? Whatever happened to joy? Whatever happened to the idea that when you do something good, when you're kind and compassionate to your fellow humans, God is smiling approval? Christ died for our sins, Eli, but isn't it more important that He spent His life telling us to be good to each other?"

Bradshaw considered the Reverend Fleming's religion of pain and suffering, despair and misery, with everything forbidden except that one narrow path, and all at once wanted to fold this woman into his arms and see the world through the gentle translucency of her faith. He smiled at her instead, and the answering warmth in her eyes was almost as good as holding her. Holding *on* to her.

A discreet knock on his door turned their heads. Mrs. Osbourne, her face pinched with disapproval, filled the doorway with a stylish blue linen pantsuit and announced, "Are we at home to a Ms. Josèphe?"

"No," Susannah said.

"That's what I told her," Mrs. Osbourne replied with deep satisfaction.

Elias knew he'd have to see Denise sooner or later. He couldn't decide, however, whether an improper communication—and, as the judge in a case involving her, it would be highly improper—should take place in secret or where others could observe. Safety in numbers of witnesses, but who knew what she might say?

"Bradshaw!" came Denise's voice from the outer office. "Let me in or I'll—"

"Not that way, miss," said Deputy Marshal Wasserman. "The door you'll be using is right behind you."

"Get your hand off me—"

"Maybe I should help give her directions," Susannah said, and left with Mrs. Osbourne, decisively shutting the door.

Bradshaw closed his eyes and rubbed both hands over his face. Wishing he had time for a hefty slug from the bottle in his desk, he stood, shouldered into his robes, prepared his mind and his magic, and went to do battle in the outer office.

Denise was still there, shrill and adamant. Pete Wasserman, Mrs. Osbourne, and Susannah had barricaded her near the hall door; they were a fortification that would withstand just about anything. Elias didn't want that to become necessary.

"Ms. Josèphe?" he said, as if he'd never seen her before. "It's impossible for me to talk to you without the presence of your attorney."

"All you have to do is listen," she snapped.

The generous folds of full black sleeves could and did hide a multitude of things; Bradshaw knew one judge who sometimes brought her cat to court, where it slept quite cozily in the crook of her elbow. What Elias hid now wasn't so benign.

Denise opened her mouth again. And no sound came out. Her eyes—green like Susannah's, but mottled with brown—opened, too, as wide as they would go.

"Very wise of you to have changed your mind," he remarked. "Marshal, would you be so kind as to open the door? Thank you."

Deprived of the powers of speech, Denise was too astonished to use any of her own powers. He'd been betting on that; she wasn't the type who could think on her feet. Wasserman had her out the door before she knew it.

"*That* was different," Susannah noted. When Elias merely shrugged, she added, "She was a lot more insistent last time."

He'd been hoping she didn't remember last autumn. "Maybe she's mellowed."

"Or maybe now that she's going to be in your court—" Susannah frowned. "Why *was* she here in November, anyway?"

For a variety of reasons, Elias Bradshaw had learned long ago to think on his feet—and more quickly than most, or so he flattered himself. Lying to Susannah came hard; it always had, but it had gotten worse the last few months.

He'd discovered it was no easier if he wasn't looking into those green eyes, the hint of blue in their depths making them almost the color of emeralds. So he met her gaze, and let a corner of his mouth quirk upward, and cribbed a page from Aunt Lulah's book of Witchly wisdom. "If I remember rightly, she wanted to turn me into a toad."

It worked. More or less. Wasserman grinned, Sophia Osbourne grimaced, and Susannah just looked disgusted.


THAT EVENING BRADSHAW CALLED DENISE from a restaurant men's room pay phone in Greenwich Village. A confrontation was inevitable, and he wanted to choose the time and the venue—*not* his chambers, or his home, or hers, or e-mail, or any telephone that could be traced to him.

"That was a stupid stunt you pulled today," he began without preamble and without identifying himself. "Don't do it again."

"Same to you, Magistrate," she snarled. "How dare you—"

"Shut up, Denise, and listen. I'm no more thrilled about this than you are."

"Then fix it!"

"Need I remind you that you don't give me orders?"

"Do it, or I'll tell them all what you really are. And I can prove it."

"Really?" he asked with genuine curiosity. "How?"

"I know everyone in your Circle. I know their names, where they live, where they work. I can ruin them all—and I intend to let them know it. Are they so loyal to you that they'll keep their mouths shut?"

"Yes," he answered with quiet certainty.

She barely paused. "The FBI may have done a background check on you before you got onto the bench, but they hardly knew where to look, did they?"

"And you think you can point them in the right direction?"

She laughed. "I know someone who was there that night in Salem, and knows what you and the others did to that man. I'm sure you remember."

"You know, I can't help thinking that you get your life confused with your books—one drama queen moment after another. Doesn't it get rather wearying?"

"If this was one of my books, I'd have you run over by a truck!"

"What appalling dearth of imagination. How do you get onto the best-seller lists? No, don't answer that—I have no desire to find out who you're screwing." He ignored her sharp hiss. "Keep a low profile, Denise. Considering the risk, I'm sure you can manage to restrain yourself. If you can't, or won't—"

"You don't give *me* orders, either!"

"That wasn't an order," he said quietly. "That was a threat. Good night."

# Fifteen

NAIROBI WAS A NOISY NEON chaos; Mombassa, on the seacoast, had been humid misery. But it was easy to forget the heat as a prop plane took her and twenty other dumbfounded tourists low over the bush toward Maasai country. From barely five hundred feet she stared down at giraffes and elephants doing what giraffes and elephants had been doing for a million years in the place where they were supposed to do it. Other countries marked the centuries and the millennia with cathedrals and pyramids, cities and battlefields; the African plains were timeless.

The seminars had gone quite well, the coordinator assuring her that Ben Wolaver wasn't even missed, let alone regretted. Kenyans took pride in their heritage—one of the richest histories on the planet, for it was the place where humankind began. Kenya's stories were essential. Ancestral tales and dreams of the future, feeling and thoughts and imaginings, everyday lives and the tragedies of the AIDS epidemic—all these things needed telling. Holly's tutorials on historical research and the uses of fiction had excited her audiences into profuse scribbles in their notebooks and hundreds of questions she answered as best she knew how.

After twelve days of cities, the offer of a photographic safari was too good to pass up. As she settled into her room at a Lake Nakuru lodge, she felt guilty glee at being *incommunicada* for a whole week, there being no computers or cell phones in the bush. There was barely even electricity, and even that cut off at nine every night. Sitting on the wooden porch, sipping brandy and listening to animals and birds she couldn't yet identify, she realized that whereas selected persons knew where she was, not even they could easily get in touch with her—something that had never happened to her before.

Five days, ten game drives, and approximately one hundred new freckles later, she'd nearly forgotten that the outside world existed. Cheetahs, lions, hippos, gazelles, antelope, elephants, giraffes, baboons—what a treasure of life this place was. Cradle of humankind, where *Homo sapiens* had learned to stand upright and make tools and communicate, one to the other. She thought about her conversation with Evan and Susannah and Elias, about dancing and art-work and song—yes, here was magic, the most intrinsic and primal magic of all. In the low rumble of a lion, in the heartbeat rhythm of drums, Holly touched, if only for fleeting moments, the most elemental source of magic. Not her magic: *everyone's*. It was the birthright of all humanity, the inner knowing that there was something greater and more powerful than anyone could ever imagine, and that a share of that *something* existed within every human on the planet.

There was *something* within her that wanted to crouch before a fire at night, rocking gently back and forth, talking tales and singing songs, weaving the life of the land and the life inside her into a single powerful whole that was deep and real and true. And she came to realize that this was her most authentic magic: the thing she could *do* rather than the thing she *was*. Blood-magic, but not the kind where she had to bleed. This was coded in the double helix over millions of years of evolution. Some people expressed humanity's innate magic in music, in the movements of the dance, in painting or sculpture or weavings; her share came in words.

She tried to write it down, to designate language that would transmit the ex-perience. Not surprisingly, no arrangement of syllables and sentences satisfied her. Sheer frustration suddenly made her laugh aloud in the thatched privacy of her little bungalow, wryly regarding scrawl-covered pages by candlelight.

Shaman? Wordsmith? Worker of sounds and symbols into pictures, thoughts, ideas? Her particular share of that *something* was inadequate to the task—but, truly, who possessed gift enough to articulate this wonder? It was enough to know the magic was real, and to feel its existence inside her as part of the whole of Creation.

The intensity would fade, of course, as all such feelings did. Yet there were fragments of it every day, like bright flecks of gemstones glimpsed at unex-pected moments: writing postcards to Nicky and Alec, finding a batik robe for Aunt Lulah, selecting a beaded necklace for Susannah; just thinking about Evan. *Maybe,* she thought, whimsy making her smile, *maybe the part of it in me re-flects the parts in them, and the light and the colors keep refracting off each other, and that's what love is. Those bits of Creation and Forever recognizing each other, making magic. And it's up to us to keep them shiny bright.*

Amused by herself and the world at large, she packed the pages away in her suitcase, blew out her candle, and went to bed.

"I AM *NOT* LOOKING FORWARD to this," Judge Bradshaw muttered.

Evan Lachlan nodded agreement. "Salmon day. Work like hell swimming upstream, and all you get is screwed." He opened the door leading to the back chambers, nodding approval when he saw the hallway was empty. "Kinda hard to leave it at the door if it's already in the courtroom when you arrive."

"I've never been seriously tempted before now. But I can hardly recuse myself without some sort of explanation."

"*That* would make interesting hearing," Lachlan chuckled.

"Well, yeah," Bradshaw said, smiling a little. "And don't worry—it's a temptation I can resist. Although I don't know how long I'll be able to resist the urge to bash all their heads together."

"I'll hold your coat."

"Heard from Holly?"

"She called at the butt-crack of dawn from Nairobi." Lachlan sighed and raked a hand back through his hair. "Somebody at the conference offered her a safari, so she's off taking pictures of warthogs. It's her way of gettin' out of writing up the invite list for the wedding."

"Hand it off to Susannah. What *will* she be wearing, by the way?"

"Damned if I know." The marshal grinned. "Personally, I've been threatening the Lachlan hunting tartan, embroidered in Day-Glo shamrocks."

Bradshaw was fighting a grin as he entered his chambers—which was exactly what Lachlan intended. This was going to be a shitty day; they both knew it; and as Evan saw it, now that he knew certain things, his job was to provide a minute or two of breathing space as well as constant protection.

Physical protection, anyway. God only knew what Denise Josèphe had stashed in her purse. From Bradshaw's description of her magical orientation, it could be anything from a few herbs to a mummified bat's skull.

Returning to the courtroom door, Lachlan vetted spectators and lawyers and reporters—who had already been through one security check at the courthouse entrance. Because it was August and muggily hot, everyone was in summer-weight clothing, which made the job easier: no place to hide instruments of mayhem beneath cotton dresses or short-sleeved shirts. He and Pete Wasserman were meticulous with metal detectors all the same. Everyone came up clean.

Supporters of the Reverend and of Denise Josèphe were pretty much identical in their wide mix of age, appearance, and social class. They could easily be told apart, however, by their choice of jewelry: crosses versus inverted pentagrams. Lachlan was sure both sides had chosen their wardrobes with the media in mind. The print reporters—no electron jockeys, thank God—annoyed Evan, but they knew better by now than to ask him for information. Instead they interviewed spectators until Pete told them to shut up or get out.

Susannah was busy behind the bench, arranging whatever it was she arranged for her boss. Her long blonde hair was scraped back in a severe chignon, her black suit and plain white blouse unenlivened by so much as a pair of earrings. Lachlan doubted she was even wearing mascara. She was gorgeous all the same.

And nervous. She fussed with Bradshaw's laptop computer—which any reporter would have sold body parts to hack into—a silver pitcher of ice water, a tall cut-glass tumbler, a gavel that had at one time been used by Joseph Story, United States Supreme Court Associate Justice from Massachusetts, who had written the majority opinion freeing the *Amistad* captives in 1841. Lachlan had been surprised, and then not surprised, to find out the gavel had been a gift from Alec Singleton when Bradshaw was appointed to the Federal Bench.

The attorneys were arrayed at their tables, seven men of varying heights, weights, ages, and demeanors, all in expensive suits. Lachlan didn't recognize any of them. They had been mightily offended when he insisted on putting them through the same security as everyone else—as if a degree from Harvard or Yale pulled more weight than the five-pointed star of a United States Marshals Service badge.

Denise Josèphe was at the defense table, inspecting her flawless fingernails. Another green-eyed blonde in a black suit, white blouse, and tightly pinned French twist—but the contrast with Susannah could not have been greater even if the accused hadn't been wearing makeup and jewelry. Seeing her in person, Lachlan now remembered her. Mainly he remembered that, at a book launch this spring, her lipstick-red dress had clashed so agonizingly with Holly's aubergine and the featured author's coral velvet that the wincing photographer told them his film was color and he didn't dare take a picture.

The Reverend Fleming arrived at last, tall and silver-maned, impeccably dressed in a black suit and tie. His side of the courtroom murmured sympathetically, ready to offer handshakes and hugs. He paused at the doorway for Pete Wasserman to run his security check; Evan watched his colleague's polite professionalism, knowing what Pete thought of this guy, who included Jews in his list of pagans, Mormons, Catholics, Muslims, Buddhists, and other sinners. But nobody would ever see it on Pete's face.

Fleming made his way slowly up the center aisle, accepting words and embraces with grace. Denise Josèphe's adherents muttered and scowled, and a few of them made complex gestures with their hands, presumably to curse him. Lachlan doubted that any would have more effect than simply giving him the finger.

The court clerk finally announced Judge Bradshaw. Everyone stood. His

Honor swept in like a nor'easter, robes swirling, face grim above the collar of a gloomy gray broadcloth shirt and the knot of probably the ugliest paisley tie Lachlan had ever seen him wear. Gaveled into session, the courtroom silenced itself and the lawyers told Bradshaw their names.

Evan had watched His Honor in all his many judicial moods: generally calm, sometimes irritated, occasionally sarcastic, rarely moved. He had never seen this expression on Bradshaw's face before, and never heard him begin a session with a single word: "Chambers."

Lachlan did what Wasserman signaled him to do with a jerk of his chin, and escorted the parties to the back hallway, ushering them through a glass-paned door. He stood guard outside, studiously not listening. Five minutes later the volume became such that he could not help but hear. Five sentences later, he decided his presence and perhaps even his weapon were necessary, and opened the door.

BRADSHAW SEATED HIMSELF BEHIND HIS desk and waited until everyone was inside. There was only one other chair in this room, over in the corner—a purposeful arrangement allowing him to use the desk as if it were the bench in his courtroom.

Now that he was close enough to smell her, Denise's little gris-gris bag was also close enough to irk him. He was familiar with the usual contents of such bags: nails, bones, Snake Root Seal, John the Conqueror root, calendula, marigold, buckthorn, skunk cabbage, bloodstone, hematite, and who knew what else that was specific to her current purposes. He had known full well she'd bring something with her, and had considered gathering a few things of his own. But he had never yet brought his magic into his courtroom, and wasn't about to start now.

"You will explain yourselves," he told the assembled lawyers, "and then I will decide whether or not your arguments will be heard in public—any more than they already have been," he added pointedly.

"There was no gag order—," said one of the attorneys.

Bradshaw shut him up with a glance. "I'm waiting."

"Simply put, Scott Fleming's death was deliberate, cold-blooded murder."

Denise's lawyer took a half-step forward. "That hasn't been establ—"

"I won't warn you again," Bradshaw snapped. "Continue."

Point man for the prosecution was Andrew Parkhurst, nephew of the congressman whose interests dovetailed so comfy-cozy with the Reverend Fleming's. Wondering how anyone with a law degree from East Nowhere God-in-His-Glory College had ever managed to pass the bar—and knowing he was being a Harvard snob for thinking it—Elias gestured for Parkhurst to begin.

"Your Honor, Reverend Fleming states that his son was not there as a Satanic participant."

"So what was he doing?"

"Testing his faith. His *true* faith."

Bradshaw was professionally compelled to maintain an impassive expression and the proper judicial distance; Susannah had no such problems. She frankly stared, saying, "I beg your pardon?"

With impervious serenity, Parkhurst went on, "As Jesus was tempted, so too was Scott Fleming. Also like Jesus, he triumphed over Satan. That's why he was killed."

"And rose again on the third day?" Denise inquired sweetly.

"That's enough," Elias ordered.

"Are you telling me," Denise's lawyer said slowly, "that he went into that house knowing full well what would go on, he was willing to participate, and did so as some test of faith?"

"Exactly. He was murdered because his faith survived the experience. They could not allow him to live and bear witness."

"The *facts*," interjected Denise's lawyer, "are that Scott Fleming went voluntarily to a ritual, participated enthusiastically—evidenced by his own semen— and when further sexual gratification was not forthcoming, threatened serious bodily harm and had to be restrained, at which point he incurred injuries that led to his death. It was an accident." He folded his arms with an air of *And that's that*.

"His neck was broken!"

"Entirely accidental."

"The Lord God knows the truth of this—and the truth of what is in your heart, Counselor. And in yours, Judge Bradshaw," he added with a portentous frown.

Denise glared. "You sanctimonious prick! You wouldn't mind if he brought his religion into the courtroom if he believed the same things you believe! You'd strew his path with rose petals every time he took the bench!"

"That's enough!" Bradshaw roared.

The door swung open. Marshal Lachlan stood there, broad shoulders almost filling the doorway, hands casually on his hips, jacket open to reveal his Glock. *Subtle*, Bradshaw thought, sardonically amused.

"Everything okay, Your Honor?"

"Nothing to worry about, Marshal. Thank you."

Lachlan nodded, left chambers, shut the door, and stood with his back against the rippled glass. It was so obvious, it was almost funny. It also worked. Everyone calmed down, with a weather eye on the powerful shoulders shadowing the glass.

Bradshaw watched the two sides face off, his eyes narrowing. He could guess what had happened. Some people got off on strangulation or suffocation during sex. If Scott Fleming wasn't one of them, then at the very least he had been introduced to the practice that night. Had it gotten out of control? Or had someone deliberately killed the boy? Considering Denise's usual playmates, he leaned toward the former. But proving it one way or the other—

The only fact that mattered was that the boy was dead. Recalling the tall, lanky, defiant youth on that hilltop the night of Imbolc, Elias shook his head. "Shall we return to the question of why this case is in my courtroom?" he asked pleasantly.

Parkhurst said, "Kidnapping across state lines—New Jersey to New York. Murder in the first degree. RICO."

"You have an interesting interpretation of the Racketeer Influenced and Corrupt Organizations Act," retorted the defense.

"These Satanists have ties to known gangsters. I have an affidavit describing the implements—candles, incense, clothing, and the like—recovered at the crime scene, and how they were purchased at a store that is serviced by a garbage collection company controlled by the de Lezze family."

Susannah said what Elias was, frankly, too stunned to say. "You mean that somebody bought stuff from a store where the trash gets hauled by a Mafia business, and that constitutes involvement with racketeers?"

"Precisely," said Parkhurst.

Bradshaw sat forward, fingers laced white-knuckled so that those knuckles could not connect with a set of perfect teeth in a face with a Hamptons summer tan. "I can guess how this case got so far so fast," he began. "Everyone has friends. I won't comment on this, as it has nothing to do with my present ruling. Scott Fleming was, by his father's admission, a willing participant in whatever went on that night. Nobody took him from New Jersey to Long Island under duress. So much for kidnapping. Regarding murder, talk to the district attorney for Suffolk County, where the estate is located. As for the RICO allegations— stop wasting my time."

Denise smirked. Bradshaw wanted to go find her Measure and shred it, thread by golden thread.

"Your Honor!" spluttered the prosecution's second chair. "You must help us expose these Satanist witches for the murderers and blasphemers they are!"

Parkhurst nodded emphatically. "United States District Court is the only possible venue for this trial, for it goes to the heart of our Constitution and our government. 'One nation, under God!'" He reared up to his full five-foot-nine, and repeated, "Under God!"

"That's the Pledge of Allegiance, not the Constitution," Denise's lawyer said. "The separation of church and state—"

"Our Founding Fathers were righteous and godly men," said Parkhurst. "They believed in Holy Writ."

At this point, Bradshaw reflected, Holly McClure would have gone into a lecture describing the divergent beliefs of Washington, Adams, Jefferson, Madison, Franklin, and any number of other icons of the Declaration and Constitution. He regretted not having her and her harangues immediately to hand.

"'There shall not be found among you any one that maketh his son or his daughter to pass through the fire,'" quoth Andrew Parkhurst, "'or that useth divination, or an observer of times, or an enchanter, or a witch, or a charmer, or a consulter with familiar spirits, or a wizard, or a necromancer. For all that do these things are an abomination unto the Lord: and because of these abominations the Lord thy God doth drive them out from before thee.'"

"Deuteronomy 18, verses 10 through 12," Elias said.

Dark eyes widened. "You are of the Faith?"

"I have an education," he replied smoothly, not adding that his education—any Witch's education—included chapter and verse of the strictures in the Scriptures. "But I think we shall render unto the Almighty the 'drive them out' part. This is a court of law, not a school of theology."

"'They sacrifice to devils, and not to God: and I would not that ye should have fellowship with devils.' First Corinthians—"

"Do we have to listen to this?" Denise complained.

"The hell you attempt to create in your pagan pageantry is laughable compared to the true Hell awaiting you."

Suddenly, for the first time in Bradshaw's experience of her, Denise said something worth hearing. In a quiet, dignified voice, she said, "There's nothing in *my* religion that says thou shalt not suffer a Christian to live."

Good point, Bradshaw had to admit, but he had to take this back into his own hands. "Ms. Josèphe." He paused, fixing her with a bleak stare. "The District Attorney of Suffolk County may do as she sees fit. Whereas there are no Federal charges here, there may very well—"

"You're out of your fucking mind!" Denise leaped to her feet, green eyes flashing. "I will *not* be charged with—"

"I have no influence over local jurisdictions. However, I will offer you a word of advice. Let your attorneys speak for you. That's what you pay them for—and it would be wise of you to let them do their jobs. For although you've been in my presence for only about ten minutes, I've taken your Measure."

Turning crimson, she shut her mouth.

"I've made my ruling," Bradshaw finished. "We're through here."

"Never!" Parkhurst exclaimed, turning red beneath his tan. "This is an outrage!"

Elias made a grab for his temper and missed. "Open your mouth again, *any* of you, and it'll be to choose between a night in jail and a thousand-dollar fine for contempt of court."

Into the abrupt silence Susannah said, "Thank you, Your Honor," and went to open the door with the grace of a society hostess bidding farewell to dinner guests. "If you'll return to the courtroom, His Honor will be along shortly."

Lachlan smiled sweetly at the people filing past him, and stayed at his post. "Y'know, I just love *not* being a lawyer," he said to Susannah, who winced before looking a question at Elias.

"Give me a minute," he said in response. When he was alone, with Lachlan's tall shadow still outside, he lowered his forehead to his clenched hands and swore. He'd done a perfectly legitimate hand-off. He was free of it. And he pitied whichever Suffolk County judge got assigned this mess.

But he *wasn't* free of it, not really. Denise would probably have to stand trial for murder—she and whoever else they could round up of the night's participants. Hedonistic morons, every single one of them. But one of them had done murder, and Elias was willing to bet it hadn't been Denise. A hundred and fifteen pounds of her against two hundred and ten of Scott Fleming?

Not his problem. Not his jurisdiction. Not until Denise's trial, and the name Elias Sutton Bradshaw showed up on her witness list—along with Holly Elizabeth McClure and Lydia Rachael Montsorel and Katherine Drummond Ramsay, and—

"Your Honor?"

He straightened quickly. "Yes? What is it, Marshal?"

"Pete says there's a pretty ugly crowd outside. We should get this over with and send everybody home."

"Or to the nearest TV studio," he appended acidly. "There's more than enough time to make the six o'clock news." Rising, he settled his robes around him. "The NYPD ought to be here, I think."

"Done," Lachlan assured him. "They're sending four cars immediately."

"Which means in half an hour, if we're lucky."

"Well, yeah. But if we space the departures right, things oughta stay fairly calm."

"I want the Reverend escorted."

"Pete and I already tossed for it. I lost."

"My sympathies."


FIFTEEN MINUTES LATER, DESPITE ALL Lachlan could do by way of verbal persuasion to get him into his car and gone, the Reverend was on the courthouse steps before a phalanx of microphones, with a crowd of at least two thousand below him. There'd been enough time elapsed since Fleming had entered the building to allow everyone to get sufficiently worked up and nasty. Banners and signs touted every conceivable point of view on the subject of witchcraft, waved by persons who had been shouting at each other for at least an hour.

Lachlan didn't like this one little bit. Neither did the NYPD uniforms assigned to crowd control. Thankful that he didn't have their job, he moved toward the Reverend.

"Sir, if you'll just—"

"I can't ignore this opportunity to speak."

"They're not interested in listening," he pointed out, exasperated. "They just want to yell. Reverend, you really need to get out of here before this gets serious."

"Perhaps I can calm them down. I must try, Marshal."

And before Lachlan could say anything more, he stepped up to the mikes. Most of the crowd quieted; Fleming threw a little smile at Lachlan, who didn't share his optimism.

"My friends, the quest for justice is not yet fulfilled, but I promise that justice will be done concerning the murder of my son. God's justice, if not the law's."

The yelling was nondenominational: people brandishing banners for Satan shouted just as loudly as those whose signs proclaimed Christ. Lachlan shook his head and peered beyond the crowd to get a glimpse of the Reverend's limo.

"I do not call myself Baptist, or Methodist, or Episcopal, or any of the other names that label churches. I am a true Christian, for I am a doer in Jesus Christ. Christian means someone who is Christ-like, not one who believes in Christ—for if that were true, my friends, if someone who believed in Christ was a Christian, then Satan would also be a Christian—for the Evil One believed in Jesus enough to tempt him! My son knew this, and my son challenged himself to be similarly tempted—"

Evan tapped one of the Reverend's lawyers on the shoulder. "Which limo?"

"He doesn't have one."

"How're you gettin' him outta here?"

"He came in my car—"

"Which goddamned one?" Lachlan snarled.

"The white Caddy over there."

"—these witches who, in the foul rite of worshipping Satan murdered my son! These whores, these murderers—seducers of innocence, despoilers of righteousness, depraved and immoral fornicators!"

Lachlan fixed his gaze on the white Cadillac, gritting his teeth while Fleming termed the woman he loved a whore.

"I know that many witches says that they do not believe in Satan, and thus cannot be Satanic. But I say unto you, my friends, there are only two forces at work in this world: good and evil. Good is obedience to the words of Jesus Christ. Evil is disobedience. It is that simple! Jesus saith unto us, 'I am the Way, the Truth, and the Life: no man cometh to the Father, but by me.' If you do not serve Jesus, you serve Satan. There is no evading the issue, no middle ground."

Cheers; angry shouts; Lachlan counted the NYPD uniforms and wished there were a dozen more present.

"Tolerance and open-mindedness do not enter into the discussion. Tolerance of wrong and wicked paths is not allowed. Open-mindedness regarding so-called other ways to God is not allowed."

Make that two dozen NYPD uniforms. *Two minutes to hustle him down the steps,* Lachlan estimated. *Just give me two minutes before all hell breaks loose —*

"Witches took my son," said Fleming, lowering his voice. The crowd had to shut up to hear him. "They stole him, they attempted to corrupt him, they abused him, and when finally they could not persuade him to their wickedness, they killed him. They are of Satan. But I say also that you must pray for Christ to show the witches that the Truth, the Way, and the Life are through Jesus, and none other. I say unto you now, any who have taken even one step down dark paths, pray with me!"

An elegant, manicured hand lifted, sunlight fracturing into a million separate rays from the diamond of his Yale Divinity ring, and the long fingers curled as if reaching for the sleeve of God Almighty—moreover, as if that sleeve were within Fleming's reach, and his reach only.

"Precious Lord, there are those here present who have disobeyed Your Word. I now ask You in Your infinite mercy to cleanse them in body, mind, soul, and spirit. In the name of Jesus Christ, I disentangle all those here who are truly penitent from any and all evil curses, afflictions, talismans, charms, potions, psychic powers, sorceries, enchantments, hexes, and spells that have been put upon them. My brothers and sisters in Christ, may Almighty God bless you with deliverance. May He bring you salvation, healing, prosperity, and happiness. Amen, and Amen."

"And may you rot in the hell you invented, you self-righteous asshole!" someone shouted.

"Curse God and die!" yelled someone else.

Videotapes of the ensuing chaos were flawed by the jostling of the camera crews by enraged citizens. Some very shaky footage caught Deputy Marshal Evan Lachlan grabbing Reverend Fleming's arm and shoving him down the courthouse steps; another shot showed how the Reverend stumbled, and how Lachlan held him upright by sheer strength. None of the cameras saw what Lachlan saw: the cold silvery glint of a gun, pointed right at Fleming.

Every news broadcast that evening clearly showed the Reverend beside a white Cadillac, turning to shout something at the crowd—and folding into the leather seat like a book snapped shut as Marshal Lachlan slugged him in the stomach.

# Sixteen

EVENTUALLY HE BECAME AWARE THAT he had to pee. Too much beer. Shoulda stuck to Scotch—the buzz came faster, lasted longer, and he didn't have to go siphon his bladder as often.

It seemed a long, long way to the bathroom. Stuff was all over the place. Stupid stuff. Coffee table, rattling with beer cans and Scotch bottles when he bumped it with a shin. Chair—what the hell was it doing here, instead of the kitchen? And boxes all over, labeled in fat black marker letters that he couldn't quite focus on. Why so many boxes? Oh, yeah, he was getting ready to move. He couldn't recall why.

His bladder was about to burst. He couldn't remember where the toilet was, either. Stupid, he'd lived here for years, but he couldn't quite—

A wave of dizziness hit him, and he propped a shoulder against a wall. Digging into his arm was something that proved to be a light switch. That would help. Harsh illumination flooded the room, and he staggered to the toilet and unbuttoned his Levi's. When he was finished, he turned—and suddenly, hideously caught sight of himself in the mirror on the back of the door.

Jesus Suffering Christ. It wasn't possible.

He looked like some big, dumb, lard-assed Mick with a two-week beard and bloodshot booze-soaked eyes.

He looked like his father.

*Caution: objects in the mirror are closer than they appear.*

He ran a hand over his belly, hating the liquor-bloat. Hating the bleariness of his eyes and the circles beneath them and the sick pastiness of his skin and the sour, filthy taste in his mouth.

Hating himself. With pretty good reason. But what did it really matter?

Nothing mattered. His career was over, gone, shot down in flames. His whole life shot to hell—no future—

Holly.

He had watched British Air take her away from him at his own insistence while telling himself he was the biggest fool ever born. He'd left a note in her luggage that said three things: *I love you. I miss you. Come home and marry me, lady love.*

He wasn't that man anymore. Dark hair, hazel eyes, big nose—yeah, all the same. But not her *Éimhín*—not anymore.

A half-smoked cigarette had burned out on the sink ledge, leaving a yellow stain on the porcelain. He had no idea when he'd left it there. Or the matches. Subconsciously trying to burn the place down? Thickheaded fool. He lit up the stub, hands shaking.

He wanted her so much. He wanted never to see her again. As he was trying to decide which would hurt worse, he heard a key in the lock and the sound of the door opening. And smelled—even above the stench of beer and Scotch and cigarettes and his own acrid sweat—the sultry sweetness of her perfume.

SHE USED HER KEY AND entered silently, fairly certain what she'd find. He was supposed to move into her place next week, and so his apartment was packed up. The living room had been denuded of most furniture and all decoration, save for the photo of him and his parents at his NYPD Academy graduation. This sat on the coffee table—a silent taunting surrounded by a repugnant litter of bottles, beer cans, pizza boxes, and full ashtrays. Yes, pretty much what she'd expected.

But as he came into the living room, cigarette dangling from his lips as he buttoned his jeans with clumsy fingers, she discovered things were even worse than she'd feared. He hadn't shaved in more than a week. Or showered, by the smell of him that assaulted her nostrils from all the way across the room. The booze showed in his eyes, in the unhealthy pallor of his skin, in the belly curving against his T-shirt. He registered her presence without surprise, taking the cigarette from his lips and gesturing expansively to the sofa—a move that nearly made him lose his balance, he who was always so lithe.

"Oh. You're here," he remarked. "How nice. Have a seat, baby."

His voice, despite quantities of alcohol, was sharp as shattered glass. She'd seen him mildly tipsy, cheerfully plastered, and owl-eyed inebriated—but never liquor-sodden. She hadn't suspected he'd be an ugly drunk. He slumped gracelessly onto the sofa, legs splayed, and ran his fingers back through his hair, exposing the long widow's peak for a moment before the lank, dirty strands fell across his brow.

Holly sat cross-legged on the floor within reach of the coffee table, and leaned over to snag a pack of smokes and a lighter. "Mind?" He answered with a shrug. She lit a cigarette, breathing in deeply. Ten years since she'd quit smoking. The rush prickled every hair on her head. Exhaling, she looked up at him through the white cloud and said, "Susannah called."

"Nice of her. Everybody's nice these days, didja notice? Everybody wants to call and talk."

Holly took off her cardigan and tossed it aside. The overnight Nairobi-to-Heathrow flight had been ferocious; Heathrow to JFK was worse. Her body had no idea what time it was. Jet-lag clotted her wits just when she needed them most.

There was a sneer in his voice as he said, "Shouldn't treat cashmere like that—oops—sorry, baby, I forgot. You can afford a hundred of 'em."

"A thousand," she retorted, and he inclined his head in sarcastic apology.

"I'm not being a good host," he said. "Not very nice of me." He leaned over for an open can of beer. "Want one?"

"No, thanks." After another drag on the cigarette, she said, "I hear you've been something of a jerk."

*"Evan hauled off and let him have it right in the gut, in front of about two thousand people—plenty of 'em reporters."*

"You could say that." He finished the beer in two long swallows, crumpled the can in one large fist, and tossed the abused metal over his shoulder. It hit the wall and then the floor, with a tinny rattle that told her this was where he'd been throwing cans for days now. "And now that you know I'm not in an alcoholic coma, you can leave." He waited for a reaction. When she gave him none, he grinned all the way across his face and jeered, "What, no bright backchat? No amusing banter? C'mon, writer-lady, break out the million-dollar vocabulary, make me a scene."

Holly pulled in a long, controlled breath. "You stupid, arrogant prick."

He nodded agreeably. "Yeah, that's me."

"You punch out some other prick, you get suspended—"

"I'm not just on suspension, baby." Sitting up with an effort, he stubbed out one cigarette and lit another. "I'm busted. I'll be lucky if I get me some files to shuffle for some rinky-dink police force in Chicken Scratch, Nebraska."

Susannah hadn't mentioned that. No wonder. After a moment she rallied. "If so, I hope you ask for a good, sturdy chair." She looked pointedly at his waistline.

"Aw, gee, I thought you liked my belly," he whined.

"When it was you, yes. Not when it's booze and self-pity."

This brought a snarl. "What the fuck would you know about it?" He put his cigarette in an overflowing ashtray and, elbows on knees, dug his fingers through his hair. "Christ Almighty—just get outta here, okay? You weren't here before, I don't want you here now—" All at once he grabbed an empty bottle and flung it against the opposite wall. The shatter made her flinch. "Where the fuck were you?"

"I'm sorry, Evan," she said quietly.

"Yeah, everybody's sorry." He flopped back into the sofa. "Everybody's sorry," he repeated. "The big boss-man marshal said 'sorry' when he took away my badge and my piece for sluggin' that motherfucker. Well, I'm *not* sorry. He deserved it. I'd do it again."

She heard the hollowness beneath the defiance, and bit her lip.

"I'm s'posed to be grateful they're not prosecuting my ass." He paused to open another beer. "Hadda pull the goddamn phone outta the goddamned wall to get people to stop tellin' me they're sorry. And the newspaper people—Jesus Fucking Christ. At least they didn't say *they* were sorry. They just wanted to know why I slugged the Rev in the gut with no procov—provocation."

"I'm sure you were provoked," she began.

"Bet your sweet Irish ass I was, baby. And now that you've said you're sorry, too, you can get the hell out."

"For somebody who's expecting me to say something about 'for better or for worse,' you've got one hell of an attitude."

"This is the worst it gets—and it never gets any better, don't you understand that?" The dragon's eyes were black. "I don't have a career. I don't have a *life*. Aw, what the fuck," he said with a pathetic attempt at shrugging it all off. "That's what I get for having an Irish temper. Anyway, whatever. You're well out of it."

"I take it you're trying to dump me."

"Before you can dump me? Yeah. You betcha, baby."

He never called her that—"babe" was an occasional, casual endearment, but this was entirely different. He was trivializing her, turning her into just another conquest, somebody he called "baby" because he couldn't quite remember her name. She decided she hated being called "baby."

"Why would I dump you?" she asked, stubbing out her cigarette and lighting another—without benefit of match or lighter. He blinked at that, and she gave him a sharp little smile. "Oh, I'll admit you look like shit and smell worse, and you're having yourself a fine old wallow—which is fairly loathsome, but you'll get over it."

He rose unsteadily, looming over her, frowning, eyes kindling with anger. He swayed slightly, reeking of sweat and liquor and cigarette smoke. "You can knock it off now, Holly. Just—cut the crap and get out. I'm nothin' you'd want—"

"You are *everything* I want," she said softly, unable to help herself.

Suddenly all the fight went out of him and he slipped to his knees before her.

She had never seen his moods change so fast. His hands almost touched her, then shied back, fingers curling tight into his palms. "Holly—darlin' Holly—" His eyes glistened. "You can't want me. Not now."

"Who the hell are you to tell me what I can and can't want?"

"This isn't the bargain you made. I'm not who you were gonna marry." He gestured to himself, the room around him. "You said 'yes' to somebody who had a career, a life, a future—it was bad enough before, the differences between us—but at least I had something to offer you. Now—I got nothin'. Abso-fuckin'-lutely nothin'. I'm not gonna let you chain yourself to a nothin' like me."

She told herself it was the booze talking, the shock, the impotent rage—anything but Evan Lachlan saying these words.

"What about *my* life?" she demanded. "The one I'm supposed to live with you?"

"Ain't gonna happen. Face it, Holly—you'd be a fool to want what I am—what I'm gonna become."

"What might that be?"

"My father." His laugh was curt and ugly. "Old, fat, drunk, walkin' a beat his whole goddamned life, heart attack at forty-nine—gives me ten years, more or less, before they retire me and I sit around gettin' fatter 'n' drunker an' whinin' about the good ol' days. That's my future, baby." He waved his hand aimlessly.

She got to her feet, standing over him where he slumped on the carpet, and swore she was going to slug him if he called her "baby" just one more time. "Am I to understand you don't much like the idea?"

"Not a whole bunch, no," he replied, trying to sound as if he didn't care.

"Then do something about it." The way he looked up at her, perhaps it would have been kinder to hit him. She took a few steps back, taunting him: "Come on, Lachlan. You've been at this routine for at least a week now. Everybody's aware that you sulk very effectively. You've made your point. Now get over yourself."

"Holly—Jesus, Holly, don't you understand?" The cry was torn out of him, ragged, desperate. "I lost *everything!*"

She stood her ground. He didn't need her tenderness; he needed her strength. "I'm staying." Then instinct stronger than reason made her take a step backward—because he surged to his feet, powerful muscles bunching beneath shirt and jeans, and his eyes were truly dragon's eyes now: vicious and feral.

"What the fuck does it take? Letters six feet high shoved under your nose?" he shouted. "Goddammit, I don't want you here!"

"Get off it, Lachlan! What good's a tantrum if you don't have an audience?"

"You bitch—!"

She supposed she ought to be glad she'd succeeded in touching off his temper after all. But she'd never known how filthy that temper could be. He surged toward her and she stumbled, one shoe turning under her foot and twisting her ankle painfully. His big hands flatted to the wall on either side of her head and he crushed himself against her. He was breathing hard, right into her face, the stench suffocating. She wouldn't have believed any man who'd drunk as much as he had would be capable, but she felt his hardness bulge against her hip.

He was half a foot taller than she and outweighed her by at least eighty pounds. For the first time ever she was afraid of him, of his size and strength, his tall body with its hard curves of muscle—and the danger within. But she wouldn't relinquish his gaze, wouldn't back down, wouldn't show any weakness.

"You stupid cunt." His gaze caught and held hers, the way dragons were said to do. "What'd you think, you could walk in and say you love me and make everything okay? 'It's all right, *a chuisle*,'" he singsonged cruelly. "'I love you *sooo* much, I can make it *allll* better!' Can you magic it all away? Huh? My own sweet Witchy Woman—c'mon, Holly, say 'Abracadabra' for me and make it *al-lll* better—"

"What're you gonna do, Lachlan—hit me or fuck me? Or doesn't it make any difference?"

It took a moment for the words to filter through the murk of alcohol. It was almost as if she could watch his mind struggle for comprehension—that such words had been said, that *she* had said them. Then his head bent, and he shoved away from the wall.

Holly sagged, sick and shaking, gulping precious air. She pushed her hair off her face and stared at his hunched, trembling figure. Somehow she couldn't feel very sorry for him. He was doing such a good job of it on his own.

"Get out," he breathed with no voice at all, arms wrapping himself, shivering as if August in New York had become December in Nome. "Just—get out."

"No."

He swung around and stared at her, still trying to catch his breath.

"You're mine," she said fiercely. "I don't much like that right now, and I don't like *you* right now at all, but you're mine and there's nothing either of us can do about it." She went to the door, defiantly not limping on her bruised ankle. "You smell like sewage. Take a shower. I'll be back in thirty minutes."

"Don't bother."

"Shut up." Without turning, her hand on the knob, she said quietly, "And if you *ever* raise your hand to me again, I'll kill you."

HE WANDERED AIMLESSLY ABOUT THE living room—looking for something, he couldn't think what. Then he saw it: the cashmere sweater, blue as her eyes. Must've been chilly when she got on the plane—

—to come home to him. To this.

Carefully he picked up the sweater, smoothed it, folded it, buried his face in its feather-softness that smelled of her perfume. He felt like a thief, stealing the fragrance of a woman no longer his.

He surprised himself by doing as he'd been told. Stripped; stuffed soiled clothes into the hamper; stood beneath a blistering shower. After wrapping himself in a towel, he shaved—the electric razor, he didn't trust his trembling hands with the straight-edge. He had to look at his own face while he shaved. The eyes were familiar, not because they were Evan Lachlan's eyes—where was the gold in them that she loved so much?—but because they were hollow, stunned, empty. He heard his own voice speaking to people whose eyes had been like this: *"I'm very sorry for your loss."*

He brushed his teeth until his gums bled, then drank two large glasses of water with vitamins and aspirin. He climbed into pajamas—an old pair, plain blue cotton, not the sumptuous black silk she'd given him for Christmas—and returned to the living room. Picking up the sweater again, he pressed his face against it and inhaled her fragrance. He took it with him into the bedroom, placing it on the bureau before sliding into bed.

Like a good little boy. Waiting for her to come back and make it all better.

Some of the alcoholic fog lifted, and as he lay there in the dark he knew that what he'd said tonight had been the truth. It wasn't going to get any better.

She loved him. Despite what he had almost done, she was still his as thoroughly as he knew he was hers. She would stay with him if he let her. But he couldn't let her. He'd made a wreck of things. If she stayed, he'd drag her down with him into this hell of his own making. Or, worse, he'd blindly seek the sweet haven of her arms, and never rise from his knees again—let alone stand on his own.

The life he could have had with her had escaped him before he'd had a chance to live it. He let himself imagine what it might have been like, coming home every night to her and the kids—he could see their red hair and blue eyes, feel their arms around his neck, hear their voices clamoring for Daddy to come see this and read that and please can I have a new bike for my birthday, and Holly was laughing at him as the kids conned him into just *one* more story before bedtime—

—and then it would be *their* bedtime, her warm giving body in his arms and her soft hair against his face, and they'd make love slow and tender or fast and frantic, every night for years and years and years until they were very, very old—

He curled on his side beneath the sheet and closed his eyes. Down on his knees—and the first move in rising was to stop regretting a future that would never be and dwelling on a past that he could do nothing about. He had to look at what was before him. Face it. Stare it down.

Without her.

HER ANKLE THROBBED AS SHE carried the grocery bags to his apartment. Bread and milk, steak and eggs, fresh fruit and greens; at twenty you could live off booze and junk, but pushing forty it wasn't so easy to bounce back. She opened the door and locked it behind her. Scents of soap and shampoo told her he'd showered and was probably in bed. She couldn't face the idea of going in to him just yet. The disaster in the living room depressed her completely, but she'd clean it up later. She was just so goddamned tired.

The kitchen was oddly pristine. Three glasses in the sink, a couple of forks, cheap wooden chopsticks still in their wrappers, and that was it. She filled the fridge, started the kettle to boil, and scrounged for coffee. He'd packed or tossed out just about everything in the cupboards, but she finally found a jar of instant coffee, with enough left for one very strong cup. She dosed it with milk and sat on the kitchen counter, legs dangling, and drank half of it before she felt braced enough to enter the bedroom.

He smelled clean and warm, tucked up in pajamas and a thin blue sheet. The thought crossed her mind that this was how his son would look when asleep— and, though she recoiled from the image, he was there before her, not the boy Evan had been but the boy he would father. Tousled dark hair, thick lashes shadowing smooth cheeks. Her heart twisted and she knelt beside the bed, setting her coffee mug on the floor.

"Heart of my heart," she whispered soundlessly. *"A chuisle mo chroi* . . . I can't lose you, I just can't—"

He slept on. She pulled the sheet up, took her cold coffee back to the living room, and began to clean.

Her ankle hurt like hell. But every stab of pain felt like penance for not being here. It wasn't right that she hadn't been here. He was supposed to have picked her up at the airport this evening. That he hadn't annoyed her only a little at the time; she was sure there'd be a message on her machine telling her he was sorry, he was tied up at work, he'd see her as soon as he could—and then his voice would deepen as he told her he loved her, had missed her, couldn't wait to get her into bed—

But there'd been no message from him. Instead, Susannah: *"Holly, call me the minute you get in—it's important."* And that was all. The first thing Susannah said was that Evan was all right—he hadn't been shot or wounded, don't worry. Holly was ashamed that such things hadn't even occurred to her. About to become a law officer's wife, and she'd never even considered—

Mindlessly she filled two plastic garbage bags with bottles and cans, boxes and ashes. When she was done she sat on the couch and lit a cigarette and smoked it down to the filter, staring at the photograph of him and his parents.

What was it she'd said once—all raw bones and big eyes—tall and too lanky, his hair too short, his nose too big for his face, years before he'd grow into that face and that strength and that heart-catching beauty. He stood there with an arm slung around his father's shoulders, grinning like a fool as the elder Lachlan smiled proudly at him. And there was his mother, blonde, lovely, oh-so-prim in her flowered dress and straw hat, not a hint in her pale eyes that she only wanted to get the hell out of there and find her next drink, her next fuck.

"It's not gonna happen for us, Holly."

His voice, calm and strong as it had not been earlier, startled her. He stood there in pajamas and an old blue bathrobe, hands bunched in its sagging pockets.

She didn't pretend ignorance of what he meant. "I love you. I want to be your wife."

"But I don't want you anymore."

She gasped with the damage of his words. "Liar!"

"I know. I'm sorry. I didn't mean it. I wish I could." He took a few steps, then stopped. His eyes were enormous, all the gleaming gold gone as if it had never been and never would be again. "Maybe what I mean is that *you* shouldn't want *me* anymore. All I know for sure is that it won't work for us. Not now."

"Why?" she cried out. "If we love each other—"

He shook his head, his voice gentle. "I couldn't live with you, not the way we planned, and live with myself. I gotta work this out. I just—I can't be with you now. I can't be with anyone." He paused. "Please."

And with that one word from this proud man, her heart broke. She looked down at her empty hands, vision blurring. "All right," she whispered. "Just— just do one thing for me, *Éimhín*, please—just h-hold me—" She lost her battle, her voice betraying her. She felt his hands on her shoulders, and looked up. Grief and guilt and absolute determination were in his eyes.

"Come here to me, my lady love," he murmured, drawing her up into his arms. He rocked her, lips moving through her hair—very tenderly, and without passion. Something in her died.

She pressed herself against him, wishing she could make them into one person. She could take some of his pain and rage and despair. She could carry it for him, she could take all of it—

No. She was strong, and he knew it, but he wouldn't let her. This was his, of his making. It had to be of his solving. She hated him for that. For being strong enough to do it—and strong enough to know he couldn't lean on her. To insist that he wouldn't lean on her.

She turned her cheek to the soft cotton covering his chest, missing the feel of his skin. She remembered the first time they'd made love, how his shirt and her blouse had ripped, buttons flying; how frantic they'd been—and how ever since that night they'd lain together with nothing but skin separating their hearts.

"Evan—"

"Shh," he whispered. "Shh."

After a long time, she pulled back. She couldn't look at him, couldn't say anything as she left him.

# Seventeen

SHE STARED THROUGH THE FARMHOUSE'S big picture window, mesmerized. They were dancing: the slight blond man caught easily, sweetly, in the arms of his tall dark lover, moving with a grace that bespoke half an eternity of knowing each other's bodies. Hands stroking lightly, possessively, gold rings glinting—matched as the two of them were matched.

She and Evan had looked like that, she told herself. Since childhood she'd thought of Alec and Nicky as the perfect couple—never mind their gender—and wanted the same thing for herself. Evan was it. He always would be.

She knew there were wardings on the house, but couldn't sense them—and neither did the wards react to her presence, for she was always welcome here. Eventually, though, the men inside felt someone watching them. Stopped; turned; saw her through the window. Alec was out the front door and with her in seconds.

"Holly! Come in, sweetheart, you're white as a ghost. Sit down." A strong arm about her shoulders pulled her gently through the foyer into the living room, into the familiar comfort of old books and Moroccan carpets and scarred leather furniture. "That's it. You sit right there and I'll get you a drink."

"Make it a big one," she heard herself say. "I'd like to be really, really drunk." Although she'd tried that last night, after getting home, and it hadn't worked.

"Uh-oh," Nicky said from the doorway.

"What's he done?" Alec added, pouring three large brandies. "Besides slug the Reverend, I mean. We heard about that."

"And read about it," Nick added, earning himself a glare from his partner. "What happened, Holly?"

"He l-left me. Goddammit—I *hate* weepy women!" She gulped liquor and coughed. "I am *not* going to cry." But all at once she was clinging to Nicky anyway, face hidden in the faded green cotton of his shirt. "No man is worth — "

"Granted, but anybody as pissed off as you obviously are has only two alternatives: cry or smash something. Is the Beemer still intact?"

She pulled back indignantly. "No man is worth my car, either!"

"Of course he isn't," said Alec.

"That bastard — does he think he'll ever find another woman like me?"

"Of course he doesn't," said Nicky.

"He'll never find *anyone* like me again, and if he's too stupid to realize it — " She drained brandy down her throat and damned near threw the glass into the empty hearth. "He's in for a shock when he's fucking some vapid little bitch with big tits and no ass, and half a minute into it he'll be bored out of his mind!"

"Of course he will," said Alec.

"Can't you do anything but agree with me?"

"My darling girl," Nicky said, "the mood you're in, we don't dare do anything *but* agree with you. You'd hurt us."

She laughed until she all but cried again. Nicky guided her to her feet and toward the downstairs bath, where he directed her to wash up for dinner.

"I'm not hungry, but you go ahead."

He pretended shock. "You can't turn down Alyosha's slum scallion!"

His partner shot back, "Slum *gullion*, you ignorant Hungarian. Come on, Holly, let's eat."

They did; she didn't. Not much, anyway. Afterward, they repaired to the living room again, and Nicky offered, "If you like, I can help you get some sleep."

"Would you? Oh, Nicky, I'm so tired — "

"Come on upstairs, then. We'll find you a nice old pair of pajamas and tuck you up under a quilt, and you'll almost think you're back home at Woodhush."

He did his best. Holly hadn't the heart to tell him his best wasn't good enough. After he murmured gentle incantations for ten long minutes, she pretended to be asleep. She heard him leave the room, and his voice as he talked softly to Alec in the hallway. But she was no nearer slumber now than she'd been last night.

Holly waited an hour or two, until the house was dark and quiet. Then she slid out of bed, pulled on one of Alec's old dressing gowns that he'd left for her, and padded barefoot downstairs with a fresh pack of smokes, a lighter, and an ashtray. The addition of a few pillows made the porch swing almost as comfortable as the bed upstairs, and she sat there smoking and rocking and staring out into the warm summer night.

"Holly, it's nearly one in the morning."

She glanced up. Nicholas, tousled and pajama-clad, looking ten years younger than his age, stood in the doorway.

"If you say so," she said.

With an impatient sigh he came outside, sat on the porch swing beside her, and appropriated a cigarette.

"Don't tell Alec," he warned as he lit it. "I quit thirty years ago." Exhaling prodigiously, he eyed her sideways. "I knew you weren't asleep, by the way."

"Sorry." She gave a little shrug.

"Sulking, I see."

"Nursing my broken heart," she countered lightly. "You'd think one of us over the years would've come up with a curing spell for that."

"Don't be maudlin." Nick sighed out another lungful of smoke. "In point of fact, I could cure it if I felt like it. Which I don't. Too much effort."

"Bullshit."

"Yes," he agreed. "But one does like to pretend one has powers beyond one's puny gifts."

"You've done all right with what you've got. Better than I have."

"Ah, but what you've got isn't something the rest of us poor drudges understand." He leaned back, making the swing rock gently. "Do you remember when you found out?"

"Like I could forget?"

"Did we ever tell you our side of it?" He put an arm around her shoulders. "I'll spin the tale for you, Witchling—a real *paramitscha,* the kind of stories told around the fire in Romany camps. And if you put it in a book, I'll sue."

"Would I do that?"

"If you thought you could get away with it, yes. All right, then. Once upon a time in a land called Virginia, two young men got lost in a snowstorm. . . ."


NICHOLAS RUBBED A SLEEVE AGAINST the pickup's windshield, but smearing condensation around did nothing to improve the view. In English parlance, rain was likened to cats and dogs; this snowstorm was lions and wolves. "I can't see a bloody thing," he complained. "Where the hell are we?"

"Virginia, last time I checked." Alec tried the wipers again; they got stuck in snow halfway up, and refused to budge.

"*Where* in Virginia?" He amended the metaphor to prides of lions and several packs of wolves.

"How the hell should I know?"

"It's your country, Alec."

"And could you navigate the wilds of Transylvania in a snowstorm?"

"Transylvania is in Romania. I'm Hungarian. I thought good little American schoolboys learn all about Virginia when they study Washington and Jefferson."

"Virginia in the 1700s—which I'll bet was the last time they did any maintenance on this road." He peered through the windshield. "Is that a light?"

"Careful. It might be Andreiu and his miraculous retractable fangs, trying to lure us."

"As long as he lures us someplace warm, I really don't care." He paused. "Warm, with a pot of hot coffee and a plate of oatmeal cookies."

The golden glow, fitful as a firefly in the storm, grew brighter. And both men's senses reeled as the light touched them.

"Impossible."

"Improbable," Nick corrected. "Remember your Sherlock Holmes. 'When you have eliminated the impossible—'"

"'—whatever remains, however improbable, must be the truth,'" Alec finished for him. "But didn't Mr. Scot say there weren't any of us out here?"

"I would say he has been underinformed. Shall I send a request for cookies and see who responds?"

"Or *what* responds."

All at once a rich scents filled the chilly interior of the Chevy. Oatmeal, brown sugar, walnuts, a delicate hint of cinnamon.

"*Az Istenért!*" whispered one voice at the same time the other muttered, "My God!"

Five edgy minutes later they struggled from the truck into the snow, gazes fixed on rectangles of golden light delineating the windows and door of a house. Two red-brick stories, with an ambitious if vaguely absurd portico-and-pillars arrangement out front; in the open doorway stood a tall woman and a little girl.

"Well? What y'all waitin' for—Imbolc? Get on in here!"

The two men slogged through hip-deep drifts. The door slammed and warmth enveloped them from a hearthfire in the room to their left.

"I don't know who you are," Alec said, "but—"

"I'm just the same as you, or you wouldn't be here," the woman announced. "Get out of those cold damp things before you drip all over Great-great-grandma Flynn's best carpet."

Meekly they did as told. She was no older than they were—perhaps a year or so younger—but she wielded authority like Catherine the Great. Tall, sturdily made, she was handsome rather than pretty, her hair a wild tangle of red-gold curls, her eyes a startling shade of blue. The child—perhaps ten and perhaps not—who peered up at the two strangers was almost her carbon copy.

Nick shed coat, sweater, and shoes. These were snatched up by the girl, who ran them into the next room and set them to toast by the fire. Soon both he and Alec were wearing ancient knitted afghans and being herded to the sofa beside the hearth.

"Welcome to Woodhush Farm. I'm Lulah McClure," the woman announced. "This is my niece. And you might be—?"

"Nicholas Orlov. My associate, Alexander Singleton."

"I'm Holly," the little girl contributed. "Do you want the cookies now?"

Alec blinked. "Uh—"

Nick intercepted the helpless glance and shrugged. "May I help?"

"If you can hurry up the percolator." The child grinned all over her freckled face. "I can't even boil water the *usual* way. And I'm sorry we don't have oatmeal cookies, like Aunt Lulah said you wanted. Will gingersnaps do?"

With coffee and cocoa and cookies laid out on a low oak table beside the fire, Lulah McClure fixed an appraising eye on the two men. "You're here after the vampires up Old Rag Mountain, aren't you?"

Nick almost choked on his coffee. "How did you—?"

"I sent a call in to the regional office," she drawled. "Sheriff McNichol and I can only do so much. Hope to hell one of you's got what it takes to clean up a nest."

"Sheriff McNichol?"

"Cousin Jesse," Holly explained. "He's Witch-folk, like us. More cookies, Mr. Singleton?"

"Thanks. Do you ever have any trouble being what you are? I mean, do any of the people around here—"

"Oh, they're more likely to eye us because we're Catholic," Holly answered with a shrug. "Not many of 'em do, since most are related to us one way or another. There's McClures and Flynns and Kirbys and McNicholses all over these hills."

"Any vampires in the family?" Nick asked blandly.

"Not recently," Holly deadpanned.

He snorted. Smart-ass kid. He rather liked her. "About this new nest—"

"Oh, it's not new," Lulah told him. "Story goes back a ways, actually. Nobody goin' nowhere tonight, so you might's well have more coffee and listen."

Back in 1932 (Lulah began), a book called *Hollow Folk* was published by a Mr. Sherman and a Mr. Henry, who wrote about Appalachia just exactly as if they knew what they were talking about. They described it as a place where people still lived the frontier life of the eighteen-century backwoods and spoke the English of Shakespeare's time. Crowded into mud-plastered log cabins, supported by primitive agriculture, illiterate, almost completely cut off from the world, these people had never seen a railroad or a five-dollar bill.

"Crap, of course," said Lulah with a sniff. "They had everything from Coca-Cola to Japanese porcelain dinnerware and Model-T Fords. But considering the mess this country was in during the '30s, they figured they were well out of the mainstream. Besides, it was a helluvalot of fun to fox the researchers. They had a fine old time playing quaint and unlettered and ignorant—before goin' home to their Caruso records and Jack Benny on the radio."

Alec grinned. "I like their style."

"Appalachia is all-American, and yet it's un-American," Lulah mused. "It's a folk culture that goes back to the earliest days of the country, but it's also the most resistant to progress—'cept maybe for the Amish. But you can't hide in Pennsylvania quite the way you can in the Blue Ridge."

What the sly hill folk hadn't known, however, was that certain influential persons decided to seize on their "uncivilized" way of life to dispossess them of their land, making their lack of modern amenities the excuse for destroying their homes and turning a vast swath of hill country into a preserve. In December of 1935, Shenandoah National Park was established. Five hundred families were displaced to "more civilized regions of agriculture and industry."

"This was exactly what the vampires wanted. Some prime land got taken over by a little family nest. Now, there've always been vampires around here— they're everywhere that ordinary folks are—but mostly they kept to themselves. They don't drink the tourists, they sure as shootin' don't guzzle local folks, and if a farmer loses a cow or a sheep every so often—well, that's farming, and the losses get spread out pretty even around the county. Peaceful coexistence, more or less."

"But this group was different," Alec suggested.

Lulah nodded, firelight striking gold off her tangled red hair. "First it was hikers and campers from elsewhere who disappeared. But then locals started to go missing. Granddaddy spent a small fortune on garlic, protectin' every farm in the area. Then he let the nest know that the sooner they cleared out, the better. Most packed up and went elsewhere, once they found out Grandaddy meant business."

Holly listened wide-eyed; this was obviously a family tale she hadn't heard. Nick reflected that Lulah McClure's version must be appreciably edited, and wondered how her grandfather had managed the eviction.

"A few decided they liked it around here, and stayed. Grandaddy saw to it they abided by the rules. Things got back to normal."

*"Ando gav bi zhuklesko jal o pavori bi detesko,"* Nick murmured.

Holly looked startled; Alec sighed. "Yet another obscure Gypsy proverb. He's got a million of them—at least. Nick, perhaps you'd be so kind as to translate for us ignorant *Gadje*?"

" 'In a village without dogs, the farmers walk without sticks.' "

"Gypsy?" Lulah scoffed. "With a Russian name and blond hair?"

"Don't ask," Alec advised dryly.

"What's a *Gadje*?" Holly wanted to know.

"Anybody who's not a Gypsy," Nick replied. "Forgive my interruption, Miss McClure, please go on. How do you think Andreiu found out about this area?"

"That's what was puzzlin' me, until you gave me his name. 'Bout two years back, a cult moved into the old Neville place. Oh, they had the whole show going—rituals, animal sacrifices—rank amateurs, of course."

"Some find Witchcraft very chic," Alec murmured.

"If it'd been just that, nobody woulda minded. We're tolerant folk, mostly. But it turned out they were white supremacists worshipping old Norse gods. The pamphlets Jesse and I found read as bad or worse than what the Klan used to print."

"Let me guess," said Nick. "After defeating one's enemies, the ancient Teutonic tradition is to drink—" Just in time he remembered the little girl's presence, and amended his words to, "—from their skulls, to absorb their strength."

"You mean 'drink their blood,'" Holly corrected. "It goes back to the Celtic tribes as described by Julius Caesar—"

Lulah sighed into her coffee mug. "I try to raise her right, the way her mama and my brother would've wanted. But she's got a brain like a sponge and soaks up the Good Lady only knows what. Anyway, Jesse and I got rid of those people. But it took us two days of hard work to clean the evil out of that house."

"Somebody there was *not* an amateur," Nick said.

"Somebody," she agreed. "We took everything out and burned it. Including a big ol' empty shipping crate with Karel Andrieu's name on it."

"*I* think there was a coffin inside it," Holly told them.

"*I* decided I didn't want to look," Lulah retorted immediately.

"I agree with Holly," Nick said. "Andreiu is known for keeping home-soil coffins in various places. What exactly has happened since he got here?"

Holly snagged another cookie. "Mr. Mallory lost four cows just before Hallowe'en, stolen right out of his barn one night. And the Widow Farnsworth, she was out hunting her Thanksgiving turkey and found a couple of deer carcasses drained of blood."

"Any human deaths?" Alec asked.

Lulah's expression turned grim. "Week ago last Monday Lucretia Houston disappeared."

"And then reappeared," Holly put in. "Most of her, anyways."

Her aunt gave her a quelling look. "Holly Elizabeth, isn't it past your bedtime?" Big blue eyes rounded and the freckled face assumed woeful lines. Lulah snorted. "All right, but if you have nightmares, don't blame me. They identified Lucretia by her dental records—yes, we do have forensic science in Appalachia. She'd been got to by animals. But there was no blood. None."

"And the increase in losses, leading up to this lady's death, directly correlates to Karel Andreiu's arrival in the area?" Nick frowned. "One kill a week isn't much."

"I'd say my partner is bloodthirsty," Alec said to Holly, "but the context is wrong. Have any more of the locals seen anything, heard anything?"

Lulah shook her head. "Not a flick of a bat's wing. I don't believe our local vampires are behind this, unless some of 'em have gone over to Andreiu's side.

Can't really see that, though," she added thoughtfully. "I've known Ben Poulter all my life, f'rinstance, and he's harmless as a butterfly."

The men exchanged glances: socializing with a vampire? Alec said, "How many are there?"

"A dozen or so. The daylight kind, anyway. There may be a few more of the allergic-to-sunshine sort. They stay pretty much to themselves, and we don't bother them, so it's worked out fine since the Depression."

"But now there is Andreiu," Nick murmured. "A true *vlkoslak*—a vampire. Do you know where he hides himself during the day?"

"Up Old Rag Mountain. I don't know exactly where. The damned thing's granite, and tryin' to see through solid rock gives me a headache."

"Of course," Alec said affably, as if he knew a score of others who could in actuality look through solid rock. "What else is up on Old Rag Mountain?"

"Just the village," Holly said. "Post office, couple of stores, two churches, a cemetery, and a school."

"Don't sneeze or you'll miss it," Alec interpreted wryly, and bent to scratch the ears of a huge ginger tabby that ignored him in favor of springing into Holly's lap.

"As you surmised," Nick said, "we're here to track down Andreiu. Our superiors are not especially fond of him or his methods."

Lulah nodded. "If you can clean out that nest up there, I'd be much obliged."

"We'll do our best." Alec finished his coffee and stretched. "Well, even if it's not *your* bedtime, Holly, it's certainly mine after driving all day in a snowstorm. Just show us to the couches, and—"

"Don't be silly." Lulah smiled. "We've been expecting you all day."

Holly confessed, "I dropped a piece of bread this morning, butter-side up. Then I dropped a dish rag. And then I got out the broom to sweep—which I *never* do," she finished with a grin.

"All three of which," Lulah told them, "mean unexpected visitors. Holly honey, run up and get extra quilts for the Wisteria Room and the General's Tent, and make sure the towels are clean."

The girl glanced at the two men. "It's not really a tent, y'know. We just call it that, from the time George Washington slept here." She laughed, fully aware of the cliché. "He really did! We got a thank-you note and everything—"

"Holly. The quilts?"

"Yes, Aunt Lulah. But they won't mind sleeping in the same bed. They've done it before. Off, Bandit." And, dumping the cat off her knees, off she ran.

Alec's face was a study before he hastily composed himself. "Umm—she's right, we don't need to muss up two beds or two bedrooms."

"Suit yourselves." Lulah rose and headed for the hall stairs. "Breakfast at eight. Good night."

It took Nick a minute to locate his voice again after she'd gone. "Alec. . . ."

"Hmm?" He seemed quite intent on watching Bandit groom a bedraggled ear that bore witness to many a hard-won victory in the field.

"Do they think we're—?"

"If they do, it certainly doesn't seem to bother them." He chuckled. "Of course, when one has just discussed how best to deal with a vampire, a little thing like that wouldn't even raise an eyebrow, would it?"

"But how did Holly know? That we've shared a bed before—out of necessity," he added quickly. "Not that we—because we aren't."

"You're cute when you're flustered, did you know that?" He grinned. "I don't know what she knows or how she knows it. I'm not even sure exactly what she is."

"That's not usual for you." Leaning back in a worn easy chair, he stretched his feet to the fire. "As a rule, you make the identification within ten minutes."

"I know, and it's driving me batty." When Nick scowled at him, he paused and shook his head. "Another ill-considered pun. Sorry."

"What about Holly?" his partner asked patiently.

"Can't say yet. The implication is that she's lousy at everything—including boiling water the usual way," he added with a smile. "Interesting kid. There's talent there, I just haven't put my finger on it yet. She has some tricky wardings—Lulah's work, if I'm not mistaken—and they're in my way. Lulah's main talent is far-sense, by the way. Nothing clairvoyant or clairaudient, but she knew where we were."

"And sensed the desire for coffee and oatmeal cookies when I thought about it hard enough."

"Seems so. I can't get a read on the girl, though."

"Let me know when you figure it out. I'll collect our suitcases. Time for bed." Rising, he grinned down at his partner. "And keep your hands to yourself."

"You're no fun."

"How would *you* know?"

"I know you, that's how I know. I'm the one who told you the name of your bookstore ought to be 'The Felonious Monk.'"

"A vile pun, and an even viler misrepresentation," he retorted. "On *both* counts." And with that he reclaimed his shoes and coat, and departed the parlor.

At the front door he nearly tripped over the cat. "It's cold out there," he told it. "Are you sure you want out?" A paw batted lightly at his shoe. When he went outside, Bandit followed.

Trudging through swirling snow to the pickup, the cat bounding beside him through the drifts, his attention was suddenly caught by a shadow of movement in a curtained upstairs window. Lulah McClure held a candle in one hand, the other gesturing lightly, gracefully, before she let the curtain drop. He shrugged, wondering why she'd been watching him—and then caught his breath. Bandit was calmly striding the gravel path between the pickup and the barn—which was as clear and dry as if it hadn't snowed here in twenty years.

He ran to open the great wooden door, then back to drive the Chevy into hiding. Carrying suitcases, he started for the house. An aggrieved yowl stopped him. Turning, he saw Bandit in the open barn door. Hurrying to close it, he muttered a thanks to the cat, who leaped into the snowdrifts and bounced around to the back of the house—presumably to his own private door.

Back inside, shivering, Nick shed coat and shoes, then climbed the stairs past what were obviously family portraits. In five paintings and a dozen photos were variations of red hair, blue eyes, straight noses, and the occasional dimple. He paused to inspect an eighteenth-century portrait of a woman at her loom, smiling at the artist's subtle inclusion of the Craft: the loom weights were painted with hexes, and the half-finished cloth was woven with sigils for warmth. Next to the weaver was a watercolor of a stern Revolutionary War officer on a huge gray horse; in the tooling of saddle and bridle were spells of protection and speed. To the unaware, all of it would seem just pretty decoration. Nick knew better.

He found Alec in the upstairs hallway, admiring a quilt displayed on the wall. Setting down both suitcases, he approached his partner and said, "Exquisite work."

Alec had leaned close to the worn, faded, still eloquent material. "Aunt Lucy has a similar one. The Double Wedding Ring pattern is traditional, but the stitching is Traditional—if you know what I mean."

"Mmm. And would you just look at all those pentagrams."

"I guarantee a good night's sleep if the bed quilt is anything like this one."

"It is," said Holly from behind them. "The Wisteria Room usually has Spring Flowers on it, but seeing as how you are what you are, I put Courthouse Steps on it instead. Integrity and strength and all that," she added shyly. "It may be a little musty—we haven't had it out since the Justice came to visit."

"Which Justice?" Alec asked.

"Which Justice do you think?" Nick answered for her, and Alec looked startled. "Thank you, Holly. Let me have those towels, and then you can get to bed. It's late, and I'm sure you have school tomorrow."

"Not with all this snow. And if you think I'd go anywhere while you're here to Work—" She broke off with a sigh. "I just wish I could help. I can't stitch or weave or brew, I'm not a Come-Hither or a Douser and I can't even Call much of a fire. But at least I can listen and watch, can't I? Please?"

"Talk to your aunt," Alec said firmly. But he winked, and she brightened, and called "Good night!" over her shoulder as she ran off to her room.

Nick paused at the doorway of the Wisteria Room to peer up at the carved lintel. "There are hexes all over this house. Generations of them."

"But no Witching spheres," Alec pointed out, nodding toward the windows. Shutting the door behind them, he stretched mightily and sighed. "Let's send down a few when we get back home, okay?"

"That violet one in Hezekiah's shop would look perfect in this room—" He broke off and blinked as Bandit hopped onto the huge oak four-poster. "Where'd you come from so fast?"

"What? Oh—him," Alec said, shucking off sweater and shirt. "He ran past me on the stairs."

Nick had learned in childhood that there were cats and Cats. Bandit was definitely a Cat. Giving the men an innocent stare, he patrolled the edge of the bed, sniffing now and then at a lump in the quilt. Nick watched him, amused, for now that Bandit had clued him in he, too, smelled the rosemary sachets stitched into the coverlet. Shakespeare notwithstanding, the herb was not just for remembrance, but for wisdom. Among other things. The scent took him back to his childhood, and for once the memories were pleasant ones. After a mighty sneeze, the Cat curled himself at the foot of the bed and promptly went to sleep.

Nick wandered about, fingering wisteria-patterned damask curtains, Irish linen sheets, and the smooth curve of an oak cheval glass.

"*Chindilan?*" his partner asked.

"Very tired, yes. Your pronunciation is getting better."

"For a *Gadje.*" Alec grinned back.

"*Gadjo,* masculine singular," Nick replied idly, inspecting a framed nosegay of dried flowers. A trace of very old magic lingered behind the glass.

"So what does your Gypsy blood tell you?"

"Not much. I'm only a quarter Rom, after all. I barely qualify."

"By those standards, I'm an outright mongrel."

"Don't ever let your Aunt Lucy hear you say that!" Nick turned and smiled. "All that fine old New England heritage, straight back to Salem—she'd string you up by your thumbs."

"What are the other three-quarters?" Alec sat on the bed, bouncing experimentally. "You never have talked about your family much."

"Oh, this and that, the usual Magyar mix," he evaded, and changed the subject. "I can't say that I've ever considered the ecology of vampires before. Somehow, I don't think that's quite what Rachel Carson had in mind when she wrote *Silent Spring.*"

"*Silent Night* would be more like it."

Both men spun tensely around when a knock sounded on the door. "Mr. Singleton? Mr. Orlov? Is Bandit in there?"

"Yes," Nick replied, opening the door for Holly. "He can stay if he likes."

The Cat trilled agreement. Holly scowled. "You," she ordered. "Out. Now." An affronted "*mroww*"; Holly propped her fists on her hips. "Bandit!"

"We really don't mind him —," Nick began.

"But you'd mind getting your nose licked raw. Bandit! Out!" The Cat landed on the hardwood floor with a thud and stalked out of the room. Holly shook her head. "He gets worse every year. Well, good night again, Mr. Single-ton, Mr. —"

"That's Alec and Nicky to you, my dear," Alec said with a smile. "Good night, Holly."

She smiled back, and was gone.

Suitcases gave up their stash of pajamas, toothbrushes, and other necessi-ties. After taking his turn in the bathroom down the hall, Nick slid into the left side of the huge four-poster and drew the quilt up to his chin. "Alec, do you ever wonder why we do this? I mean, I could be back in New York right now, mind-ing the store —"

"—selling first editions of Sayers and Poe at exorbitant prices —"

"—and translating six different languages into comprehensible English —"

"—and getting paid damned well for that, too." His partner smiled down at him. "I could be a full-time lawyer instead of having Fairleigh and Bradshaw think I'm a hopeless dilettante with the partnership potential of a circus flea." He sat on the bed and traced the angular pattern of the quilt with one finger.

"We both know why we're here," Nick said wryly. "Mr. Scot gave us that *look* of his."

"Ah, yes — The Look. The one that makes you feel as if sitting in your nice cozy office is an affront to nature. We do what we do, Nick. Ours not to ques-tion why." Drawing back the covers on his side of the bed, he slid in, reached to turn off the lamp, and snuggled down. "G'night."

The next morning was pleasantly spent in the kitchen, sampling Cousin Clary's herbal teas, formulating and refining their plans, and engaging in a pleasant intellectual debate about whether or not a storm could block out enough sunlight for a *wampyr* to feel safe. They were also shown General Wash-ington's note to "*Mistress Margaret Flynne for her gracious hospitality and the sweet quiet hush of her woods*," framed on the wall of the room he'd slept in.

"That's when we got our name," Holly informed them. "We were Flynn's Hope before that, but by 1785 all the letters are addressed to Woodhush Farm. How can you resist getting your house named by George Washington?"

After lunch, Lulah's meaningfully arched brows sent Holly grumbling off to her textbooks. Alec and Nick went upstairs for a nap, reasoning that if they were going to spend all night chasing vampires, they'd need the rest.

Nick woke before dusk to three distinct sensations. He was alone in bed; he was more rested than he'd felt in ages; and he was being watched. Opening one eye, he saw freckles, red hair, and inquisitive blue eyes. "Hello," he said tentatively.

"You slept well," she observed. "It's a good quilt." Then, with the devastating simplicity of children, she asked, "Why do you hold a pillow when you sleep, when you want to be holding *him?*"

# Eighteen

HOLLY STARED. "I really said that? I don't remember."

"*I* do—vividly." Nick hugged her closer. "I damned near had a coronary."

"I should've set myself up as a matchmaker—life would've been less compli-cated."

"If you say so. But that talent wasn't the one we found out about that night."

"*That*, I remember. Vividly."

LULAH FED THEM AN EARLY dinner of lamb chops, potatoes, green beans, and rhubarb pie. They went upstairs to dress in their warmest clothes and arm themselves, then came back down to find the McClures at the front door. Night had fallen, the snow had stopped, and two horses were saddled and waiting out-side beneath the portico.

"Faster than the pickup, believe me," Lulah told them. "You never know when the snow's gonna reach up and grab you—and a truck tire can't kick free. I'm assuming y'all can ride?" When they nodded, she made a pleased sound in the back of her throat. From a pocket of her cardigan sweater she drew two tal-ismans on long strands of leather. "Umpty-ump Great-grandpa Goare carried this during the Revolution," she said, handing one to Alec. "And this—" Giving the other to Nick. "—comes from Holly's Griffith ancestors, who were horsey folk and swore by turquoise." Nicholas examined the chunk of sky-blue stone about the size of his little fingernail, set in iron. Alec's, he saw, was a carnelian paired with a bloodstone, similarly clasped by iron.

"Holly, would you do me the honor?" Alec asked gallantly, and bent so the girl could slip the leather thong around his neck.

The talisman slipped from her fingers; she made a grab for it in midair, and as she closed her hand around it exclaimed, "Ow!"

"After two hundred years, you'd think the rough edges would've worn off that iron," Lulah said. "Let me see, Holly."

"It's okay—it's already stopped bleeding." She held up her palm, where three tiny punctures showed on the heel of her thumb.

Alec enclosed her small fingers in his and kissed the back of her hand. "Wounded in the service."

"Kiss it and make it better?" she asked, shrewd eyes flashing at Nick, who winked at her. "Alec Singleton, y'all're a flirt and no better than you should be."

"And you, little miss," Lulah admonished, "are an uppity child who doesn't get spanked near enough. Go clean up supper and *maybe* I'll let you stay up to wait for them."

"Aunt Lulah!" she wailed. "How could I sleep?"

Nick donned the turquoise, tucked it beneath his sweater, and shrugged into his coat. "We're likely to be gone all night. Neither of you should—"

"We'll wait," Lulah said succinctly, and that was an end to that.

Holly walked them outside into a sparkling cold night, the stars so brilliant that they seemed to reflect on the gleaming snow. Nick inhaled sharply, his breath coming out in a cloud of white.

The girl checked saddle girths, saying, "The chestnut is called Lazybones, but don't let the name fool you. He's fast when there's need. The palomino is Featherfoot. He's a sweetie, once you let him know who's boss. Y'all be careful."

"We will." Glancing at Alec, he added, "Lazybones is unquestionably meant for you."

"Cute, isn't he?" Alec observed sourly to Holly, who laughed. He used one gloved hand to smooth the palomino's shoulder and the other to ruffle Nick's hair. "Growing our winter coat, are we? Two shaggy blonds: Featherfoot and Featherhead. Go on back in the house, Holly, it's cold."

"Oh—that reminds me. We tied a couple of blankets to the saddles, in case it gets any colder than it is now. Happy hunting!"

Lulah had been correct; the horses were much more practical than the Chevy. Chillier, but more practical. When Nick complained of the cold, Alec laughed.

"This from the kid who walked five miles to school in the snow?"

"Ten," he shot back with a grin. "Barefoot."

Directions up to Old Rag, past silent white fields and shadowy woods, had been specific. But they never got that far.

"Nick . . . ," Alec ventured, reining in about ten miles uphill from Woodhush Farm.

"What?"

"Correct me if I'm wrong. . . ."

"You usually are, but go ahead."

"Don't bats come out to feed at about twilight? And isn't it full dark right now? And have you ever seen a bat that big?" He pointed with a gloved finger.

"*Sheka!*" The damned thing was the size of a California condor.

"Hungarian cussing is bad enough," Alec muttered. "When you switch to Rom, you get really foul. Come on."

They left the road, horses plunging through the snow, and followed the bat. It worked as hard as the horses, for there were no thermal updrafts to float on and immense wings must beat vehemently against the frigid wind. The bat came to rest at last atop the stone skeleton of what might once have been an elegant antebellum home. Glaring balefully down twenty feet at the two men on horseback, it heaved for breath, exhaling great white fetid clouds they could smell even from the ground. Alec swung down, stumbling a little in the snow, and glared up at the bat.

"Andreiu!" he shouted. "Come down from there!"

Great leathery wings unfurled—blacking out the starlight, casting shadows onto Alec. A piercing hiss issued from between gleaming fangs.

"You expect me to be impressed?"

Nick slid from his saddle, landing lightly in knee-high drifts. "I expect he expects you to go away and leave him alone."

"Andreiu, you've been a very naughty *wampyr*, and Mr. Scot wants to have a little chat with you. Do we do this the easy way or the hard way?"

The bat laughed. More or less. Listening carefully, Nick decided that the wheezing, stuttering chirp was indeed laughter. It wasn't quite so vile as nails-on-chalkboard, but it was an annoyance all the same.

"Alyosha, I'm freezing. Just get him down from there and let's go, all right?" Delving into a pocket, he came up with two sets of silver shackles and dangled them from gloved fingers. "Hurry it up, would you?"

"You want me to drag him down by the fangs?" To the bat: "Andreiu, we both know this is ridiculous. I work a few illusions, you struggle and get distracted, I spell you into changing back into a human, my friend here does his thing, and you're down here wearing these seriously fashionable silver bracelets. Personally, I'd rather not tire myself. Be a good little bloodsucker and spare us both, okay?"

Nick snorted. "I'm beginning to think you intend to talk him into submission." He stamped his numbed feet. "If you won't expend the energy on a Working, then why *don't* you climb up and wrestle him down?"

"Even if I could find a toehold, there's about a ton of stone wall that could collapse any second—"

Nick knew that sudden silence, that abrupt glitter in brown eyes. "Alyosha?"

His partner strode forward, boots crunching confidently in the snow, one hand fumbling at his neck. With the carnelian-and-bloodstone talisman clenched in his right fist, he began to murmur, left hand gesturing swiftly.

The old building shuddered as if the stones were trying to shrug off the *wampyr*'s weight. Snow cascaded in miniature avalanches that spewed clouds of white. The bat screeched, wings flailing as its perch trembled. Rock chittered alarmingly against rock—and then the whole ramshackle construction shook it-self apart and toppled with a muffled rumble of stone.

Right onto Alec.

Who stood there quite calmly, absolutely untouched.

Of all the things Nicholas Orlov had witnessed in his admittedly bizarre career, this sight stopped both mind and heart. Alec ought to have been buried, crushed and bleeding, beneath that onslaught of stone. Instead, he casually brushed snow off his shoulders, narrowed his eyes, and stepped elegantly out of the rubble.

Andreiu—in human form—lay half-in and half-out of a pile of rock. Alec snapped his fingers for the silver handcuffs; Nick shook himself out of his daze and tossed them over. He fastened the leg restraints onto the *vlkoslak*'s ankles himself, fingers not quite steady. Andreiu lay there, stunned by the fall and the abruptness of transformation. The silver woke him up, raising welts on hyper-sensitive skin, an allergy that would weaken him enough to prevent another shape-change. As consciousness returned, Andreiu struggled to reassume his bat form—a hideous sight, with leathery black skin and fangs and sharply pointed ears fading in and out of view. A painful process, too, judging by his ag-onized grimaces.

"Give it up," Nick advised, wondering idly why it was that every *wampyr* seemed to be devastatingly good-looking and built like a brick battleship. "Or we'll stake you right here and now."

"He's fed tonight," Alec reported. "And on a human. Look at his eyes." Planting a booted foot squarely on Andreiu's naked chest, he asked, "Who were you after? You don't need sustenance. It's someone special that you need to be at full strength to take. Tell me who you drank from, and who you're after—and I wouldn't advise lying. I have this strange little quirk for knowing a lie when I hear it."

Huge eyes glowed red for an instant, then faded back to dark brown as sil-ver sapped his strength. "You!"

"No," Alec said with the unwavering certainty that was one of his gifts. "Not either of us. You're out alone, without the nest to back you up. So it must be somebody you don't want them to know about—somebody you fear."

"I fear no one and nothing!"

"Another lie. Well, Mr. Scot will sort it out. Nicky, I hate to break up a matched blond set, but do you think Featherfoot would object to having a vampire slung across his back?"

Featherfoot was not, in fact, pleased. He rolled his eyes, laid back his ears, bared his teeth, and looked as though he'd love to batter that aristocratic face with his iron-clad hooves. Nick could coerce humans, not horses; he pondered a minute, then took off the turquoise talisman and hung it from the saddle horn. "Better?" he asked the horse, stroking and calming him. Featherfoot snorted, but settled down.

Alec heaved Andreiu over the saddle and draped a blanket over him. Nick perched behind his partner on Lazybones for the ride back to Woodhush Farm, Featherfoot's reins in his hand and an eye on Andreiu at all times. They found the road again without too much trouble.

"Good thing it's still fairly early," he told Alec. "Holly will get to bed on time."

"You really like her, don't you? I'll admit to a weakness for red hair and freckles, myself."

Andreiu growled, shifting on Featherfoot's back, across which he was slung like a sack of grain. "Quiet down," Nick advised, putting some magic into it just so he didn't feel quite so useless. "And don't even think about biting the horse. He's likely to bite back." To Alec: "I didn't know you liked redheads that much. Your last five girlfriends have been blondes."

"Always at the top of my list."

Which included, Nick reflected peevishly, every conceivable hair color, eye color, and cup size known to New York City.

The horses picked up the pace, recognizing the road home. Soon enough the men were unloading their cargo onto a hay bale in the barn. "If you're cold, I'm sure we can find another blanket," Alec said with mock solicitude. "A bit horsey-smelling, but one makes do with what one has."

Nick unsaddled Featherfoot, who seemed relieved to be rid of his burden. "Where's the garlic?" he asked.

"I thought *you* brought it."

"Damn it, Alec, must I do everything?"

Further censure was prevented by the timely entrance of Lulah and Holly—the former with a silver crucifix, the latter with a long braid of garlic.

"Got him, I see," Lulah remarked, nodding her satisfaction. "You gonna do the garlic-in-the-mouth and stake-through-the-heart routine, or just leave him out in the sun tomorrow morning?"

Nick blinked at her casual ruthlessness. "We'll take him back to D.C. for the proper authorities to deal with."

"Hmm. Pity. Well," she continued, hanging the crucifix on a nail by the door, "if y'all throw him in the back of the truck, Holly can circle him with garlic."

Andreiu never took his eyes off the girl. As Nick retrieved the turquoise from Featherfoot's saddle, something itched in the back of his mind, some nagging warning of danger. Silver, garlic, crucifix—Andreiu was safe enough in his hay nest in the back of the pickup until morning, when they'd throw a tarp or something over him for the drive.

But he couldn't get over the feeling that there was something they'd missed.

Back in the house once more, the tale of the capture was told—quickly, in deference to the hour. Alec promised Holly embellishments at breakfast. Then they finished Cousin Clary's chamomile tea and said their good nights.

Upstairs in the Wisteria Room once more, Nick finally gave words to what had been churning in his mind since capturing Andreiu. "You nearly died tonight."

Alec shrugged. "You're overreacting. I didn't get a scratch."

"But you should have. Doesn't that bother you?"

"Not particularly."

Nick sat on the bed and scowled at his partner. "Emerging unscathed from having a stone wall fall on you doesn't seem the least bit odd to you?"

"It's better than *not* emerging *exceedingly* scathed."

"Alec, will you be serious?"

"Okay, okay." From his pocket he pulled the talisman Lulah had given him. "Observe that the stones are bound with iron, which protects against evil spells."

"Andreiu is a *wampyr*, not a Witch."

"But we'll agree that he *is* evil, and the hypnosis and so forth that true *wampyrs* bring to bear are spells, of sorts. We have carnelian for luck—that's Basic Phylactery 101. Protection against stone walls is carnelian, too. One wonders why umpty-ump Great-grandpa Goare worried so much about walls falling on him, but maybe he was in charge of a fort during a British bombardment."

"Stop babbling," Nicky said severely.

"I'm not babbling, I'm lecturing. Your education was sorely neglected. By the way, there'll be a quiz next class period, so pay attention." He dangled the charm playfully in front of Nick's nose. "The bloodstone felled the walls that the carnelian protected me from. Of course, carnelian also reveals hidden talents. Maybe I've got a hitherto undiscovered knack for dealing with vampires."

Stubbornly serious, Nick retorted, "Alec, I can't understand why you walked away completely untouched by something that should have killed you."

"When you can tell me why this is a bad thing, we'll resume this conversation." Kicking off his shoes, he retrieved his pajamas from the closet. "Until such time, I'm tired and want to sleep."

"Very well. Answer me just one thing, though. Why did your spell work perfectly?"

This time there was no glib reply, no *"Because I'm so brilliant at what I do,"* no *"Maybe there's something to old Grandpa's jewelry after all."*

"You're good," Nick went on softly. "But nobody's *that* good, to drop a *wampyr* so quickly and cleanly. You said yourself he'd just fed. He was at his strongest. *Why did it work?*"

"Fuck if I know," Alec snapped.

The obscenity both surprised Nick and warned him that his partner was on the thin edge of exhaustion. They dressed for bed in silence.

". . . AND YOU KNOW WHAT HAPPENED next."

Holly repressed a shiver, tried to cover it by lighting another cigarette. Nick sensed it anyway. He always did.

"It's a long time ago, Witchling," he murmured. "Shall I finish? Or would you rather not — ?"

"I'd like to hear it from your point of view. If that's okay."

"Of course." He settled back in the porch swing. "Andreiu got out of the barn by breaking the truck window and crawling through to the cab. He must've used the tire iron under the seat to break the silver chains."

"I hope it hurt like hell," she said viciously.

"It probably did. But never discount powerful motivation."

"It's so nice to be wanted," she retorted.

"Don't be impudent. Then he hot-wired the truck and drove it past the garlic and through the barn door with the crucifix on it. We only knew he was in the house when your window broke and Bandit howled."

"And all hell broke loose."

NICK COULDN'T SLEEP. Silently rising from Alec's side ("*Why do you hold a pillow?* . . . "), he pulled a sweater on over his pajamas and left the Wisteria Room. On the tour this afternoon, Holly had shown them a small library downstairs; this was his goal. Specifically, a volume on jewels.

It was a square, slim book, no more than fifty pages: *Gemstone Essentials*. Obviously intended as a primer rather than an encyclopedia on the subject, the text was terse and to the point. He clicked on a reading lamp beside a worn leather chair, sat, and began to explore.

In the next few minutes he learned that agates healed scorpion bites, fire agates enhanced night vision, snakeskin agate diminished wrinkles, and moss agates not only assisted in making and keeping friends but gardeners were advised to wear them—presumably, he thought with a snort of derision, to gain the affection of their vegetables. Tourmaline came in black, blue, green, pink, red, orange, yellow, and watermelon (of all things) varieties, and each color had different properties. Black was suggested for easing neuroses and obsessions. He considered informing the American Psychiatric Association.

Thinking of the stone he'd worn tonight, he found turquoise and read:

*Primary holy stone of Native Americans; warns of danger; protects against evil. Luck, happiness, good health, prosperity; pledge of friendship when given as a gift. Protects horses.*

Another snort died aborning as he recalled how Featherfoot calmed down when he'd hung the talisman on the saddle. Could there really be something to this? Had Alec been serious? He flipped back through the book, looking for *Carnelian.*

*Joy, protection, energy. Activates and energizes personal power, revealing unsuspected gifts. Wish stone. Courage, joy, peace; heals grief; protects against falling walls; suppresses blood loss.*

"Falling walls," he murmured, shaking his head. Shifting uneasily in his chair, he found *Bloodstone —*

*Favorite talisman of soldiers. Stops bleeding; wards off accidents. Courage, vitality, wisdom, generosity. Brings honesty to relationships. Heals wounds; opens doors; topples stone walls.*

—and decided that when he returned to New York he would be spending quite a bit of money in a rock shop. Taking the turquoise from beneath his shirt, he frowned at it. He supposed that his education *was* sketchy in this regard. Still, the Rom who raised him hardly had access to the variety of jewels taken for granted by the son of an ambassador and the grandson of a judge. He imagined Alec as a little boy, sitting with his grandmother in the parlor of that old Boston mansion, sparkling gems sifting like rainbow fire through his fingers. During those same years, Nicky had crouched in the dirt beside his grandmother—or a woman who said she was, anyway—learning to hold *real* fire in his hands.

Yet that was what made the two of them so excellent a team, as Mr. Scot had decided four years earlier. For all that Nick was the bookstore-owning scholar of the pair and Alec dealt in the numbingly practical details of contract law, their talents were opposite to their professional personae. Alec dealt in fine esoterica; Nick, in utilitarianisms. Alec wove the subtlest of Illusions; Nick Summoned with brutal efficiency. And tonight—tonight, Alec had cast the spells, while Nick had brought the silver.

*Silver, garlic, crucifix*—he reassured himself that Andreiu was safely penned for the night. But the sensation that something was wrong became a clamoring in his head—*"Turquoise . . . warns of danger"*—no, ridiculous—but sky blue had darkened to muted, muddied blue-green—

Shattering glass and an anguished yowl brought him to his feet. He was halfway up the stairs when he heard Lulah McClure scream her niece's name.

Alec blocked the door of Holly's room, both hands white-knuckled around the doorframe. Lulah stood behind him, disheveled and shaking, not even noticing when Nick looked past her shoulder. Holly huddled against the headboard of her bed, blue eyes fixed in mindless terror on the gigantic black bat perched on the footrail. Between her and it, claws sunk into the quilt, was Bandit: arched, spitting, fur standing on end so he looked twice his usual size.

"Sweet Mother of All," Lulah breathed, "what does he want? She's only a little girl—"

"He wants to make her one of his own," said Alec, and the bat hissed with laughter. "She's the one he was after tonight."

Nick knew how Andreiu would take her: blood, soul, and body. Sliding gently past Lulah to stand shoulder-to-shoulder with Alec, he said, "He'll not have her," and saw the same vow in his partner's quick, fierce glance.

Lacing his fingers with Alec's in their habit of working support, he waited for energy to flow between them, palm to palm in ever-steadier heartbeat rhythm. Together they took a step forward, and then another.

"Holly," Nick murmured, his voice pitched low and precise, power thrumming through him. "Holly, look at me."

The girl's mind and will were imprisoned by the creature poised at the foot of her bed, and it was the Cat who responded to Nick's words. Eyes like green chrysoprase flickered toward him, and for an eerie unanticipated instant he was thinking Bandit's thoughts.

"No—!" Nick broke free of his partner and lunged forward as a blur of ginger fur flew at the bat, claws and teeth sinking into the leathery black neck. The *wampyr*'s furious shriek was answered by Holly's scream. Knowing himself nine times a fool, Nick grabbed the outstretched wings from behind. The massive head was flung back and a gurgling noise rattled in his throat, but Bandit hung on tight. Nick could only do the same—fighting instinctive revulsion as steely wing-bones and tough hide quivered beneath his fingers. As the bat-shape shifted to human, the bedpost splintered, throwing Andreiu off-balance. There was no advantage in it; the speed and strength of a *wampyr* were as advertised. Nick lost hold of one wing; its flailing raked a talon across his cheek and stabbed his right eye.

Crying out, still he dug his fingers into granite biceps. The instant the change was complete, Andreiu was on his feet, one hand tearing Bandit from his neck and the other arm smashing back. Nick twisted, but not fast enough; the point of Andreiu's elbow cracked his rib like a matchstick. Still he clung, and his fall tumbled them both to the hardwood floor. The *wampyr*'s weight crushed all the remaining air from his lungs.

For a long time there was nothingness. Then nothingness and pain. And then only pain.

"Nick? It's over. Come on, *Miklóshka*. Look at me."

Alec. He opened his eyes—and remembered he probably had only one eye left to open. An involuntary gasp of denial sent agony howling through his chest.

"Just one broken rib, as near as I can tell," Alec said, voice unnaturally calm. "You're lucky you don't have a punctured lung. Stay still and breathe shallow."

He obeyed. A soft cloth wiped at his cheek, skirted gently around his eyes. The cloth came away from his face smeared with blood. He wanted very badly to take a very deep breath to calm the sudden pounding of his heart. Squinting with his good eye, he saw his partner kneeling at his side.

"Holly's all right," Alec told him. "Andreiu . . . isn't." He glanced to his left.

Nick turned his head and saw the split end of a length of oak sticking up from Andreiu's back. There were scars in the polish, as if from claws. Of course; what remained of the oak bedrail. How very practical of Alec. Nick wished he had breath enough to tell him so.

"That was a damnfool thing to do, going after him with your bare hands," Alec chided, his voice not so steady now. "What were you thinking, you idiot?"

"It's . . . all right . . . ," he managed. "Worth it." He tried again, taking small breaths. "I'll look . . . rather dashing . . . with an eyepatch. . . ."

Holly's voice came from the doorway. "I want to see Nicky—"

"He'll be all right, I keep telling you," Lulah replied. "We have work to do."

"I want to see for myself." And then she was kneeling beside him, all wild hair and huge eyes, with Bandit purring contentedly in her arms. "Nicky?"

Alec rose, moving toward Andreiu's body. Nick tried for a smile that was a very bad fit. "I'm only scratched. You were very brave, Holly."

"I was scared to death," she reported frankly. "If you and Bandit hadn't— Nicky, what did he want?"

He was spared having to answer by the noise of a body being dragged across the floor. Bandit hissed. Distracted, Holly glanced over at the dead *wampyr* and shivered—less with fear than with revulsion, Nick saw, and was relieved.

"Holly," Lulah said briskly, "get Clarissa Sage on the phone and tell her we've got an eye injury and a broken rib. She'll give you a list of things. You bring them all up here right away."

"Y-yes, Aunt Lulah." She patted Nicky's shoulder—tentatively, as if touch might hurt him further—and ran to do as told.

The next thing Nick knew, his partner had gently gathered him up and was carrying him to Holly's bed. "Alec—"

"Shut up. And eat more, you scrawny little Rom."

He was carefully settled atop the quilt and covered with a blanket. "Give me something so I don't bleed all over everything," he murmured; he'd gotten the knack of how deep to breathe, and could manage a whole sentence without having to gasp in the middle.

"Here." A clean washcloth was provided. As he pressed it to his cheek, Alec asked, "Will you be okay while I dispose of Andreiu?"

"Fine. What will you—?"

"I'm going to shove garlic down his throat till it comes out his ass," he snapped, "and leave him out so the sun fries him to a crisp."

No sooner had Alec left than Lulah came in, Bandit at her heels. The Cat leaped onto the bed and tucked himself around Nick's feet.

"You need a hospital and an ophthalmic surgeon," Lulah said, delving into the deep pockets of her green velvet dressing gown. "But for now you'll have to put up with some old-fashioned Witch doctoring."

He winced his appreciation of the dry joke, then winced in earnest as his torn cheek throbbed. "I'm not in a position to argue."

"Good. Don't."

She emptied her pockets, and he forgot some of the pain in fascination. What she planned to do with a willow switch, a blue candle, a flat oval of malachite, a sycamore pod, and a bottle of aspirin was utterly beyond his comprehension. Except maybe for the aspirin.

"You don't like to say much out loud, but you have a talkative face," she told him, and he was taken aback—he who had always prided himself on the impassivity of his expression. Lighting the tip of the willow switch, she let smoke waft through the air for a moment before touching the tiny flame to the blue candle. A scent of sage tickled his nose. Then she extinguished the willow and placed it with the candle on the bedside table. "To answer the question you're too polite to ask—yes, this crazy lady does know what she's doing, with a little guidance from a specialist. That's Clary. We all study with her for at least two summers, over at her house near Monticello. All this stuff has to do with healing, magic, and sight." Pausing, she cocked her head at him. "No guarantees, but I'll do the best I can. Trust me?" Then she snorted. "As if you have much choice."

"Exactly," he said wryly.

"I admire your calm."

"Hysterics would seem to be counterproductive."

Her lips twitched, and her fingers reached beneath his pajama shirt and brought out the turquoise talisman. "Your pardon for getting fresh," she said, a muted twinkle in her eyes, "but I need this, too."

"Umm—think nothing of it," he answered, bemused.

"I've got everything I could find," Holly called from the doorway, and as she came toward the bed delicious scents came with her. "Cousin Clary said one bulb of garlic is enough. We don't have any elder flowers or fresh chervil—"

"Yes, we do. Elder's in the pantry, upper shelf, same place as the cayenne. Get Alec to reach it for you—you'd only fall off the ladder. The chervil's in the winter herb pots, right next to the comfrey. Bring me the whole pot, Holly. Let's see," she went on, inspecting the contents of the basket Holly placed on the bed. "Fennel, lavender, bay, caraway, sage—"

She named each of the tins, boxes, vials, and muslin bags as she organized them on the quilt. Holly paused long enough to drag over her desk chair so her aunt could sit down, then vanished, calling for Alec to come help her.

"—marjoram, thyme, coriander, eucalyptus, cayenne, angelica—"

Sweat was drying on Nick's skin in little shivers of cold. He was grateful for the warmth of the quilt—and Bandit curled soothingly at his feet. He watched Lulah take a pinch of this and a bit of that to rub gently onto the malachite and the turquoise around his neck, her long fingers swift and sure.

"I remember some of these from my childhood," he said, as much to distract himself from the shakes as to remind her there was a human being involved here.

"Herbal lore is herbal lore, whether you're an Irish Witch or a Gypsy. You'll have to tell us about that one of these days, you know." A finger touched his lower lip and he opened his mouth reflexively—and two aspirins he hadn't seen her take from the bottle were shoved onto his tongue. "Although a little modern medicine can't hurt," she said as his whole face screwed up with the bitterness.

"Hmm," said Alec, coming in to stand on the other side of the bed. He was carrying a small terra cotta pot with something green growing in it. "Clove, cinnamon, allspice, nutmeg—are you about to make him into a pumpkin pie?"

"We have sayings around these parts, too," Lulah retorted dryly. "One of them goes, 'Dimple in chin, Devil within.' Did you take care of that offal?"

"Yes, ma'am. And we found the elderflower and the chervil, too." He handed over the pot. Lulah began to pinch off stems and squeeze juice onto the malachite as Alec continued, "Water's boiled, things are steeping, and Holly and I found a secret stash of Belgian chocolates. So what say we have a tea party at midnight?"

Nick frowned. Alec was looking much more chipper—without much reason that Nick could tell. But it wasn't a front for his benefit, that much was obvious when his partner smiled at him. The expression was effortless, unguarded. It made Nick deeply suspicious.

"Aunt Lulah . . ." Holly spoke hesitantly, standing at Lulah's shoulder with a small earthenware teapot cradled between her hands. "We have an idea, sort of. At least, Alec has an idea, but he won't tell me why."

"And this idea might be . . . ?"

The girl gave her aunt the teapot. Taking a deep breath, glancing at Alec for reassurance, she scratched at the heel of her thumb to open the slight scabs of the early evening's little accident. Nick stared with his good eye, blinking back reflexive tears as Holly took the malachite oval into her hand, her blood smearing the deep green striations.

Lulah turned away, biting her lip, pretending to fuss with the teapot. Alec watched Holly with a look of bleak gratification. Nick didn't understand any of it. When Holly wordlessly held out the stone to her aunt, Lulah shook her head.

"You do it," she said gruffly. "Nick, this will hurt."

Before he could ask, Holly cautiously but firmly placed the malachite atop his swollen right eye. It did hurt. The weight, the icy chill, the sudden sting of salt tears and blood and herbs and red cayenne pepper.

Without warning his whole body quivered, rousing to awareness of something other than pain. He could smell the willow, the sage oil from the blue candle, each distinct herb and spice rubbed onto the stones. He could taste the acrid remnants of aspirin on his tongue, and the coffee with chicory he'd drunk after dinner. He could feel the warmth of his partner's fingers enfolding his own, and hear Bandit's purr and Lulah whispering something too low and soft for understanding. But more than anything else, he was aware of the rapid beat of Holly's heart.

No—her heart*blood*, thrumming through her veins, pulsing against his eyelid. His own heart began to keep the same time.

And then the pain was gone. All of it. Everywhere.

Someone removed the heaviness. He opened his eyes. Both of them. And took in a deep, easy breath.

"Yes," he heard himself say, looking up at Alec.

HOLLY SMILED IN THE DARKNESS. "You do have such beautiful eyes, Nicky."

"My sight back wasn't the half of what you gave me that night," he replied.

"Ah, yes—the malachite," she teased. "Something about one's heart's desire, wasn't it?"

"Here I'm trying to thank you, and you're making fun of me."

"Thank me for what? Besides Alec, I mean?"

He took the cigarette from her fingers and smoked it awhile in silence. Then: "I believed in the power of the mind, the manifestation of will. Everything else was nonsense. At least I thought so until that night. Gems, herbs, scents, and so forth—they provide cues to which the subconscious mind cannot help but respond. They awaken parts of us, of our magic, that would otherwise lie dormant. It wasn't the smell of the sage or the feel of the elderflower infusion washing my eye clean. It was what those things and all the others represented to my subconscious."

Holly laughed a little. "You're the only Witch I know who intellectualizes magic."

"But the heart has to be considered, as well," he said gently. "The heart also responds. It's the instinct that tells us a new acquaintance will become a friend. It's the feeling that swells inside you when you hear a glorious piece of music for the first time—you know it will become part of you, that you'll never get tired of it, because of what it awakens inside your heart. It's love at first sight."

"That's chemical."

"Okay," he agreed, "pheromones. Why is it different from how the smell of fresh-baked bread makes you respond? There's magic in everyone and everything."

"That's what you and Alec gave *me*, you know. My magic, and my freedom."


"YOU KNOW NOW, DON'T YOU?" Nick asked quietly.

His pajamas sweaty and slightly bloodied, he had changed into a T-shirt and boxer shorts to sleep in. But he had never felt less like sleeping in his life. He sat cross-legged in the middle of the Wisteria Room's big bed, watching as his partner, too, traded his snow-wet pajamas for something clean and dry.

Alec came to his side, touched his brow with fingers that shook just a little. "Are you sure you're all right? There's not even a hint of a scar on your face—"

"Alec," he warned, drawing back from the touch. "What is she?"

He sighed. "Spellbinder."

"You aren't serious!"

"Aren't I? Do you honestly believe in the curative powers of herbs and spices and a lump of malachite? Do you truly think I could've brought down a stone wall—and stayed alive when it fell on *me?* It was her blood that quickened the magic. Andreiu wanted her because she's a Spellbinder."

"To kill her." Nick traced the outline of an oak leaf stitched into the quilt around a tiny sachet of cedar that embellished the meaning. *For courage,* his memory identified at once, the voice of a Rom wisewoman reciting names and attributes like a catechism. *Courage,* he thought again, *too much courage demanded of a little girl who doesn't even know what she is.* "Andreiu knew that if her blood was used to work a banishing against him, or something worse, he—"

"No, that's not it at all." Alec shook his head, dark hair falling into his eyes to be brushed irritably away. "He didn't want her dead. He wanted her *un*dead."

*"Fasz kivan!"* Nick shuddered.

"If she became a *wampyr,*" his partner continued ruthlessly, "if they took her, drank from her regularly, used her blood to bind whatever spells and hexes they wished—if she was theirs to do with as they pleased—"

"Why didn't you keep him alive enough to burn tomorrow?" Nick demanded.

"Don't you think I wish I had?" was the savage retort. "For her, for what he did to you—"

"I'm all right," Nick said automatically, taken aback by Alec's vehemence.

"Only because Holly is what she is."

"Does Lulah know?"

"She might've suspected, but she wasn't sure until tonight. The wards on Holly aren't specific enough." He walked to the window and pulled aside the heavy curtain, staring out at the snow-wrapped fields.

After a time, Nick asked, "How did Andreiu find out?" then answered his own question. "Her blood must smell like nectar to a *wampyr*. And she said herself she's clumsy—a skinned knee, a cut finger—Alec, what will it be like when she reaches menarche, unable to hide the scent of her blood every month?"

"I hadn't thought of that." The muscles of Alec's long back clenched. "You're the scholar—can we protect her using her own blood to seal the work?"

"There's not much literature on the subject, such people being vanishingly rare."

"She's in for it, then, isn't she? When Mr. Scot finds out about her."

"But we're not going to tell him, are we."

Alec said nothing.

Nick threw back the quilts and got to his feet. "We can't. Think what her life would be—could you see her caged?"

"Mr. Scot wouldn't do that." He didn't sound very certain of it.

"He'd have to, one way or another. Every practitioner in the world would be after her. And there's only so much blood in the veins of one little girl. For her own protection, she'd have to be kept under glass."

"When she's older, she'll be able to make her own decisions about what she is and who she wants to be. But for now—"

"No!"

"She's too isolated here," Alec argued, turning to face him at last. "She needs to be someplace with thousands of people, preferably millions, where her scent will mingle with others and—"

"No!" he repeated, feeling a chill that a dozen quilts, hexed and sacheted and spelled or not, wouldn't help. "We're talking about taking her from everything she knows and loves. We can't do that to her, Alec. It was done to me. I won't see her go through the same thing."

"She'd have Lulah, and us."

"She'd be miserable. If we can keep her safe here—"

"How?" Alec asked hopelessly. "This house is spelled six ways to next Lammas Night. Andreiu still found her. So will others."

"We use those same spells and hexes—only we seal them with her blood. If we work on the house and not her specifically, on her clothes and the like, it'll work." He hoped it would work.

"Oh? And how would we test these hexes? Find another vampire to attack her?" He pivoted on one bare heel. "Or maybe invite the exquisite Madame Liao from Hong Kong to try a few spells on Holly the way she did on you last year?"

Nick ignored the sudden dark anguish in his partner's eyes, ignored his own instinctive cringe of memory. "I won't exile Holly from her home."

"Was it really that horrible for you?" Alec asked softly, unexpectedly.

"What do you think?" Nick retorted, too angry to protect himself with any sort of façade. "I was about Holly's age when it became clear what I was. And publicly, too—in front of half the town." He remembered clearly only two things about that day: the absolute certainty that he could make the Russian policeman drop his gun, and the absolute horror on his mother's face as the Kalashnikov hit the cobblestones. "After that, it was either the Soviet camps or the Rom camps for me."

"*Miklóshka*—"

"Hungary was well and truly under the Soviet bootheel—*gulyás* Communism with its hodgepodge of capitalism and collective didn't last long, you know. What do you think it would've been like for me, Alec? The bastard son of a Gestapo rapist and a Hungarian girl—"

"Gestapo? . . ." Alec looked sick.

"You wanted to know about the other three-quarters—well, half of it's German. I didn't get the blond hair and blue eyes from Sergei Orlov. He wasn't my father. This—" He ran a hand through his hair, and finished bitterly, "—is pure Aryan. Polluted, of course, by Magyar and Rom, though you can't tell by looking at me. You're not the mongrel, Alec. I am."

"*Miklóshka*," he said again, whispered this time as if in pain.

"The Soviets would have experimented on me or executed me as a freak. My mother understood that, and gave me to her mother's people. Two days after I left, the area commissar arrived to investigate the rumors. My mother vanished—perhaps to a labor camp, perhaps to an unmarked grave. Sergei Maximovitch couldn't protect her. I learned years later that he tried, but—" Suddenly spent, he sat back down on the bed. "She made the right choice—for me. And she paid for it."

"So did you," Alec murmured. "You lost everything."

"I'm alive, aren't I?"

"And you don't want to hear Holly say that in twenty years—not in that tone of voice. Well, neither do I." He sat on the bed beside Nick, hands clasped between his knees. "All right. We'll say nothing. We can work with Lulah on protections for her, and come back to renew them every so often."

"You'd do that?"

"I'd do more. I *will* do more." He hesitated, then touched Nick's arm lightly. "Holly, I can protect. You—" He shook his head. "I wish I could have, *Mik-*

*lóshka*. In almost four years you've never told me half so much as you just did about your childhood."

"I—I don't think of it much."

"But it shaped you—*bludgeoned* you into who you are now."

He shrugged, uncomfortable. "Whatever I am, I—"

"No, I said *who*. You were born what you are. Like Holly, like the rest of us. But *who* you are is the sum of what's happened to you, how you've reacted to it. What it did to you and what you refused to let it do."

"Is this by any chance your philosophical hour?"

"Knock it off." He shook Nick gently. "I'm trying to tell you that I hate what happened to you, but I happen to love who you are." Smiling a little, he fingered the talisman still around his neck, and there was a warmth and a gentleness in his eyes that Nick had never seen there before. "I should mention another trait of carnelian."

"Which is?" Nicky asked a bit breathlessly.

"Worn next to the heart, it has the power to fulfill one's dearest wish. Has our Holly *that* much power as a Spellbinder, to make it real for us?"

"YOU'RE NOT GOING TO STOP *there!*" Holly exclaimed.

"The rest is none of your business," he replied with a smile.

"Nicky!" she cried, outraged. "You *have* to tell me what happened. I mean— did you? That night?"

He drew back, genuinely shocked. "In your house? With a little girl right down the hall? Good grief, no!"

"So when—?"

"You're relentless, you know that? It was about a week later, actually." A faint, reminiscent smile played about his lips.

As sure of indulgence now as she'd been all those years ago, she mused, "You were both amateurs, I know that much. I gather you both improved with practice."

"Watch your mouth, young lady."

"Hey, you're talking to the person who spelled that quilt for you two."

She remembered sitting around the quilt-frame with Lulah and the other ladies, practically hugging herself with glee at what she knew and the innocents of the sewing circle did not. Careful to do the *real* stitching on it when alone, she would sit up late, pricking a finger for the blood-drop on a silver dagdyne, a Witch's sewing needle four generations old, to sew in miniature fragrant sachets of lavender for luck, rose for joy, and sweet basil for good wishes, *knowing* all would spell true.

"Not that you needed any magic from me. You two were so perfect together that it practically screamed at me."

"What about you and your Evan?"

"He's not mine anymore. If he ever was. If he had been, he still would be."

"I'm sure that will make sense once you've had some sleep."

"I'll try," she said, and followed him inside the house.

# Nineteen

THE NEXT MORNING AT ABOUT nine, Nick found his partner seated at the redwood picnic table in the backyard, a black cloth spread before him. Alec was weighing a black velvet pouch gently in his hand, as if trying to make a decision.

Nick made it for him, in a way. "You haven't done this in a while."

Alec glanced up with a little shrug, and opened the pouch's drawstring. "Don't think I didn't see you eyeing the plain white porcelain cups."

Nick snorted. "So we're both worried about her. She's still asleep upstairs, by the way."

"I wouldn't be at all surprised if she sleeps all day. It'd be good for her, poor lamb." He spilled the bag's contents onto the cloth, staring down at colors glistening in the summer sun. "I can't think what to ask," he said plaintively.

Standing behind him, Nick rubbed the sturdy shoulders soothingly. "Shall I play Gypsy before you play with pretty rocks?" He paused for effect. "On the other hand, don't forget I'm the one who predicted that Al Gore would win the election."

Alec half-turned, pointing an admonitory finger. "Do *not* get me started!"

Nick grinned. "Sorry. But one has to be careful and specific. If I'd asked 'Who will be the next President—'"

"I mean it, Nick!"

"Okay, okay. Why don't we try it simultaneously?"

Gathering up the thirteen rocks, Alec let them flow back and forth from hand to hand. Click-click, click-click-click. At length he nodded. "Go boil water."

Nick had set the kettle on and was retrieving the special stash of China tea when something occurred to him. Slipping off his shoes, he soft-footed it up the stairs, careful to avoid the creak on the third-from-the-top, and eased open the door of Holly's room. Sound asleep, right enough. He smiled, resisting the impulse to brush her hair from her cheeks, and found the black scarf she'd been wearing when she arrived last night.

Back in the garden, he set down the tea tray and gave the scarf to Alec. "This might help. It's hers."

"I married a genius. This is perfect."

After tea leaves were measured and water was poured, Nick tucked a foot under him and glanced over Alec's preparations. The black velvet had been exchanged for the black silk scarf, and the stones were lined up at its edge. "That's always been my favorite." He pointed to the moonstone: milky white, about the size of a thumbnail, and carved with a moon face.

"I like the aquamarine—summer blue, a hint of leaf-green. Like your eyes."

"Restrain your poetic impulses, please."

"That wasn't poetic, that was romantic. Impulses to which you've never had in your life."

"You do it well enough—and often enough—for both of us, Alyosha." Idly stirring the tea deosil with a silver spoon, Nick inventoried the stones. Apache tear, duskily translucent; solid black onyx; aquamarine, smoky quartz, and garnet; indigo-dark beryl and rose quartz that looked like child's marbles. Green bloodstone, flecked with red that gave it its name; a lopsided chunk of golden amber. The malachite and carnelian matched each other, both being flat ovals. Moon-faced moonstone, and a tall, pointed phallic symbol of an amethyst, sliced off a geode.

"Why are you using that one?" Nick asked. "Holly's a girl."

"Who's got man-trouble," Alec retorted. "Hurry up and guzzle your tea. We wanted to do this at the same time, remember?"

"It hasn't steeped yet. What's the rush, anyhow?"

Alec only shrugged.

They sat quietly for a time, until Nick decided the tea was ready and started drinking. Resisting the urge to gulp it down fast so they could get started, he asked, "Have you decided the question?"

"How specific should we get?"

"Let's just think about Holly, and leave it open from there."

"Okay." Alec put all the rocks back in their pouch, cradling it between his hands as Nick finished the tea. Nodding his readiness, Nick swirled the remaining spoonful of liquid in the cup three times sunwise, then turned it over onto the saucer. At the same time, Alec let the stones fall one by one onto the black scarf.

East came up black, blue, and red: onyx, aquamarine, and garnet. "Ideas, inspirations," Alec muttered. "Definitely a journey for creative purposes . . . a good trip, she'll enjoy it. . . ."

"That means Florence again," Nick stated.

"Hush. I'm concentrating. Devotion is there, but to what? A bit of aimlessness, I think—that's it, travel for the sake of travel, to escape. We've got separation of lovers—no surprise—but I can't tell whether it's defensive to repel the darkness or if it'll end up binding them closer—"

"South," Nick said. "Tell me what's there." Besides the malachite and the bloodstone—both green, the color of healing.

"More travel. We won't be seeing her for a while, Nick. But it will help her. She'll start seeing things differently. That's the bloodstone." Alec propped his chin on one hand, staring at the Western quarter. "Here it gets tricky. Five stones, all clustered together—which one's which?"

Nick waited him out. Eventually there was a sharp nod.

"The Apache tear is just that—grief. Which doesn't take many smarts to figure out. But she'll get past it if she looks inside herself. The amethyst is interesting—it's the stone of atonement, but it also ensures faithfulness. And, as you so charmingly pointed out, it's definitely a masculine stone—so he's not going to stop loving her, Nicky. She's it, for him."

"We knew that already."

"Yeah, well . . . his problem, and hers, will be to get beyond the anger. Ah, but then there's the moonstone for rebirth." He pointed to the Northern quadrant. "There's her writing. Communication, creativity, confidence, success—"

When he broke off, Nick leaned forward. "What? It's the Center, isn't it? What's there?"

"Profound confusion," Alec replied, his voice deceptively light. "Stones in the Center are the negative or positive influence on the rest of the casting. Smoky quartz, overcoming depression with common sense. And carnelian to change your luck and protect from negative emotions. Both are good. But look where the two blacks are in relation to the Center. Black stones are always six of one and half a dozen of the other when it comes to positive and negative influence."

"English, please."

"She's in for a bitch of a time." After staring at the configuration for a few moments, he swept all the stones into his palm and stashed them in the pouch. "Your turn," he said gruffly.

Nick gazed for a moment at the Limoges stamp on the cup bottom for something to distract him from a sudden pessimism, then shook himself mentally. Distraction would not do. Upending the cup, he looked at the pattern of leaves.

"Well?"

"Patience." Nick wished he didn't see what he saw. "You tell me," he said suddenly, holding the cup so Alec could look. "Is that an arch or a bridge?"

"There's a difference?"

"Both are journeys, but the bridge is a favorable journey."

"It's a bridge," Alec decided. "Ties in with what the stones said."

"What else do you see?"

Black brows arched, he peered dutifully into the cup. "Is that a mushroom?"

"Sudden separation of lovers after a quarrel," Nick said dully. "It's close to the rim, which is the immediate future. The closer to the bottom of the cup, the more time will elapse before whatever it is comes true. See this, right at the bottom? It's a kettle—there's the spout."

"Looks more like a camel to me. Or maybe a swan. Or—"

"Kettle. Who's the Rom in this family?"

"All right then, *ves'tacha*," he said, using the gypsy word for *beloved*. "Tell me what the kettle means."

"Death."


HOLLY WOKE AT NOON, PULLED on clothes, and went downstairs to an empty house. A note on the coffeemaker read: *Foraging for food. Back by 2. Love, Alec.*

He wasn't kidding. Not moldy crust or curdled milk or yet a solitary egg was to be found. She settled for handfuls of cereal from a box *best sold by FEB 97*, taking coffee and a fresh pack of cigarettes out to the back porch.

The ashtray was still there, overflowing. She thought over what Nicky had told her the night before—not about him and Alec, but the memory he had evoked of sewing their wedding quilt, back when her magic was new and felt good. Other people took joy and pleasure from their talent. She knew plenty of them, Alec and Nicky included. She tried to remember how that had felt, and couldn't.

Through childhood and adolescence, she'd been wrapped in cotton-wool. Going away to college, she might have expected to feel threatened, but her only insecurities were those shared by every freshman. Would she make any friends? Would she flunk out? And what about boys? Her magic hadn't really been an issue. If she'd sensed herself different, it was because of her accent, her clothes, her relative poverty among the wealthy blue bloods, and all her goddamned freckles.

She'd smoothed out the accent and learned to live with the freckles. She hadn't even minded much when, during grad school at UCLA, the California sun popped new ones. (Although she'd been expecting to get a real tan, so that all the freckles sort of merged together; vain hope.)

Back then she'd enjoyed magic. Healing, Banishing, Scrying, Grounding, Centering, Initiating, Mourning, Handfasting—she had participated in versions of them all and more besides, taking pleasure in the magic and her contribution to it. But she'd never really *felt* it. While others saw and heard and experienced and lived their magic, she stood by. Watching. She, who made it all happen with an intensity they never could have achieved without her, truly participated in nothing.

At Woodhush, magic was in the quilts and the paintings, the herbs in her dresser drawers, the carvings on the furniture and lintels, the horseshoe above the barn door. Keep the last egg laid by an old hen as a charm to protect the poultry; always ask the faeries' permission before taking a cutting from a hawthorn tree; myrtle, rosemary, and parsley grow best if planted by a woman; a saltcellar overset between two friends is a sure sign they would quarrel. Things were just things, ordinary and commonplace, in the way a New Yorker would hear on the TV that a demonstration at the U.N. was going to foul up his crosstown commute. Magic was as normal as oatmeal with cinnamon sugar on a winter morning.

Even after Alec and Nicky came to Woodhush Farm and discovered what she was, Holly hadn't truly *known* what she was until the first time she participated in a Circle, the first time she extended her finger for someone else to stick with a silver needle and her blood was the seal and the binding for someone else's spell.

But in the last few years it seemed to her that almost everyone in her life wanted her blood—literally or figuratively. Except Evan Lachlan. He was the only man in her life who didn't want her to bleed.

Nicky had been right, early this morning: all life was magic. Especially love. To her, it was the only magic that ever really worked. And she was damned if she'd give it up.

A scrap of empty envelope in the kitchen sufficed for a note to Alec and Nicky: *Gone home. Thanks for everything. Love you. Holly.*

JUST INSIDE HER FRONT DOOR was a sealed envelope with her name in his handwriting on the front.

Her hands shook as she ripped open the envelope. His writing was clear, though the long tail on every *y* told her he'd written very fast.

Holly—

I don't have words, not the way you do. All I can think of to say is that I can't be with you. Nobody can help me with this. Not even you. If you're here I won't even take the first step, or if I do it'll just be because I have you for a crutch. I can't do that to myself and I won't do it to you.

This won't be forever. I promise. What's forever is that I love you.

Evan

Holly sat on the cold tile floor, his letter on her knee, and stared at nothing. It seemed about a year before she felt chilly, and shivered, and wondered what had happened to her cardigan.

The door chimes made her glance up incuriously. She didn't care who it was, because never again would it be him.

"Holly? Come on, Holly, open up."

Susannah. Holly pushed herself to her feet, opened the door. "Come to view the corpse?"

Susannah's face was a study in compassion—and wariness. "Evan called a couple of hours ago. He said you'd probably need—"

"What I need," Holly enunciated carefully, "or, more properly, *who* I need, has just thrown me away like a dead cell phone. If you intend to join me in getting drunk, come on in. If not, shut the door on your way out." Turning on one heel, she went to the living room for the bottle of Stolichnaya.

"The usual," Susannah said behind her. "The one with my name on it."

After she found the Cuervo Especial, she sliced two limes into wedges, put out a salt shaker for Susannah, and poured into cut crystal glasses. "*Sláinte mhór.*"

They tossed back the liquor, coughed, wiped their eyes. Holly poured again while Susannah licked salt off the back of her palm and sucked on lime. After a moment Susannah raised her glass and said, "Men: may every single god-damned one of the motherfuckers rot in hell."

"Amen, sister," Holly agreed, and they drank.

"I should've called you in Kenya, I know," Susannah began.

"So I could come home and do what?" Holly asked pointedly, lighting a cigarette.

Susannah did likewise. "God, that tastes good. Holly, I honest to God thought he was gonna be all right. I was stupid enough to believe that Evan would be fine. Sooner or later." Susannah raked dark hair back from her eyes. "Then Fleming and his allies started yelling for his head. Pete threatened to re-sign if they fired him. Frank Sbarra called everybody he knows—"

"And everybody else tried their best, including you and Elias. And now that I'm back, what would you suggest—that I write a letter to the editor?"

"Cynicism isn't really your thing, Holly. What you can do is be there for Evan."

"He doesn't want me. Do you know what he said? That he had to do this on his own. That he can't use me as a crutch. And he's right, damn him. I hate him for it, but he's right."

"Holly, he'll come back to you."

"I told you—either drink or go away."

Susannah tossed back the tequila and held out her glass for more.

"Good choice."

"I think I figured out why he did it," Susannah said after a while. "I heard Fleming sermonizing to the crowd—toxic bullshit, really stirring them up. Evan got him down the steps, but he started yelling again. That's when Evan slugged him."

"Lachlan doesn't like preachers, with or without Roman collar." Unwillingly, she remembered the day Elias had formally sentenced Father Matthew.

*"What the hell are you doin' here?"*

*"I love you, too, Lachlan." She nodded to Susannah as her friend went past into the courtroom. "I'm here," she said more softly, "because I wasn't here before."*

*"Holly—you don't have to."*

*Needing something to do with her hands, she straightened his tie. She'd watched him dress this morning, but until this moment hadn't realized she'd matched her clothes to his. They both wore black suits.*

*"I know you don't need to me hold your hand," she said. "But maybe I need you to hold mine, you know?"*

*"I don't want you even breathin' the same air as that bastard." A few moments later, though, some of the tension left his face. Briefly, gently, he touched her cheek with his fingertips. "Okay. Come on."*

*They stood unobtrusively in the back of the courtroom. Sitting behind the prosecution were a dozen or so women of varying ages, early twenties to late fifties. All were more than usually good-looking, and all of them looked bruised.*

*The priest was brought in. Whatever allure this man might once have had, it was gone now. Remaining was an aging, nondescript nonentity who had hurt and warped and destroyed. She felt Evan tense beside her, every muscle rigid. She wanted to touch him and didn't dare.*

*"Before I impose sentence according to the arrangement made with the prosecution, does the defendant wish to make a statement?"*

*"Yes, Your Honor." He turned.*

*Holly felt the long body at her side draw in on itself without moving a single muscle.*

*"I want to tell everyone how sorry I am. I don't deserve your forgiveness, and I'll pray every day of my life for God's."*

*For a moment his gaze lit on Evan, and then Holly—and he was interested. Despite where he was, what he had done, and that he would be spending the next twenty years in prison, he wanted her. She met him stare for stare—and the furtive, faded eyes flinched. His head turned—quickly, as if to avoid a raised fist.*

*She glanced up at Evan, found he was looking at her, his eyes wide, startled. Only then did she realize that her lips had curved in a little smile. For the priest.*

*Who had looked at her and flinched.*

*Shaking her head, she slipped out of the courtroom. Gulps of cold water from the drinking fountain got the taint out of her mouth.*

*"Holly?" Susannah came up to her. "Come talk some sense into him—he's gone back to confront the man."*

*A quick walk through a side hall to the holding cell; slowly, careful to make no sound of breath or footstep, Holly went closer.*

*"Those women trusted you," Evan was saying. "And you raped them. What gave you the right to do that?"*

*Holly pressed her spine against a wall, unable to see Evan. His words were hoarse, roughened by pain and anger. Yet there was an entreaty deep in his voice, a tremor that begged for understanding of why this man had done these things.*

*"God trusted you to help people. Instead, you helped yourself to as many women as you could, and when they didn't want you anymore—how do you live with what you did?"*

*Pete Wasserman entered the hall, giving Holly a glance and a nod before opening the holding cell. A moment later she heard him say, "Let's go," and the priest was taken away. Handcuffs and leg chains rattled. The watery gray eyes saw her, and the defiant lift of his head disintegrated into another flinch.*

*She knew she wasn't smiling now. She wondered what was in her eyes. She watched the priest being taken away, thinking,* Evan's been running for years—from you, his mother, his childhood, even himself sometimes—but it stops now. You can't get to him without getting past me. And nothing will ever get past me.

*She walked toward the cell. Behind the iron bars stood Evan. He saw her, and very slowly his right hand reached out for her. She went inside. His fingers were chill, his grip almost painful. It was a long moment before he spoke.*

*"Given the chance, you woulda killed him, wouldn't you?"*

*Her brows arched. "For you? Of course. Him or anyone else."*

*His lips curved in a flicker of a smile, and light returned to his eyes. "Good thing looks can't kill, or I'd have to arrest you." He squeezed her hand, his fingers warm now, alive. "You can be pretty scary, McClure."*

*"Never underestimate an Irishwoman in love, Lachlan." She tugged at his hand. "Can we get out of here, please? We're on the wrong side of these bars?"*

She remembered her vow of that morning: that whoever and whatever would injure Evan Lachlan must get past her first. But something *had* gotten past her, she reflected bitterly. Evan himself.

Susannah was saying, "He didn't punch the Reverend just because he was monumentally pissed." The fine green eyes were watching her, waiting for her to see whatever-it-was for herself.

"The Reverend's the type who milks it till it moos," she said slowly. "The crowd was getting uglier by the minute—but that wouldn't have troubled him, he'd just keep on while they—"

Susannah interrupted impatiently. "Would it help if I told you that the NYPD's haul during the arrests included eleven guns?"

"Oh, no," Holly whispered, seeing it at last. "He decked the bastard to get him out of the way before somebody could kill him."

"Which isn't to say Evan wasn't furious and didn't want to belt him just on general principles."

They drank in silence for quite a while after that.

When the phone rang, Holly flinched. After one heart-thudding instant she realized it wouldn't be Evan. She got up and answered it, grateful that her first experience of liquor had been the Widow Farnsworth's moonshine at age thirteen. A good healthy slug was Aunt Lulah's sovereign remedy for menstrual cramps.

Elias said, "Holly? Is Susannah with you?"

"Yep."

A pause. "You've both been drinking."

"Yep."

"And you're going to keep on drinking, aren't you?"

He surely did have a keen grasp of the obvious. "Yep."

"So I won't be seeing Susannah tomorrow at the office."

"Nope."

Another pause. "Don't let her drive home."

"Nope."

"Look, Holly, I'm sorry about—"

"Night, Elias." And she hung up on him.

Susannah sat up straight. "That was Elias?"

An equally keen grasp of the obvious—it must be catching. Holly sat down again, propping her feet on the coffee table. "Sure was."

"He's gonna be mad."

"Tough shit. I wonder just how sick we're gonna be tomorrow."

"How much've we drunken—drank—," she corrected herself, frowned, and amended, "—had to drink?"

Holly held up the Stoli bottle and sloshed it experimentally. Susannah did the same with the Cuervo. "A lot," Holly said at last.

"This gonna become a habit with you, McClure?"

"Over Lachlan?" She laughed bitterly and lit another cigarette. "Fuck 'im."

"Speaking of which, I been meaning to ask. He any good?"

"Well, Counselor, to tell the whole truth and nothing but the truth—he's so great in bed he yells his *own* name." She drank straight from the bottle. "But there ain't a man in the universe worth turnin' into a drunk over."

"Amen, sister." Sprawling long, jeans-clad legs, Susannah rested her head against the back of the sofa and stared at the ceiling. "Glad to hear you say it, Holly. Evan would kill me if I let you destroy the woman he loves."

" 'Destroy'?" Holly laughed again. "Melodrama is *my* gig, Wingfield. And it's 'loved'—past tense."

"I'll believe it when he looks at some other woman the way he looks at you. In fact—" She seemed to lose her train of thought, swallowed another tot of tequila, and chortled softly. "In fact, I'll bet you my diamond bracelet that he comes back to you—against all your sapphires if he doesn't."

Holly tried to sort that through. "Huh?"

"I'll part with the bracelet when Lachlan does what I know he's gonna do," Susannah explained. "But if he doesn't, I want serious consolation for being wrong. Ergo, the sapphires. Besides," she added impishly, "Elias says I look better in your sapphires than you do."

"You look better in anything than I do, you bitch! So what's the time limit on this wager?"

"Mrs. Osbourne predicts they'll change their minds about firing him, but he'll be doing confiscated property inventory for two-and-a-half to five."

Holly winced. "He's good at his job, Suze, they can't possibly stick him in some do-nothing position—"

"He's lucky he's still *got* a job," was the bleak rejoinder. "And I think that galls him more than almost anything else. You know him, Holly—he's got pride enough for a dozen. Even a dozen Irishmen. And his pride tells him that until he gets his life together, he's got nothing to offer you. And the last thing he'll ever do is justify his actions by explaining them. With Evan, either people trust him and believe him, or they don't."

With difficulty, Holly said, "My trust and belief aren't the issue."

"Exactly. Right now it's his belief in himself that's at stake, that he can get through this on his own."

"If he needs me or anybody else, he can't be a real man," she interpreted, and her friend nodded. "And if I was some helpless, faint-hearted little thing who couldn't hardly think for herself and needed him to make every decision, then he wouldn't've left, because he'd have to stay and be strong for me, right?"

"Holly, if you were some pathetic clingy type he had to take care of, he wouldn't've been with you at all."

"Why are men such morons?"

"Nature of the beast. But it's not entirely his fault. He's been essentially alone all his life, you know. 'Dysfunctional' is a polite term for his family. When he's in trouble, it's instinct to handle it alone." She squeezed an already limp wedge of lime into her glass and mused, "For a hot-tempered Irishman, he does a great impersonation of the next ice age. Nobody gets in when he's like this."

"Not even me."

"Especially not you. He's a fighter—and he goes into the ring alone."

"But he doesn't have to!"

"A lifetime's conditioning is hard to break. Once he's convinced he's done it on his own, and he's got something to give you, he'll be back."

"And until then, I do my Statue of Liberty imitation. Terrific."

Susannah hesitated. "That's up to you. But that torch may get awful heavy."

"I'm stuck with it," she replied bleakly. "It's got his name on it."

"Well, anyway, I'd bet on about six months before he comes back to you. Have we got a deal?"

"We got a deal, Counselor. But make it a year."

"It won't take that long."

They sealed it with a clink of bottles and long swigs of liquor. Holly sat back again, regarding her friend. "You really love that bracelet," she remarked.

"I know. But I really love you and Evan more." In lousy imitation of Holly's Virginia accent: "Holly 'Lizbeth, honeychile, y'all gonna look so purdy wearin' them thar diamonds on y'all's weddin' day."

Holly's eyes flooded with tears. A sound escaped her, harsh and desperate. She bent her head, fist crammed between her teeth, trying to muffle the cries that clawed her throat, terrible gasping cries that she couldn't stop. A moment later Susannah gathered her close. She hid her face on her friend's shoulder and wept.

*Twenty*

THE NAME ON THE DISPLAY of hardbound novels leaps out at him. This is why he hasn't willingly been inside a bookstore in over a year. But the United States Marshals Service has jurisdiction over escaped fugitives, and this suburban New Jersey bookstore's horrified owner has discovered on this fine Friday afternoon in October that last month she hired a wanted felon. So here he is—but only because his name was on the original case file, and somebody had neglected to adjust for new realities.

When the senior deputies arrive, he gives his report tersely and quietly. They know who he is. Was. They know he was put back on the job after an incident across the river that ultimately resulted in a sixty-day suspension. They also know that he used to be assigned this case—and they all expect him to do their work for him. And they're waiting for him to make a mistake. But he doesn't make mistakes. Not anymore. He does his job, but not theirs. He refuses to let his mind worry at puzzles—when they present themselves. That isn't too often. Not anymore.

When the senior deputies tell him okay, we'll take it from here, he goes to the front of the store. He takes a copy of the book to the desk. The owner is still shaky. She stares at the twenties he hands her as if she's never seen money before, then snaps back into her job. As he has been hoping she would. When the criminal world intersects with the conventional world, the sooner someone gives the victims something familiar to do, the sooner they calm down.

He waits for her to make change and bag his purchase, and nods when she asks if he's read the author's other books. Yeah, he says, I've read everything she's ever written. The woman—firmly back on familiar ground, her world righting itself—says she really likes this writer's work, too, she read this book when it came out in June, it's really good, really sad but really good.

He is tempted to say, *Really?* but restrains himself. She is a victim, and he is always gentle with victims. He will not do the other marshals' job for them, he will not play the catch-the-perp game, because that's not why he's still in this business. He doesn't care about catching the bad guys, not the way he did before. He cares about the victims now. This is a change in him, and he recognizes it with a mixture of amusement and fatalism. He'd felt like a victim for a while himself.

He heads back to the office, finishes his paperwork, and goes downstairs to his locker to change into street clothes—jeans, shirt, jacket left over from that other life—and heads for the nearest bar.

In that other life, he would have gone with somebody else from the office. A few drinks, a few bullshitting hours winding down. Now he goes alone. For a single beer. It is all he can afford—not monetarily, for his apartment rent is cheap, and he has never been an expensive person. A single beer is all his body can afford, because any more than one—or any fewer than a dozen—and he feels himself weaken, and he is prey to things he doesn't want to feel, and he gets even less sleep than usual, because the nightmares come.

He has his usual single beer, staring all the while at the bag beside him on the bar. He can read the title through the thin paper, and the name of the author. He turns the bag over, and can almost but not quite see the picture on the back cover.

He starts to open the bag, then shakes his head. Later. When he's alone. He knows that feeling is going to flood him, and if he drowns, he doesn't want anyone to see. He'd been stupid enough a few months ago to reread his favorite of her books, and it was like hearing her talk to him in that low, quick, husky voice. If this book is what he thinks it is, and he's certain it is, he must be alone when he reads it, where no one can see him.

But where? Not his apartment. Except for her books, and one blue cashmere sweater tucked away in a drawer, there is nothing of her in that place. She doesn't belong there. Her letters and postcards, Granna Maureen's ring, the art books from Italy—none of it. He doesn't even have a photo of her, not even buried somewhere in his desk. The one he does have, the only one, is with the ring in his safety-deposit box. Someone took the picture at her alumni party, and she gave it to him in a silver frame. She is in a glittery green dress; he is in a dark blue business suit and white silk shirt. He sits on a bar stool, she stands behind him with arms wrapped around his chest, chin on his shoulder. He can hear echoes of her laughter whenever he looks at it. Which is not often. As for him—the look on his face in that photo is one he hasn't seen in a very long time. He looks happy.

If not his apartment, maybe the roof. Cindy Ramirez has a garden up there, trees in pots and vegetables in long wooden troughs, safe playground created for her fatherless children. He helped her put together a jungle gym last fall, and this spring found some discarded barrels in an empty lot and dragged them upstairs for roses. She isn't into herbs, which is a relief. Too many memories connect with the scents.

In his apartment, he pours a Diet Coke, tucks the book under his arm, takes an ashtray and two cigars and climbs up to the roof garden. Cindy is there, tending tomato plants. He plays catch for a while with Eduardo Junior and Rita. Cindy smiles, and he thinks that in the year since he moved into the building Cindy's face has grown younger. Widowed at thirty with two little kids to raise, she used to look ten years older. Perhaps she is finally recovering from her grief. He hopes so. She is a nice woman, a good woman, who deserves a good man in her life again. They talk sometimes, she of her husband, he of the life he'd left behind.

That can't be your dinner, she scolds, eyeing the Coke and the cigars. When he shrugs, she tsks. She goes downstairs with the kids and ten minutes later comes back up with a bowl of spaghetti, half a bottle of Chianti, and a glass. He protests; she tells him to hush up and eat, there's plenty. She stands with fists on hips for a minute or so, to make sure he does eat, then returns home to feed her children.

He eats because she's a good cook and because a severe cutback on alcohol has reduced his weight. All that liquor, months of it—though never on duty, he's not that stupid—was detrimental to his blood pressure as well as his waistline, and his annual physical provoked the medical version of the riot act. He's been careful since March, and it shows. So he eats Cindy's spaghetti and drinks her Chianti, and finally, with the late sunset, lights a cigar. The roof lights have come on, one right behind his deck chair. He opens the bag and takes out the book.

*Jerusalem Lost*, it says, and her name below it. The picture on the back cover is black-and-white, but memory fills in the colors of hair and eyes and mouth. This is not the cat-and-sweater photo, where she was smiling. She wears a dark shirt and her mother's pearls; her hair is scraped back, all its soft curl repressed, to expose the stubborn square jaw and chin, the high rounded Celtic forehead, the fine arch of brows, the ruler-straight nose. She seems to be assessing whoever might be looking at this picture, her eyes seeking, questioning—but knowing there is only one person who can give her the answer she craves.

That person is staring at her picture right now.

The sight of her hollows his chest, makes him ache with need. He closes his eyes and unwisely allows himself to remember . . .

. . . the perfume of her skin, her soft sigh of his name in Gaelic, her fingers cradling his face in tenderness and her body moving sweetly and powerfully beneath his, and the brandy and coffee and *her* of her mouth—

—the stench of sweat and liquor and cigarettes on his skin, the cruel jeering of his voice, the fear-bunched muscles of her shoulders as he shoves her against the wall, and her blood from where her teeth cut her lip when he tries to rape her.

He opens the book and begins to read.

## EPILOGUE

*She had always looked down on men. From the high window of her tower chamber, as they strutted and pranced and fancied themselves lords of all creation; from the top of the stone stairs into her father's great hall, shy when she was young, then pausing to collect their gazes as she learned her power; from her gilded chair, looking down on the drunkards and the boors and the merely stupid.*

*Only one man had ever made her lift her gaze to meet his. She could make them all look at her—look up at her. All but him.*

*In seeing him, she had also seen limitless sky and wild wind-chased clouds and the sweet infinity of the stars. Sky, wind, stars—poor substitutes for him, but she was used to that.*

*Perhaps he would have been happier had she died of the wanting of him. But it was the only life she knew how to live, after all these years: to survive, strong if not whole; to live, wanting him.*

*He rode away from her for the last time, long back and proud shoulders rigid, obstinate conviction in every line of him. He knew he was right, as surely as she knew he was wrong. If he was hers, then he could not still be his own. What a fool he was. She had been his these many years—had it crippled her, caused her to be a thing less than herself?*

*"I have nothing left to offer you, Elisabeth. Nothing to give—"*

*"Except yourself. Do you think I would be content with less?"*

*"I think that you deserve more."*

*"What is this 'more' you talk of? Wealth I have, and possessions, and name and rank, and such power as is granted to women. What 'more' can you offer me that I would ever need—except yourself?"*

*And though she might offer herself, gladly and willingly and with pride in the giving—strength to strength, need to need—he would not take what was his. If he needed, only he would know of it. His life was his own, and he would live it alone. For he had nothing to offer her except himself.*

*All the loving that had been his for the taking lay in the gutter, to be washed down into the middens with the next hard rain.*

*She wanted to hate him. But she had spent so much of herself loving him that there was very little left within her with which to hate. She would have this last sight of him, of his proud back and strong shoulders and graying dark head with the red glints of Hell's fire still bright in the sunshine. And that was all. Some part of her wanted it so, was glad she had sent him away. Perhaps without him there could be peace, of a sort. But it would be lonely, this life, a thing of bleak bitterness, knowing there was no man worthy of her gaze who could lift her eyes and her heart and her soul.*

*There was still sky. Wind. Stars. And she was used to loneliness.*

*Finis*

THAT JUNE SHE STAYS IN New York long enough to attend launch parties for *Jerusalem Lost*, do a few signings at her favorite bookstores, and take Susannah to a lavish lunch that becomes a pleasantly drunken dinner during which a certain name is never mentioned. She visits Mugger, who now lives quite happily with Alec and Nicky at the Connecticut farmhouse. She stays most of July at Woodhush with Aunt Lulah. And then she returns to London, where the book had been written last autumn and winter. She has spent much of 2003 anywhere but Manhattan: Spain, her beloved Florence, California. She has repeatedly told herself that she deserves time off, especially after the exhaustion of finishing *Jerusalem Lost*.

On August first, Lughnasadh, she participates in a ritual with the London Circle. It is the first magic she has done in a year. The Magistrate is Mr. Scot's granddaughter, and she figures she owes the woman a favor in the old man's name.

Her British publisher never has figured out why she went into a funk but is certain he's found the perfect man to bring her out of it: a tall, black-eyed Irish playwright whose accent is all emerald hills and bardsong. He is charming, witty, intelligent, fun, everything she enjoys in a companion. After she's known him longer than the requisite month, she decides to take him to bed. But if not him, then someone else. Anyone else. It's been a long time.

Yet she hesitates, and escapes London's heat with long drives into the country. She visits cathedrals and medieval ruins and great houses, for once making notes on nothing, researching nothing, simply being in these wonderful places for herself and not for any book.

*Jerusalem Lost* is spending more time on the best-seller lists than she had any right to expect. She knows it's a good book. It just isn't the book she'd meant to write. She is bleakly amused to find it is competing with Denise Josèphe's newest fangs-and-fanatics novel. In all honesty, there is no such thing as bad publicity. Denise has legal problems, which her lawyers have long delayed with multiple continuances, and her name is often in the news.

At last, one Saturday night early in October, she invites the Irishman to dinner. He suggests Luigi's, a favorite of the late Princess Diana, where he points out several semi-scandalous faces and amuses her with gossip. She purposely drinks too much. He comes back to her suite at Durrant's, undresses her, and begins to make love to her quite proficiently. But she makes the one unforgivable mistake. She calls him by a name not his own.

He has compassion enough—or ego enough—to stop. He listens to her stammered apology, then smiles, touches her cheek, and tells her that when she's ready, he'll be here. And then he dresses and leaves.

Humiliated and furious, she pours herself a very large cognac. At length she falls asleep. But being in a man's arms for the first time in more than a year wakens the memories of her flesh, and she dreams.

*He laughed—exultant, triumphant, knowing she is at her limit. She cursed, and he laughed again, and finally allowed her to blaze down to ashes in this fire of his gleeful making. When it was over, and she lay gasping beneath him, he was still hard within her, his satiation secondary to hers, sensitive fingers soothing the frenzy he had created. She roused herself, touching him, greedy for the feel of sleek flesh and hard muscles and sweat-damp skin, muscles contracting along his length, and it was her turn to laugh as his eyes became green-gold dragon's eyes and his head arched back on his long neck and he spent himself within her, crying out her name.*

*As she recovered her breath she opened her eyes to see him propped on one elbow beside her. His hair was tousled, his eyes gleaming, his lips and cheeks flushed, and she felt her heart ache with his beauty. No man had ever loved her like this: with his heart as well as with his body, their souls and minds and spirits all interwoven in this perfect making of love.*

*"A chuisle mo chroí," she whispered, "my love, only mine—"*

*He smiled at the litany. "Just like you're mine. And in case you need it proved to you again—"*

*"You're insatiable. Incorrigible." She ran a hand down his belly to his groin and he hardened once more beneath her caressing fingers. "Indestructible!"*

*"It comes with a lifetime guarantee, babe," he purred. Then he laughed, and pulled her atop him, and kissed the breath out of her.*

*He tastes of good Chianti and fine cigars.*

She wakes up with the memory of a stranger's hands and a stranger's mouth, and cries herself to sleep.

She dreams just before dawn, about a gigantic black grand piano, gleaming with polish and perfect in every respect but for the keys, which ripple and flutter like loose shingles in a gale. Suddenly they begin to fly from the board, short black and long white shards that sound their assigned notes even though they are no longer connected to hammers that strike strings. She lunges to catch them, knowing she must put them back in the proper order, and when she wakes to the ringing of the phone she is sitting up in bed, staring at her empty hands.

She has no tears left when, from an ocean away, Elias Bradshaw tells her that Susannah Wingfield is dead.

———

HE HAS NOT BEEN BACK across the river in over a year. But today he has to go. He's not sure why. Maybe because he doesn't want to think of her as that hard, bitter woman in the book—or of himself as that grim, bitter man. There are memories to be found, good memories that will take the taste of those words out of his mouth. If for a time it hurts even more than usual—well, the words hurt worse.

His few hours of sleep the past two nights have been anything but restful. He thinks with weary longing of when she'd last slept beside him, when the nightmares caused by memories of his mother and the priest vanished as if they'd never been. When the world she'd created for him gave him rest, and peace.

He doesn't dream about the priest anymore, about running and running and never stopping. That is an old hurt, and cannot compete with nightmares in which he cannot move, cannot speak, can do nothing but scream soundlessly with the panic that never wears a face. He has tried to teach himself how to trigger wakefulness, how to turn the dreams deliberately so they can't master him. But he has never quite gotten the knack, and he always wakes with his face buried in a pillow, shivering with sweat, his body clenched with need, with longing, with hatred of his own impotence.

He fears the nightmares, the pain and the panic of them, and for a time last year thought that sex would be an antidote. He was wrong. The first time had been a failure—the first of his life, humiliating him. The second time he'd managed it, but only by squeezing his eyes shut and pretending. Afterward, nightmares had come, and it was months before simple physical desperation had driven him to the bars, and the bed of some woman whose name he didn't know and didn't want to.

There is liquor, of course. There is some measure of oblivion to be found at the bottom of a bottle, but what it did to his body and his mind was, eventually, not worth the hours of sodden sleep.

He's not sure why, but he thinks maybe he'll find something here this bright Sunday morning that will let him sleep tonight. Something is drawing him here, to a tiny part of the world he shared with her. He walks where they once walked together, remembering long talks and laughter and sudden crazy races back to her place so they could make love.

Nothing has changed in the Park. But he is different. He created a hell for himself, and managed somehow to survive it, and now that he has finally come out on the other side he sees that other Evan Lachlan who loved a woman with his whole heart, and shakes his head with incredulity that this man could have been so colossally stupid as to let her go.

He also sees what he did not fully see back then. She offers him everything. Whatever he wants, whatever he needs. He has thought all this time that their private world was of her sole creation. Now he understands that although she was its conjurer, the magic was theirs together. He was always the exact center of that world, and it does not exist without him.

He thinks about something a psych professor said a long time ago. *"The pet theory of a colleague of mine is that there are four kinds of people in the world: Creators, Consumers, Guardians, and Destroyers. Those who choose to work in law enforcement are obviously Guardians. Keep the Consumers safe, let the Creators do their work, and catch the Destroyers before they do any more damage."*

He knows now that she made that world because she needed to. She could no more choose not to create than she could choose not to be born. He was to have been that world's Guardian. Instead, he has been its Destroyer.

He knows that no woman will ever love him like that again. There had been affection from others, tenderness, sometimes real caring, but never this encompassing love that enfolds him even now that he is parted from her. For despite what he did in shattering their world, her loving stays wrapped around him. Pride told him he must get through his self-made hell alone. What he has not realized until this very moment is that she is with him, she has been with him all along. If he has risen from his knees, and stood, and walked, and found his way through, it is partly because she has been beside him.

He knows this now. Accepts it, with gratitude. It is not weakness, to admit this need. That would be the same as believing that he is a lesser person because he is right-handed or hazel-eyed. The man in that book, with his own Jerusalem forever lost, with his rigid pride and his terror of loving—wrong, so wrong. Loving her and needing her are as much a part of him as his skin, his blood, his bones.

He can see that other Evan Lachlan catch her in his arms and whirl her around and around, laughing. When she escapes him, he runs after her. And this, he thinks suddenly, is what has changed most about him: he has stood, and walked, but he no longer runs. Not like that other Lachlan, with his eager uncomplicated joy.

Suddenly his legs ache to run. He isn't wearing the clothes for it—the T-shirt is okay, but the jeans are too snug. He runs anyway, pushing himself harder and faster until his lungs are on fire and his thighs are screaming. He slows, eventually stops. Hands on hips, bent over, gulping air.

A voice says to him, Legs that long aren't meant for sprints, you know—you're built for distance.

He looks up. Barely five-five, thin as a rake and carefully sculpted, no hips to speak of, blonde ponytail. The eyes are greenish, and for a moment he is reminded of Susannah—but the face is all wrong, the lips too full and the cheekbones too sharp. She is dressed for jogging in barely legal shorts and a cropped halter top that expose toned and honed stomach muscles and artfully tanned skin.

Distance, huh? he says. What'd you have in mind?

She looks him over once again, and likes what she sees, and replies, How about the five blocks to my place?

He puts a grin on his face, but inside he is reeling. This easy? Twenty-five words or less, and they'd be in the sack? But it has been a long time.

The apartment is pricey, self-consciously decorated, and smells of some odd, nose-prickling incense. The bed is huge. He lifts her effortlessly—she weighs nothing—and splays her across the velvet bedspread. He strips her clothes off without preliminaries, using every trick ever learned, every technique, until she finally begs for mercy.

As she sleeps, sprawled on her stomach with her face hidden in a pillow, he lies on his back, late afternoon sunshine streaming down from a high window. His body is sated, his soul unsatisfied—just like all the other times. Those falling-down-a-well-into-the-mud times when he's been so starved for touch and warmth or just plain sex that he took whatever was offered.

But it turns out there is a difference with this one, because there was no softness, not even inside, where a woman is usually warmly yielding. It was like fucking a sweat-sheened marble statue: alive, the blood hot within her, but ultimately hard. Repressing memories of another body, strong but soft and giving (that is what he's missed, more than anything else: the givingness), he draws the sheet over her and goes into the bathroom.

There is no light in his eyes. No look of sheer exhilaration, of shared ecstasy. Of being happy. Leaning on the sink, hands gripping the porcelain, he squeezes shut his lightless, lifeless eyes and smells the woman on him and whispers, "Holly . . ."

*"You're mine, Evan Lachlan—"*

He remembers the first time she said that. When it had startled him, and for a few moments he had shied away from it, until he understood what she meant.

*They finished dinner, with the choice of brandies to be debated before they went to the bar for cigars. A woman in a tight black dress approached and mentioned something about special reserve Armagnacs—but she didn't get around to naming them because she recognized him. And he recognized her.*

*Hi-how-are-you-what've-you-been-doing. Holly sat patiently waiting for him to remember his manners and perform introductions. Glancing over at her, he did so. And wished to God he was anywhere but here.*

*Sherry smiled with the smug superiority of prior knowledge; Holly smiled with the poisonous sweetness of current possession. He made a hasty escape to the men's room, telling the women to order whatever they thought he'd like. Christ Almighty—there was nothing worse than an old girlfriend running into the new one. If they didn't shred you right in front of your face, they hacked you up without saying a single word, just by smiling.*

*Five tactful minutes later he returned to the table. Sherry's voice could have blighted every newly budding tree in Central Park as she told him his friend was waiting in the bar. He nodded thanks, and didn't say he'd call her real soon.*

*Holly, perched on a tall chrome bar stool, had already lit her cigar. She gestured to the cognac and Cohiba waiting for him. Her perfect serenity made him deeply suspicious.*

*He smoked, sipped, and waited. At last, able to stand no more, he asked, "What the hell did you say to her, anyway?"*

*She shrugged. "All I did was tell her that I'd greatly appreciate it if she'd wipe the drool off her chin."*

*He choked. "McClure!"*

*"Well, what else could I do? She had the gall to ask not only how long we've known each other — with biblical implications to the verb — but whether it's still impossible to wake you up in the morning, with the further implication that she could wear you out like no other woman in the world." Holly took a long draw on her cigar. Fragrant smoke trickled from her lips as she went on, "To which I replied that I don't bother trying to wake you up before noon. Any more former girlfriends among the staff here?"*

*"None that I know of. Why?"*

*All at once her eyes were fierce. "You're mine, Evan Lachlan, in case you hadn't noticed yet. And if any more of your women show up —" She didn't have to finish the thought. A smile was back on her face, but this time it was the smile of a predator anticipating the gratifying crunch of bone.*

He'd seen that smile only one other time: when she looked straight at Father Matthew. By then he'd known what it meant. But the first time, he hadn't known whether to feel smug and delighted or trapped and appalled — until he abruptly understood that the other thing she meant was, *"I'm yours, Evan Lachlan, in case you hadn't noticed yet."*

He is still hers. And the flesh that has just spent itself within another woman disgusts him. Just his body, he tells himself as he strips off the condom and showers himself clean. Nothing to do with his heart. She is still here, still beside him, and even with the feel of another woman lingering on him despite his efforts to wash her off, he can sense warm fingers slide into his palm and hear soft laughter as her head rests on his shoulder. She is still here. She always will be. And despite what he has just done with his body, the truest part of him is still hers.

He returns to the bedroom for his clothes. The girl is still sleeping. Nice, he thinks sourly, to know a pushing-forty out-of-shape deputy marshal can wear out a twenty-two-year-old marathon runner.

He gets into his clothes, hoping she won't awaken. She does. She stretches, and turns over — and all at once her face is different, altered, older, sickeningly familiar. The last time he saw it was inside Elias Bradshaw's courtroom.

Still don't believe in magic? she asks, grinning. She sits up in bed, shaking out long blonde hair. I have to say it was worth the trouble it took to bring you to Manhattan today.

Bring me—? he asks, voice thick with disgust.

Unlike your former playmate, I know how to use what I've got. I got a late start Friday—you remember that murder charge? Continuance after continuance, but Friday I had to be at the courthouse for some tedious interview. But once I got back here— She gives a little shrug. Complicated, and I expected you Saturday, but well worth the effort and the wait. I Called, and you came, and— She breaks off, laughing. Did she ever do you as well as I just did?

For a moment he thinks he's going to throw up.

Her brown-mottled green eyes strafe him. You're not quite as impressive as that time we talked at Starbucks. Body by Nautilus, back then. Now it's more like Body by Budweiser. But you're still a choice lay, Marshal. And my choicest trophy, even better than beating that bitch on the August best-seller lists.

Somehow he manages to leave her apartment. This is worse than the other times he's found a woman to fuck. Infinitely worse. For the first time he understands how Holly must feel when her blood is used for someone else's magic.

Back across the river, there is a message waiting on his answering machine. The time-log says it has been here since noon. He plays it, then plays it again, thinking he has heard wrong, that Pete is mistaken. God, no—it must be a mistake—not Susannah—

Tears blur his eyes. He can't take this. Not after that book, not after this day. With a blind, mindless need he wants Holly—to be with her, to hold her while she cries, to rock her in his arms and cry with her, to talk of Susannah, to mourn her—

But he has no right. Especially after what he's done today, he has no right.

In his apartment across the river, a place he has never even begun to think of as home, for the first time since his self-imposed moderation he gets thoroughly, senselessly, retchingly drunk.

# Twenty-one

HOLLY FLEW INTO HARTFORD for Susannah's funeral with no very clear idea of how or even when she arrived. Another classmate picked her up at the airport and categorically forbade her to stay in a hotel. So Holly and her luggage rode out into the suburbs, then the countryside, while darkness fell and Jemima Stapleton Rowell filled the silence with details of tomorrow's memorial.

Jemima had inevitably been known during childhood as Puddleduck, a nickname unused at college for the simple reason that she threatened frightful vengeance on anyone who even thought about calling her that. The only person who ever got away with it was the man she eventually married—and Joshua dared only "Puddin'" or "Ducks."

The Rowell residence was forthright New England clapboard outside, and on the inside a chaos of toys, discarded sweaters, skates, schoolbooks, half-eaten peanut butter sandwiches the mutts hadn't yet found, and other effluvia of a family of three boys and three girls. Jemima herself had grown comfortably plump, presiding over the turmoil with the benign neglect of the absolute monarch who doesn't have to prove it. When she escorted Holly through to the kitchen, the Babel of sons and daughters instantly moved itself elsewhere when she hollered, "Out! And take the cookie jar with you!"

Holly sat in numbed silence, watching her old friend bustle, not thinking at all until Jemima spoke. "Her mother wants us to sing tomorrow, you know."

"I couldn't."

"Me, neither. I'll get us out of it, don't worry." Seating herself on the other side of the kitchen table from Holly, she poured coffee and dispensed macaroons. "She gave me a piece of music Suze had written—it was in her jacket pocket when—when they found her. Holly, it's the most dreadful thing I've ever seen."

Holly shrugged dully, circling the edge of her coffee mug with one finger. "We both nearly flunked Composition."

"When I think of what a glorious voice she had, I just can't believe she'd write something so awful. I didn't even know she noodled around with writing music."

"She didn't."

Joshua Rowell—six feet of former hockey star, with the twice-broken nose and capped teeth to prove it—came in, greeted Holly, kissed his wife, and said, "I'll ride herd on the kids tonight, Pudds. You and Holly don't stay up too late, all right?"

"Thanks for lending me the spare room, Josh," Holly replied.

"No trouble. I already took all your stuff upstairs—third door on the right. The girls should be out of their bathroom by seven thirty for school, so you'll have it to yourself." He smiled, poured himself a cup of coffee, and left the kitchen.

"I could do with a bath tonight," Holly said. "I'm all stinky from the planes."

"The kids will be in bed by nine," Jemima replied. "More or less. Are you sure you don't want something to eat? Okay, but if you get hungry in the middle of the night, you know where the fridge is. Everything's fair game except the pies—they're for the reception tomorrow."

"Aunt Lulah used to bring a couple of jars of moonshine for after a funeral."

"Jesus, I remember that stuff! You got the most interesting care packages from home I ever saw. How is your aunt? And those two hunky uncles who used to take you out to the most expensive dinner in town on your birthday?"

"All fine. Alec and Nicky are retired now. Aunt Lulah's got a new mare at Woodhush, sweetest gallop you ever rode." Holly scraped both hands back through her hair, still unused to how short it was. "Jimmie, I'm not ready to start going to my friends' funerals."

"Nobody ever is. I should call Mrs. Wingfield and let her know you've arrived safely. And think up some reason why we won't be singing tomorrow. And especially not singing that thing Suze wrote."

"Okay, I can take a hint—let me look at it while you talk to Mrs. Wingfield."

While Jemima spoke softly on the telephone, Holly examined the single Xeroxed sheet of something written on a yellow legal pad. The original was undoubtedly still with the cops, bagged as evidence. Jemima was right: the piece was musical gibberish. Four/four time and a treble clef were the only things that made any sense. The rest of it didn't even have the virtue of a twelve-tone experiment; it was simply irrational. Holly read through Susannah's scrawled notation, memory automatically supplying the scene of her dorm room the night before their Composition project was due, when they'd loaded up on coffee for an all-nighter and despaired of ever coming up with anything that would—

"Hellfire and damnation!"

Jemima hastily concluded her conversation with Mrs. Wingfield. "Holly? What's wrong?"

"Paper and pen—quick."

"Inspiration hit?"

"In a way." While Jemima rummaged her kitchen drawers, Holly stared at the rioting ivy wallpaper, deliberately blanking her mind. When a stack of construction paper and a selection of Magic Markers were set before her, she jumped.

"Hell of a time to be thinking about your next book," Jemima offered, a fond hand on Holly's shoulder taking the sting from the words. "I couldn't find anything but leftovers from Becca's last project."

"It's okay. It's fine. This has nothing to do with a book, Jimmie. It's something Suze and I cooked up in college." She began ruling off one of the blank pages into two columns and twenty-six lines. "Remember Professor Dominguez? No, you wouldn't, he left before you took Comp. He was a big John Cage fan, anything that fooled around with the way music was written. Anyway, Suze and I sat up until dawn figuring out a way to impress him. And we came up with this."

She wrote out the alphabet, then started at H, and in the next column marked down a D and a half-note symbol. "The first seven notes are easy. Whole notes correspond to letters. But once you get to letters eight through twenty-six—H through Z—you have to use half- and quarter-notes to make it work."

"Half of a D? No—double it, get eight, and that's H!"

"Exactly. Four times two gets the eighth letter of the alphabet. Some have more than one way to do them—"

"A quarter-note quadruples the value, right? So a quarter-note B gives you H as well," Jemima said briskly. Seating herself next to Holly, she grabbed paper and another Magic Marker. "Do your chart and then dictate Susannah's letter."

"Thank God for clever friends!" As she worked at completing the guide, she said, "We did 'I Am the Walrus' this way for Dominguez—which ain't easy, because there's letters in it that you can't get with this code. Like M, which is more essential than you know until you can't use it. But if you play with the phonetics, you can usually get the meaning across."

Jemima had been doing some calculations in her head. "No prime numbers above seven, so no S, either. What did you do, use a TH and call it a lisp?"

"Clever *and* snide," Holly retorted. "We used C. And the W was just that—a double U."

"And two Ns for M?"

"Yep."

"What about ends of words? You couldn't have done it like a telegram and used 'stop.' And it couldn't have been the end of a bar or a measure, either."

"Well, we were thinking about using a bar of silence, but the thing was ugly enough without making it even longer. The words sort of fell into recognizable patterns."

"Even if the music was crap. I am *so* not disappointed that this never occurred to John Lennon. You ready?"

With Susannah's pages to her left and the chart to her right, Holly began. Jemima wrote in neat capital letters with no spaces between—occasionally drawing a backslash when a word became clear.

"E whole, C half, C three-quarter—ELI." Holly paused. "Elias Bradshaw. Susannah had been seeing him."

"I know. Her mother told me about him—the judge with the sailboat, right?"

"He likes to sail, yes." Giving the lie to the old one about Witches being unable to cross water. Susannah had loved Long Island Sound of a Sunday afternoon; Holly begged off the twice she'd been asked along. She did get seasick.

"Mrs. Wingfield wants to scatter Susannah's ashes at sea. They're renting a launch or something in a few days. Anyway, Elias Bradshaw will be here tomorrow. Sorry—go on. First word is 'Eli.'"

They continued, with Holly muttering to herself and reciting letters. What emerged bewildered Jemima, but sent a fiery flush of terror through Holly.

ELI / HALLOEEN / THREAT / HOLLI / BLOOD / RITE / LEADER / NOEL / NOX / INCARNATA / REGRET / DONT / NO / LOCALE / ELI / DEAR / HEART / NO / GRIEF

"And this means—?" Jemima asked.

*That by the time she finished this, she knew she was going to die.* "Nothing I can explain right now, and nothing you'd want to hear about anyway."

"Who's Noel?"

"Damned if I know."

"'*Nox incarnata*'—incarnation of night? My Latin's a little shaky these days."

"Works just fine," Holly replied grimly. "Jimmie, I have to use your phone. In private."

"Believe it or not, there actually is such a thing as privacy in this house," Jemima added with a slight smile. "Try Josh's office. The door locks."

HOLLY NEEDED TO KNOW EXACTLY what had happened to Susannah, beyond the finding of her body in Central Park and the fact that her neck had been broken. She couldn't consult Susannah's mother, or Elias Bradshaw—the former hadn't been able to talk much on Sunday night when Holly phoned her from London, and she wasn't ready to deal with Elias. So she called Sophia Osbourne.

Ten minutes later she curled up in Joshua's oversized desk chair, arms wreathing her knees, and thought over the conversation. A recital, actually, of the police report, with tears thickening the redoubtable Mrs. Osbourne's voice.

Last Friday afternoon Susannah left Elias's chambers to have lunch with a friend in the Manhattan D.A.'s office. That was the last anyone saw of her. Who took her, where, how, and why were mysteries likely to remain unsolved. An early-morning jogger found her body on Sunday, beneath the three cypress trees of Strawberry Fields. She was dressed in the beige linen trouser suit, blue silk shirt, and hosiery she'd worn Friday, with four little splinters of wood stuck in the trousers at the left knee. The clothes were stained with grass and soil, but no blood, except at that knee. Her purse, shoes, and briefcase were gone. Her neck had been expertly snapped: clean, quick, painless. There were no signs of rape, no bruising, no physical trauma. The medical examiner's first cursory appraisal had revealed a needle-mark on her right hip; toxicology would identify the drug used, but obviously this was how she had been subdued for the snatch. She wore pearl earrings, gold chain necklace, and her class ring; in her jacket pockets were about an ounce of dirt and a diamond bracelet, a felt-tipped pen, and a crumpled page of musical notation.

The dirt was being analyzed. "That girl knew evidence," Mrs. Osbourne had said. "I bet they took her shoes to prevent this very thing—there are too many cop shows on television these days, any idiot knows about trace evidence. But that dirt in her pocket, that'll tell us something. And the splinters, too."

Holly wasn't counting on it. Too easy—way too easy. But Mrs. Osbourne was right about Susannah's perfect grasp of the importance of evidence. She stared at the note, laid out on the desk. A blood ritual on Hallowe'en—old Samhain—led by Noel, whoever he was. *Nox incarnata*. She thought about the presence of dirt, note, jewelry, and splinters; the absence of shoes, briefcase, and purse.

"Absence of evidence is not evidence of absence," Holly muttered, quoting the archaeologist's credo. Too, there was "the curious incident of the dog in the nighttime"—the dog whose silence had told Sherlock Holmes so much. There was an absence of evidence here, or an evidence of absence; certainly something about this constituted a curious incident.

ELIAS FLED THE CHURCH IMMEDIATELY after the service. He couldn't go to the Wingfield home to pay his respects. He simply couldn't. He'd been asked to join the family to scatter the ashes, but the thought of being in some boat with all that was left of Susannah horrified him. The beautiful, passionate body he'd held in his arms was now soft gray ash and fragments of bone in a green-glazed Japanese urn.

Would he rather have known her to be whole and untouched and six feet beneath the ground? Lying in black silence, hands folded, until the years and the cold had done their work and the fine bones of her fingers showed through crumbling skin and the wheat-gold hair tarnished and—and—

He couldn't think about that, either. Not thinking about it, he nearly threw up onto the carefully manicured lawn.

The October afternoon was a glory of sapphire sky, shimmering sun, and a freshening breeze off the sea to stir the leaves hinting at their glorious autumn show. Picture perfect, this white church with its postcard steeple and austere stained glass. How many weddings, baptisms, funerals, and staunchly Protestant Sunday services had occurred here? Thousands upon thousands. Susannah had returned home to her ancestors. Why couldn't they at least have been Irish? Then he could've gone to a wake, with a socially acceptable excuse to get mindlessly drunk—

"Elias?"

He turned. Holly McClure wore a plain brown dress, a white scarf draped around her shoulders—a relief after all the black. She was heavier than he remembered, and her hair had been cut short around her cheeks and neck. Her eyes were red-rimmed and she looked exhausted.

She took his elbow and walked him across the lawn toward the ocean. He resisted for a moment, then heard others coming out of the church and decided this was as good an escape as any.

Though why Holly was providing it, he had no idea. The last time he'd seen her, she'd been screaming at him about Evan Lachlan. He hadn't seen her since. She hadn't seen Lachlan since, either, judging from something Susannah had said a couple of weeks ago—

It hit him then, how soon "a couple of weeks" would become "a couple of months," and then "a couple of years"—and he'd never see her again, never touch her, never take her out sailing and watch the wind play with her hair, never—

"I won't allow you to hate yourself," Holly said softly. "Not when Susannah loved you so much."

He shook his head.

"Don't do it, Elias," she warned. "I won't profane her memory by letting you hate the man she loved."

"You're not usually redundant. Lost your writer's touch?"

"I'll say the same exact thing a thousand times if that's what it takes to get through to you." Holly tugged him along toward the shore, over the dunes, tall sea-grasses shifting in the breeze.

"I don't know why you give a damn."

"Because she did love you."

"As much as I'd let her, and more than I deserved." The beach stretched out on either side of them, reeds lazily waving, blue water beyond. "Her mother asked — my sailboat — she always talked about how much she loved sailing — "

"I'm glad you said no." Holly paused a minute. "Mrs. Wingfield wanted us to get a few of the Chorale together. We begged off, too — I think Jemima said that we couldn't possibly choose among Susannah's favorite songs." She sighed quietly and stared out to sea. "Your sailboat, the songs — they wouldn't have been for her, Elias. They'd be — I don't know, glimpses of her for other people to see, people those things don't belong to. Not even her family."

He took the hand resting in the crook of his elbow and squeezed it gently, grateful that she understood. Susannah's mother had not. It occurred to him that Holly McClure was possibly the only person who would understand.

"The candles were for her, though," Holly said.

"Your idea?"

She nodded. "Twelve around the — the urn, to protect her. Nothing evil can cross into a circle of lighted candles. I told her mother it was an old Irish custom."

"You did the candles yourself? Magic?"

"Last night, when they brought her to the church."

They stood watching the sea in silence. Then Elias said, "I need a drink. Care to join me?"

"No. You don't need a drink." She bent, slipping off her shoes, tucked them into the lee of a dune, and wriggled bare toes in the sand. "Come on. Let's walk."

After a moment's hesitation, he shrugged. Shoes and socks off, he loosened his tie for good measure, and after about a quarter of a mile of walking found he was holding Holly's hand. He wasn't sure who initiated the gesture. But he figured he ought to say something. "I'm sorry about what happened with Lachlan — "

"We're not here to talk about him. Elias, I have to know if you'll be all right."

He shrugged. "Eventually."

"That's what I said, too."

He stopped, turned her to face him. Her face was grieving and older and much harder than he remembered. He stood with her in the shelter of a dune, reeds humming in the wind that ruffled her curling russet hair.

"Holly, I *am* sorry. Let me finish. I don't know if there was anything more I could've done. All I know is she fought like hell for him. Not only for your sake, but for his. But it just — it wasn't going to happen."

"I don't want to talk about it, Elias," she said fiercely. "I mean it."

Again he shrugged. "Okay."

"Tell me what to do for you," she said, almost pleading. "I won't see you make wreckage of yourself. She'd kill me."

"*I* killed *her.*"

There. He'd said it out loud.

"How's that again?" she asked, a dangerous note in her voice.

"I should've protected her. I should've told her what I am, what the risks are."

"You, you, you!" she shouted, wrenching away, abruptly furious. "What makes you so fucking important? What makes you think the world revolves around you, Bradshaw? I think Susannah *did* love you too much! Just because you were the center of her world doesn't mean the whole of Creation turns on what you do!"

The tears came then, as they had not in all the long days since—since. They hurt; he hadn't cried since his mother's death twenty years ago. He didn't know how to weep anymore.

Holly didn't try to hold him. She simply stood there, blue eyes bleak with understanding. But after a time he reached for her. She was real and warm and she had loved Susannah, too.

She was too tall. Her hair was too short, too curly, her shoulders were too square, her body too rounded. Doubtless she was thinking similar things: not tall enough, not broad-shouldered enough, not anything she truly wanted to hold.

She wasn't Susannah Wingfield. He wasn't Evan Lachlan.

But when he looked at her—at her eyes that were the wrong color and her face that was the wrong shape and her mouth that was the wrong curve—he kissed her anyway. She parted her lips, and kissed him back.

And if, on that stretch of deserted windblown beach, with his jacket for a bed and the long grass to hide them, either of them called out for someone who was gone, no one else knew.

After, they silently smoothed rumpled clothing and walked back up the beach, not touching.

"Amazing, isn't it?" she said all at once. "To realize you're still alive." She slanted a look at him. "I have this feeling I ought to thank you."

"Depends on why that happened."

"Compassion?" She looked amused. "Altruism? Not bloody likely. I'm not that nice a person, Elias—and neither are you."

"Comfort, then."

She shrugged.

"What about Lachlan? Where does he fit in?"

"He doesn't," she said flatly. "This wasn't about him."

"Then why did you say his name?"

"Habit. You called me 'Susannah.'"

"Did I? Christ." He raked his hair back. "What a hell of a situation."

"Why? You don't really want me, and I don't really want you. We both just had to make sure we were still alive."

"You make it sound so damned cold."

"I'm sorry you see it that way, because it didn't feel like that to me at all. And there's no 'situation,' Elias. None at all." She smiled briefly. "You don't have to send me a dozen red roses."

He swore softly, remembering now that Susannah had shared that bit of his grandfather's credo with her.

Holly rummaged in her purse for a comb, and gave it to him. While he was dragging it through his tangled hair, she said musingly, "Last weekend I made a try at convincing myself I was still alive. Still a whole human being. I wasn't much good at it. In the past year I haven't met anyone I'd care to spend ten minutes with—let alone half an hour on a sand dune." Another little smile as he gave her back her comb. "But I know you, Elias. I feel comfortable with you. Because there's never going to be a repeat. You know it, I know it. We're just not each other's type."

"Yet she loved us both."

"Susannah knew how to love. So few people saw that in her. The dedication to whatever she chose to do, whatever she found worthy of her. The work, friendship, loving . . ."

He tried to lighten things. "Sounds as if there's a book character in this."

"Oh, no," she said very seriously. "I could never do her justice. And I've discovered that you can't transpose people that way." She hesitated, and suddenly her eyes were hard and cold again. "This wasn't vengeance against Evan, Elias. That was published in June."

"I know. I read it."

They kept walking, up the beach to find their shoes, then to the church. The parking lot was deserted but for Elias's Lincoln Town Car.

"Where can I drop you?" he asked.

"Where are you staying?"

He shook his head. "I'm not."

"You can't drive back to Manhattan today. We have to talk."

"We already did."

She opened his car door and slid inside. "There's something else, Elias. About the people who kidnapped Susannah. And the one I think killed her."

"Why the fuck didn't you say something before?" he roared.

"Because I wasn't sure you'd be able to hear it yet. Now I'm sure— Magistrate." She slammed the door and folded her arms, jaw set and rigid.

He stood where he was, so angry, he shook to the bone. His title asserted its own identity, then demanded his full awareness. "All right, Spellbinder," he muttered, striding to the driver's side. "Your way or no way, as usual."


JEMIMA AND HER HUSBAND WERE at the Wingfield home. The kids were in school. Elias and Holly had the big rambling house to themselves. In the kitchen with coffee brewing, she told him flatly, "She left a note."

"How the hell could she have—?"

"Shut up and read." Taking the Xerox page from her pocket, she handed it over. Musical notation. "Translation is on the back."

He read. And read again.

"We had a project in college for a composition class. She used the code we made up then, which I won't bother to explain, to write that. As for Noel—I think I finally figured out who he is."

Holly told him about her visit to the store, and Nick and Alec's worries, and reminded him that she'd asked him to check it out last year after she'd recognized the scent in Denise's bedroom as incense or oil from Noel's collection. "And do you remember that night my Witching Sphere went psychotic? Alec did a read while he was cleansing and respelling it. The main feel to it was Voudon, which logically leads back to Denise. She hates me and she knows what I am."

"How does that connect with this Noel?"

"She bought things at his shop. She knows him. *Nox incarnata* sounds just like her kind of homefolks, doesn't it? He might even have been there the night Scott Fleming was killed."

"If so, why not trade him for immunity or a lesser charge?" he objected.

"I'm supposed to know this how, exactly?" she snapped. "Who knows what goes on in her little pea-brain? But consider this: Fleming and Susannah both had their necks broken. Some forensic comparison might be interesting."

The thought of reading Susannah's autopsy report made him want to smash his fist into a wall. "You're a novelist. You—"

"I make up stories for a living? I'm also a biographer. Is that a little more precise and scholarly for you, Your Honor? I can recognize a coincidence when one bites me in the ass. Blood rites on Hallowe'en—when the veil between worlds is vanishingly thin."

"A vanishingly thin connection."

"We're not in your courtroom. The rules of evidence don't apply."

He flattened his hand on the note. "How many people have touched the original?"

Holly stared, perplexed. "What?"

"Susannah, the cops who found her—who else?" he asked impatiently.

"Well—the crime scene people, and somebody put her personal effects together, and made the copy to give to her mother—"

"It might be possible," he muttered.

"What are you talking about?"

"Lydia."

Holly got to her feet. "You're crazy. We don't know what happened to Susannah. We don't know what it might do to Lydia, to sense her memories. And how will you get hold of the original?"

He only looked at her.

"Okay, okay," she conceded. "Stupid question."

Elias finished his coffee, rose, and said, "We have to get moving on this. I'll go back tonight, and—"

"You'll stay here in town," Holly shot back, "and get a decent night's sleep. I'll drive back with you tomorrow morning. We can phone the others from here. Don't fight me on this, Elias. We're neither of us in any shape to do the drive and then get ready for this kind of Work."

"*We* are not going to do anything. *You* are going to go home and stay there until Samhain."

Holly slammed her coffee cup down on the table. "If you think you're going to wrap me in cotton and stash me away, you've got another think coming!"

"It's a damned good bet that he knows you're a Spellbinder. You can't risk—"

"Don't even try, Elias," she warned. "You'll need me for Lydia's sake."

"Since when did you ever give a shit about Lydia—or the rest of the Circle, for that matter?" When she turned pale beneath her freckles, he made a little shrug of apology. "Sorry. I'm wound pretty tight. At least go stay with Alec and Nick."

"No. In fact, I think we should all go about our normal business, because if Noel is watching—and you know he is—anything out of the ordinary might tip him off that we're aware of him."

Bradshaw grunted reluctant agreement, and almost asked if she'd taken fool-the-perp lessons from Lachlan. At the thought of whom, an idea formed.

"We have to do this right," Holly was saying. "That means preparation, and caution, and waiting until we're all rested and ready. I'll bleed buckets for this if necessary, but not for some half-assed attempt that gets tried too soon because you're in a rage. After all, it's *my* blood we're talking about here."

There was no replying to that.

She acknowledged it with a wry half-smile, and sat back down at the table. "I've already made a few contingency plans. I called Pete Wasserman. He says the lab reports on the dirt in her pocket will be in on Friday."

"How'd you like to make yourself useful?" he asked, a contingency plan of his own developing. "I'll have him okay it with the lab to release the reports to you. Go pick them up on Friday."

"Why me?" she asked, suspicious.

"We're holding a sale on excuses and justifications today," he countered. "Which one are you buying? I could say it's because I want you surrounded by law enforcement as often as possible, or because everybody in the office is going to be hellishly busy and I want this report picked up in person instead of getting lost in the bureaucracy. Or maybe because giving you something to do will keep you from going crazy."

"How about because you *asked* me to, instead of issuing an order the way you usually do?"

"Works for me," he said with a shrug.

It worked even better when he made a brief call later that afternoon, when Holly was busy with her friend Jemima. *Contingency plan A,* he thought to himself, and really smiled for the first time since Sunday morning.

# Twenty-two

HOLLY WAS AT One Police Plaza by eleven o'clock Friday for the results of the soil analysis, Pete Wasserman having called in a favor with a friend in the NYPD labs. If the dirt in Susannah's pockets had come from some obscure and unique area, they'd be a step closer to finding Noel—or at least one of his haunts.

The dirt turned out to be just dirt. Long Island dirt, but—just dirt. She thanked the clerk who gave her the report, hiding her frustration. Not that she'd expected much to come of this; she'd told herself Tuesday that it would have been too easy. Still, there'd been a hope. She felt it die inside her, a wretched little death. Reaching to punch the elevator button, she saw the glitter of diamonds on her wrist.

Susannah had lost her bet. Her mother had known nothing about that, of course, when she gave Holly the bracelet.

*"We have to go see them. Elias, five minutes. Just to pay our respects. Neither of us showed up after the memorial yesterday. Her mother will be hurt."*

*"Do I look as if I care?"*

*But he drove to the Wingfield house anyway. They arrived to find the sisters, brothers-in-law, nieces, nephews, and various other relatives preparing to go home. Mrs. Wingfield would soon be all alone in the house. Holly felt guilty about that, though she knew what she and Elias planned to do would mean more to Susannah's mother than a few hours of their company.*

*In the midst of a reserved New England chaos, Mrs. Wingfield took Holly and Elias aside. "The police returned her things. In her will she left this to you." She fastened the bracelet around Holly's wrist. "There are a few other things—and for you, Judge Bradshaw. Just some tokens to remember her by."*

*As if Susannah was forgettable. Holly saw the flinch in Elias's dark eyes, and hastily thanked Mrs. Wingfield, made their excuses, and escaped.*

*In the car, Elias said, "I could hardly look at her. I kept seeing Susannah in thirty years."*

*"I know," Holly murmured, fingering the bracelet. "Me, too."*

*"I should have given her that." He nodded at the jewelry.*

*She considered a moment, then said, "It was the roses that mattered, Elias. The red roses, and everything that went with them."*

Now the diamonds shone up at her, and she knew without even thinking about it that she'd always wear them. Just as she knew Evan still wore the St. Michael medal, and always would.

Everything came back to him in the end, even after more than a year. She couldn't still be thinking this way, not after all this time. But her body still ached at the thought of him, and the heart he'd broken bled anew.

Giving up on the sluggish elevator, she headed for the stairs. Seven flights — but she could use the exercise. Settling into a rhythm that didn't quite plod, she tried to listen to her footfalls instead of her thoughts.

He should've been the last man she'd fall for — and she'd fallen hard. But why him? She liked them tall and lean; highly educated and perceptive; men of style, elegance, and sensitivity. How had it happened that her heart had been irrevocably stolen by a big, broad-backed, blunt-spoken Irish Deputy U.S. Marshal?

Educated? He knew the streets, he knew people, he knew himself. And her.

Perceptive? He'd plowed through her books, genuinely liked them, and discussed them with her so astutely that she found new insights into her own work.

Style? Elegance? Nothing could outclass him in a tuxedo, naked he was glorious, and anything in between was a privilege and a pleasure to look at. Except for those ostrich-hide cowboy boots . . .

A sound halfway between laughter and a sob escaped her throat. Evan Lachlan and his godawful ostrich-hide cowboy boots . . .

. . . And his long fingers, so gentle as they framed her face. And his strong arms, wrapping her in warmth and safety. And his impossible grin. And his tenderness, and his deep searching kisses, and his powerful, generous body —

This was ridiculous. No man could possess such a glamour, in the sense of the old Gaelic: to cast an enchantment. This past year she had imbued him with qualities he'd never possessed —

Who was she trying to fool? He was everything she'd ever wanted. He'd given her strength for strength, fight for fight, loving for loving. And she'd lost him. Somehow all the pieces had come together and fallen apart. His fault, her fault, their fault — it didn't matter anymore. She'd loved him and she'd lost him.

Damn him for doing this to her. For having this much power. For leaving her and yet never leaving.

She'd been terrified he'd come to Susannah's memorial. She had no idea what she would have done if he had — except that she wouldn't have taken that walk with Elias. She still wasn't entirely clear on why she'd even tried to help him, other than that Susannah would have wanted her to. There'd been more than three hundred people in the church, but somehow Holly had felt herself an alien with all of them except Elias. Three hundred people—but not Evan. Maybe nobody had told him. He wouldn't have stayed away just because Holly would be there. He'd been too fond of Susannah, admired her too much. Maybe he knew, but had to work.

She emerged from the stairwell and bumped into a bulky lawyer-type who snarled at her and hurried on his way. Apologizing to the man's back, she hiked her purse over her shoulder and continued through the lobby.

And stumbled when she saw him. Hair a little longer, tall body sleek in a black suit and white shirt and those godawful cowboy boots, moving with that powerful saunter that always took her breath away. There was gray in his hair now, silvering his temples, and a few lines around his eyes, and he was maybe ten pounds heavier—and he was still the most beautiful man she had ever seen.

A frantic hand to her hair—would he like it short?—and a glance down at her clothes—how completely perfect Fate's joke was—she wore the brown Armani suit—he always said it made her look like a goddamned lawyer—

He saw her then, and stopped walking midstride. He caught his balance easily—she had forgotten how supple he was, especially for a man his size. His height and breadth of shoulder and the strength of him made her bones go all hollow. His eyes narrowed, brows quirking downward as if not believing it was her, then went wider than ever. And the gold came into them, brilliant with joy.

Her heart thundered and her body cried out and the suddenness of it put tears into her eyes that she damned because they obscured the sight of him. She scraped them away with a goddamned brown pinstriped Armani sleeve. He saw the tears, and his eyes grieved that she could even think of crying. He shook his head slightly, and the sweep of dark hair fell across his brow. She made her legs move, walk toward him. He started walking, too—faster and faster, and the sudden embrace suffocated whatever breath remained in their lungs.

But she found voice enough to whisper, "Evan—*a chuisle*—"

And after a short, sharp inhalation, as if the sound of his own name wounded him in some way, he answered in a voice that shook with the pounding of his heart, "Holly—oh, lady love—"

She tilted her head back to look up at him. Those eyes. Those incredible hazel-green gold-lit long-lashed luminous dragon's eyes . . .

Helpless. Just like before. Damn him. How she would love to hate him for his power over her.

His voice was low and quiet, his face deadly serious. "Are you free?" She saw it in his eyes: *Is there anyone else? Is there?* She couldn't speak. "Are you?" he insisted. *Are you free of everything and everyone—except me, the way I've never been free of you and never want to be?*

"Yes," she whispered. "Oh yes."

The gold in his eyes began to burn. He took her elbow, guided her outside. The wind was blowing hard, and she stumbled as if she had no strength to resist any force of nature—especially not him. His arm around her waist steadied her. His touch was a pleasure almost too painful to be borne. A taxi appeared in front of her, and he opened its door, and she got in. She didn't hear what he said to the driver. She turned, trembling, unable to think of a single word to say.

"I'm still yours, Holly. If you'll still have me."

She hid her face against his chest. He rocked her in the old familiar way, and for the length of the cab ride they simply held each other. At last she stopped crying. He gave her a handkerchief to wipe her eyes and nose.

"All right now?"

She could only nod, and sniffle.

"God, you're silly-lookin' when you cry. Don't do it again, okay?"

"Oh, shut up," she muttered, her voice still thick with tears.

"After all this time, all you can say to me is 'shut up'?"

"All I can say to you is *yes*."

The cab stopped, and Evan paid, and they got out, and it was a hotel. There were mirrors in the lobby. She peered into one while he strode ahead to the reception desk. Mascara down to her chin, swollen nose, freckles like splotches of sepia ink, red-rimmed eyes—she fled across to the ladies' room, splashed cold water on her face. Powder, more mascara, comb for the windblown wreckage of her hair—

She looked like something no self-respecting cat would even consider dragging in.

Emerging from the ladies' room, she saw him standing alone in the middle of the vast lobby looking almost frantic, almost scared. He caught sight of her and his face changed, and he crossed the floor in five long, quick strides.

"Don't disappear like that again," he said, deep voice harsh with relief.

"I won't—I'm sorry—" She shook her head. "I just—I look—I'm a mess—"

"You're the most beautiful thing I've ever seen."

He took her arm again, and the shock of renewed contact nearly staggered her. She snuck a glance at him, not daring to believe it was as overpowering for him as it was for her—but it was there in his eyes, the shock and the wonder of it.

As they walked to the elevator she made an effort, trying for the old banter. "The Waldorf, in the middle of the day, with no luggage?"

"I had a helluva time deciding whether to register us as 'Smith' or 'Jones,'" he teased back, and she laughed. Strange that laughing hurt.

In the elevator he held tightly to her hand, his mood changing again. "It has to be new," he said very softly. "We can't go anyplace we were before. Not yet."

He didn't look at her. She couldn't stop looking at him—his profile, the curve of his lower lip, the pulse pounding so fast in his long throat.

He had trouble with the card key; his hands were shaking. Inside the locked room, they faced each other silently. She let her purse drop to the floor, then her jacket. Buttons catching, material snagging, fingers trembling badly now, at last they stood naked to each other for the first time in more than a year.

The same, he was just the same. Pale smooth skin over long bones and hard muscles. Broad shoulders, long legs, sleek curves and strong lines—and the need rising as his eyes devoured her. But the look on his face was different now: openly yearning, wise with the memory of suffering.

"My God, you're so beautiful," he whispered. "I just want to look at you."

Again she tried to rally. "You'll do more than just look, or you're not the Evan Lachlan I knew."

A brief smile touched his mouth. "I'm not—but we'll talk about that later."

All at once she hid her face in her hands. He was with her instantly, stroking her hair and her shoulders.

"What is it, babe? What's wrong?"

"You ripped my heart out, damn you, and I still love you so much—every day without you clawed into me—and now you're here and I can't believe it—"

"Believe it, lady love," he said, and took her hands from her face and kissed her lips.

They remembered each other's rhythms, sensitivities, secrets. She had thought it would be hard and quick and fierce, after so long apart. But his fingers sought her gently, delicately, renewing his memory of her, just as her lips traveled over every inch of him from high forehead to absurdly narrow ankles, rejoicing in what had been denied her so long. She wanted to taste him, to swallow him whole. He wouldn't allow it, instead entering her with poignant tenderness, his big hands on either side of her head to cradle her face as he gazed down into her eyes.

"Love you," he chanted. "Love you, love you—"

"Evan—p-please—"

"Holly—shh, slow down, take it easy—I want to make this last forever—"

"Don't make me wait—now, please now—" She arched against him, whimpering, crying out as he came to rest within her. "*Éimhín*—!"

"That's it—sing for me, lady love, it's been so long—" He laughed low in his throat, gloating, triumphant, just as she'd remembered he could be when he'd driven her past sanity. The dragon was in his eyes, fiercely arrogant. She dug her fingers into his back, his hips, urging him on, pleading without shame or hesitation for what she'd wanted every night and every day for more than a year.

After he had finally given it to her, and they lay tangled around each other, she clung to him, trembling. His hands soothed her, and eventually she calmed.

"I'd almost forgotten . . . ," she whispered.

"—that it was that good with us," he finished for her. "I didn't forget. I just had to try so damned hard not to remember."

She pressed her lips to his chest, where the St. Michael medal rested near his heart. The beat was strong and solid, slowing down from raging need. "Evan, how can this be happening?"

"I kinda have a confession to make. I knew you'd be there today. Bradshaw called the other night."

She looked blank. "Elias—?"

"All he said was where you'd be at about eleven—he wouldn't let me ask anything, didn't explain why—just said that if I wanted to see you, Police Plaza's where you'd be."

"What's he up to?" she asked, tensing.

"Ask me if I care," Evan replied, wrapping his arms around her.

She looked down at him, frowning. "Why did you come?"

"Because I need you," he replied simply. "And I'm sick of pretending I don't."

That simple. Nothing was ever that simple.

"Okay, I know. You want it explained." He gave her a rueful little grin. "God forbid you should ever just accept what I tell you."

"If that's what you want me to do, I'll do it."

"No, you won't," he told her. "I know you, McClure." His fingertip caressed the curve of her left breast. "God, I missed you. You're even more beautiful—"

Holly felt her lips twist in a crooked smile. "Yeah—me with my gray hairs and secretary spread—"

"I'm goin' gray, too, lady love. And I never did like girls who're built like boys." He was quiet for a moment, then said, "I almost stayed in Jersey today."

"Not because you were scared," she said, knowing him.

"No. It's just—it's been a long time. I didn't know if I could mean anything to you again."

"You never stopped."

"I saw that, looking at you, that first second—it was all over your face." The joy in his eyes held not a hint of the old smugness: only gratitude, strangely humble. She supposed he had indeed changed, if this could be in the dragon's eyes. "You were there, just standing there, all red hair and freckles and blue eyes, like I'd dreamed you or something, and I just about lost it. But the way you looked at me—" That new smile was back, achingly tender and sweet. "Most other women—hell, *any* other woman—woulda slugged me or told me to go take a flying fuck—or both."

"Are you asking why I didn't?"

"I already know why." And there was no trace of the old self-satisfied glint as he finished, "You love me. God only knows why, but you do."

"There's a third alternative, you know," she mused. "I could be stringing you out just long enough to make sure I could hurt you, and then leave you."

His eyes showed no anxiety that she might do just that. "Not you, Holly."

"Give me one good reason why I shouldn't! Do you know what this did to me?" She jerked out of his arms and sat up, turning her back, hugging her knees to her breasts. "I laid siege to every Federal building in New York for you. I ranted and raved and made a total fool of myself with the Marshals Office, the mayor, anybody I could think of—"

"You did that?" he asked incredulously. "You fought for me?" His hand ran gently down her spine. She shifted away.

"Stop it. Don't touch me. If I had the sense God gave a gerbil, I'd do exactly what I just said—make sure I had you hooked good and solid, make you as much in love with me as you ever were—and then throw you out."

"Like in the book." His voice roughened. "How'd it feel, Holly? Doin' that to us?"

"Oh God," she whispered. "You read it?"

"It was gonna be *our* book. Of course I read it." He took a long breath. "It hurt like hell, but I got through it. You write when you get angry. But by the end of it you weren't anything but tired and sad. I think that hurt worst of all."

"That book wiped me out. I holed up in London and wrote like a madwoman. Gained ten pounds while I was at it, too, and another ten afterward, when I had to quit smoking again. I thought I'd gotten rid of you by getting the book out of my system. Shows how stupid I am. When it came in proofs, I read what I'd done to you and me in it and cried for a week."

"But you couldn't write it that way now. You couldn't leave, or send me away—not even in a book." He sounded so damned sure of it.

"You want it all, don't you?" She turned her head. "No, I couldn't do it. You've been hurt too much. I've been hurt too much. If I didn't love you the way I love you, I could lead you on and then throw you out. But I do love you, more than I ever thought I could love any man. And the next time you leave me, Lachlan, it'll be in a pine box."

"Darlin' Holly, it won't even be then. I'll come back and haunt you."

"The way you've done for the last year? No thanks." But all at once she felt everything drain out of her—all the anger, the pain, the hopeless longing. "It doesn't matter anymore, *Éimhín*. It might, before we've talked it all through— but right now it's meaningless. You're here. That's all that matters to me."

"I'll always be here," he promised, reaching up to stroke her cheeks.

"With any other man, I would've pounded down his door, forced him to let me back in—but I couldn't. You made the decision for both of us—and you're as strong and stubborn as I am, and that's saying something."

"I know," he said wryly.

"But what made me crazy was that I trusted your decision. When you said you had to work it out yourself, I couldn't fight something you were so sure about."

" 'When you truly love a man,' " he said softly, " 'you don't twist him into knots.' "

"Christ, Lachlan—don't quote me to me!"

"But you knew that already," he insisted. "Before you wrote it."

She wiped away the last of the tears, watching his eyes. "If you read the book, then you know that all I ever wanted was you. I've given up wondering why you couldn't see that."

"I did see it, lady love," he answered, taking one of her hands, stroking the palm with his thumb. He was silent for a long time, staring down at their clasped hands. "I thought—I don't know, that I'd be stronger somehow, that I'd become somebody you'd want in spite of everything." He glanced at her briefly, then away. This was new, as well: before, he would have looked her straight in the eye, challenging, daring her to stare him down. She waited him out, wondering what else about him had changed, that he had put aside that wary defiance. "I had to prove to myself that I could do it on my own. That I didn't need you the way I was scared to need you. For a long time I thought I was doin' it all on my own. But then I realized you were with me every step of the way. I could feel you beside me, but I never really knew it." His gaze lifted again, darkly troubled. "I know that doesn't make any sense."

"It shouldn't," she agreed. "But it does—if it means I'm part of you—"

Quick gleam of gratitude. "I could no more not need you than—aw, dammit, it's not comin' out right. One day I woke up to it, that needing you is the same for me as breathing—" He broke off, shaking his head again. "And that was the day you were *really* gone."

"And yet when Elias called, and told you where I'd be—"

"I had to see you again. Susannah—all I could think about was that if it hurt me that much, you must be—" He stroked her cheek with his fingertips, and she turned in to the tenderness. "I had to see you, even if I couldn't make things right."

"You're the only one who can," she murmured.

Evan got out of bed and poked around the floor for his jacket. "Here," he said, sitting on the bed. He held a small crimson velvet box. "I got it out of the bank this morning. Lucky charm," he added. He opened the box, fingers not quite steady. Within was a very old, very familiar ring. "And this time I promise the diamond won't fall out."

She wanted to laugh, but couldn't. Gently she took the ring from the box, watching it sparkle. "Do you still have yours?"

"Yeah." He held up his left hand, and she wondered why she hadn't noticed before: the gold claddagh she'd brought him from Ireland. He wore it with the heart's point toward his wrist, sign that he was spoken for. "I tried it on one night when I was really, really drunk—and y'know, I just couldn't seem to get it off my hand. I wonder why that was," he finished dryly.

She smiled back. "I wonder." She gave him the diamond. "Ask me."

"I already did."

"I want to make sure you still mean it." But then the banter failed her and her eyes flooded again. "Oh, damn it to hell!"

"Holly, will you for Chrissakes shut up?" He took her hand and slid the ring onto her heart-finger. "Marry me."

"You're not going to take it back, or—"

"I'm yours, I keep tellin' you. Marry me."

"You're sure—tell me you're sure, Evan, I couldn't bear it if—"

"Holly Elizabeth McClure!" Exasperated now. "Shut up and marry me."

Somehow she regained a little poise. Blinking tears away, she tucked the corners of her mouth into a smile and nodded.

"Say it," he ordered.

"I thought you wanted me to shut up."

"Say it—" This time in a threatening growl.

"Yes. Yes yes yes yes—"

A while later, Holly murmured against his shoulder, "Susannah was right. She said you'd come back. I just hope she knows it."

He drew her even closer, pressing his lips to the top of her head. "I know you don't have the kind of faith I do, but I swear she knows, Holly. She knows."

# Twenty-three

IT WAS LATE AFTERNOON WHEN he woke. He glanced at the bedside clock, squinting to bring the numerals into focus. *Need glasses soon,* he thought with a sigh. *Pushin' forty—gettin' old.*

And he didn't care a bit. The peacefulness of Holly was back, settling all around him. He hadn't slept this well in all the time they'd been apart. He smoothed the short curls all tangled around her face, liking them. And there *was* silver in her hair, threading back from her forehead. Gently he drew back the covers, taking inventory just as he used to. She had indeed picked up a few pounds, but he'd outgrown skinny twenty-year-olds long ago. This woman who rested so deeply before him, this woman who would bear his children within her body—he'd seen faces more beautiful on his pillow, and bodies more beautiful in his bed, but this wasn't just a face or a body. This was *Holly.*

All at once she blinked owlishly up at him, and as he tapped the tip of her nose he said, "Hey. Did you think you'd dreamed me?"

Her lips twitched at one corner. "Oh, no. You're damned good, lover-man, but even *you* ain't that good in dreams. It *had* to be you, for real."

He laughed and ruffled her hair—something he could never do when it was longer. "I like this. When did you cut it?"

"This spring. But it grows fast—"

"No, I like it," he repeated, running his fingers through its thickness. "Makes you look like a little girl when you're asleep."

"With all this gray? You've learned some new lines, Lachlan."

"Just for you, writer-lady."

"I guess we have a lot of catching up to do," she ventured at last.

"Yeah," he acknowledged. "How's the farm, and your Aunt Lulah?"

"Fine. And Alec and Nicky, before you ask. What about your father, and Maggie and her family?"

"The old man died in January. Don't be sorry; he wanted to go. He started downhill after I got busted. But he didn't blame me—said he woulda done the same thing. I think it was the only thing I ever did—aside from becoming a cop—that he completely approved of."

"He did love you, Evan."

He shrugged. "Maggie and Nate moved to Pennsylvania when he retired from the army. She's in real estate, and he plays golf and rebuilds old Mustangs. And the kids are great. How's Mugger?"

"Fat and sassy. He lives with Alec and Nicky now. I spent so much time away that it was better for him to have a real home."

"How about the books? You workin' on anything special?"

And so it went on, exchanging bits and pieces of the lives they'd led apart. None of it really mattered all that much. It was just stuff they had to deal with before resuming the reality of their lives, in *their* world. In all this time, he'd never really *talked* with anyone. Now the whole of it spilled out of him without qualm or pause. *"If you close your heart and thoughts to me, how then will I know what I love?"* He could remember *Jerusalem Lost* with much less anguish now.

"Evan . . ." She was apprehensive, not quite looking at him. "I don't want to make a thing of it, but—I know there must've been other women—"

"Not as many as you're thinking," he responded. "One-night stands, all of 'em. And nobody in the last four months." *Oh yeah?* said a snide little voice in his head. *What about that bitch Denise, just last Sunday?*

"You?" She snorted. "Go without for more than twenty minutes?"

"Knock it off. It just wasn't worth it, Holly. I couldn't take it when I woke up and I wasn't next to you. You know what I'm sayin'?"

"Yeah, I do," she admitted. "For me, it was one man, once. Honest Injun, as they say—and since I'm part Cherokee, you can believe it!"

Just once? But he understood. "Better to do without—except that sometimes I missed you so much I thought I'd go crazy—all the nights alone in bed, when I couldn't stop thinkin' about you and I'd—" He broke off, and felt his cheeks burn.

A snicker, muffled in his shoulder. "You, too? Oh, Evan! Believe me, lover-man, you're a *whole* lot more satisfying than a small personal appliance! And a girl can get damned tired of self-inflicted orgasms—"

"McClure!"

"Just promise me you didn't like you doing it to you half as much as you like *me* doing it to you, and I may decide to let you live." She snuggled in close again. "Know what? You're nicer than you used to be. Not as tense. You're not fight-ing the whole world anymore—or yourself." Her fingers began to drift along his body, and suddenly she giggled. "Oh, good! It's still there!"

"Huh? Oh. Well, what'd you think, we'd wear it out and it'd fall off?"

"Moron. I meant your belly. I missed it. And don't you dare say you'll get rid of it. Nothing should ever be perfect—not even you, *a chuisle*."

He'd waited so long to hear her call him that again. It went through him like wine and fire and heartbreak. "I love you, Holly," he breathed into her hair. "I love you so much—just say you forgive me for everything I put you through—"

"Yes," she whispered. "Everything, anything—always."

His eye was caught by the sparkle of diamonds on her wrist. The swirls of delicate gold were unmistakable. "That's Susannah's."

Holly nodded, then scrubbed her fingers back through her hair. "It was in her pocket when they found her. She left it to me in her will."

"Why?"

"We had this stupid bet—"

"No," he interrupted, "why was it in her pocket? Shouldn't she have been wearing it? I remember when she bought it, and she never took it off. There's gotta be a reason—"

"I thought so, too. I've been over it and over it, Evan, and I can't think why she'd put it in her pocket." All at once Holly rocketed out of his arms and grabbed frantically for clothes. "Oh, *shit!*"

"What?" he demanded, wide-eyed.

"There's this thing I have to go to—Susannah's charity—a cocktail party, starts at seven thirty—I'll be back by nine, I promise—"

"You don't want me to go with you."

She stopped in midmotion, trousers halfway up her thighs. "I—I didn't think you'd *want*—"

"Not if you don't want me there."

*"Of course I want you there!"*

"Okay, then. Where is this thing, and how fancy?"

"Palm Court at the Plaza. Tux." When he groaned, she hurried on, "Evan, you don't have to if you don't want to—"

"I told you I want to. I can rent a tux this afternoon. Will you relax? There's plenty of time. What's the occasion?"

"Breast cancer."

His heart stopped and he went cold to his marrow.

"Not me, Evan." She came to sit beside him. "I'm fine, love, I promise. I had my annual mammogram in July. Absolutely clear."

He nodded, able to breathe again.

"It runs in Susannah's family. She lost an aunt and two older cousins to it. This thing tonight—I wasn't going to go—I've been in London—"

"But you changed your mind."

"Some friends were talking after the funeral on Wednesday, and since this was already planned, we decided to make it something special in her memory. Elias will be there, and a few other people from the office." She leaned over and kissed him. "Come on, we have to check out of here and get you a tux."

"Right *now?*"

Holly rose and tucked her sweater into her trousers. "Oh, that's it, Lachlan—make big eyes at me and look all sex-starved!" Snagging her jacket from the floor, she made a face at him. "At least *that* hasn't changed. Ever the sex maniac."

"With you in the room? Damn betcha, lady. What time do I pick you up?"

"You're really going to go with me?" She took a step, then another, as if wanting to come to him but fearing he'd suddenly vanish. "You won't leave me again—it would kill me, Evan—"

"Holly." He held out his arms and she sought his embrace blindly. "Shh. It's all right, lady love. Where would I go, if it wasn't someplace I could be with you?"

She hid her face against his chest. "I hate clingy females," she muttered.

"You don't have to be strong *all* the time, y'know. I finally figured that out." She knuckled her eyes and smiled ruefully. "You did, huh?"

"Yeah." He took her face between his hands. "I'll *be* there tonight. And every night from now on."

THEY PARTED IN THE HOTEL lobby. He went to the Ralph Lauren store in the old Rhinelander Mansion, ending up with a classic peak lapel tux, wing-collared pleated shirt, and black silk bow tie. What the hell, he thought, trying not to notice the numbers after the dollar sign. Marriage to Holly McClure would find him in need of a tuxedo. Or two.

He picked up other stuff, as well: shoes, underwear, socks, jeans, a shirt for work. He winced at the further damage to his plastic, but he didn't want to go back to his place in Jersey ever again—though he knew he had to. This way, because he had a suit and tie and needed only a clean shirt for work on Monday, he could put it off as long as possible.

It was well after five when he got to Holly's apartment. Mr. Hunnicutt smiled and let him in with a "Good to see you back, Marshal Lachlan."

"Good to be back," he replied. He paused a minute. "How's she been?"

"Lonesome," was the succinct answer, which told him all he needed to know.

*One man, once.* He couldn't help wondering who she would choose, after him. Still, he could shrug it off, and even pity the man, whoever he'd been. After all, Evan was here and the other guy wasn't.

It felt strange to ring the door chimes. He still had her key someplace in his desk. Isabella answered the door, smiling bright as a new penny.

"Come in, come in! She said you were back! And about time, too!"

"Lookin' good, Isabella—I like your hair that way."

"Sweet-talker!" she chided. "You want something to eat while you get dressed? Sandwich?"

"Do you still make the best iced coffee in the world?"

"Better," she announced, taking his shopping bags. "I'll put all this out for you while you clean up. The right-hand bedroom's all ready for you upstairs." She paused, then added, "She wasn't the same, with you gone. Don't you ever leave again, okay?"

"Not a chance. Thanks, Isabella."

He took a long, hot shower, and when he emerged with a towel slung around his hips he found that Isabella had left not only a tall glass of iced coffee but also a slice of hot-from-the-oven pound cake. He missed the sight of Mugger sniffing around the table, convinced there must be *something* for him to eat. Lachlan thought about the cat for a minute, then decided that whereas a Witch might require a feline familiar, for himself he wanted a dog. Something big and spirited for him to take for a walk while Holly gnashed her teeth over a book, but patient and gentle enough for the kids to roughhouse with. . . .

Did she still want children? He experienced a fierce desire to find her and make love again and again until they knew she was pregnant. She wasn't yet forty, but they didn't have time to waste.

*I'm sorry, Holly. But it had to be this way. For me, anyhow. I'm just sorry I put you through it, too.* If only she'd been just a little bit weaker, he could have stayed. But if she hadn't been as strong as she was, she wouldn't be Holly, and he wouldn't have loved her in the first place. It would have been so easy to just lean on her— let her do all the work, take all the anger and hurting away—

He couldn't have done that to her. To himself. To them. And as deeply as he regretted the year they'd lost, the man he'd been had compelled him to do what he'd done—and it had been the only way to become the man he was now.

After scraping his face smooth of whiskers and attending to all the other requirements of getting gussied up, he climbed into the tux, ran a comb through his hair, made a defiant face at the gray, and went downstairs.

"Holly? You in yet?"

No answer. In the living room nothing much had changed—different books on the tables, a new painting to admire. Thinking back over what she'd told him, he realized she hadn't been here to change things—and abruptly recalled he'd never heard anything about her time in Kenya. A postcard he'd never read had been forwarded to his new address in Jersey a month after he'd moved. Her souvenirs of Africa were on a shelf behind the bar: three exquisite little beadwork baskets, a carved wooden bowl whose handles were giraffes bending down to drink. What had she seen there, what had she thought and felt and learned? He didn't know.

He glanced at his watch and sank into an armchair. It was 6:30 and he knew she'd be late. But worth it. They'd gone out classy a dozen or more times—but nothing she had ever appeared in prepared him for what glided into the living room now. Thin indigo velvet flowed from half-bared shoulders all the way to the floor. No bra confined her breasts, and inside he laughed, for as their eyes met her nipples hardened. The dress fit like skin to the hips, where she wore a belt of linked silver plaques with Celtic knotwork designs on them, with matching earrings, Susannah's bracelet—and Granna Maureen's diamond ring. Her hair was tucked back on one side behind her ear. The whole effect was elegant, romantic, medieval.

He unfolded himself from the chair and drawled in bad imitation of her Virginia Southern, "Y'all shore do clean up nice, ma'am."

"Many thanks, my lord." She gave him a curtsy and looked him down and up. Her admiration was gratifying, even though he hated like hell being done up in a tux. "And thank you for choosing a big bow tie—a man with a nose the size of yours couldn't possibly wear a skinny one."

"I'll choose to believe you're complimenting my taste instead of insulting my nose." Ambling closer, hands in his trouser pockets, he continued thoughtfully, "Y'know, there's only one way that dress could look any better."

"Yeah?"

"Yeah. If it was on the floor of the bedroom."

"Voracious," she accused, eyes dancing. "Ravenous. Absolutely a glutton."

"There you go again, with all them big fancy words," he complained. "You know a big dumb Mick like me ain't got the smarts to—"

"Big dumb Mick, my ass. I've seen your college transcripts. Shall we go?"

"You have to make a speech, right?"

"Yes. But I don't know what I'll say."

"You can rehearse in the car." He grinned. "While I drive."

"You missed that goddamned BMW more than you missed *me*," she growled.

"Yep," he said—and got out of her way, fast.

ON PRINCIPLE, AND OWING TO experience, Lachlan never used valet parking if he could avoid it. More often than not a car returned to its owner at least one dent the worse, and sometimes minus a few gallons of gas. Tonight he parked the Beemer himself. Others were of similar mind; there was a steady flow of gowns and tuxedoes heading for the elevators. Holly hadn't mentioned what the ante was per head, but he was inclined to be impressed by the money tonight would raise.

"Upmarket crowd," he murmured to Holly. "Y'know, I'm actually glad I'm wearin' a tux."

"You are absolutely, totally, shatteringly gorgeous, Lachlan."

He was surprised by how proud her proud smile made him. To cover it, he said, "Two-drink maximum. You want to make sense when you make this speech you don't know what you're going to say in."

"I adore your sentence structure. Actually, I adore *all* your structures."

"Good evening, Holly, Marshal Lachlan," said a familiar voice as Elias Bradshaw, lean and elegant and edgy, joined them at the elevator.

"Evening, Your Honor," Lachlan said, unable to think of a single thing to say about Susannah that wouldn't sound trite or foolish, or end up hurting people who were already hurting. Still, he gave it a try. "I didn't get the chance the other day to tell you how sorry—"

"Yeah, I know." The brusque interruption was marginally gentled with a brief smile that didn't touch his eyes. "Thanks."

Holly slid an arm around Bradshaw, and as he hugged her lightly about the shoulders she asked, "Did you get any sleep last night?"

He shrugged. "Some."

"For a lawyer, you are one lousy liar."

Their easy physical intimacy astonished Evan for a moment, but then he reasoned that the loss of Susannah had doubtlessly brought a truce.

The elevator ride to the Palm Court was a crush of rustling dresses and a skirmish of contradictory perfumes. Evan handed Holly out into an only slightly less crowded foyer. She caught sight of her publisher, glanced an apology up at Lachlan, picked up her skirts, and began sidling her way through the throng. This left Evan alone—relatively speaking—with the man he could never decide whether he truly loathed or just didn't like.

"I see you took my advice," Bradshaw murmured. "Not that I did it for you."

"For Holly," Lachlan replied.

Bradshaw shook his head. "Susannah. Because she fought for you—and I didn't fight hard enough. And if you tell Holly any of this, I'll deny it to my last breath. There are things happening that require somebody who knows—well, somebody who knows. We can talk about it later," he finished gracelessly.

"Let's talk about it now," Lachlan invited. He nudged His Honor toward a comparatively unpopulated corner.

"No. Not tonight."

"Still paranoid, huh?"

"With damned good reason," Bradshaw retorted. "I need your particular expertise. There's a lot going on that makes tonight the last breather any of us will have for a while. You'll know what you need to know when you need to know it."

Lachlan supposed he really had changed—because a year ago this choice bit of arrogance would have set his temper off like a brick of C4 explosive. Now, he merely regarded Bradshaw with frank admiration for the man's ability to arrange the world to suit himself. "So you're making me an auxiliary member of the Circle? You are the most unpredictable son of a bitch I ever met."

"Holly needs you. And so, in fact, do I."

Evan had no time to reply, even if he could have thought of a swift comeback for this startling admission, for Holly had reclaimed his arm. "What a zoo!"

Bradshaw pasted a smile on his face. "Holly, you long tall drink of Irish whiskey, since you roped me into this I'd better make good use of my entry fee and go schmooze. See you later."

Lachlan watched him go, still stunned.

"Hey." Holly jostled his elbow. "What happened?"

"Huh?" He looked at her, then shook his head to clear it. "Nothin'."

"Bull me no shit, Lachlan. What did Elias say that's got you looking like you've been hit in the gut with a two-by-four?"

"More like a steel rebar," he answered. "Tell you later."

She favored him with a look that vowed he would indeed be telling her, and in abundant detail, then started for the coat-check.

Someone in the main room was playing the piano, and very well, too. He couldn't quite recall where he'd heard the particular riff before, but as a bluesy voice began to sing, he remembered all too clearly.

*They'd chosen to hold the annual alumni party at a karaoke bar, of all places. Mercifully, most of the singers were pretty good, and getting better as liquor kept flowing. Lachlan was actually enjoying himself, and decided double-dating with Susannah and Bradshaw wasn't so bad after all.*

*Then some Wall Street type with his designer tie askew brought the cordless microphone to their table. The two women held a whispering, giggling consultation, then asked for a second mike. Lachlan and Bradshaw traded glances, and for the first time in their acquaintance their reactions were in perfect agreement: horrified amusement and equally horrified apprehension.*

*"What the hell do you think you're doing?" Bradshaw demanded as the women rose, smoothed their dresses demurely, and grinned pure wickedness.*

*Lachlan asked, "Do you really want to find out?"*

*"Men's room's over there, Marshal."*

*"Lead the way, Your Honor."*

*Both got to their feet, only to be shoved back down onto their chairs by their Significant Others, who ordered them to keep their sorry asses put. The song came up: driving drumbeat, thundering bass line. Holly, in her glittery green dress, and Susannah, in creamy white silk that bared shoulders and back, with Holly's sapphires gleaming at wrists and ears and throat, turned into honky-tonk singers right before their eyes. The voice Holly had likened to an angel's was clear and pure and strong, but Lachlan would have bet Holly's farm that Susannah had never belted out a number like this in college choir—every raunchily suggestive word of it directed at Elias Bradshaw.*

*By the last chorus ("We be gnawin' on it, baby—yeah, gnawin' on it"), they were laughing so hard, they could scarcely get the words out. Raucous applause was swiftly followed by whoops and hollers of approval as Lachlan took his revenge by hauling Holly down onto his lap and kissing the wits out of her. From the other side of the table he heard Susannah—so demure and circumspect at the office—demand of Elias, "So where the hell's my reward?"*

"Evan?"

He looked at Holly. And thought about Susannah. And realized for the first time what her death meant to Bradshaw. *If I lost you as completely as he lost her—*

"Evan!" Frowning worriedly, she placed a hand on his chest. Her eyes widened; he knew she felt the sick thudding of his heart. "What's wrong?"

He slid an arm around her waist and somehow managed a smile—and kept himself from crushing her close in mindless gratitude. "Y'know what?"

She searched his eyes, then smiled. "I love you, too, *a chuisle.*"

"Is that gonna be your speech for tonight?"

"Don't remind me."

"You'll do great."

"I just hope I don't trip in these heels."

He made his voice a throaty purr and whispered in her ear, "Pretend all you've got on is those shoes and that little black thing you have the nerve to call a slip—"

She choked on a stifled giggle. "Evan!"

"—and you're comin' into the bedroom on a rainy night—"

"Stop it!" Holly hissed. "I'll never be able to keep a straight face!"

"—and it's all candlelight and that '82 merlot and those white silk sheets—"

"You'll pay for this, Lachlan." She swayed a little against him as her knees started to buckle. Ever the considerate gentleman, he held her elbow to keep her upright—because he had a great finish planned.

"—and *I'm* in bed waitin' for you, with this bow tie and a really, *really* big—"

She glared at him.

"—smile," he concluded with unabashed glee.


NINETY MINUTES LATER, HER SPEECH given and applauded, he was idly finger-stroking her bare silken shoulder while people he didn't know came by to chat and check him out head to foot while wondering who the hell he was. Sharply curious eyes saw a tall, fortyish man in an elegant tux, with no clue as to what he did for a living or anything else other than that he was H. Elizabeth McClure's escort. He smiled and said very little—and held Holly tighter.

On impulse he pressed his lips briefly to her temple. She looked up in the middle of what she was saying, a question in her blue eyes. He noted with a

smile that with that one gesture he had managed to make her forget whoever it
was she was talking to as well as whatever it was she'd been saying. Center of
her world; reason for its creation.

"So you're finally going to do it," said Elias Bradshaw—who was developing
a habit of appearing rather suddenly. "Nice rock," he added by way of explanation, nodding to Holly's left hand.

"I know," she replied.

"I liked your speech." His eyes said he more than liked it. Then, with a half-
step to one side that revealed a young woman standing nearby: "I don't know if
you've met Deputy Marshal Leah Towsley."

"I've been nagging His Honor all evening to introduce me," Towsley said,
moving forward to shake hands. She was about five-foot-four, African-American, dressed in a slither of red and white sequins, and, to Lachlan's discerning
eye, built like a brick dollhouse.

"Thanks—but it's not a gown, it's a costume!" Holly laughed in response to
Leah's compliment on her dress. "I write medieval, so people expect to see medieval. Frankly, I'd kill to be able to wear that masterpiece you've got on—
vintage Halston?"

Elegant brows arched. "You have a good eye. It was a real find—I picked it
up in a retread shop last year. Judge Bradshaw, do me a favor and stand between us—I feel like half of a flag!"

"I have a question for Holly," Bradshaw said as he duly placed his tuxedoed
self between the red-and-white dress and the blue one.

Leah Towsley interrupted with mock severity. "Not before I read her the
riot act about *Jerusalem Lost*. It kept me up all night—best cry I've had in years."

"Sorry about that," Holly said ruefully, as Bradshaw turned an incredulous
look on his marshal.

"So you're my replacement," Evan remarked, smiling.

Holly gave a start. "Oh, good grief, I'm sorry—Marshal Towsley, this is my
fiancé, Evan Lachlan."

As they shook hands, Towsley said, "Congratulations on your engagement.
And I didn't replace you—I just kept the bench warm." She cocked an eyebrow
at Bradshaw.

"Nothing of the kind," he assured her. "I need Marshal Lachlan for a special
assignment, that's all."

"Special—?" Holly began, but the judge interrupted her.

"Why didn't you tell me about establishing this fellowship in Susannah's
name? Why did I have to learn about it in your speech? And why the hell did
you make me one of the trustees?"

"Well . . ."

As she launched into explanations, Evan gazed down a foot at his fellow marshal's dazzling dark brown eyes. "So how do you like workin' with His Honor?"

"Beats inventorying confiscated property in New Jersey," she replied, which let him know she knew all about him.

"I'm not after my old job back, I promise."

"I didn't think you were. Anyone who'd consciously volunteer to babysit Elias Bradshaw is nuts. Despite what I've heard, you don't look that crazy to me."

He laughed. "Appearances can be deceiving."

"MY GOD, YOU'VE MELLOWED!" Holly exclaimed in the car. Her shoes were off, and her belt, and she was stretching her shoulders and spine in ways he would have liked to appreciate with more than a sidelong glance. But he was driving.

"Yeah?" he said, negotiating the Beemer through late-night traffic.

"Yeah. Used to be I could hardly get you to stay at those things for an hour. But you were very sweet and obliging tonight."

"Uh-oh. Does that mean you think I've turned into a wimp?"

"No," she replied solemnly. "I think you've become one very fine man. You started out that way—but purest gold can't shine brightest until it's been through fire."

He gave her a crooked smile. "We both oughta be 24-karat by now."

It was probably ridiculous—no, it was definitely ridiculous—but the fact that she'd never changed the seat settings he'd programmed into her BMW really got to him. Nobody else had made it far enough into her life—but more important, no matter what she said, deep inside she'd known he'd be coming back. It was funny and silly and touching, and it made him realize that for the first time in more than a year his entire world was *right*.

"So Elias had ulterior motives," she said suddenly. "What did he tell you?"

"Not much. We're going to have a little chat soon."

"I couldn't get anything out of him, either. But obviously he thinks you can help find out who killed Susannah."

He was too good a driver to allow the car to swerve with his reaction. "I think," he said quietly, "that you and I better have a little chat *tonight*."

She talked; he listened. Of all the things she recounted—Long Island dirt, splinters, code, Noel, and so on—his instincts kept snagging on the bracelet.

"I had the same feeling," she said when he mentioned it. "Only there's no reason."

"And no reason for her to take it off and put it in her pocket, either. Come on, Holly. Susannah was a very sharp lady. Tell me everything you know about the bracelet, starting with the day she bought it."

"I drove us to Connecticut. Suze spent that night with her mother and took the train back to the city. I went to see Alec and Nicky. But there wasn't anything special we said or did."

"Just tell me what happened." Knowing it was there without knowing exactly how he knew; it was the same feeling he got whenever all the little dance steps his fugitive quarry did were finally coming together, and he *knew* that one more move and he'd have the whole pattern.

"We left early—it was a Saturday. We stopped for breakfast in some little town, and did some shopping. There was a place that sold pewter, and a quilt shop, antiques—the usual touristy stuff. And a jewelry store. That's where she bought it."

Lachlan pulled the BMW into the garage and parked. "Keep thinking," he said as they left the car and walked to the elevator. "Pretend it's a movie and you're watching the scene."

Casting him a doubting glance, she shrugged, leaned back against the elevator wall, and closed her eyes.

*"Oh, c'mon, Suze—you've always wanted one. It's a great price, and I've never seen another one like it. The craftsmanship is gorgeous."*

*"I don't know. I mean, it's beautiful, but—"*

*"Well, if you're waiting for Elias Bradshaw to cough up, forget it. He has all the earmarks of a man who doesn't know that diamond jewelry is like chocolate. Women not only want it, they need it!"*

*Susannah laughed and consulted her checkbook balance. Holly took the artisan aside, ostensibly to ask about a brooch in another case, and murmured that it would be a very good thing if he knocked a bit off the bracelet's price—and passed him four crisp fifties. When they returned to Susannah, he lowered the price by three hundred dollars—saying it was because of Susannah's beautiful smile.*

A touch on her arm opened her eyes. Evan guided her out the elevator and down the hall to her door. "Anything?" he said when they were inside her foyer.

She shook her head. "I just don't remember." Taking off her coat, she draped it on the hall tree and started for the kitchen.

He followed. Relentless. "What was the name of the town?"

"I don't know."

"The place you had breakfast?"

She took refuge behind the pantry door, rummaging for something to eat. "I don't remember that, either."

"Goddammit, Holly—"

"Maybe she put it in her pocket so they wouldn't steal it!"

"They didn't take any of her other jewelry, did they?" he shot back. "Did the jeweler say anything? What'd he look like? What was the name of the shop? What was *his* name?"

Holly slammed the pantry door. *"I don't fucking know, okay?"*

"Yes, you do. You just don't know that you do."

"Will you quit being a cop?"

"I did," he answered, low-voiced. "Not of my own choosing, but—" With a shrug: "Turns out it's like you with the writing—it's not just that I do it, I *am* it." He shrugged. "You ready to think some more about this, or should we call it a night?"

She stood straighter, bracing herself. "Are you saying you want to go?"

His brows knotted. "I told you I wouldn't leave."

"But do you want to *stay?*"

"McClure, what the hell am I gonna do with you?" he snarled, taking her left hand. "See that?" he went on, pointing to the ring. "Remember what it means?"

"I know what it means to *me*," she replied.

"So what did that bracelet mean that Susannah wanted you to remember?"

"Christ on a kayak, Lachlan—you never stop! All right, all right, we're waiting for the jeweler to finish with her check, and looking at other pieces . . . they were all one-of-a-kind, mostly nautical themes, seashells and fish . . ." She closed her eyes again, picturing the shop. "She asked about a starfish pin, and the jeweler said he was Portuguese, he'd been in the fishing fleet for twenty years, then retired to make jewelry—San Jacinto!" she exclaimed, looking up at Evan. "He named his store after the patron saint of sailors!" Triumph was there and gone before she could really feel it. "But what's that got to do with anything?"

Evan was looking the way he did when he'd polished off a four-course dinner and was anticipating the sweet trolley. "Oh, yeah—Susannah was a *very* sharp lady."

"She was, but I'm not," she snapped.

"Jacinto?" he repeated, brows arching expectantly. When she stayed stubbornly silent, he relented. "Hyacinth, writer-lady. Hyacinth."

"So? Hyacinthe Rigaud was a French painter at the court of Louis XIV. There's a Vermeer called 'Girl in Hyacinth Blue.' There's—"

"No lectures, please." He held up both hands in surrender, smiling. "The dirt from Long Island is just dirt from Long Island. But 'hyacinth' tells us where on Long Island."

"It does?"

"Yeah. Got a map? No, forget it, we'll hit the computer." And he was striding through to her office before she could say another word.

She made coffee, then joined him. He was leaning back in her desk chair, and glanced around when she came in. "Got it," he said.

"Is it something she saw out the car window?"

"Nope. There's a St. Hyacinth's Catholic Church in Glen Head. But that's not the reference. I checked out all 'hyacinth' references to make sure. What she wanted us to know, where she was directing us—it ain't no church."

She peered at the computer screen. A real estate site, but having about as much in common with the average Realtor as Sotheby's had with the local junk shop. There, in full color, was a photo of a Victorian mansion, the kind built by stupendously wealthy New Yorkers wanting a seaside escape from the city's summer heat. That whole section of Suffolk County was known as the Gold Coast. And the turreted, towered, crenellated mansion in the picture was known as The Hyacinths.

Twenty-four

LACHLAN HAD BEEN INSIDE Elias Bradshaw's house five times: twice into the living room, once to the kitchen, once to the hall bathroom, and once just to the foyer. Now, on Monday night a week after Susannah's death, he went up the stairs holding Holly's hand, and was admitted to a room without electrical outlets, telephone jack, lamps, or any other modern technology. The only light glittered from a single white candle burning in a silver holder on a small table.

Holly left him to go speak to a blonde woman over by the fireplace. Feeling a little lost, Evan glanced around. The floor was inlaid with a five-pointed star of pale wood within a circle of what might have been mahogany. There was a hearth without a fire, wooden chairs without cushions, and a heavy iron-bound chest without a lock. The only attempt at comfort was the small one-armed sofa over in a corner. From a garment rack hung robes in various colors; rainbow-hued candles were arranged on a shelf.

"Welcome to the sanctum sanctorum," said Nicholas Orlov, approaching with a slight smile and a double handclasp that Lachlan returned rather nervously. "Did Holly remember to bring something for you to wear?"

"Uh—I don't know."

"I brought my extra," Alec Singleton said, proffering a black robe that smelled faintly of cinnamon. "Don't worry, Evan, we'll all look just as silly as you."

"I'll just pretend I've been promoted to judge, or got my Ph.D., or something." Alec smiled. "The rest will be some time getting ready. Come sit down."

He followed Holly's honorary uncle over to the hearth. Nick joined the others in setting up the space, placing various stones from his pockets at what Lachlan figured were the cardinal points of the compass.

"The tall black guy with the sword-sized athame is Martin," Singleton began. "He'll be in the South."

"Fire and St. Michael, right?"

"Very good. But I think you learned most of what you know on your own, didn't you? Holly's rather casual about things she doesn't have to be involved in, such as Calling the Quarters."

"Not casual," he protested. "She knows why she's here—"

"—and you don't much enjoy the idea of her bleeding whenever Elias requires it of her."

"Not especially." He shrugged.

"The other Quarters will be Ian in the North—the one in green, he's Martin's partner the way Nick's mine—Nick in the West, and myself in the East. I usually take the South, but tonight we're improvising. The blonde lady is Kate, our Apothecary. She'll be in the Southeast. Simon is the wily codger with the chalice, and tonight he'll take the Northwest. Elias will be in the Northeast, and you'll stand Southwest. Shall I describe the process to you?"

"I think I remember most of it from Beltane with Holly."

"I just bet you do. This Circle is already laid out in the floor—which is why this room is off-limits to everyone *but* the Circle, since it's been spelled to them. Elias spent this afternoon including Nick and me and you. It's nine feet, with boundaries of stones, incense, and candles. Because you'll be in the Southwest, we've chosen a purple candle—a mix of red and blue—which also nicely calls the protections you'll need."

"Which are—?"

"It's Male, for one thing," Alec smiled. "It shields from danger, especially magical danger. It's symbolic of the law, as well. As for the rock—I chose one from my personal stash that I thought would do you the most good. And the moonstone connects you with Holly, and with me." He fingered the milky white gem hanging from a silver chain around his neck.

"I know it's kinda late to ask, but—does all this really *work*?"

"Nick can give you his lecture sometime. The short version is that yes, it does, but not for the reasons one might expect."

"Actually," he admitted, "I'm not sure *what* I'm expecting."

"Don't even try," Alec advised. "Not tonight. Magic isn't inherent in stones or scents or chalices, it's inside *us*. Some people hear music in color, for instance."

"Is that why they call it 'the blues'?" Lachlan smiled.

"Could be! Ever see *Fantasia*? The colors used for Bach's *Toccata and Fugue in D Minor* had to come from somewhere. That they feel right to most of the rest of us may mean there's something going on inside our brains that equates certain colors with certain sounds. The medical term for it is "synesthesia." Most people never recognize or develop the instinct.

"There are places in our brains we can't begin to understand," he went on. "Combine a scent, a color, maybe the ringing of a bell, words that evoke images, some sort of rhythmic chant, and something in your brain wakes up and responds to the stimuli—and that's magic, for lack of a better term."

"Proust," Lachlan said suddenly. "The madeleines."

"Precisely. Smell is primal—it's why we give off pheromones, which make us respond at a visceral level. Nothing to do with the parts of our brains that think and reason. We perceive, but not with our conscious minds. And sometimes your brain fights so hard against what consciousness perceives as irrational that—" He broke off and resettled himself in the hard wooden chair, crossing long legs at the knees under his white robe. "And to think I accuse poor Nick of lecturing," he said wryly.

"Believe me, I'm used to it," Lachlan replied in the same tone.

Alec laughed. "Okay, then—heard the one about the itchy palm? The old saying has it that you're about to get some money. What if your brain is picking up something from the person signing the check and putting it in the mail? Because you know the tradition, and you have no other way to rationalize or process this 'something,' your brain tells your palm to itch."

Lachlan frowned. "So to work magic, you pick a combination of objects that will provoke the response you want inside your own head?"

"That's the theory. One must experiment, of course, with exactly what causes which reactions. Which music coaxes us out of depression, what we find to be comfort foods. For instance, it's well-known that chocolate stimulates the same chemical changes in the brain that happen when you're in love. Nick can go on about this stuff for hours. But the whole thing boils down to: Magic is Life, and Life is Magic."

"Now, *that* I can relate to," he replied, glancing over at Holly.

"I thought you might." Alec's expression changed as a slight, almost fragile young woman entered and chose her robe from the rack. "Lydia Montsorel," he said softly. "Whose gift is almost as rare as Holly's."

"What exactly is she?" Lachlan asked, unconsciously lowering his own voice.

"She's a Sciomancer. She sees the future in shadows. When the stimuli are right—as we hope they will be tonight—she can read the past as well. She's one of our finding, mine and Nick's."

"Like Holly."

"Yes. Lydia's is a life that nearly turned tragic. She spent her first six years afraid of daylight, not knowing why. By the time we found her, her parents were frantic. Her grandmother had an inkling—her own magic, untrained though it was, kept her alive through the Holocaust."

"Holly said Lydia's grandmother was a Survivor. She didn't say much else."

"I don't think she knows. Sylvie managed to hide her family for three years during the Nazi occupation of France. She knew when evil approached—felt it, sensed it. They were caught near the end of the war, on a day when Sylvie was sick in bed with a raging fever. The family was separated, and Sylvie alone survived the camps. She emigrated, married, had children—and Lydia is the only one who inherited the magic. In her, it manifests in shadows. She can feel the presence of evil, like her grandmother, but she can also see it."

"Afraid of the daylight," Evan murmured, shaking his head, thinking of his own children, his and Holly's; hoping that if they inherited magic, it would be a more benevolent kind.

"Time and teaching showed her what to avoid. Electric light has no impact on her. But sunlight, fire—even a lighted match can do it if she's not careful. With help, she learned control, and how to prevent seeing and sensing if she wishes. And she has a wise and loving husband looking out for her, as well."

Lachlan said nothing for a moment, watching the dark girl in the yellow robe as she moved around the room, graceful as a dancer. "Is that where I come in, with Holly? I mean, it's not as if Bradshaw told me where I could find her last week out of the kindness of his heart."

"Like David with Lydia, Holly's physical protection is up to you, yes. Magically—" He shrugged. "We do what we can. She's valuable."

"For her blood," Evan muttered. "Not for who she is, or what she's made of herself, but for something she was born with that she—"

"Stand down, Marshal," Alec advised. "She is what she is. But think of it this way: if she wasn't a Spellbinder, if that hadn't influenced every decision she's made, would she *be* the person she is now?" Singleton got to his feet. "I think we're ready. When this is all over, remind me to tell you the tale of a vampire, a freckle-faced little girl, and how two Witches found her—and each other."


THE MAGISTRATE'S CIRCLE—PLUS TWO who were not of it, and one who had no magic at all—took up positions. In the East, Alec stood as the Truthseeing Warrior in the domain of Raphael and the Air of which shadows were in part made. South, Fire, and Michael was Martin, a pendant of red amber glowing on his breast, Warrior of the Spirit. To the West, Nicholas represented Gabriel, in his hands a chalice filled with Water in which rested a small chunk of aquamarine the color of his eyes, stone of tranquillity and protection despite his function as Warrior-Coercer. North was Ian, Warrior of the Sword, wearing Earth green, standing for Ariel.

At the cross-quarters were Kate, Evan, Simon, and Elias. The Magistrate took the Northeast, symbolic dividing line between darkness and light, the place where the Circle would be opened if necessary, and the place most vulnerable in the way that Hallowe'en was vulnerable: the place and time where the veil between the worlds was thinnest. Directly opposite Bradshaw was Evan, whose lack of magic was supported by Elias's abundant power.

Lydia seemed the antithesis of shadow; in pale yellow and with a large opal glinting from her finger, she was a creature of air and light. As she spoke to each Guardian, she turned to each of the men, black hair tumbling over her shoulders as she bowed to those they represented.

"I call on Air's pure breath to inspire me, on Fire's warm brilliance to illumine me, on Water's cool sweetness to cleanse me, on Earth's solid strength to support me. I call on the Guardians to protect me." She sighed softly. "I release my fears."

Lachlan, watching her, wondered if it could possibly be that easy.

Calmly, in a voice so soft it seemed weightless, Lydia went on, "I'll start with Susannah, and go forward as far as we need to. Holly, did you bring something of hers for me to focus on?"

Holly unfastened the diamond bracelet. And dropped it. Lachlan expected the clumsiness to evoke an *Oh, shit!* but Holly seemed incapable of speech. Lydia bent, straightened with the gold and gems enclosed in her palm. After a few moments, she nodded and handed the jewelry back.

"Thank you. That was quite powerful. Only you and Susannah ever wore it."

Holly managed a nod, fumbling to fasten it back around her left wrist.

"Kate, could you begin, please?"

The Apothecary went to the altar and from the pockets of her robe brought forth four small bags. "Parsley, sage, rosemary, and thyme—believe it or not." She smiled. She upended each bag of fresh leaves in a different bowl, saying, "Parsley, a grave-offering in Roman times. Sage, against negative energy. Thyme for divination. And rosemary, of course, for remembrance. She who is remembered, lives," she finished softly, and returned to her place.

Lydia censed the Circle with a sweet-smelling smoke Lachlan couldn't identify. Simon used a small twine-wrapped bundle of leaves dipped in his chalice to sprinkle water gently around. Then the long wooden stick Ian held sprouted a flame at its top without his having touched it with a match; if Lachlan hadn't seen Holly do this, he would have flinched. Each of them finished the assigned task with the words, "She who is remembered, lives."

Gradually he became aware that Bradshaw was studying him from across the Circle. His Honor looked even worse tonight than he had on Saturday. Grief had aged him, carving lines on his face like fine Chinese calligraphy. Having observed him in the courtroom, Lachlan had thought that most of his gravitas came with the black robe and the gavel. Now he saw the power Elias Bradshaw wielded as a Magistrate. Harsh, dedicated power; more often ruthless than compassionate.

"I conjure and invoke the Sovereign of the East, the power of Air," Bradshaw said suddenly, raising his athame to sketch a pentagram over the tall yellow candle on the floor beside Alec. But he did not continue to the South, as Holly had done at Beltane; instead he moved to Ian in the North, then Nicholas in the West, and finally Martin in the South. Counterclockwise—widdershins, Holly termed it. Lachlan wondered why the Quarters had been called backwards—maybe because Lydia was trying to sense the past?

"The Circle is now cast," Bradshaw finished. "We are between worlds, beyond the boundaries of time, where night and day, death and birth, sorrow and joy, ending and beginning meet as one."

Again, a difference. Holly had used the same words, only the pairings had been expressed in reverse.

"In this place," the Magistrate added, "let she who is remembered, live."

"So mote it be," responded his Circle, including Alec and Nick.

Holly unwrapped a large square of black silk, and slid the wrinkled original page of music notation onto the altar without touching it. With her great-grandmother's silver dagdyne she pricked her left ring finger—the wedding finger, where his own grandmother's diamond was, the finger said to have a vein connected directly to the heart. She touched the drop of blood to a dry, leafy tree branch. A pause while more blood welled; she smeared this on the leaves, and again, and again. Her hands were shaking. She called fire to the branch—differently than he had ever seen her do it, the flame leaping to the leaves from the white candle on the altar. Bone-dry wood and desiccated leaves ignited at once.

"She who is remembered," Holly whispered, "lives."

Placing the branch in a tall cut-crystal vase, she stood to the left of the altar, folding her hands inside flowing white sleeves.

Lydia overturned one bowl of herbs onto the page, gazed by the light of Holly's strange torch, and shook her head. She blew the crushed leaves away and tried the second bowl. And the third. With the fourth, a spark from the branch sputtered onto the herbs. Smoke rose. Lydia caught her breath, then shook the embers from the singed paper before they could ignite.

Smoothing the page flat on the altar, she paused, hands spread over and then onto it. Her huge dark eyes fixed on the shadows dancing over the page, and when she spoke it was with Susannah's clipped New England accents, dryly sarcastic.

"Oh, good, you're back. I was getting a little tired of counting the rats."

A small wounded sound came from deep in Bradshaw's throat.

"This? Just writing some music—I do that when I'm bored, and you left me my briefcase. Did you think I wrote the ransom demand for you?" Lydia's delicate fingers clenched, crushing the paper as Susannah must have. "What do you mean, making notes for my next book? What're you talking about?"

Lachlan bit both lips, abruptly knowing what must come next.

"Oh, God—you mean you think I'm—" Her voice changed, and with cutting authority she said, "You've made the most pathetic mistake. My name is Susannah Wingfield, and I work for Judge Elias Sutton Bradshaw. I suggest you release me before this becomes any more preposterous than it already is."

There was another brief silence. Then: "You must be Noel. Will you please tell your pair of village idiots they got the wrong blonde?"

All at once Lydia's voice changed again: deeper, menacing. Masculine. "Did you think to check a book-cover photo before you grabbed a green-eyed blonde from the courthouse? Did you bother to think at all?"

A minute passed, then another.

Susannah again, this time in a whisper. "Don't go stupid on me, Holly—you have to remember—"

Lachlan could almost see it, and a glance at Bradshaw confirmed that he *was* seeing it: Susannah retrieving the paper, stuffing it into her pocket where it would no longer contact her skin or retain her memories—thank God. Because the next person to touch it would be the cop who found her beneath the cypress trees.

"Poor girl. She looks a bit like my youngest, doesn't she, Glen?" Pause. "Looks like her neck's been snapped. At least she went quick."

Lydia drew in a long breath, let it out slowly. Her hands unclenched from the page. She glanced at Holly, then Elias, as she said, "Nothing else."

Holly plunged the last smoldering leaves into a crystal bowl to extinguish the fire. She was sickly pale, her freckles smears across nose and cheekbones. Evan wanted to go to her, but Elias was speaking again—and in a voice that reemphasized the power Lachlan had sensed in him earlier.

"I thank the Guardians of Air and Fire, Earth and Water, for watching over us this night. As we re-enter the world of birth and death, day and night, joy and sorrow, beginning and ending, we remind ourselves: she who is remembered, lives."

"So mote it be," Holly responded gently.

A few minutes later, when everyone had moved from their places in the Circle to put away implements, Lachlan figured it was okay to join Holly beside the altar. She looked up at him, eyes brimming, and leaned into the shelter of his arm.

Just that simply, they were back in the world. The room was nothing more than a room with an interesting pattern on the floor. Lachlan wondered why he didn't feel a little more wobbly about it—why, indeed, he didn't feel any sort of dislocation at all. Glancing at the other members of the Circle, he mused that perhaps this was because *they* all treated this as perfectly normal, perfectly natural.

If you saw a camel, your reaction would depend on the circumstances. At the zoo or in Egypt, a camel wasn't a big deal. In Gramercy Park, however . . . He grinned to himself, for he'd just seen a camel, right here in Gramercy Park, and it hadn't freaked him one bit.

"Elias," Holly was saying, "do you need us for anything else?"

What suddenly startled him wasn't the camel; it was that he was included among those who found the camel perfectly routine.

"Not right now." Bradshaw, looking weary, pinched the bridge of his nose with thumb and forefinger. "Lydia and I will be working on some things for the next couple of days. Keep your head down, Spellbinder."

"Understood," Lachlan replied for her. "C'mon, Holly, let's go."

She had the decency to wait until they were in the car, then let him have it. "Don't you even begin to think I'm going to be locked up like some animal in a zoo!"

As he pulled the BMW away from the curb, he said, "Bradshaw pulled strings and got me a new assignment—and you're it. Like it or lump it, lady—"

"The perfect bodyguard, is that it? What, he figures I'll be so busy with your body that I won't notice I'm being guarded?"

"Pretty much. Alec and Nicky are coming over later, by the way." He grinned over at her furious scowl. "Tomorrow they'll redo all the wardings at your place. I invited them to stay for the duration."

"Goddammit, Lachlan—"

"Yeah, that's my redheaded powder keg," he approved. "I'll take the long way home so you can get it all out of your system before we go to bed, okay?"

"Don't work me, Evan!" she snarled.

"Don't play me, Holly," he advised. "You'll lose."


DENISE HAD NOT LEFT HER apartment since hearing Susannah Wingfield was dead. Fear kept her inside, pacing, unable to sleep—unable even to lie down in the bed where she'd had Evan Lachlan. She knew who had killed Bradshaw's girlfriend. Instinct, magical awareness, whatever—she knew Noel was responsible and she knew she was in danger.

He hadn't communicated with her at all after the disaster of Beltane last year. She'd been too spooked by that night, and then too furious over her legal woes, to think of him with anything but a cold shudder, positive that if she tried to trade him for immunity, he'd come for her and kill her, too. Once the prosecutors backed off from Bradshaw's court to huddle over whether they had enough to indict in Suffolk County, she'd been legally able to leave the state. Fleeing to New Orleans, she laid low and decided to get in some serious study with a local griot. The Magistrate, Jean-Michel, had issued a warning about causing any trouble whatsoever, informing her that he knew Elias Bradshaw had her Measure. Denise had behaved herself perfectly, immersing herself in esoterica and finishing her next book.

Which, when it came out, sold so well that it prevented Holly McClure's pathetic little historical potboiler from rising any further than number six on the best-seller lists. Confidence restored, lawyers optimistic, and skills enhanced, she returned to New York. Though she still didn't know who had given her name to the police—she suspected Bradshaw himself, it would be just like him, the bastard—the death of Scott Fleming was ancient history. Noises were still being made about indictments, and the Reverend was still getting mileage out of the tragedy and the contretemps with Marshal Lachlan, but Denise sensed herself safe enough.

And, remembering Marshal Lachlan, she spent what time she could spare from signings and parties cooking up something really luscious. Needing a few supplies, Denise had steeled herself and visited Noel's shop. He wasn't there. But the second week in September he phoned, telling her he was planning a little get-together for Samhain, and would she like to be there? He actually had the balls to say he again wanted her to be the Altar.

She hung up on him and changed her phone number.

Then Susannah Wingfield was killed.

Denise was terrified, but she had to get out of her apartment. She'd go insane if she didn't. Just a walk down to the corner bar for a drink—the sheer ordinariness of the idea was too compelling to resist. She dressed, ensured she had not one but three protective pouches—two in her purse, one in her pocket— and left her building.

She paused beneath the awning, shaking her head when the doorman offered to flag down a cab. She shivered slightly, underdressed for the crisp autumn day. The season had abruptly changed in the days she'd been shut indoors, and her jacket was inadequate to the wind off the river.

"Good afternoon," said a pleasant voice at her shoulder, and she whirled around to find a tall, graying, roguishly handsome man smiling down at her. "Heading down the street to the bar, were you?"

Queasy with dread, she could only nod.

"You look a little chilly. Perhaps I might persuade you to consider taking refuge in the warmth of my car—ah, here it is," he beamed as a silver Mercedes pulled up to the curb. His touch on her elbow was as light and as inexorably persuasive as his deep voice. "Allow me," he said, opening the passenger door. "There, that's right. Mind your head. Seat belt fastened—good." He slid into the backseat and finished, "All secure. Let's go."

She was whisked away from the building before she could string two thoughts together. The driver was a man with blond hair and a chiseled profile, whose slender hands on the steering wheel bore a thin gold wedding ring on the left and a garnet on the right. She had no idea who he was.

"Nicholas Orlov," he said suddenly. "I don't read minds. It was simply the obvious question. My friend is Alec Singleton. We are associates of Elias Brad-shaw, who would like very much to hear what you have to say."

She had lots to say—mainly about getting the hell out of this car—and could give voice to none of it. Orlov flicked a glance at her from very blue eyes, a tiny smile playing around his lips.

"But, as you may have noticed, you won't be saying it just yet."

Denise was as silent and helpless and furious as she'd been when her Mea-sure was taken. What did the Magistrate know? What did he expect her to tell him? Could she bluff her way through this? But why conceal anything? Brad-shaw could be her best—her only—defense against Noel.

She relaxed a little, and crossed her legs—wishing she'd worn a skirt in-stead of trousers, because even though the driver and his friend were a little old for her taste it never hurt to have an attractive man or two on one's side.


"NICE WORK," BRADSHAW COMMENTED AS Denise was brought silently into his house. "No muss, no fuss."

"Always hire professionals," Alec Singleton intoned pompously, dark eyes twinkling. "Where do you want her?"

"The living room will do."

A few minutes later, Denise was seated on a brown corduroy sofa, and Sin-gleton and Orlov had taken up position to one side of the empty fireplace. Brad-shaw perched on the arm of an easy chair.

"Comfortable, my dear?" Alec asked, and shrugged a little apology when she glowered at him. "Forgive our method, but the Magistrate does need to talk to you."

Elias didn't care if she was comfortable or not, and resented Singleton's in-trusion. "Denise, you're going to tell me everything you know, and you're going to do it now—without commotion and without concealment. Do you under-stand me?"

Sulkily, she nodded.

"Nicky!" Alec admonished.

"Oh—sorry," he said, not sounding it in the least, and flicked an index finger.

Denise gave a violent start, then sucked in a huge lungful of air as if she hadn't breathed for days. "It wasn't my fault!" she began, predictably enough. "Noel killed that kid—put his hands around his neck and snapped it!"

This wasn't quite the topic Bradshaw had in mind, but it would do for a start. "I never did think you killed Fleming. You don't have the balls for it, liter-ally or figuratively. I want to know everything you know about Noel. Every-thing. Now."

"He just showed up at The Hyacinths that night—I didn't know he'd be there. I haven't seen him since. I went to his store a while ago but he was gone. That's all I know."

Orlov shifted slightly by the fireplace, but said nothing.

Bradshaw went on, "He functioned as High Priest at Beltane?"

"Yes. I was—I was the Altar."

"Perhaps," Nick said, "he wishes you to play the same role at Samhain." When Denise flinched, he added, "I knew she was leaving something out."

"Okay, okay, he called me! I hung up on him!"

Elias nodded. "Tell me about the weekend Susannah was killed."

She looked if she wanted to turn him into something appreciably slimier than a toad. "My lawyer was in Manhattan, in court for something else. I met him there to talk about the Suffolk D.A."

"Keep talking," Bradshaw advised. "There's magic to mention, isn't there?"

"Yes!" Denise wrapped her arms around herself. "I was in the middle of a spell, changing my appearance a little—" When Orlov arched his brows, she snarled, "There was a man I wanted, okay?"

This was the second time the partner who didn't Truth-See had behaved as if he was the partner who did. Elias puzzled at that for a moment.

"So that's why Noel's people didn't recognize her," Alec said.

She aged ten years. "*Bon dieu de merde*—they were after *me?*"

"Yes," Bradshaw said flatly. "You didn't see any of them?"

"Would he have killed me?"

"Not likely. He wants you for his ritual, remember."

Alec said, "The snatch was a little early for Samhain, don't you think?"

Bradshaw dug his hands into his trouser pockets. "Perhaps Noel only wanted to talk to Denise in person. Persuade her to come willingly at the end of the month." He regarded her again. "Continue. Tell me what happened next."

"I went home."

"And?" Orlov prompted.

"All right! I finished the spell that evening—I expected him—the man— Saturday but he didn't show up until Sunday. I heard on the news that night—" She broke off with a shiver. "That's all. I'm telling you the truth!"

"I have a question," Nick said. "Does Noel know what Holly is?"

"He—he may have guessed. I'm not sure—dammit, don't *do* that!" she cried, cringing away from him. "I told him there's a Spellbinder in New York, but I don't know if he knows it's her."

Elias saw Alec nod fractionally, and knew Denise was telling the truth. "Well, you're what he wants, for the moment. And he's going to get you."

"What?" she exploded. "Are you out of your fucking mind?"

He drew from one pocket a length of golden cord. Denise turned white. "I think you'll do as we ask. You're fully aware that I know how to use this." He smiled a tiny feral smile, and tucked the Measure away.

She could be convinced arcanely, of course, but despite the gathered expertise of three skilled practitioners, he didn't care to trust to spells. Denise he trusted not at all, except to look exclusively to her own welfare. But sufficiently convinced in what passed for her brain by a combination of the Measure's threat and irrefutable logic—if he took care of Noel, she'd never have to worry about him again—she would do what he required, and of her own free will. All he need do was point out that their goal was basically the same: neutralize Noel. She seized on this instantly, which told him just how frightened she was.

"But I'm not going there alone," she insisted. "Somebody has to protect me."

Singleton exchanged glances with his partner. Bradshaw shook his head, saying, "You're both too powerful. He'd feel it in an instant."

"And not you, either," she stated.

"I think I know someone who'd do, if he agrees." Rising to his feet, he glanced out at the rain. "Go home and call Noel. If you can't get him, leave a message. He'll call back, I guarantee it. Tell him you've changed your mind and will be there at Samhain. He'll be at The Hyacinths again, I assume?"

"How should I know?"

"When you find out where the ritual will be held, I'll arrange for you to send me a message. Don't phone or come over."

"She's not stupid, Elias," Alec murmured. "Be nice."

Nick shot him a speaking look; Denise, incredibly, almost smiled. After an incredulous second, Elias realized she thought she'd made a conquest—which evidently was just what Alec wanted her to think. And, he grasped an instant later, why the pair stood close together while Nick pretended to be reading her—even if she felt the trajectory of the magic, she couldn't pinpoint it. Alec could do his work without seeming to, and then deploy the charm he also possessed in abundance.

"Who's going to protect me?" Denise was saying. To Alec. With green eyes wide and entreaty dripping from her voice like sap from a tree.

Bradshaw smiled sweetly. "You'll just have to trust me, won't you?"

"I think," Nicholas said in baleful tones, "it's time we took her home."

As Alec escorted her through the front door, Elias arched a questioning brow at the Hungarian and murmured, "Nice act the two of you have. Any specific reason for it that I should know about?"

"He likes to confuse—not difficult with that one," Nick grunted. "Delightful girl. Do you have in mind the person I think you have in mind for her protection?"

"I can't think of anyone better, can you?"

Twenty-five

EVAN LEANED BACK IN HIS chair and blew out a long, long sigh. Even with all access restored and updated, Noel remained a mystery. Lachlan couldn't even get a last name for him that stuck longer than three forged pieces of identification.

"No parents, no birthplace, no childhood, no schooling, no employment history, no arrest records, no goddamned motherfucking *anything!*"

Holly looked up from her laptop, squinting at him across the partners' desk. "If *you* can't find him, then he isn't going to be found."

"I appreciate your faith, lady love," he replied with a crooked grin, "but I'm not *that* good. Most criminals are fairly stupid, when you get right down to it. They always make a mistake—let something slip, return to an old haunt, forget to get rid of a piece of paper that'll nail 'em."

"But Noel's not just a criminal, is he? I mean, the real sociopaths never seem that way to anybody else. You're always hearing in interviews about what a nice, quiet, polite guy the local serial killer was, before he started killing serially."

"Maybe I'm goin' at this wrong," he mused. "Nick gave me what he got when Noel bought the shop, but none of it checks out back more than five years." He shut down the computer and got to his feet, stretching. "What're you workin' on?"

"My last will and testament."

He scowled at her. "Not funny."

"I'm just e-mailing Aunt Lulah to see if anything's come up—I asked her to check with people she knows. Nothing will come of it, but I had to do something."

They were waiting for Alec and Nick to return from Bradshaw's little tête-à-tête with Denise, to which they had firmly not been invited. Just as well. All Evan lacked at this point was another encounter with that blonde bitch.

"This is making me crazy," Holly fretted. "I'm tired of sitting around waiting for something to happen. We've been working on all this for—" She peered at her desk calendar.

"—two solid weeks and we're no closer to finding out who or where Noel is. We can't even find *him!*"

He heard what she hadn't said. "But you think you know what he's up to."

She sipped iced coffee and wouldn't meet his eyes. "Let's say for a minute that we believe in what he believes in, and especially in what he can do. Apparently he drew power from that boy's death. He's got a store full of esoteric books about deities willing—or unwilling—to supply power. Elias said that Lydia's collection of symbols ties in to some of the nastiest entities anybody ever regretted hearing of."

Lachlan snorted. "He wants to become God? What for?"

"I've never understood the impulse, either," she agreed. "Power to make the world the way you want it—" She shook her head. "All the creator-gods gave humans free will. Take away that, and you're left with the mindless devotion of inferiors and everything going along just the way it was planned—which would get pretty boring pretty quick, even for a god."

"Maybe he wants to destroy everything and start over." He made a show of squinting at the windows. "Look like rain to you?"

"Been there, done that, Noah-honey." She grinned. "Next time's supposed to be fire, isn't it? Trying to predict when God will get cheesed off enough to end the world has occupied clerics of all persuasions for thousands of years."

"Makes 'em nervous. End the world, they're out of a job. But I don't think that applies to Noel. Maybe killing Scott Fleming was his first taste of power over life and death, and he wants more."

"I don't understand *that* kind of warp, either," she admitted. "But we have to think in terms of Samhain. It's the night when the border between worlds blurs. That could mean that on any other night he wouldn't have the chops to call up whatever it is he wants to call up."

"Even with your blood."

"Yeah, well, there's that." She chewed a thumbnail, then said, "Nobody ever did tell me about the night Scott Fleming died. Or why Denise got blamed for it. Or why she didn't trade Noel for immunity or whatever."

Evan shrugged, determinedly not remembering the scant moments on Beltane when it had been Denise Josèphe's face he saw, not Holly's. "Bradshaw thinks the place was sanitized magically. It's the only way there'd be no evidence—and I mean *none*. No fingerprints, no trace for DNA, not even the family's prints or DNA—"

"Which you'd expect to find."

"Which you'd expect to find," he agreed. "Fleming's body on the floor was it.

End of evidence. The only thing the cops did get was a pile of sworn statements from thirty-two witnesses that the owners were absolutely elsewhere."

"Let me guess—everybody was everybody else's alibi."

"It stank to the Suffolk County detectives, too, but they couldn't shake anybody loose. The only print they found was Denise's, on one of the kid's ear-cuff charms. Was Noel was good enough to wipe out everything else but not that? Not fuckin' likely. She got set up."

"Couldn't happen to a better person," Holly growled.

"Granted. As for why—maybe he wanted leverage with her. Maybe he got pissed at her for some reason and left her print so there'd be somebody to blame for the murder. As long as it wasn't him, what did he care? It was a couple of days before the daughter discovered the body—or so they claimed. She went into hysterics, her folks had her committed for the summer, and then they put the house on the market and moved to Florida."

"Keeping her out of the way during the investigation, and tagging her as delusional so even if she accused Noel, nobody'd believe her."

"You have a twisted, diabolical mind, you know that?" He grinned.

"It's why you adore me." She gave a start as the doorbell chimed. "They took long enough!" She ran to let Alec and Nick in.

Coffee was poured as Nick reset the alarms—both electronic and magical—and soon they were in the living room. Alec gave them the essence of Denise's story, then fixed Evan with an inquisitive gaze. "How'd you like to make yourself useful?"

"What did you have in mind?"

Alec told him, finishing with, "You'll have every protection we can give you without making it too obvious."

"I thought Bradshaw wanted me to guard Holly, not that slut."

Nick arched a brow. "You know her?"

"Seen her once or twice at book parties," Lachlan said with a shrug. And because no one would ever suspect him of being less than truthful where such serious business was concerned, they were unaware that he wasn't *exactly* lying.

"You're not leaving this building, Evan," Holly told him.

"Darling girl," Alec said, "it's not as if he'll be walking into the middle of a Working. He just has to pretend he's a Satanist so he can find and arrest Noel."

"With Denise as a complaining witness," Nick added, "Evan can read him his rights over the murder of Scott Fleming. It's thin, but it'll be enough to keep him locked up until after Samhain."

"Forty-eight hours to arraign or release," Evan agreed. "So Denise leads me to this guy, I flash my badge, cuff him, haul him off to jail, and that's it." Slanting a look at Holly, he had the nerve to grin. "You've got that look in your eye."

"Which one?" Alec asked, fighting a smile.

"Which look, or which eye?" Evan countered.

Holly's jaw hardened. "Has it occurred to you that a year ago you were, shall we say, somewhat visible in the media? What if Noel recognizes you?"

He was just as glad that luring fugitive felons had taught him strict discipline over his expression, and let somebody else answer her.

Alec obliged. "Good point, but it's my opinion that Noel hasn't even been in the city this last year. A visit to the store last July revealed that his assistant manager—a nice young lady who didn't tell a single lie—had been left in charge while he was on vacation. As this holiday coincided with the indictment of Mademoiselle Josèphe, I think it can be assumed he skipped town in case she ratted on him."

Nick went to the bar and poured a tot of Drambuie into his coffee. "We also went to his residence the day after we arrived in New York. No food in the fridge, no clothes in the closets, no computer, and a landlord who was persuaded to tell us that Noel's mail has been redirected since last July to General Delivery in some dreary little town—Moose Drool, Montana, or something equally improbable. We also left a little something that would stick to him—"

"Think of it as the dye that explodes in a wrapped stack of stolen cash," Alec suggested.

"—but we haven't been able to track him down," Nick finished. "He must have sensed and negated it."

"Speaking of cash," Evan said, "the owners of The Hyacinths withdrew fifty grand two days after Beltane. That reeks payoff to me. He takes the cash, holes up in Buffalo Chip, Wyoming, or wherever for a year—he couldn't have seen any of the media. So I'm okay." He grinned. "Who should I be—Dillon, Wyatt, or McCloud?"

Baffled, Nick looked at his partner for enlightenment. Alec began to laugh. "The man has no shame at all."

"And no sense, either," Holly snapped. "You're not doing this, Evan."

"Nicholas," Alec said decisively, "come with me to the kitchen. We need more coffee."

"I'm fine, still have half a—" His eyes widened. "Ah . . . yes. You're right, I do need more coffee."


AS THEY REMOVED THEMSELVES TACTFULLY to the kitchen, Alec muttered, "We'd still hear her yelling even if we went all the way back to Connecticut."

"I don't think there'll be much yelling, actually," his partner mused.

"That's not so good. When she doesn't rant, she's *really* mad. How d'you think she'll start? 'Don't you even consider it' or 'What, you think you're immortal?'"

"I'm betting on 'Why does it have to be you?'"

Alec hitched a hip onto a stool at the breakfast bar, nodding. "At which point he'll say he graduated two academies, swore oaths to protect and serve, it's his job, he won't risk her or anybody else, and what kind of man could he call himself if he refused?"

Nick glanced around from the coffee grinder. "*Jerusalem Lost* was a novel! Life imitating art imitating life? Do me a favor! She's no medieval damsel embroidering tapestries while her White Knight fights the Crusades."

"How many medieval damsels really just sat around embroidering tapestries? With the men gone, there were castles and farms to run, justice to be meted out, serfs to be flogged—"

"Spare me the history lesson," Nick snapped. "Holly has to be protected. She's too important."

"I agree. And now the one man to whom *she* is vitally important—in the only ways she really wants to be important—is going to do this crazy thing."

"At our behest."

"At Bradshaw's behest. You'd have objected if you didn't agree with him. Holly will have to wait until it plays out, just as Elisabeth did with Guillaume."

"With happier results, I trust." He measured fresh grounds into the coffeemaker, frowning. "Oh, very well. You and I will take up guard duty while poor Evan gets in touch with his inner Lucifer so he can play his part. Which all could have been avoided, if—"

"Don't say it, Nick."

"Say what?"

"That this is your fault to begin with because you sold the store to Noel. He would've found her anyway. That's the way life works."

"Is it?"

Hearing the bitterness in the softly accented voice, Alec murmured, "Yes. That's the way life works. That's why they call it 'life' instead of 'art.' Life is messy and complicated, with outrageous coincidences that would get Holly laughed out of an editor's office if she put them into a book. What are the odds, for instance, that a Mayflower descendant and a Hungarian Rom would stumble across each other?"

"You're forgetting the magic of it, Alyosha." Nick smiled. "Which of course was precisely your point, yes?"

NOBODY HAD HEARD FROM DENISE by the next afternoon. Holly pretended not to notice. Alec and Nick spent the day renewing old wards and setting up new ones; Evan observed for a while, then took out his frustrations in the basement gym.

Mr. Hunnicutt, carrying a large padded envelope, arrived at Holly's door at the same time Evan returned. Thanking the former, she wrinkled her nose at the latter.

"Bathtub, stinky."

"What's that?"

"Stuff."

He growled and strode off to her bedroom. She ripped open the package, poking a finger in to rummage the contents, and inhaled deeply of the scents within. She hoped Kate had provided everything requested by phone this morning—

"What's that?"

Evan's words, Nicky's voice. She turned too quickly, saw him coming down the stairs, dropped the box, and swore.

"One did hope," Nick said as he helped gather up all the little silk bags strewn across the floor, "that you might outgrow tripping over your own feet, *béna.*"

"Stop calling me clumsy. You startled me."

He untied one of the pouches. "Sea salt? Holly Elizabeth, what do you have planned?" Then he sat back on his heels and gave her his most adorable smile. "You're going to Work some magic!"

Cramming the envelope full, she went into the living room knowing he would follow. "You told Evan you're protecting him. Well, I don't see any signs of it yet, so I'm going to make myself useful. Don't go away. I'll be right back."

At the door of her bathroom, she paused for a steadying breath. Evan always took off his St. Michael medal for a shower or bath, in case the chain broke. It would be simplicity itself to purloin it from the countertop. As she opened the door, he surfaced from a dunking to rinse his hair and burst into song, a gruesomely off-key rendition of "New Kid in Town." Holly winced.

"Enough!"

He glanced around, hair dripping. "Oh, c'mon—I hit most of the notes."

"Not the ones the Eagles had in mind."

"Bradshaw call yet about Denise?"

"Nope. Tell me, love of my life," she went on, casually leaning against the sink counter, one finger just barely touching the medal's silver chain, "how can you possibly not sound as bad to yourself as you do to everyone in a five-mile radius?"

"Bitch, bitch, bitch. Why don't you join me? I'm gonna be in here a while— I think I pulled something," he added in aggrieved tones, stretching a shoulder.

"You didn't happen to see my cell phone anywhere in the bedroom, did you?"

"No, I haven't seen it—or anything else in that mess."

"Bitch, bitch, bitch." She escaped, the medal clasped in her hand.

Back in the living room, she found Nick lounging in a chair by the hearth, the contents of Kate's package on the worn carpet at his feet. Holly sank down near him, ignoring his analytical gaze as she sorted supplies. At last she could stand it no longer and looked up at him.

"Are you going to help me or not?"

"That's contingent on one or two things. A commitment, for starters. An acknowledgment of the gift you've been given, and your responsibility to use it prudently. Perhaps even wisely."

"I've never refused a bloodletting," she retorted bluntly.

"And you've never really participated in a Circle, either, have you?"

"Are you going to help or not?" she repeated.

"Oh, I'll help. But the Work has to be yours."

"What Work?" Alec asked, entering with an armful of logs from the service porch bin.

"Protecting Evan," Holly snapped. "Nicky, please!"

He leaned back, folding his arms. "Evan is your responsibility. Which of course is exactly the way he feels about you. Is he trusting anyone else to do what he knows *he* can do better than any one of us?"

"I need you to help me!"

Alec, crouching by the hearth to lay a fire for that evening, glanced over his shoulder. "No, you don't. You just think you do. But you don't."

*"Feri ando payi sitsholpe te nayuas."* Nick laughed gently. "'It was in the water that one learned to swim.' Put another way—*Bi kashtesko merel i yag.* 'Without wood, the fire would die.'"

"Stop mixing your obscure Romany metaphors," Alec chided, "and tell her what you *really* think."

"Are you going to help or not?" she snarled for the third time.

"You don't need us, *cailleach*," Alec soothed.

"Since when do you speak Gaelic?" Holly muttered.

"I know the word for 'witch' in sixteen languages."

"And I know it in twenty-nine," Nick said. "We'll call a Circle, how about that? The rest of it is up to you."

It was as much as she was going to get, and she knew it. Pushing herself to her feet, she said, "All right, a Circle. Facing South."

"Fire and Michael," Alec interpreted, nodding.

"And Brighid," Holly added. "The real, original, accept-no-substitutes Irish *cailleach*. You'll find candles and things over in that cabinet."


FRANKINCENSE. BLACK POWDERED IRON. Sea salt and oak moss. Sandalwood oil on a large white candle. *Think clearly about what you need. Set a goal. Avoid distractions. Use meaningful symbols.* Oh, she knew the hows of spellcasting; she just didn't trust much to her own ability to Work one and make it stick.

This time, she would have to be sure.

Her uncles cast a Circle, waiting for her to enter it before closing it. She sat facing South, the St. Michael medal in her palm, and lit the white candle—with only a thought this time, eliminating the gesture that was a holdover from needing to be visually reassured.

With mortar and pestle she ground all the dry ingredients together. Then, on a bit of parchment, using red Dragon's Blood ink that smelled of white wine and cinnamon, she wrote Evan's full name, once in English, once in Gaelic. Rolled and tied with a black thread, she set the parchment aside.

She wrote his name again along the white candle with the tips of four different obsidian arrowheads, using each to inscribe a pentagram on the candle as well. These she placed at the base of the candle, aimed at the cardinal points of the compass.

Alec and Nick, who had taken guardian positions in the West and North, watched without expression or comment. She was grateful for that; she had enough trouble concentrating, keeping everything in proper sequence, remembering to keep a corner of her mind chanting Evan's name in two languages.

Because she felt nothing.

Urgency, yes; fear; anger. But not magic. Not the steady flow of arcane strength and calm power and even delight so often seen in other practitioners of the art. Her Work here was no humble petition for bright protective wings to fold around her beloved; she would beg, demand, storm heaven and earth alike to keep this man safe.

Why? Because she loved him? Inadequate reason. Worse, presumptuous. Who was she to command the safety of one man merely out of love?

She wanted him safe because it was right that he should live, grow old, father children, teach them to love what was beautiful and know what was right and to be like him, to have his honor and courage, his humor and strength. *Éimhín*, her Evan—he deserved the notice of the All-Mighty because he was a good man.

All at once the fire laid in the hearth caught, and blazed. Holly stared at it, into it, and felt herself slowly rocking, back and forth, back and forth, to the rhythm of her chanting of his name, of her own heartbeats. Of her own blood. This wasn't what it meant to be a Witch. This was what it meant to be *human*. To connect; to listen, and know that even if you didn't consciously hear, something inside heard anyway, and understood. What she had felt in Kenya stirred within her, elusive but real. Scents of cinnamon and sandalwood, of wine and burning pine logs, of the woolen rug on which he and she had made love—the heat and brilliant light of the flames, the silver oval clasped in her palm, the sound of her lover's name in her ears and its taste on her lips—

*Magic.*

With each whetted arrowhead she pricked her left ring-finger, smearing blood down each fire-sheened black length before replacing them at the compass points. Squeezing up more blood, she ran her finger across the letters of the name carved into the candle. She pressed her fingerprint to the parchment and to the silver image of St. Michael holding a sword. Finally she placed the parchment into the bottle, sifted in the herbs and iron powder, and corked it. The candle she lifted from its flat glass holder, tilting it so the wax dripped to seal the cork as she turned the bottle widdershins. All the while she rocked gently, whispering.

*Éimhín Liam Lochlainn*
 *This Work I do for thee alone*
 *Flesh or blood, breath or bone,*
 *No hurt shall come to thee, my own,*
 *From secret foes or enemies known.*
  *This geas bound by power of Three*
  *As I will it, so mote it be.*
*Éimhín Liam Lochlainn*
 *This thing I swear to thee alone*
 *Flesh and blood, breath and bone,*
 *No hurt shall come to thee, my own,*
 *From secret foes or enemies known.*
  *This geas bound by power of Three*
  *As I will it, so mote it be.*
*Éimhín Liam Lochlainn*
 *This spell for thee, and thee alone*
 *Sealed by blood, writ in bone,*
 *No hurt shall come to thee, my own,*
 *From secret foes or enemies known.*
  *This geas bound by power of Three*
  *As I will it, so mote it be.*

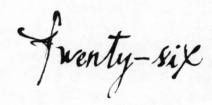

# Twenty-six

AT ONE IN THE AFTERNOON of the thirty-first of October, Denise Josèphe was picked up by taxi for the drive to The Hyacinths. That this taxi was driven by a tall young black man Denise vaguely recognized did not help her mood.

"I know you. Where have I seen you before?"

"Sweetness, I'm so tickled that you remember." He grinned and bowed her into the cab with an exaggerated flourish. With the sound of his voice, she did remember—and cursed under her breath. He was the one who, with Holly, had taken her Measure.

"Lovely weather we're having," said another voice, smooth and cold, from within the cab.

Denise flinched back from Evan Lachlan. "*You're* my protection? *You?*"

"Me," he replied, his eyes taunting her to challenge him.

Rebellion was the last thing on her mind. True, he had no magic—but if anything was guaranteed to bring Holly McClure to the ritual, her lover's presence was it. Once she was there, Noel would have what he wanted and Denise would require no protection—and could get away from Noel once and for all.

Leaning back with an air of exaggerated ease, she remarked, "When Bradshaw said to tell Noel I'd be bringing along a good-looking stud, I had no idea it would be you."

The driver opened the sliding window between the seats and said, "We have a little planning to do, so listen up."

Arrive, identify Lachlan as a friend and fellow celebrant, listen to Noel's plan for the Samhain rite, agree to whatever he said, and get out—yadda yadda, who the hell cared? She could smell Lachlan's body, remembered vividly from the Sunday afternoon she'd laid him.

Had he told Holly? For a delightful minute she fantasized the scene: his protestation that he'd been tricked by a shape-changing spell, her mortification that Denise was her superior in magic and in bed as well as in prose. The vision faded as she remembered the day she decided to pursue Lachlan, after literally bumping into him at the bookstore.

"Does Noel know who you are?"

"Why should he?" His voice was silk, his eyes stone.

She wanted to smack him. This was *her* life he was playing with here. If Noel recognized him, and knew him for a cop— But if Noel remembered him at all, it would be as a customer. That would lend credence to her claim that he wanted to join the Samhain ritual. Denise relaxed a little. If she played it right, she just might come out of this ahead after all.

GO IN, GET THE DETAILS, get out. That was all Denise knew about this afternoon's little outing. As for Holly—as far as she knew, Evan would immediately arrest Noel and that would be the end of it. Lachlan, however, had a different agenda: evidence. *Something* was going to link Noel to Susannah's murder. She'd done her best with the handful of dirt, but her geological gamble hadn't paid off. Courtworthy evidence was needed; even if Noel turned out to be a talkative egotist who wanted his genius admired, Lachlan wanted to nail him with physical proof. Just what that might turn out to be, he had no idea. He was open to inspiration.

Someone had been caring for The Hyacinths during its long months of desertion. The lawns and hedges were tidy, the gravel drive free of weeds, and the beds where, presumably, the namesake flowers grew in their season were neatly kept. For the rest—size and sumptuousness didn't impress him much.

Neither did Noel, who appeared at the front door and sauntered out to meet the taxi. Lachlan remembered him from the bookstore, and hoped brazenly that Noel didn't remember him. Tall, lanky, with cold silvery-blue eyes and lots of hair raked back from his face, there were faint grooves cut into his forehead now and framing his mouth, as if the last eighteen months had been a strain. Lachlan supposed that hiding out in Elk Fart, Idaho, hadn't been a picnic.

Evan made a show of paying the driver, who arched a questioning brow at him; when he shrugged by way of reply, Ian grimaced and nodded. "Thanks, buddy. Have fun," he murmured, and drove off—but only to the main road, where he would wait out of sight.

"Denise! Good of you to come," Noel was saying. "And this is your friend?"

"Dillon," Lachlan supplied, shaking the long, thin hand extended to him and suddenly wishing he'd worn gloves. Not that he was chilly; a black cashmere sweater and leather jacket were keeping him warm. He just didn't like the way touching Noel's skin made him feel. "When we gonna rock 'n' roll?"

"Ah, the enthusiastic type." Noel grinned. "After nightfall. Come in, let's get started." As they entered the foyer, he added, "I'll show you the venue—you've seen it before, Denise, but I've made a few alterations. Dillon, if you have any suggestions, I'd be pleased to hear them."

"I'm kinda new at this," he admitted, looking around the foyer. All the furniture had been cleared out; remaining were some unlit wall sconces and an appalling chandelier dripping a gazillion multicolored crystals. "I've done a couple before, just along for the ride. If it's okay, I'd like to get more involved, y'know?"

"Great!" Noel clapped him on the shoulder, and again Evan had to hold himself from recoiling at the contact. "I can guarantee you the time of your life."

He led them down a long hallway where all the doors were closed except the one leading to the stairs. Lachlan wondered which room Susannah had been held in. Someplace with a chair to sit on, and a table to write on, and rats to kick—he swallowed hard and reminded himself to look as if he were paying attention to Noel.

"—the usual attire, nothing fancy. We'll meet in the hall as we did on Beltane, then relocate belowstairs." He opened a heavy wooden door and lit their way down with a fat black candle. "I replaced the couch with one of the stone benches from the back garden—we'll need the organic power of the granite."

"Sounds cold, hard, and miserable," Denise remarked testily.

"I admit it's not cozy, but I'll make sure it's comfortable."

"You'd better," Lachlan put in, as if solicitous for the lady's well-being.

They entered the cellar. Lachlan couldn't keep an exclamation from leaving his lips; the place was huge, icy-cold, and as bare as the rest of the house but for the promised stone bench, a slab of black rock he assumed to be the altar, and candles. Hundreds of them, ink-black, standing virgin and unlit on every available surface. In window recesses, crowded onto shelves cut into the rock, on steps up to an outer door, in a semicircle around the stone bench, at each corner of the altar—tall tapers, thick columns, votives, pyramids, spheres, squares, and pillars of black wax clustered everywhere.

"Holy shit," Lachlan muttered. "You wanna burn the whole place down?"

"The fire department would be outraged," Noel agreed. "Why don't you try out the bench, both of you? You can tell me how many cushions we'll need."

"Silk, stuffed with feathers," Denise put in. "If you're determined to go organic."

Lachlan stepped over the half-circle of candles around the bench and paused to turn slowly around. Vaulted ceiling, stone pillars to hold it up, arches on the far wall where wine racks must once have stood, and a small rickety table with some black glass bowls on it. He could picture Susannah seated there. Writing that strange coded note; hoping Holly would get hold of it and recognize it for what it was; scraping her knee against the table leg when she kicked at scurrying rats—

If the wood matched the splinters in the knee of her slacks, and if a bit of her skin or blood lingered, Evan could prove she had been held here. For all the good it would do, he told himself morosely. Bradshaw had hypothesized a magical scrubbing after Beltane, and the same had probably happened after Noel murdered Susannah. No wonder there were Magistrates to deal with miscreants within the community; ordinary law enforcement didn't stand a chance.

Denise pushed past, gathering her burgundy velvet cloak around her, and sat on the bench. "It *is* cold," she complained.

"Dillon? What's your opinion?"

Lachlan seated himself beside her. "It needs more than a few pillows."

"Yes," Denise seconded, "where's the couch we had at Beltane?"

Noel bent to touch a lighted match to one of the candles on the floor, straightened, and looked at them unsmiling, his eyes as flat and cold as a frozen window into an empty room. With a single sweeping gesture he lit all the candles around the bench.

"What the—?" Lachlan tried to stand. He couldn't. His muscles pushed and strained against something that wasn't there. He felt neither weak nor drained; his ass was simply stuck to the bench as securely as if he'd been glued to it. Neither would his hands lift from where they rested on his thighs, nor his arms move from his sides, nor even his toes wriggle in his boots. He could feel the Glock nestled at his ribs. Useless.

Denise blurted with surprise, struggling just as ineffectually beside him. "What is this? What have you done?"

"What do you think?" Noel inquired, as if sincerely curious. "While you contemplate your duties as the altar, Denise, you can also think up a really good explanation for why you brought a United States Marshal with you." He stayed beyond the barrier of candles, regarding his guests with scorn. "Did you think I didn't know? Did you think I wouldn't remember? I catalog every single person who comes through my shop door! Waiting for the right people, searching them for power—you have none," he directed at Lachlan, "but you reek of those who do. When *she* came in—" There was no doubt he was not referring to Denise. "—I could smell you on her. *What is she?*"

Lachlan tried shifting his body to one side, leaning into Denise to push her off the bench. She was as stuck to it as he was, and cried out as he shoved her again, harder, with no result.

"Stop that, goddammit! Noel, I don't know what you're talking about!"

"Tell me what she is," he said.

"Just let me go, I promise I'll get her and bring her back here—"

He regarded Lachlan quizzically. "Can she really be this dim-witted?"

Evan discovered he could shrug his shoulders. "It's a gift."

"What a relief to know she didn't have to pay for it. Come on, Denise," he cajoled. "Tell me."

As she drew breath to speak, Lachlan warned, "Say it, he'll kill you anyway."

"Denise isn't the Sacrifice, Marshal. I need her living, breathing, and un-damaged. Now, for the last time: What *is* that woman?"

Denise spat the word. "Spellbinder!"

Noel looked startled, then laughed. "Of course! Absolutely perfect. At Beltane you mentioned there was one in New York, but I never dreamed she'd walk into my bookshop! I've still got her credit card number in my computer— her address won't be any trouble." Cocking a brow at Lachlan: "You think you're the only one with resources?"

"I think you're going to be in a world of hurt if we don't show up when and where we're supposed to."

" 'We'? How gallant of you, Marshal. 'We' all know you don't give a rat's ass about this bitch." He frowned, slitting silvery eyes to scrutinize Lachlan's face, as if trying to see inside his brain. "You smell of her. She gave you something. Very recently. What is it? Something of magic—" He moved forward, then caught himself just before he reached the boundary of candles. "I suppose it doesn't matter. When this begins, nothing will protect you."

"IF HE'S NOT BACK BY FIVE—"

Alec didn't bother to glance up from the book he was reading. "Dear heart, do sit down. Or, if you must do your decapitated chicken act, get out a vacuum and do something useful."

Holly plopped herself down on the sofa. "What're you reading?"

"*Seabiscuit.*" He turned a page. "Hush up—I've just gotten to the 1938 Santa Anita Handicap."

"It's not as if you haven't read it twice already—"

"Three times. It's one of the few books—besides yours, of course—that I en-joy rereading."

Holly walked to the window, flicked a finger at one of the witch spheres, and walked back to the hearth again. "You realize I could have you arrested for false imprisonment. In my own home, no less."

"Protective custody." He turned a page.

"I'm going stir-crazy."

"No, you're not. You're just scared."

"You're goddamned right I am."

"Good. I worry about people who aren't scared when they ought to be."

"Oh, *that's* helpful!"

He set the book aside and mimicked her posture of folded arms and baleful stare. "He'll be fine. He's not stupid."

"Denise is." She marched over to the bar for a club soda. She wanted a cigarette so badly, she was ready to claw the plaster off the walls. "Drink?"

"Glenfiddich, please."

She poured and brought it to him. "Where's Nicky?"

"Taking a nap. We're not as young as we used to be, you know—and watching you fret yourself into a nervous breakdown is rather exhausting."

"What are we going to do about Noel?"

"Oh, I'm sure we'll figure out something," he said airily. "Ever been to the Gold Coast, where the rich folks live?"

"No."

"You really don't get out much, do you? You shop, you do the restaurants and theaters, museums and parks—but you don't participate in the city's real life. The day-to-day New York."

"I'm a country girl. Big cities make me nervous."

"Bullshit. You've lived in them before."

"Maybe I simply agree with Dickens: 'All that is loathsome, drooping and decayed is here.'"

"Bullshit squared. He only visited. Why don't you read Walt Whitman sometime? He actually lived here."

"And not in an ivory tower like me, is that what you mean?"

"Well, there's a whole world going on in New York that you stay fairly insulated from. I'm not saying it's wrong. I was just wondering."

Capitulating, she said, "I don't understand this city. I've never figured out how so many people can live in such a small space and pretend that it works."

"And L.A. *does* work?" he asked wryly.

"They're all spread out, so they can fool themselves better. There's a natural insulation of space. Plus everybody lives in a car, which is a galvanized steel metaphor. But here, there's so *much* of everything. So many lives, all separate—you say I'm not connected to New York, but is anybody here really connected to anybody else? Outside of family and friends, I mean. There's *contact*—hell, walking down the street is a contact sport—but is there *connection*?"

"I think the intertwining is not often acknowledged. New York is the greatest city in the world—which means it's the most excessive city in the world. Wealth, poverty, art, ugliness, generosity, violence—all outsized. But it weaves together."

"I think the word you want is 'tangles,'" she retorted. "And no tapestries, please—the image is uninspired. Okay, I can see that after 9/11, yeah, connections were made. Martin told me that he and Ian realized it was the first time in their lives they didn't feel hyphenated. Not African-Americans, but *Americans*. The United States finally became their country—and they descend from slaves who goddamned *built* half the United States!"

"We were all shocked into seeing each other. It's a disgrace that it took 9/11 to do it, because we've all been here living with each other all along."

"Not 'with,' Alec. 'Among.' The connections were made out of hideous necessity. Some still exist, I'm sure. But—"

"Life can never be the same. I know it every time I see that great gaping hole in the sky. I would argue that because we're never more human than when death is breathing down our necks, 9/11 opened our eyes—"

"—to each other's fear?" she interrupted. "That isn't how it should be! It's unpardonably sappy of me, but why can't we see each other for reasons that celebrate our common humanity instead of—?"

"Let me ask you this. To how many people can you be truly visible?"

"Rephrase that. I don't understand."

"Is there a limit to the number of people you can know? Really know, I mean, not just nod to at the bank or the market. How many people allow you to see them—and how many do you allow yourself to be seen *by?*"

"Very, very few," she mused. "I could do a whole lecture about socialization within the family, tribe, and clan, and keeping relationships structured—"

"And then I'd have to yell 'The point! The point!' and you'd get pissed off."

They exchanged brief grins. "The *point*," Holly resumed, "is that evolution didn't wire us for an infinite number of connections. In a city like this we guard our personal space, and that means seeing only a finite number of people. But when we do look at each other, we should see the *possibilities*."

"We have to be willing to be seen, you know."

"Yeah." Holly settled on the couch and dug her hands into her trouser pockets. "I had dinner once with a group that included a rather well-known mistress. No, I'm not going to tell you her name or whose mistress she used to be. She was the wariest person I've ever met. People had been wanting things from her all her life. Her body, her influence, gossip about the rich and famous. People were always trying to slice off bits of her. Anyway, there's this weird dynamic that goes on between a woman who's made it on her brains and a woman who's made it on her back. Each secretly envies what the other has, each is not-so-secretly contemptuous of what the other lacks. I hadn't expected that in myself. But I expected nothing from *her* except some conversation. It wasn't until dessert that we finally hit on a topic we were both interested in. We became *visible* to each other, to use your term. Then she suddenly realized it, and I could practically hear the portcullis slam down. I haven't thought about her in years—but what you just said reminded me, Alec. She didn't *want* to be visible. And who could blame her?"

"Life does that to some people," he agreed. "I imagine it has to do with figuring out how visible you want to be. After all, life can be controlled by *not* making connections."

"So we circle back around to me," Holly observed. "This was your and Nicky's ivory tower—an equally uninspired image—before it was mine."

"Yes, and he holed up in it the same way you do, when he had the chance."

"Until you. But that was Mr. Scot's doing, or so I've been told."

"And no coincidence. Like the one about the writer whose college friend works for a judge who used to be with my father's firm, and whose official protection is a big hunk of an Irishman—" He laughed. "I see you take my point. Fate? Destiny? Maybe even magic?"

"You've become insufferable in your old age."

"And *you*, sweetheart, have become more real than you ever were before. *Visible.* Especially to Evan." He sipped his Scotch. "I've been meaning to tell you, by the by, how relieved Nick and I are that he likes us. He's remarkably without prejudice."

Holly giggled slightly. "You mean for a Catholic heterosexual male law enforcement officer? Except that lesbians confuse him. I think he just can't wrap his mind around the idea that a woman could prefer another woman to a man— meaning, of course, *him!*"

"He's that good, is he?"

"Uncle Alec!"

Eyes twinkling, he asked, "So what do you think we ought to do about Noel?" He waited for an answer, then added, "Has anyone ever told you that you do a first-rate imitation of an astonished goldfish?"

"Why the hell did we sit here blithering when we should've been—?" She fixed him with her fiercest stare; he only smiled. "Have you been *managing* me?"

"My love, you are outrageously left-brained and never met a problem you didn't tackle with words, words, and more words. All I did was give you the chance to talk yourself out of a potential panic while we wait."

She hunched down and said nothing for a full five minutes. Alec returned to the 1938 Santa Anita Handicap. His nonchalance infuriated her, all the more so for its being calculated to produce just that effect. *Visible?* To him she was an open book—hell, she was a whole encyclopedia. *Holly Elizabeth McClure A–Z.*

"You're sulking," he observed at last.

"Does such acuity come naturally, or did you take lessons?"

"You're an uppity piece of work." He turned another page.

"Celebrated in song and story," she shot back.

The front door chimed. Every nerve in her body cringed. But that was insane, her instincts were playing her false, it was Evan finally home—

Nicky entered the living room, wordlessly handing her a note.

I HAVE LACHLAN. I WOULD RATHER HAVE YOU.

# Twenty-seven

IF DENISE HAD BEEN A moron to come here, Lachlan figured he had been doubly moronic to come with her. In fact, if he was any stupider, they'd have to water him twice a week. On the other hand, he hadn't expected to get stuck like a wad of gum to a stone bench.

Noel had left them alone in the gathering twilight. Denise was currently treating Evan to a moderately impressive prima donna tirade bordering on hysterics. Her voice ratcheted up a couple of octaves, her breathing was quick and erratic, and she was really starting to get on his nerves.

"Knock it off," he said at last. "This isn't helping anything."

"Help? There's nothing anybody can do to help! I'm going to die here—"

How he wished he could slap her. "Noel won't kill his altar."

"What the fuck do *you* know about it?" She tried to twist her way off the bench again, and failed. "If I hadn't left my purse upstairs, there are some things in my gris-gris bag that might have helped us out of this."

"So it's voodoo?"

"The term is 'Voudon,'" she retorted haughtily. "Holly hasn't taught you much, has she? There are as many different Traditions and variations as there are types of magic. I'd explain them, but you could never understand."

"We're stuck on a stone slab and there's a madman upstairs who wants my fiancée's blood for some sick ritual to accomplish God knows what—make *himself* a god, for all we know. Can you lose the attitude, please?"

"You never told her about me, did you?" she asked unexpectedly.

"No, and *you're* not gonna say anything, either," he warned.

She shrugged—movement above the waist was possible, or they wouldn't be breathing—and shook back her long blonde hair. "I got what I wanted. So did you, if you recall." With a sly, sidelong smile, she added, "She'll come for you, Lachlan. Even if Elias tries to stop her."

He stared bleakly at the candles. "I know."

BY SEVEN THE CIRCLE WAS assembled at Kate's house on Long Island. Her menagerie was banished to their various crates and cages, her furniture was cleared from the living room, and her electricity and telephone were turned off at their sources. Holly called fire to candles and a substantial hearth blaze, at which Martin and Ian warmed themselves after a long drive in the Porsche with the top down. Simon busied himself drawing the drapes. Nicky brought in and unrolled Holly's sisal rug from her Beltane celebration with Evan. Elias and Alec were in the dark foyer with Lydia, keeping her away from any shadows.

Kate's touch on her arm turned Holly's head. "You received my package?"

"Yes. Thanks. I hope it works."

"It will." She hesitated. "Your poor friend. Dead for a stupid mistake."

"That's what hurts so much," Holly murmured. Looking down, she fingered the diamond bracelet around her wrist. "She didn't have to die, dammit—"

"Well, nobody else is going to," Kate said briskly, "especially not your Evan. This Noel person seems oriented toward Satanism. That's probably the form his ritual will take, and we know how to deal with that. But from what Elias says about the sigils Lydia saw—" Kate shook her head, tendrils of blonde hair coming loose from her ponytail. "It may get pretty nasty at The Hyacinths."

". . . ALWAYS HATED THE COLD, AND Alaska's no tropical resort. After the battle at Attu, while one detail was settin' up wooden platforms for the tents on the beach, Granddad went around to the enemy foxholes. After makin' sure the dead Japanese really were dead, he took all their big, thick, fur-lined parkas back down to the beach, and that's how my grandfather ended up with the only fur-lined tent in the United States Navy." Lachlan paused. "Okay, your turn."

"I'm tired of this, and I'm tired of you." Denise's earlier hysterics had exhausted her, but he needed to keep her awake and reasonably sharp for when Noel came back. Thus they were telling stories.

"C'mon, the deal was that I tell one, then you tell one, and so forth. You're supposed to be a big-time author—you must have a couple more saved up."

Her shoulders shifted. "My back hurts, my feet are numb, and I don't feel like telling any goddamned stories."

"Suit yourself." He subsided into silence.

About five minutes later Denise suddenly said, "Once upon a time there was a woman who was captured by a lunatic who held this big ritual on Hallowe'en where he killed her and the cop she got captured with. The End. Are you happy now?"

"No wonder you're on the best-seller lists."


EVERYONE WAS SEATED AROUND THE sisal rug in a loose, informal circle. Elias looked at each of them in turn, summarizing them in his mind. Ian, the Spirit Warrior; Martin, the Physical Warrior. They would, he hoped, take care of an attack. If any came, Simon the Healer and Kate the Apothecary would tend to injuries. So far, the usual in his Circle. But tonight Lydia the Sciomancer was there to warn them of coming evil—if she could. Elias worried about her, as always, about her fragility and the inchoate terrors that could come upon her without warning. He was comforted a bit by the presence of her original protectors, Alec and Nick. But the two men had other duties tonight that might distract them from protecting Lydia. Alec, with his truth sense, was to be Elias's monitor for what was real and what wasn't; Nick the Coercer would have to focus his strength on containing Noel as far as possible. As for Holly—he didn't want her here at all. But short of knocking her out (magically, of course) and stowing her in a closet, he was stuck with her.

Kate lit incense in a small iron pot and passed it around the room. Each person cupped a hand to waft smoke near, inhaling lightly of herbs and spices.

When Holly's turn came, she sneezed. "Sorry," she mumbled.

Bradshaw cleared his throat. "This is by tradition the night when the partition between the worlds is at its weakest and most vulnerable. Samhain, All Hallows' Eve, whatever they call it in Mexico—"

"Los Dias de los Muertos," Martin supplied. "But it's the not the dead we're concerned with here; it's the living."

"I beg to differ," Alec said mildly. "It's spirits—ghosts, demons, angels."

Holly rubbed at her nose and said, "I only had one look at his bookstore, but the titles in it covered every Tradition I've ever heard of and then some. If tonight parts the veil between other worlds and this—"

"He wants the powers of a *god*?" Ian stared.

Lydia corrected him. "Gods of death and destruction. When I saw those sigils, I had an overwhelming impression of that quality of darkness."

"Charming," Elias rasped. "So we have one objective: prevent him from calling up any of these Powers."

"And if he does?" Lydia asked.

"Send them back where they came from."

"Uh-huh," Ian murmured. "One thing, Elias. What if they don't want to go?"

———

LACHLAN HAD NO IDEA WHAT time it was when Noel came back down to the cellar. All he knew was that it was pitch black but for the glowing circle of candlelight, and he was sick of listening to Denise breathe.

An oil lantern in Noel's hand cast a spuriously warm golden radiance into the shadows. The long narrow face wore a smile that hinted at a slowly building excitement, a tremulous anticipation that would intensify to a hard throb of exultation. *Like he's about to take Viagra and then pop an ecstasy,* Lachlan thought. *The guy really looks as if he's about to have the greatest fuck of his life.*

"The Spellbinder should be here soon," Noel said. "I remember her now. Not half the beauty you are, Denise," he added with mocking gallantry, "but I remember thinking at the time that there was something about her—as if she'd been around magic but didn't Work very often."

"She doesn't," Denise said bluntly. "She's dead meat."

"Except for her blood," he mused almost fondly. "Pints and pints of it—"

Lachlan forced his mouth into working order. "Didn't know you were a vampire, too."

"I'm not. Sordid condition, though I'm told the sex is phenomenal." He delved into a pocket and produced a thin length of polished wood. "Know what this is? I've had it with me since I first encountered Sammael, but I didn't know until tonight how appropriate it would be. It's carved from the wood of a holly tree." He laughed—restless, eager, fingering the wand. "I find the congruence of names both madly appropriate and more than a little funny. As if we truly were made for each other: Holly and Noel."

"Hilarious," Lachlan remarked. "Look, if it's Denise you want to screw, why don't you just do it?"

"And you can vouch for her competence, can't you? I gave her the original shape-shifting spells. I didn't know it was you she wanted, though."

"Yeah, lucky me. Why don't you just spread her and get it over with?"

"Sex is part of it," he acknowledged. "A really major orgasm gives a glimpse of eternity. Your sense of self fades, and you're alone within the Abyss. Sex and Death are intimately related."

*This guy is absolutely bug-fucking nuts. "Alone" is the* last *thing I feel when I'm with Holly.*

"Of course, most people never learn that orgasm becomes truly sublime when it's part of a ritual designed to touch the Eternal."

"Uh-huh," Evan said, with a glance at Denise. She looked bored.

"It's simple, really," Noel told him. "Death-in-Life. The ego dies in the oblivion of orgasm, and infinity is revealed—and what is Infinity but God?"

"The lesson you taught that kid, Scott Fleming," Lachlan said suddenly.

"I believe that a ritual's participants must understand its purposes. But I must say, Marshal, I didn't expect you to experience the insight in advance of the fact."

And just that simply, Lachlan knew that it wasn't Denise that Noel was planning to kill.

ELIAS BRADSHAW WAS VERY TEMPTED to feel sorry for himself. It was proving problematical to hold command of his Circle, and impress its members with the gravity of the situation, when one of them kept sneezing.

"Here," Kate said at last, tossing Holly a small silk bag of herbs. "Sniff this."

Stifling another sneeze, Holly pressed the bag against her nose, inhaled — and promptly had a coughing fit.

"As I was saying —"

Holly whooped in two huge breaths, catching everyone's attention, and failed to produce the anticipated sneeze. She sniffled, looked apologetic, and pressed the herbs against her nostrils again.

"Go on, Elias," Alec said, his face perfectly solemn. "You were about to tell us about —"

Colossal sneeze.

" — Sammael."

"So," Martin asked brightly, while Holly wiped her streaming eyes, "who's this Sammael when he's at home?"

Bradshaw resisted the impulse to grit his teeth. "The sigil Lydia drew was the most definite — the others were hesitant, as if they faded in and out before she could properly sketch them. But Sammael's is strong and firm. Some say his name means 'blind to God.' It can also be read —"

Supplementary sniffling. Nick had pity and ushered Holly out of the room, presumably to have her blow her nose.

Back in charge of things, Elias continued, "It can be read as 'venom of God,' for he carries out the Almighty's death sentences by dropping poison into the condemned's mouth from the point of his sword."

"Longfellow," Ian said suddenly. " 'The Golden Legend.' When the rabbi asks Judas why the dogs howl at night, the answer is: 'In the Rabbinical book it sayeth / The dogs howl when, with icy breath, / Great Sammael, the Angel of Death, / Takes through the town his flight.' "

"So Sammael works for God?" Simon asked.

Lydia gave a tiny shrug. "Some say he was sent to take Moses to God when the Lawgiver's days were ended. But in Qabalistic tradition, Sammael is chief of the ten Sephiroth. And they are evil. He was the highest Throne Angel before the Fall, but became a prince of demons."

Elias took over. "He can be a handsome man who loves art and helps magicians in their rituals, and he can be a twelve-winged serpent who destroys the solar system. Revelation, Chapter Twelve."

"Angel and demon, good and evil," Kate mused. "He's the dichotomy of how people feel about death. It can come as a welcome release from suffering, an end to earthly life that brings union with the Eternal. Or it can be the destroyer, carrying the poisoned sword."

"Or both," Simon added. "Friend and enemy, simultaneously anticipated and dreaded. But it seems to me that the question is whether or not this Sammael does or doesn't work for Jehovah."

"Exactly," said Martin. "If Sammael is the one Noel plans to call on, how do we treat him? Friend, enemy, or neutral?"

"I don't plan to let it get that far," Elias informed him.

"THAT WHICH IS ETERNAL," Noel said as he busied himself arranging four big three-legged iron pots, presumably for incense, "is not truly alive as we understand life—because life ends in death. The Eternal exists beyond Time, within Chaos, the Abyss of the Collective Unconscious. It's where monsters and angels and demons live. Where God lives. Master Chaos, and the primordial energies are yours."

"Swell," Lachlan muttered. The guy talked almost as much as Holly when she was on a tear.

Denise roused slightly. "Do you know what you'll be calling down?"

"Thinking of your Voudon practices?" Noel smiled over his shoulder. "The Summoner possessed by that which has been Summoned?"

"Sounds like fun," Lachlan said.

"I hear scorn in your voice, Marshal. You think power is evil." He turned from a window. "But it's why we both want the Spellbinder. Her power."

He was careful to keep the muscles of his face still, careful to meet Noel's gaze calmly. But he was startled to realize that in a way it was true—though the word Lachlan would have used was "strength". Same thing as "power"?

"Hers is the rarest and most valuable of all. I wonder, does her blood smell different to the truly perceptive? Am I the only one who can sense it?" He shrugged, not really expecting an answer. "But we were discussing power," he went on, distributing incense into the burners, and setting each alight without benefit of matches. "In itself, it's neutral, neither good nor evil. There is no moral nuance. It is simply Power."

Lachlan arched a brow. "I'm sure you know the old one about corruption."

"Interesting theological point. God has absolute power—is God absolutely corrupted? You're one of the ignorant masses after all. You fear power. And you really shouldn't. All the images that come down to us—all the totems, if you will, the wolf, the bear, the buffalo, the lion, and so on—they're fearsome and fascinating at the same time. We watch them so avidly—when we're safe from them, when they're behind bars in zoos. Do you know why they beguile us? Because our ancestors knew that their kind of strength was essential to survival. The more powerful the magical image—the archetype—the more vigorous the magical result."

Denise spoke up again, asking acidly, "And you're going to become—what? Bambi? Thumper? No, wait, I know—Lassie."

Noel regarded Lachlan for a long moment. "You actually went to bed with her?"

Evan gave a shrug. "She didn't say much. I guess she was too busy keeping her face on."

"THANKS, UNCLE NICKY," HOLLY SAID, swabbing her nose with a dampened paper towel. "I'll be okay now."

He leaned against the kitchen sink, looking pensive. "What set you off?"

"I only sneeze like this—oh, shit, here comes another one—"

Nick retrieved and held out the box of tissues swiped from the hall bathroom. "Careful, you'll rub your nose raw," he said. "You've had fits like this before?"

"Twice. Denise's apartment and Noel's bookstore. It's the patchouli. Kate was telling me what she used tonight, and it's supposed to be protective. But try telling that to my sinuses." After blowing her nose yet again, she wadded tissues and towel to throw in the garbage. "I'm going to the little girls' room. Go on back—Elias is probably being eloquent about demons or something."

She headed for the bathroom, bringing a candle with her, went inside, and stared at herself in the mirror. Her nose *was* red, and it *did* itch. There were dark circles under her eyes, freckles stained her pallor, and in sum she looked like crap.

After washing her face, she extinguished the candle before opening the door. Halfway down the hall was the coat closet. Holly kept to the plain blue runner extending the length of the hall, boot heels silent on the rug. She had no fear that the closet hinges would squeak; she'd been careful to listen earlier when putting away her purse and coat. Both items were in her hands within moments.

The kitchen was still dimly lit by a few plump, fragrant candles. She tiptoed, barely breathing, and got as far as the back door before a soft voice said, "You devious little shit."

She spun to find Nicky watching her, candleflames striking gold and silver from his dark blond hair. "Yeah? And who'd I learn it from?"

"Don't blame us for your stupid impulses."

"Gonna rat me out?" she challenged.

A small enigmatic smile twitched his mouth. "I'll get my coat."


"THE ARCHETYPES WERE SEEN AS evil," Noel explained, "because those who called on them couldn't control them. Primeval powers, when let loose, terrify those who don't understand." From the rickety table he took a black glass bowl. This he placed carefully on the floor and filled from a plastic bag of—birdseed?

Lachlan nodded, just exactly as if he wasn't convinced that Noel was indeed absolutely bug-fucking nuts. "But if you protect yourself, and if you're careful, the power can be used."

He threw Lachlan a great big smile of approval on his way to getting a second black bowl. Enough incense had burned by now to produce a slithering gray cloud that hovered about four feet off the floor; he paused to cup some smoke in his hand and inhale deeply. "Do you know how hard it's been ridding myself of millions of years of fear generated by the superstitions of lesser minds? Minds that could never understand the power of death, of sex, of anything!"

"Yeah," Denise jeered, "the collective unconscious can be a bitch."

"You ought to know," he shot back, moving into the far darkness. There was a spitting sound of water from a long-unused spigot as he went on, "You use it in your book—you prey on your readers! Appealing to the primal terrors of the cataleptic masses—you confirm and justify all their fears. You're a parasite, Denise."

There was more in this line, but Lachlan tuned him out and sought a few minutes of escapist sanity. All the reading he'd done when Holly had first told him she was a Witch rattled in his head like marbles in a jar. Traditions, techniques, meanings, methods—none of it coalesced into a protocol he could deal with. In a way, it was kind of like all the laws he'd had to study: as an officer in the NYPD, he'd had a certain mind-set that changed when he became a United States Marshal. Legal minutiae, procedures, jurisdictions, rules and regulations . . .

Didn't it all boil down to Right and Wrong? And here, in this cellar, with his ass plastered to a stone bench, didn't it all end up as Good and Evil? In spite of what Noel said about interpreting power as evil because it was frightening, wasn't there wisdom in that fear? After all, look at how power was used: death and destruction and suffering.

Evan wasn't fool enough to believe himself infallible on the side of Right in his job. He had done things that, while not exactly Wrong, could most charitably be called unscrupulous. Nor was he about to delude himself that he was Good and Noel was Evil. But the impetus behind his choice of career—that he trusted himself to do the work—held true here as well. He believed in his own knowledge, instincts, ethics, and experience. As he thought this, an image flirted with the edges of his vision: himself, the Knight in Tarnished Armor, striding with a blazing sword and a shield bearing the Lachlan crest through a field of purple hyacinths.

*Uh-oh.*

Though he coughed to clear his lungs, the incense was already in his blood, inside his head.

"—open a vein and bleed all over your spells for you?" Denise was saying.

Lachlan was distracted from Noel's answer by the sudden and vivid mental picture of blood dripping from Holly's throat. He shook his head violently.

"—she is the key to achieving my final goal." Noel's voice sounded funny, as if gloved fingers were flicking at the strings inside a piano. "It'll be incredible!"

Thunk, plink, twang. "'Final goal'?" he asked, his tongue thick in his mouth.

"Don't you get it?" Denise's voice was weird, too—not the sound of it, but the little droplets that drifted out of her mouth, like slow-motion spit. It wasn't spit. It was poison, and he knew it, and tried to angle away from her. "All this shit about power and death and sex is all because he can't get it up."

Noel burst out laughing. "Isn't she priceless?"

In between trying to avoid toxic dewdrops and trying to make sense of plopping and clunking words, Evan told himself that nobody would go to this much trouble just for an orgasm. Then he tensed as Noel reached into a pocket and brought out a folded penknife.

"I need a little sample, Marshal," the man said almost apologetically. Almost. "One mixture of herbs requires a special bonding agent." He stepped behind the bench, behind the semicircle of candles, and leaned close to Evan.

Who couldn't move, even as the familiar surge of adrenaline trembled in his muscles and cleared his head some. The three-inch blade that appeared before his nose looked wicked shining sharp. "I thought—I thought you needed a ceremonial blade," he managed. His heart raced, providing nicely distended veins in his arm or neck or wherever Noel planned to stick a spigot.

"Not all of us make our implements obvious." He tucked a finger beneath the high neck of Lachlan's sweater, drawing it down, stroking skin. Lachlan braced for sudden piercing pain. Instead there was a dull chime of metal on stone as the blade clattered from its casing to the floor.

"Oops," Denise said.

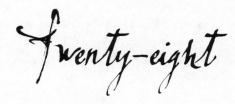

# Twenty-eight

"HAVE YOU ANY IDEA WHERE you're going?" Nick asked as they crept outside toward the BMW. "Failing that, have you a plan?" Stony silence. "Ah, well. Familiar enough. I'll drive."

"Familiar?" she echoed as they got into the car.

"Of course. Alec never plans anything either." He started the engine and pulled quickly out of the driveway, narrowly missing Elias's Lincoln.

Holly stretched out her legs; the passenger's side didn't have a memory, except of the last time a certain long-limbed marshal was in the car. "Why didn't you tell on me?"

"Well, I could say it's because they'll come after us the instant they hear the engine, anyway," he said, giving her a sidelong smile. "But in truth, it's because this *is* familiar. I've been in your position, and I've done the same thing."

Holly nodded slowly. "It's not . . . *endurable*, you know? I mean, Elias getting all studded up like Special Ops heading for Tikrit to find Saddam. I've been playing the what-will-Noel-anticipate game and it's driving me crazy. Will he expect the Circle, will he expect just me, will he expect us to expect him to expect whatever—?"

"—and you end up thinking 'Oh, the hell with it,'" he finished for her. "So you're going to give him what he wants. Your blood."

"Yeah." She mimed pricking a finger and held it up. "Come 'n' get it, honey. I brought me a large-bore needle."

"Distracting him, while I do something scathingly brilliant to save the day— not to mention Marshal Lachlan." He sighed quietly. "If this were one of your novels, I'd say let's go for it. But you can't script this, Holly. You can't plot everyone's moves."

"Maybe not," she admitted, "but I can make some good guesses. Denise will be looking out for Denise, end of story. The best thing would be to remove her as quickly as possible so she doesn't screw up anything else."

"Agreed. Evan, on the other hand, will be looking out for you. So it would behoove us to get him out, too."

"And by that time Elias and the cavalry will arrive to take care of Noel. So we really don't have to worry about *him* at all."

He cast her a sideways glance. "Darling girl, if you believe that—"

"Yeah," she replied glumly. "I know."


"*DAMN* THAT WOMAN!"

"And that sneaky little Rom," Alec added to Elias's outburst. "Come on," he said, heading for the hall closet. "Nick and Holly both drive like maniacs. We'd better hurry."

"I won't rush anyone into this. We have to be ready. If they're determined to go haring off on their own—"

Shouldering into his overcoat, Alec asked, "Are you telling me you'd allow that much risk to your Spellbinder? And let's not even mention my partner."

"One of the hundreds of things you don't yet know about Sammael is that like all manifestations he's attracted to specific things. He likes—"

"I thought the idea was to keep him away, not Summon him with arcane associatives."

"—certain woods," Bradshaw continued grimly. "Primarily oak and holly."

"You're reaching." Alec started for the front door. "It's just her *name*, Elias. And I don't care if he's attracted to caramel lattés. You can catch up when you've talked it into the ground."

"You're not leaving. What you don't know can kill any or all of us."

All the smooth cream charm of the man turned to hydrochloric acid. "I know Nicholas Orlov and I know Holly McClure. That's enough for me."


"HOW FAR IS IT?" Holly asked, peering through the windshield into the night.

"Not very."

"That's helpful."

"Mmm."

"Don't get lost, the way Ian did on the way back this evening."

"I won't."

"I know he was upset and all—what with Noel coercing him into leaving with that note—which reminds me, do you think your Come-Hither will work on Noel?"

"Possibly."

"Nicky, *talk* to me!"

"Lovely weather for October." When she growled, a tiny smile crooked one corner of his mouth. "Very well. I'm curious about something. You never even turned your head to look when we passed the World Trade Center location tonight."

"What's *that* got to do with anything?"

"I was just wondering. After all, looking is compulsory. As if we're all hoping it was all a nightmare, and the Towers are still standing."

"And the fear and anger and grief come back all over again when we see that they aren't. I don't like reminders of failure. Especially not tonight."

A surprised snort escaped him. "'Failure'? In what way?"

"Why can't we ever do anything useful?" she burst out. "Why can't whichever of us who can look into the future see the important things, the catastrophic things?"

"Why aren't any of us omniscient? Because then, my dearest, we'd be gods."

"Now comes the oration about how we're only human, and people not like us don't understand that, and that's why we hide. Heard it all before, Nicky."

"While obviously paying no attention whatsoever. Why did none of us foresee 9/11? The answer might be that we weren't looking. Maybe we wouldn't have believed it if we saw. Who *would* have believed? Or perhaps the answer is that anything so unspeakably evil—call it a miasma surrounding it, so that anyone even glimpsing it must needs look away or be infected by that evil."

"You believe that?"

He was quiet for a time. Then: "I believe in Creation."

"Creation," she echoed, watching his face.

"Yes. We come closest to Deity when we create—whether it's a work of art, a friendship, a baby, a marriage, a satisfying meal, laughter, the smile on the face of a child." He broke off with a shrug. "Don't most of us venerate, in one form or another, the Creator of All? Something results from a creative act. Destruction is just the opposite. An emptiness is left, most obviously on the skyline, most terribly in people's hearts."

"The Eagles," she said suddenly. "'There's a hole in the world tonight—'"

"But with what do we fill the void? More hatred? More destruction?" He shook his head. "That's not what we're here for."

"*Why*, then?" she cried. "What's the point? So I create something, I write a book—big fucking deal!"

"That book is read by thousands, maybe millions, the vast majority of whom will learn something, see something differently, be inspired to go looking for more information, or simply have a good time during the hours they spend reading. You add to people's lives. What you create touches them in some way."

"That's not why I write, Nicky," she protested.

"I know. But it's the result you end up with all the same."

"That still doesn't answer my question—"

"Why do we never do anything useful?" When she nodded, he gave a quiet sigh. "We are what we are, Holly. Society labels us Witches for convenience' sake, just the way it pigeonholes everyone. Gay or straight, able-bodied or handicapped, religious or atheist, patriot or traitor—most of the categories are opposites, and that's for convenience' sake, too. We subscribe to it because we're part of society. Us, the Witches—and Them, the Normals. But why should any group hold more responsibility than any other?"

"Responsi—"

"That's what you're getting at, whether you realize it or not. Because of our magic, do we have a greater responsibility? Should any of us have foreseen—?"

"People with gifts, whatever they are, have an obligation to use them."

"Ah, but who decides how those gifts ought to be used? The state-run 'from each according to his abilities' tactic has been tried, and it didn't work. Millions died in the purges and gulags before it was finally admitted that it didn't work."

"So we all have to make the choices and decisions for ourselves?"

"Yes. We do. So," he went on, slowing the car and pulling it to the side of the road, "is any individual's responsibility to humankind greater than any other individual's? No."

"It's the Good Samaritan story," Holly blurted. "The man categorized by everyone as outcast was the only one who helped. He recognized his obligation."

"Thereby saving a life, which is creation of a sort."

"But he did something more," she insisted. "What he created was a connection—the old Chinese saying that if you save a life, you're responsible for it."

"It's better to be responsible for a life saved than for a life destroyed." Switching off the engine, he said, "And now to create a diversion, so we can get your marshal and that silly woman out of this mess. Do you know she actually had the impudence to flirt with my Alyosha?"


ALEC SINGLETON HAD HOT-WIRED THE Lincoln and was gone before Elias had even fully explained to the others that Holly and Nicholas had left. What remained of his Circle—Kate, Ian, Martin, Simon, and Lydia—readied themselves with renewed determination for what Elias now knew would be a battle royal. The six of them got into Kate's SUV and Martin's Porsche for the drive to The Hyacinths, uneventful but for Martin's missing a turn. Kate slowed, waiting for the Porsche to catch up again, and as Elias squinted into the side-view mirror he began to swear under his breath.

"Problem?" Simon asked from the backseat.

"Of course not," he growled. "Life is wonderful. Everything's just peachy. Kate, pull over."

She did so, mystified, parking just beyond a streetlamp. Elias jumped down and stalked over to a white Mercedes that rolled to a sedate halt in the gravel beside the road. From the driver's side emerged a tall, distinguished, silver-haired gentleman who approached Elias with both hands outstretched like Christ beckoning the little children to come unto him.

"Reverend, what the hell are *you* doing here?"

"THIS IS QUITE POSSIBLY THE most pretentious house I've ever seen," Holly commented as she and Nick walked through wet grass toward The Hyacinths. The place was minimally lit by outdoor floodlights that accented a turret here, a tower there, a goodly section of walls, and most of the courtyard.

"Snob," Nick accused. "You just naturally incline toward white columns, Spanish moss, and verandahs."

"I've been known to hanker after a castle or two in my day. D'you think it has secret staircases and hidden passages and everything?"

"Restrain yourself, child. Let me concentrate."

They circled the house. Occasionally Nick stopped to stare up at a turret or a spire, then shake his head. Apart from the sporadic floodlights there was no illumination, and this place needed lamps glowing from every window or risk major spookiness. The breeze, faintly smelling of the nearby ocean, got colder. Holly hunched her shoulders inside her heavy wool coat, balled her fists inside her pockets, and wished she'd brought gloves.

They were almost back at the front, not having found any useful points of entry, when her sinuses began to itch. Nick turned suddenly, caught her rubbing her nose, and grinned in the gloom.

"Sure you don't have some Southern bloodhound in your ancestry?"

"What?"

"Follow your nose."

WITH A DRAWLING INDIFFERENCE DISTINCTLY at odds with his mood, Lachlan said, "Guess you'll have to wait for the Spellbinder's blood."

"Shut up," Noel ordered. "Why did this happen? This isn't supposed to happen."

Denise was staring at Lachlan, eyes wide with speculation. Her look made him antsy, a feeling aggravated by the reeking incense that wisped around the cellar like an inversion layer of smog. Noel's hand came back around within sight, naked blade gripped between forefinger and thumb. Lachlan drew away as far as he could. It wasn't far. But the movement was enough to jostle Noel's arm, and the steel glided harmlessly across skin.

Lachlan smelled the man's breath as he hissed his exasperation, and though not exactly foul, neither was it minty-fresh. It just smelled weird. Noel dug his fingers deep into Evan's hair, dragging his head back and to the side, exposing his neck like a Mithras bull's for sacrificial slaughter. From this angle Noel's face was visible: lips stiff with annoyance, pinpoint pupils centered in the arctic blue of his eyes. So he *had* taken something. Lachlan wondered what it was.

"Third time's the charm?" Denise asked sweetly.

Noel was so startled that he dropped the blade. Its point caught in a link of the chain around Lachlan's neck. He plucked it free and tugged at the necklace. Lachlan felt the medal just below his breastbone move fractionally and then stop as if snagged on chest hair. Which was ridiculous, because he didn't have much chest hair. Noel worked a finger beneath the chain at Evan's collarbone, pulling. The medal stayed where it was.

"What the fuck is that?" he demanded, moving back.

As it had been earlier when they'd shaken hands, when Noel had slapped his back, when he had touched him the first time to try for his blood, the lack of him was an acute relief. Evan rolled his head, trying to ease the muscles.

"The necklace." The hands were back, feeling through his sweater. "Just above the diaphragm," Noel muttered. The knife sliced through luxurious cashmere, from the neck halfway to Lachlan's waist. "This is what I sensed earlier. *She* gave you this, didn't she? There's magic all over it."

"St. Michael," he offered, trying to sound helpful. Pretty sure he sounded drunk. He *felt* drunk. "Patron of law enforcement. It's from Rome—it's even been blessed by the Pope." He wished he could cross himself, just to see the reaction.

"I said *magic,* not religious trickery! I can smell her blood! When did she give you this? What does it do?"

"Whaddya mean?"

Denise giggled. "Can't you feel it? No, course you can't." She tilted her head around to smile mockery at Noel. He backhanded her. She cried out, blood gushing from her nose.

"That make you feel like a real man?" Lachlan snarled furiously. "You gotta knock a woman around before you can get it up?"

All at once Noel darted from behind the bench. "What's that?"

"What's what? I didn't hear anything. Did you hear something?" Lachlan kept talking to cover up any noise Noel might actually have heard. The flush of anger seemed to have cleared his head again—he'd have to remember that adrenaline could be very useful. "Might be a deer or the wind or somethin'—"

"Shut up! There's someone outside." Noel cocked his head, listening intently.

This time Evan heard it, too: one ordinary, everyday sneeze.

WHAT REVEREND FLEMING WAS DOING there did not enter into his explanation of how he had arrived. Kate's house being at the end of a cul-de-sac, it had been simplicity itself to wait on the main street, unobserved, for cars to emerge. Holly's black BMW had excited conjecture, but no other cars had followed. Then had come Bradshaw's Lincoln, but without Bradshaw inside it; the Reverend had almost followed, but only a few minutes later the SUV and the Porsche left within moments of each other, making the same turn as the first two cars. So he'd set off in pursuit.

Simon assumed a harmless, genial, absentminded professor demeanor. "Reverend, I sympathize with your loss. But I can't understand why you'd be following any of us at all. We're just going out to dinner."

"I've been following Judge Bradshaw, or having him followed, ever since I heard about the death of his paramour."

Elias growled low in his throat. Simon hastily asked, "To what purpose? What makes you think — ?"

"Please, sir, spare me the prevarications." The hand wearing a Yale Divinity School ring waved away Simon's protestation like a bothersome insect. "I know where you're going tonight, and it isn't to a restaurant. You are heading for The Hyacinths, and on the night of Hallowe'en."

Now, Elias thought, they would be treated to a tirade on the Fundamentalist Christian condemnation thereof. "I don't have time for this," he snapped. "Reverend, I strongly advise you to go home and minister to your flock—among which I am *not* to be counted. Simon, Kate, get back in the car. We're out of here."

"Please."

Bradshaw turned slightly, looking at the man over his shoulder. "'Please'?"

"It is not a word I use often," the Reverend admitted. "But I want to know who murdered my son. I want—I *need*—to see his killer brought to justice. And so I say to you—please."

Kate threw Elias a speculative glance, then moved toward the preacher, the lone streetlight shining on the pale blonde of her loosened hair. "I don't think you understand," she said gently. "Two people are held hostage. We can't call in the police—this man would escape them. He is beyond the reach of legal authorities."

Fleming was silent for a moment. Then: "You intend to kill him."

The others looked at Bradshaw or looked away. As well they ought, he told himself; he was, after all, Magistrate. The decision was his.

"You must not kill him," insisted the Reverend. "You would be no better than he is—and his soul would burn forever in Hell."

"This is not your concern," Bradshaw began.

"Every life is precious!"

"I know where you're going with this, and you won't get there with me marching in lockstep alongside," Elias snapped. "Life is what we do with it — and the man is a murderer. He killed your son and my Susannah, and—"

"You must not!" the Reverend thundered. "In the courtroom they address you as 'Your Honor.' As a man of honor, if not a man of God, you must not kill him! I know I can't persuade you with Holy Writ—"

"Please don't quote John Donne," he interrupted wearily. "I can't see any way that this man's death would diminish me or anyone else. The bell can toll all night long — I'll pull the rope."

"I hate him, too, Judge Bradshaw. But his death would indeed diminish me, for I would be left with my hate. Until I can look him in the eye and forgive him, and know that *he* knows of my forgiveness—"

"Does he want it? Would he accept it? Don't make me laugh!"

"He has to *know* that I forgive what he did to my son! In that is his hope of salvation—and mine. And yours, whether you want to admit it or not! We diminish ourselves with hate and exalt ourselves with forgiveness, with love, with joy—"

*"Whatever happened to joy?"*

Bradshaw turned away from him, not wanting him to see how his use of that word, Susannah's word, shook him. "This isn't your pulpit, Reverend. Save it for next Sunday." He was about to impress upon all of them once again that there was no time for any of this, when a new arrival made Elias's day an unqualified triumph. A big green Jeep Cherokee with a blinking red dashboard light appeared around a bend in the road, slowed, passed them, turned, and finally came to a stop with its nose two inches from the white Cadillac's grille.

From the Jeep slid a slim dark woman wearing jeans and a brown leather jacket. "Nice try, Your Honor," said Deputy Marshal Leah Towsley. "But the next time you throw a party, pick someplace warmer."

"HERE," HOLLY SAID. "It's strongest right here." She sneezed.

She and Nick had been around the mansion once again, peering in dark windows when they dared, the floodlights showing them the house had been stripped of furniture. Twice now she'd buried her nose in her woolen sleeve to smother a sneeze. Now they paused at the far end of the house, where the servants' hall and kitchen would have been in bygone days. Steps led down to a service door; nearby there was an iron drawer where coal had been delivered a century or so ago. Next to this was a series of arched windows draped by black cloth and locked tight.

"Now what?" She squinted at Nicky in the darkness, absently rubbing her irritated nose.

"Now I find out if I can bring him out here." Treading lightly down the stairs, he tried the service door. "Marvelous. It's unlocked, but I can't open it. And no, it isn't stuck by paint or rust or anything else." Beckoning her down the steps with one hand while the other delved into a pants pocket, he said, "My dear, I'm going to have to ask you for a little blood. Do you mind?"

"Of course not. What for?" Holly dug in her coat pocket for needle and alcohol swabs.

"I still have that turquoise from all those years ago." He held it up, the nearby floodlight glancing off the opaque blue—and several other stones, she saw with surprise. The bloodstone-and-carnelian token Lulah had given Alec, a lump of raw amethyst, and a ragged little branch of pink coral all depended from a short silver chain. Nick took the needle to hold while she opened a sterilizing pad and swiped it across her thumb. "These have proved very useful, one way and another."

"Which do you want, Spellbinder? Or maybe all of them?"

"Well, I don't know that we'll have much use for the bloodstone's protection against scorpions and gallstones, but I would like to open this door." He chuckled softly. "Then again, the part about strengthening the sense of smell might be hazardous to your poor nose. Pity one can't pick and choose what one unleashes."

From the brick walkway above them Alec Singleton said, "I, on the other hand, am perfectly capable of picking you both up and choosing to haul your asses out of here."

"*Mi a kurva'k fassza't keresel itt?*" Nicholas exclaimed.

Alec descended the steps. "What the fuck I'm doing here is pretty much what the fuck *you're* doing here. I'd expect dim-witted behavior from Holly, but I thought *you* of all people would know better than to—"

"Oh, shut up, Alyosha," Nick said. "I assume Elias and the rest are hot on your heels. Let's get this done."

Taking the needle from Nick, Holly pricked her thumb and squeezed up a drop of blood. "All of them, or just the bloodstone? And I'm sure there's a pun in there somewhere, but I'm not inclined to go looking for it right now."

"You shut up, too," Nick admonished. "All the stones. We'll divvy them up." When the five stones were blooded, he unlatched the chain and let them slide into his palm. "Alyosha, take the coral and the turquoise. I'm keeping the bloodstone and carnelian. Which leaves the amethyst for you, Holly—appropriate, it's February's birthstone."

"It'd do more good protecting one of you," she argued.

*"Az Istenért!"* he snarled. "Take it!"

She did, meekly, knowing that when he spoke Hungarian—or was that Rom?—more than usual, things were grim. She clenched her fingers around the amethyst for a moment before putting it in her pants pocket.

"Now," Nick said, "we begin." He faced the door, holding the carnelian and bloodstone in his left hand. With his right he drew a pattern in the air, while under his breath he muttered a few syllables. Hinges creaked, wood splintered, and the door flung itself open to slam back against the interior wall.

"Not bad," Alec remarked.

"You're welcome," Holly replied, scratching her nose in earnest. "Can we get on with this before I need a respirator?"


EVAN FELT A HOLLOW TINGLING begin in his chest, more or less like the sensation he sometimes got when a lure-and-lasso was about to get sticky. He slanted a look at Denise. "How's your nose?"

"Hurts." Denise sniffled and tilted her head back. "I think it's stopped bleeding, though."

"You're getting a black eye."

"Wouldn't be the first time."

"I'm sorry I couldn't stop him." He surprised himself by meaning it. A little, anyway.

*"Que vous êtes gallant, Monsieur le Mareschal.* I've been hit harder. Bet you have, too."

Lachlan shrugged. "He's been gone awhile. Maybe he got lost."

"Or maybe Holly really is here." She slanted a glance at him. "What a wound to your machismo—a woman riding to your rescue."

Lachlan only smiled. The expression felt a little wobbly on his face, as if the signals to his nerves were off-kilter. He tried to squirm, imagining that he might be stuck a little less adamantly to the bench. No such luck. After a moment's silence he offered, "What time do you think it is?"

"Maybe midnight, maybe not. Like it matters."

She was neither hysterical nor particularly loopy; Noel's fist in her face had unleashed some adrenaline in her, too. Lachlan reasoned that he could gauge how loaded they both were if he kept her talking. Not that he was terribly interested in anything she might say. "The bit about the animals was kinda weird. You do a lot of that with Voudon?"

"There are prototypes—"

"Archetypes," he corrected. Jeeze, he was getting as pedantic as Holly.

"Stereotypes, genotypes, typographical errors, what-the-fuck-ever. I never expected a cop to be such an intellect—oh, but wait, you hang out with the Professor, right? She give you a pop quiz now and then, just to make sure you're paying attention when she lectures?"

This didn't deserve a comeback—especially as he'd just been thinking more or less the same thing—so Lachlan let his attention stray to the cellar. Before hurtling up the stairs, Noel had waved a hand to light every candle in the place, and the heat of the flames added to the stink of incense was stifling. The light showed him something he hadn't noticed until now: black statues of birds, none more than a few inches high. Some stood with outspread wings, and others hunkered down like pissed-off parakeets. Idly he began to count them, and wondered what significance attached to the number sixteen. Song lyrics began to drift around in his brain: sixteen candles, sixteen tons and whaddya get, sweet little sixteen—

Suddenly Denise said, "At Beltane last year, he killed Scott Fleming right at the moment of orgasm."

"The 'sex and death' thing." With a sigh and a shake of his head, Lachlan said, "Y'know, I really don't *believe* this guy."

"Be better if you did. Something else I remember from Beltane. He thinks it's harder to hex somebody who believes, because he's protecting himself."

"Watching his step," Evan interpreted. "Taking no chances."

"Somebody who doesn't believe, he's easier. He shoves any instinctive fear deep inside where it can fester and work against him."

"Leaves him open to the workings of the curse," he interpreted.

"Very good, Marshal. There may be hope for you yet."

But fear wasn't something that could invade from outside. It was already there. You could choose to control it, and not to let it be used against you. Or use it yourself. Anger wasn't the only emotion that triggered adrenaline.

Suddenly the house spasmed around them, stone grinding on stone. Evan watched plaster dust sift down through the smog layer of incense smoke, and realized that a nice, healthy surge of his own fight-or-flight chemicals wasn't going to be all that difficult to accomplish.

BRADSHAW PACED TO THE BROKEN white line, seething. Somehow, this was Holly's fault. He wasn't sure quite what her responsibility was, but he was certain it would all come down to her in the end. Just his luck: the only Magistrate to have a genuine Spellbinder on call, and she'd caused him more trouble in the scant two years he'd known her than anybody else in his entire life.

Three Witches of his Circle stood beside a country road arguing with a fundamentalist reverend. Two Witches had escaped him completely and were doing who-knew-what to free a woman he detested and a U.S. Marshal he didn't much like, either. Two more Witches were gallivanting around Long Island in a Porsche convertible, lost. His Spellbinder was behaving like a jackass, as usual. And now his very own United States Deputy Marshal had arrived, which put the cherry atop the icing on the cake.

Hell of a Hallowe'en.

"This is ludicrous," he muttered. And, for the first time in a very long time, he cast the kind of spell that had gotten quite a few ancestors—who also should have known better—into interesting predicaments. With both hands he built a precise framework of Power around everyone and everything before him. With the strength of a fine, disciplined mind he constructed lattices linking Kate, Simon, Lydia, and Reverend Fleming into an edifice of absolute stillness and absolute silence.

Turning, he fixed his gaze on Leah Towsley, who alone of them all could still move. In fact, she *had* moved. Her jaw had dropped.

"We're leaving," Elias told her. "Now."

She looked at the four people beyond him, blinked, faced him again, all but saluted, and got back into her Jeep. Bradshaw swung up into the passenger's seat as she gunned the engine.

"Not a single question," he warned. "Not one. Drive where I tell you, Marshal."

"Absolutely, Your Honor."

Finally, he thought, a woman who did what he told her to.

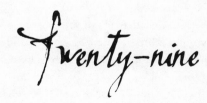

# Twenty-nine

ALEXANDER SINGLETON SURVEYED THE WRECKAGE of the stone steps and the kitchen's outer wall. Nick's emphatic opening of the door had been presaged by an ominous rumbling; Alec had barely hauled his partner and Holly up the steps in time. Now, waving a hand to clear away the dust that had Holly sneezing in earnest, he cast a sour look at his partner.

"That wasn't exactly what I had in mind."

"High-octane blood. But perhaps we'd better do this from outside."

"Aw, gee—ya think?" Holly asked, rubbing her nose.

"What I think is that we probably got Noel's attention."

"Well, then, why don't you continue your little home improvement project, and I'll go see what Evan's up to?"

"Nothing doing, girl," Alec ordered. "You stay with us until Noel appears and we've dealt with him. Then you can rush to the rescue."

Though she looked rebellious, she followed the two men around back, where a glassed-in octagonal garden room protruded onto the lawn.

"Now *that*," Nick mused, "would make a perfectly lovely crash."

"Musical, even," Holly agreed a bit ruthlessly.

"Restrain yourselves," Alec advised. Speculative sidelong glances from two pairs of blue eyes ought to have warned him, but he couldn't keep from catching his breath on a curse when the stonework traceries between windows rasped, shuddered, and collapsed, the glass shattering with them.

Even Nick took a few startled steps back, but the grin he turned on Alec made him look about twelve years old. "No wonder you never let me play with the bloodstone. It's fun!"

"Yeah, no wonder I never let you play with it," he retorted, ducking reflexively as more splintered panes tinkled down from twisted and sagging framework. "We can't go around demolishing things at random. There's such a thing as load-bearing walls. You're the only one with protection, Nick."

"Spoilsport. Let's see if I can coerce him out into the open." But a few moments later Nick shook his head in frustration. "I can't read him. There's something between him and the rest of the world, some sort of personal murk."

Holly gave him a little smile Alec didn't understand, and said, "I'm told that happens sometimes. Don't push it. When he comes out of hiding, and you can actually see him—"

"Maybe it's not him," Nick mused. "Maybe it's this place. More than one murder was done here. It's as if the deaths were absorbed by the stones, and pulling them apart has set free some kind of—I don't know, *corruption*."

"He can't keep ignoring us," said Holly. "Sooner or later he'll have to come out and see what's going on. Nicky, do your thing again."

They started around the house once more, striding through damp grass, searching for something else to demolish. "How about that turret hanging off the second floor?" Nick asked.

Standing well back from the round projecting tower, Alec scrutinized it, judged it safe to demolish, and nodded to his partner. Nick gripped carnelian and bloodstone, muttered a few words, grimaced with effort. The turret shivered, stone dust sifting, trickling, and finally pouring from loosened joints. With a scraping groan, the tower separated from the house and crashed to the ground.

"I do hope their insurance is paid up," Nick remarked. "What will they attribute this to? Termites? No, it's mostly stone. How about a freak hurricane?"

"Deeply as *I* worship and adore you, *Miklóshka*," Alec grinned, "I doubt you qualify as an act of God. My own hope is that The Hyacinths isn't on the National Register of Historic Eccentricities or something else that'll get you into trouble."

"Me?!"

As they walked shoulder to shoulder, scanning for more targets, Alec said, "One more crash, and then try to suss him out again, okay? Holly—"

But when he looked around for her, she was gone.

---

*Those fingers in my hair, that sly come-hither stare.*
*That strips my conscience bare—it's witchcraft.*

At first Lachlan thought he was hallucinating again. Then he realized that somebody really was singing. Not Denise; the song came from the stairwell. Peering through the thick mists of incense, he blinked several times as the hazy image of a gigantic purple hyacinth flower swayed languidly about three feet in front of his face. Yeah, he was hallucinating.

He was positive of it when Holly sauntered into view on the stairs as if this were a cocktail party. Lachlan had seen her do this a dozen times: take a casual step, pause as she scanned the environs, and then decide whether or not there was anyone here worth talking to. This time the blue eyes considered the candles, bird statuary, bowls, incense burners, stone bench, Denise, and finally Lachlan himself. A little smile touched her lips, and her heeled boots clicked softly on the flagstones as she took another two steps down.

"Hi, darlin'," she greeted him.

"Hi, yourself," he replied. Delusion or not, it sure was nice to see her.

She scratched her nose, and all at once gave a ferocious sneeze that sent her stumbling, grabbing for the wall, and falling hard down the last two stairs to her knees, swearing vilely the whole time.

Denise stirred vaguely beside him. "The Ego," she announced, "has landed."

Holly sat on the bottom step, sprawling long legs, and scrubbed at her nose with her fist. The crown of her head was just below the level of smoke. She peered at Evan, then at the incense burners all around the room. A gesture incinerated every remaining speck of incense, four huge gouts of flame erupting in a gush of heat that brought sweat to Lachlan's face and bare chest. An instant later, nothing was left but cinders and a smell of scorching.

"Well, fuck a duck, as they say in Oregon," she muttered. "You okay, Evan?"

"Sure. How 'bout you?"

"Oh, just great. What's with her?" She nodded at Denise.

He turned his head, and found that Denise was swaying lightly back and forth, as far as the spell would allow, a singularly vacant expression on her face. The smeared blood from her nose had dried, giving her a kind of second mouth above the first one. It wasn't especially attractive. "Busted nose, maybe. He got a little pissed off."

"Is there some reason you two are sitting there like lumps on a log?"

"Yep." He would have said more, but the flower was back—hugely purple, dripping black pearls of dew that fell splat onto the stone floor and sent up sparks.

"Evan! Stay with me!"

"Mmm?" His attention, such as it was, returned to Holly. She was crawling toward him, keeping well below the lingering clouds of incense. "Whatcha doin'?"

"Time to open a window. If I was a real Catholic, I'd have calluses on my knees from all that praying and this wouldn't hurt so much. Not to worry about Noel, by the way. Alec and Nicky are keeping him busy upstairs. With some luck, a wall will fall on him." Right on cue, the building vibrated again, and bits of loosened cement drifted down to swirl in with the cloudy incense. "Trouble is, I don't know how much either of them knows about architecture— supporting walls, braces, buttresses, all that stuff."

"Y'know," he observed, "your buttress looks pretty cute, stuck up in the air like that." She threw him a grin, and he wanted to grin back, but something was nagging at him. He wished he could raise a hand and wave away that stupid purple flower; it loomed closer, distracting him. The black pearls were piling up on the floor, and he worried that Holly might bruise a knee or a palm. Or burn herself from the billion dancing sparks. And just how stupid was it, anyway, to fret about a bruise or a singe when Noel would be back any minute to gouge holes in her to get at her blood? Then he reminded himself that Holly was about as real as the monster hyacinth. Which made everything okay. Sort of.

"Evan? Come on, lover-man, keep talking to me."

For an illusion, she sure was as high-maintenance as Holly. Of course, his experience of her would make an illusion of her just the way she usually was, so that didn't mean anything. He wasn't sure what *did* mean anything anymore. If only that goddamned purple hyacinth would move out of the way. Squinting, he tried to focus on Holly where she crabbed across the floor, and blinked as he saw the twinkling lights sparked from the dewdrops slither up and swoop through the air to loop around her right wrist and swarm atop her left ring-finger.

"Evan, don't you dare zone out on me."

Diamonds, they had all turned into diamonds, Susannah's and Granna Maureen's, pulsing like a heartbeat. Like that Witching Sphere in her window, the night he'd figured out that Elias Bradshaw was all magicked-up, too.

"Hey," he asked suddenly, "are you real?"

"I hope that's not an existential question. Yes, I'm real, *Éimhín.*" She was very near the bench now. The throbbing light of the diamonds became brighter, timed to the rhythm of his own heart. "I hope some fresh air clears your head. I need your help."

The diamond glow illuminated all the little black birds. Some twitched their feathers. Definitely the incense was loaded with something outrageously potent. He heard himself chuckle. "Hey, Holly. Guess what? I'm stoned."

"I figured."

"No, *stoned,*" he insisted. "Not just wasted on the smoke. Stuck to the bench. Petrified. Stoned!"

She gave a long sigh. "Terrific. By the way, is there some reason your turtleneck is now a cardigan? Not that I don't appreciate the scenery, but I gave you that sweater and I was kind of fond of it."

It was too much trouble to explain, and anyway he was reminded of something else she had given him. "What'd you do to my St. Michael medal?"

"Later," she told him. "Sorry, but you're going to stay stuck for the time being. I have absolutely no idea how to unWork whatever Noel did."

"And here I was hopin' to get loose before I'm the main event at the ritual."

"I kinda thought that was what Noel had in mind. I have to tell you, though—as a sacrificial altar, that bench will never compete with Stonehenge." There was a pause, and he tried to listen for her movements behind him. "Where the hell is the catch?" Holly griped, startling him. She sneezed again, just as the house quivered and more dust dribbled from the arched ceiling.

Glass shattered behind him, the building staggered, cold night wind blew past him, and Denise suddenly keened like a hyena in mourning.

"Where is she?" Noel shouted down the stairwell. "*Where?*"

"I DON'T LIKE TO BE nosy, Your Honor, but—"

Elias didn't even glance at Leah Towsley. "It would take much too long to explain. Turn here. Yes, right up the driveway—no point in skulking around." Alec, Nick, and Holly were already here, and creating grand bloody havoc from the looks of things. The outdoor floodlights showed him dust rising into the breeze from a toppled tower and a smashed glass greenhouse.

"I guess a low profile would be fairly pointless," the marshal said laconically as something at the back of the house gave way with a resounding boom. Pulling the SUV to a stop, she shut off the engine and continued, "I forgot to mention it earlier—nice robe. Not exactly standard issue for judges, though."

Bradshaw eyed her sidelong. "Can I trust you to stay outside and not meddle?"

"Depends."

"I'm armed," he said, parting the front of the robe to show the pistol tucked into his belt.

"So am I—but what I saw back there probably means a howitzer wouldn't be much use tonight."

He grunted acknowledgment, and winced as another muffled rumble came from the rear of The Hyacinths. The floodlights flickered and died. "There's something I have to do, and I can't be worried about protecting you from trying to protect me while I do it. Stay here. You'll be safe—"

"—as long as I don't go for a stroll," she finished for him, gesturing to the fallen turret. "Judge Bradshaw, I'm not making any promises. But I'll make you a deal. You go do whatever it is you feel you have to do. I'll give you ten minutes."

"Half an hour."

"Fifteen."

"Who works for whom, here?" he snapped.

"*I* work for the United States Government, which has a vested interest in your continued health and well-being," she snapped right back. "You've got fifteen minutes, and then I come get you—and call for backup."

"You just said traditional firepower would be absurd in this situation, and you're right. No backup."

Dark eyes regarded him steadily. "You'd have *so* much more explaining to do if others got involved, am I right? Okay, fifteen minutes, no backup—but if some concerned citizen has already called in random acts of destruction, all deals are off." As he opened the car door, she pointed a long finger at him. "And no messing with me like you did those people back there, Harry Potter."

Tight-lipped, he got out of the Jeep and slammed the door. The gun digging into his stomach would be completely useless, he well knew, but some of the other things stashed away about his person were not. Extracting one of them from a deep, commodious robe pocket, he muttered a few words, and smiled grimly at Towsley's magnificently furious face. He watched her yell at him for a moment as she struggled with doors that would not open unless or until he allowed it. After all, she hadn't said anything about Working on the car.

His wand safely back in its pocket, he strode for the house. *Harry Potter, indeed!*


HUDDLING BELOW THE WINDOW SHE'D just smashed open, Holly cradled her stunned elbow and wished she could become invisible. She could have done just that, had she a nice-sized opal and an expert Witch to cast the spell, plus a bit of her own blood. Speaking of which—shirt, sweater, and heavy woolen coat had protected her from the glass, but she'd knocked her funny bone on the frame and she badly wanted to shake the resulting wriggly tingle out of her arm. And she knew she could not move a muscle, not even blink, or Noel might see her.

She breathed as deeply as she could, trying to clear her brain of the incense. As briefly as she had been exposed, she could still sense it dancing like a gleeful demon at the corners of her vision, ready to claw her brain if she relaxed her guard.

The swift breeze through the shattered window had guttered many of the black candles. Swaths of darkness complicated the architectural shadows, disorienting her; she hoped Noel shared the sensation. She couldn't see him, which meant he probably couldn't see her where she crouched in the window arch behind the stone bench. On the other hand, how many cats had she watched stick their heads into bags and believe that because they couldn't see out, nobody could see in?

The sea-scented wind was dispersing the itchy odor of incense. Whole sides of the house must be yawning wide, creating a draft. But Noel had abandoned his quest for whoever seemed bent on toppling every stone of The Hyacinths, and as the building settled again with a rasp and a quiver, he made his demand again.

"Where is she?"

"*Je ne sais pas* shit, shugah," Denise drawled, leaning comfortably against Evan's shoulder. Holly wanted to kick her into the middle of next week.

"Whole lotta shakin' goin' on," Evan said all at once. His voice sounded firmer, and Holly hoped the incense was losing its hold on him. "Any other windows break?"

Blessing him—and congratulating herself for choosing a man who had a brain and knew how to use it, even when he was stoned—she tried to make herself smaller and hoped Noel would buy the excuse for the sudden breeze.

He didn't appear interested in explanations. "She'll come. She has to come," he grumbled, his voice echoing weirdly in the stairwell. Holly risked movement, peeking around Denise's shins. Noel was descending the last of the stairs into fitful darkness. At the bottom step he froze, thin nostrils flaring. "What is that?" he whispered. His fingers delicately probed the wall, as if testing it for validity. He inhaled deeply. Then he wiped his palm with tender care across the corner stones. "She's here—or she has been," he chuckled. "Her blood is on the wall."

Holly looked down at the heel of her right hand. Sure enough, a nasty scrape that only now, when she knew it was there, began to sting a little. There wasn't much blood. There was enough.

Noel moved to the center of the room. As he passed her line of sight, she noted with relief that his silvery-blue eyes were focused inward. Still, she hardly dared to breathe as he turned a slow circle, widdershins, and ended by facing West.

"I am armed! I am strong! I summon Bayemon, and command the Western Regions and the Waters! The phrase I conjure and command you with is *tacere*, as all will *keep silent* and tremble at the touch of my mind! Your power of mysticism belongs to me! Come, Krokar and Kuzgun, Cigfrain and Bran!"

As he spoke, every candle in that Quarter shivered to new light. So did other things, shining iridescent black things—four of them, all in the West, shaking out their feathers. The birds hopped and fluttered toward Noel, black beaks wide as they *kaw*ed, throat-feathers angrily fluffed. He pointed to the glass bowl of water, and they bent their heads to drink.

He turned to the South next, as Holly had known he would; Elias would have Worked sunwise, but this was not white magic. From his robe Noel drew a knife—not so small as a bolline, nor double-edged like an athame, nor so long as a sword. Again the candle flames ignited, and again four birds came alive and leapt across the cellar floor, approaching him on black-taloned feet that shifted in a dance of impatience, in perfect time to Noel's chanting.

"Let Amayon, King of the Southern Regions, and the beings of Fire cower before the Fire of my Sword! The phrase I conjure and command you with is *velle*, as I have the *will* to see deep into the Abyss! Your power over Time belongs to me! Come, Korakas and Fiach, Cuervo and Karasu! Come!"

Noel positioned the blade on the floor of the South quadrant. Candlefire leaped and licked along its length and the birds fluttered around it, wings outstretched as if bathing their feathers in blue-black flame.

*Cuervo*—she finally recognized the Spanish, and belatedly the Irish and the Welsh, for "raven," and chided her own stupidity. Susannah's favorite tequila had been Cuervo Gold 1800. Untimely and inappropriate tears welled up, and she almost choked. Damn it, she was getting as loopy as Evan. Incense, it was the incense, she wasn't really seeing this and it wasn't real and Noel couldn't possibly be bringing these raven statues to life.

But his palm had cradled the black glass bowl of water, and the hilt of the blade—his palm that had her blood on it. Not much of her blood. Enough.

Ravens, what did she know about ravens? A mental filing cabinet of odd and generally useless information collected over half a lifetime of research began spewing out associations. If the ravens ever left the Tower of London, England would fall. The Valkyries wore raven feathers in their hair, signifying their role as Choosers of the Slain. Celtic Morrigan, the Death Crone in the form of a raven—

East came next, and the robe yielded another implement: a length of pale polished wood tipped with an obsidian arrowhead. "Let Lucifer of the Air draw back at the waving of the Spear! The phrase I conjure and command you with is *noscere*, as I will *know* what it is to hear the music of eternity! Your power of traversing the infinite belongs to me! Come, Kolkrabe and Holló, Corbeau and Gaagii, come!"

The spear-wand was positioned, and white smoke rose from the candles for the quartet of ravens. Two on either side, they whisked at the air with their wings to disperse the cloud upon each other.

Finally the North, where another black glass bowl rested. "I summon Belial, Prince of Trickery, and imprison the spirits of Earth! The phrase I conjure and command you with is *audere*, as I *dare* to taste the power of a god! Your power of binding belongs to me! Come, Vron and Fitheach, Corvus and Kruk, come!"

Four more ravens alighted and began to crack seeds with their beaks. The word "trickery" activated a prompt in Holly's mind: Raven was archetypical kin to Coyote the Trickster. Both were shape-shifters and entirely slippery customers. But they were also teachers, shamans, emissaries of change. What was Noel after? She tried to sort through what Elias had said about Sammael, and power, and now the ravens with their implications of transformation and death, and the widdershins summoning of four sinister Guardians, and could make no sense of it.

Noel stood in the center of his Circle of candles and implements and ravens, raising both arms in jubilation. "I am armed! I am strong! I am more powerful than the Lord of Time! I who was nothing deny all that I was; I who am everything affirm all that I shall be!"

"Good luck," Holly muttered soundlessly, and got to her feet. She was unconcerned now with being seen. It didn't matter. Noel stood within his Circle; she and Evan and Denise were outside it.

This suited her just fine—until Noel flung back his head, howled like a *bean sidhe*, and called out again and again, *"Sammael!"*

The house shuddered; cement dust rained down. With Noel's back to her, and with his Circle demarcated by candles and ravens, she could risk moving. So she pushed herself cautiously to her feet.

*"I have opened the way! I am come!"*

His voice was different. Her musician's ear heard something deeper, richer, something akin to the low note of a Japanese temple gong. She froze, watching for some kind of physical transformation to match that change in his voice. Nothing happened—not that she could discern, anyway.

Every nerve in Evan's body twitched as she whispered his name. "Don't touch me," he warned. "Get outta here—"

"Can you move at all?"

"Not below the elbows."

"Oh, then it's all right, as long as I don't touch the bench." She put both hands on his shoulders, caressing powerful muscles through leather jacket and cashmere sweater. "It's all right, *a chuisle*. Alec and Nicky will be here soon."

"You're real?" he asked, rubbing his cheek to her arm. "Really real?"

"Really real. And you'll be safe, I promise." She slid her hands down his chest, fingering the chain of his St. Michael medal. " 'Flesh and blood, skin and bone, no harm shall come to thee, my own.' " Hugging him, pressed snugly to his back, she added, "Very bad poetry, but it got the job done."

Noel cried out again, startling her. *"My heart is the heart of Abraxas!"*

Evan quivered a bit with laughter. "Isn't that an old Carlos Santana album?"

*"My face is the face of Set! My eyes are the eyes of Eblis, god of fire! My lips are the lips of the Destroying Angel Abbadon! My tongue is the tongue of Baalberith, Canaanite Lord of blasphemy! My teeth are the teeth of Eurynome, who feeds upon corpses!"*

"Yeucch," Evan muttered. "Holly, you gotta get outta here. He'll want more of your blood—and that wand on the floor, it's made of holly—"

*"My legs and feet are the legs and feet of Shiva, who dances the end of the world! My bones are the bones of the living Gods!"*

Holly held Evan tighter. "He's Calling avatars. Power. Bits and pieces of old gods, to make one seriously bad-ass deity."

*"My arms are the arms of Malphas, the vast black wings of a raven! My kteis is the kteis of Thoth, supreme god of magic! There is no member of my body that is not the member of some God!"*

Denise stirred. "I," she announced petulantly, "am sick of this *cochon*."

"Take a number," Holly muttered.

# Thirty

"THOTH, HMM?" ALEC MURMURED. "That's some schlong he wants for himself."

"Don't be vulgar," Nick reprimanded. They were standing outside the closed stairwell door, having entered through the mess of the greenhouse. Noel's bellows of triumph were giving Nick a headache. "And don't underestimate him," he went on. "Have you heard who he's Called? He's done his research; give him that."

"Personally," Elias said from just behind them in the darkness, "I'm not disposed to give him anything."

Nick exchanged glances with his partner. Bradshaw had snuck up on them as if they were novices without a spell to their names instead of senior Witches with nearly a century's combined experience. Alec turned a bland smile on Elias. Nick merely arched a brow. Neither would give the Magistrate the satisfaction of seeing them taken aback.

Elias gestured to the destruction around him. "This was meant as a distraction, I take it?"

"It worked—for a while, anyway," Nick said, forbidding himself to sound defensive. "Holly got in," he added, neglecting to mention that she had been just as silently sneaky as Bradshaw. Perhaps he and Alexander were getting too old for this sort of thing.

"So what's keeping you up here?"

Nick gestured to the closed door. "Noel shut it rather effectively."

"Well, the front door is standing wide open. I don't like the feel of the entry hall, by the way. Avoid it." He waited a moment, then said, "Get on with it, then."

"As thou will it, so mote it be," Alec retorted, and reached for Nicholas with his left hand, where his wedding ring shone; Nick matched his left hand with Alec's, lacing their fingers together so the identical rings touched. Together they faced the door. It had been many years since they had first done this, since circumstances dictated an interweaving of power that both viewed warily, neither wanting to give over control—only to find a pure and elegant joy in the sharing. Nick reveled in his partner's strength, directing it to the door, willing it to open.

"*Fasz kivan!*" he spat, feeling his face flush with angry effort. "Whatever he's done—it's so foul, it shields itself with its own malevolence. I've only felt this a few times, this kind of *mahrimé.* I can't find a way in."

"There's always a way in."

Elias pushed them both aside. Nick stopped him with a hand on his arm, and pressed into his palm the blooded stones. Alec hesitated, then gave over the other two rocks. Stepping back, he watched Bradshaw draw a slow, centering breath and spread his arms wide. An instant later he reeled, shoulder colliding with the wall.

"Christ!" he said shakily. "You're right—it's like—everything that ever died in the history of the world is stinking down there—"

"*Mahrimé,*" Nick said again. "Not just impure, Elias. Something intensely polluted. Something evil—and Holly's in the middle of it."

"*I am armed!*" roared Noel's voice from below. "*I am strong!*"

Elias pushed away from the wall. "So am I," he muttered, grim-faced.

It was true. Armed with magic and determination and four small bits of Earth, fury blazing in his dark brown eyes, hands clenched bloodless, every muscle rasping against every bone, his hate matched itself against Noel's evil.

The wooden door splintered. Elias laughed.


NOEL PIVOTED SLOWLY, HIS BREATHING erratic, his cheekbones flushed crimson, and pointed one long finger at Denise. Holly resisted an impulse to shrink back into the shadows; he didn't seem to see her anyway. Or maybe he simply wasn't interested anymore. He had enough of her blood to Work with. Denise tottered up from the bench, trembling, white to the lips with fear.

Evan hissed in a breath through his teeth. Holly felt him struggle, trying to move, and tightened her arms around his shoulders. Denise dropped her cloak onto the floor, stumbling as she slowly shed the rest of her clothes. Sweater, blouse, brassiere, shoes, trousers, opaque black tights—she walked naked into the Circle of candles that were rock-steady, no breeze from the shattered window plucking at the flames. Holly suddenly realized she could no longer feel it on her skin, that breath of cold sea air, and understood with a sick grinding in her guts that she had made a mistake. The Quarters meant nothing. She and Evan were not outside the Circle. They were not safe. Noel and the Powers he had invoked had encompassed them within a realm of his conjuring. The breeze could no longer pass through the open window. Nothing else would get into this Circle, either.

Denise fumbled with the clips holding back her hair. A few strands caught, and with an uncaring yank she pulled them free. Noel raked her body with a dim and feral gaze, a tiny smile touching his lips.

*"I am He that lightnings and thunders! I am the Lord of the Storm and the Shadows! I am your Lord!"*

Not even the Widow Farnsworth's 'shine had ever made her feel this drunk. *Not real, not real,* sang a little mocking voice in her head; the preening ravens, the shimmering candles, the naked woman and robed man before the black marble altar, the lingering whiff of incense—*Not real not real not real!*

The solid strength of Evan's body argued otherwise. She clung to him. *He* was real. *She* was real.

When Noel spread his arms wide, robes billowing purple-black as raven's wings, he was real, too.

THIS TIME ALEC HAD WARNING of new arrivals. He tore his attention from the disintegrated door and Bradshaw's eyes that danced with glee at his own cunning, and nudged Nick's shoulder. "Keep him here," he mouthed, and his partner nodded vigorously.

He returned to the foyer, where, as he had suspected, all precincts were now heard from and accounted for: Lydia, Martin, Ian, Kate, Simon, a tall silver-haired man Alec recognized as the Reverend Fleming, and a young African-American woman with coldly furious eyes. Martin was carrying his sword at the ready, hilt grasped in both hands, as he demanded, "What the hell's going on here?"

"It's kind of complicated. I can't say I'm glad you're joining the festivities."

Kate said severely, "If you don't tell us what's going on right this instant, I'll—"

"No, *I'll,*" Martin snapped. "I'm the one with the Sword. And slicing holes in Elias's spells tonight has given me just enough of a warm-up."

"Evidently," Alec remarked, eyeing the younger man's martial stance. "You might as well keep that thing ready. You're not going to credit what Noel has Called on down there."

"Where's Elias?" Lydia asked, glancing around the ruined foyer.

Alec pointed to the servants' corridor. Then he turned to the unknown young woman and smiled. "I don't believe I've had the privilege and the pleasure." She confronted him with a glower that convinced him he'd have more luck trying to charm a starving panther, and safer conversations with his straight razor.

"Deputy Marshal Leah Towsley," Kate supplied. "Martin got her loose, too. We may need her. Oh—and this is Reverend Fleming, whose son—"

"Yes, I know," Alec interrupted. "My condolences, Reverend. We shall probably be needing you, as well." He glanced around, made a quick count. "All together, we're thirteen—very good."

"Thirteen?" the Reverend echoed, scowling.

"Twelve plus a leader," Kate murmured. "The way the Order of the Garter is organized, the original Round Table—"

"And Christ with the Disciples," Fleming snapped. "I know the mockery you people make of Holy Scripture, and I will not be a part of it!"

"Reverend," Alec told him with unfeigned compassion, "you may not have a choice."

*"THE—ACT—OF—WORSHIP,"* Noel said, his lips moving in weird slow-motion now, as if unfamiliar with the English language.

Lachlan knew what that had to mean: Noel had successfully cobbled together a composite godhood chunk by chunk, and was ready to rape Denise. And Lachlan could do nothing about it.

He felt Holly clutch his shoulders, felt her shivering a little. He turned his cheek to her fingers, wanting the comfort that their bodies always communicated, one to the other. As he shifted, he felt the pull of the shoulder holster beneath his leather jacket. If the petrifaction spell didn't extend that far up, and if Holly could get the gun, she could shoot the son of a bitch. He opened his mouth to tell her so.

But suddenly she wasn't there anymore. She was walking around the stone bench, shedding her coat as Denise had done, and there was a flash of diamonds, Susannah's and Granna Maureen's, and of cold delicate steel from her left hand.

"Running a little low by now, aren't you?" she asked mockingly. "About ready for a refill?"

"Holly!" Evan shouted. "No!"

She paid him no mind. Noel's gaze swerved from Denise to her, and Denise sagged against the altar like a string-snapped marionette. Holly brought the needle toward her right thumb and went on taunting him.

"Only a taste, now, you wouldn't want to drain me dry." She pricked her thumb and a ruby drop welled up. "Just what every god needs, a surefire stone-cold guaranteed way to work miracles."

*"I—AM—God!"*

"And you need to be worshipped, right? I never did understand that part— why an omniscient, omnipotent, omnipresent Being would want us trivial little humans to grovel mindlessly in hopes of coercing favors—but, hey, that's probably just me. At any rate, Your Divinity, why bother with her? She's got a trifling sort of magic, granted, but *I'm* the one you needed in order to become whoever it is you've become. Why not indulge yourself with somebody who really counts?"

Lachlan ground his teeth with frustration. He knew what she was doing: trying to throw enough words at Noel to confuse or at the very least delay him. Where the hell were Alec and Nick?

Holly was still talking—not that this surprised him. He squinted at Noel's face, which seemed to be locked in an expression of vast confusion: mouth slightly open, brows pinched, pale eyes with their pinpoint pupils fixed on Holly as if he'd never seen her before. And still she kept talking.

"—what really gets me? When any mere human presumes to know the mind of God. I mean, how is it possible? Our paltry little brains can barely conceive of deity, let alone comprehend it. That's why we're humans and God's God." She paused for breath. "So I guess you can now understand me perfectly, whereas I don't understand the first thing about you, right? I mean, nobody really understood Christ, either, when you get right down to it. It's an ancient paradigm, an individual taking on himself all the sins of the world, and there have been sacrificial kings for thousands of years, but Jesus is the one who got all the press. And yet nobody really comprehended who or what he might truly be."

She was like a general on a battlefield, marshaling words instead of soldiers, sending them out to feint, attack, flank, skirmish—but her enemy would not engage. All Noel did was stand there, watching her with those pale, uncomprehending eyes, and whether his not-quite-humanness was a result of the drugs he had taken or the gods he had called to take him over, Lachlan didn't care to speculate.

BRADSHAW TOOK A STEP TOWARD the open door, still smiling. He felt a presence behind him, a hard grip on his arm, and shrugged off both. What he hated, what he wanted to destroy, was down there wallowing in death. What had Nicholas called it? *Mahrimé?* Noel was a walking, breathing pollution.

"Elias!"

He barely heard his name, and certainly did not respond to it. All that he had deliberately not felt since losing Susannah grew within him, as if that corruption so nearby acted like manure. Grief, loss, abandonment, the bitter ache of longing—he felt all these things at last. Yet even as they ripened, they withered. None could compete with the hatred, could be as powerful as the anger.

*His* hatred. *His* anger. He sensed them grow and thrive—

"Elias!"

That aggravating presence again, that voice scratching at him with magic; he moved away from it, down the stairs, inhaling deep of scorched and acrid air that smelled of power.

Lovely things, the anger and hate, luxurious and commanding. They reached for and twined tight all the Power in him, like those two men upstairs clasped each other's hands, giving and receiving until they didn't know where one ended and the other began, a perfect swirling Möbius strip of eternity. His emotions and his ability served each other, fed from each other, until he laughed again.

His body was improbably light, buoyed by power. But as he reached the fifth step, he growled as he sensed a barrier between him and the cellar. The structure screened anything going on within it; skillful Work, Master Class, in fact. But not even remotely in *his* class. *Shut* me *out, will you? Not fucking likely!*

Pocketing the gemstones, he felt around the edges of the obstruction, contemptuous of the tiny burning flashes that plucked at his fingers. With both hands he pushed at the barrier. It resisted, like a gigantic sparking bubble.

He pushed again. This time it contracted. One inch, two—

"—HELD A GREAT BIG SOLEMN meeting at Chalcedon in four-hundred-and-something to debate whether the Nazarene was human with a spark of the divine, divine with a spark of the human, or half human and half divine."

She hadn't talked this much since her lectures in Nairobi.

"And you know what they came up with? You'll never guess. Christ was both fully human *and* fully divine. Now, this does show some largeness of imagination, but it's the idea that humans could decide such a thing in the first place that's really remarkable. What absolutely luscious arrogance!"

She'd never lectured a god before, either. Or gods. She wished somebody—anybody—would interrupt with a question. She wished she had a glass of water to soothe her scratchy throat. She wished Noel would get that befuddled look off his face. Whoever he was, or thought he was, seemed pretty much all hat and no cattle at the moment. Most of all she wished Alec and Nicky would hurry up.

"What's the line about if there was no God, it would be necessary to invent him? I guess that's what you've done here, with bits and pieces of some of the real biggies. And the ravens are a nice touch. Most cultures venerate ravens."

Denise sank to the floor in a welter of long limbs and blonde hair, staring at Holly with a stunned expression on her bloodied face. Holly didn't dare look at her except from the periphery of her vision. She had to keep eye contact with Noel, keep him occupied. She put her brain on automatic pilot and dredged up more of the trivia that clung to her memory like kudzu to a split-rail fence.

"Huginn and Muginn belonged to Odin. Mostly they're translated as 'Thought' and 'Memory,' but the more accurate version is 'Thoughtful' and 'Mindful.' The Romans thought ravens were birds of prophecy, because their kawing sounded like *cras*, which is Latin for 'tomorrow.'"

She heard a faint sizzle, and from a corner of her eye saw a flicker. It had to mark the edges of the Circle. She felt slightly weak-kneed with relief that the thing didn't encompass the whole house.

"'Tomorrow and tomorrow and tomorrow, creeps in this petty pace from day to day—' Which reminds me of how right dear old Billy was, if he really was William Shakespeare and not the Earl of Oxford. 'What a piece of work is a man.' Yeah, what a piece of work we are, forsooth. The only animal who blushes, or needs to. The only animal that fouls its own nest, the only one that kills for sport—"

Noel's glazed eyes flickered with renewed life. She lost her thread for an instant, then talked louder and faster.

"—but I prefer an idea proposed to me just this evening by a very shrewd friend. He reminded me that humans are the animals that create—and in the process of creation glimpse what true deity is. Not what it's like to *be* a god, but—"

Something tingled against the elbow she'd bruised earlier. It made her flinch and take an involuntary step sideways—which brought her into contact with what felt like a waterfall of that same almost-electricity, all along her arm and ribs and leg.

"—who among us trivial pathetic humans can even imagine what it must be like to be—to be omnipotent, and omniscient, and—" *Stop repeating yourself, dammit! Catch his mind again, or what passes for it.* "—but you'd know much better than any of the rest of us, wouldn't you, with parts of gods now part of you, so you can create or destroy at will—all that power, all-knowing and all-consuming—"

Fleeting embers danced around her, across her clothes, seeming to tangle in her hair and the diamonds at her wrist and on her finger. But she kept talking. She had to keep talking.

"—but what is it you're thinking of creating? Or are you beyond that now? This thing we mere humans have been doing since before we could walk upright without tripping over ourselves out on the savannah—"

Tiny pinpricks of heat and ice and low-voltage shivers passed through her, spiking every nerve in her body.

"—a lot of what was created was lost in the intervening millennia, but it had to've been going on all that time. After all, it's not as if thirty thousand years ago somebody just woke up one morning and said, 'Today I'm going to do some really gorgeous cave-paintings, and I know the perfect spot at Lascaux—'"

BRADSHAW HEARD IT, BUT HE couldn't believe it. *Christ on the Cross with a Crown of Thorns — the woman is* talking *again! Still. Yet. For-fucking-ever! Does she never shut up?*

It reminded of him of his birthday at Chanterelle, when she'd driveled on and on and *on* like a pompous doctoral candidate defending her dissertation, and he'd looked across the table at Susannah —

"Why do we make things beautiful when all they really need to be is *things?* We make tools. So do chimpanzees. But we're the ones who decorate our tools, make them into works of art as well as function."

Anger, newly fueled by a monumental exasperation at the Spellbinder he was here to rescue, shriveled when confronted by pain. Susannah, so perfect that night, wearing a blue silk dress and Holly's sapphires and a blush when she and he both realized Holly had deserted them on purpose —

"I mean, a chert knife cuts just as well whether or not it's got a design on the handle. So why make it satisfying to look at? Why decorate it with an invocation to divinity? We obviously can't deny the impulse, or maybe it's a compulsion —"

— leaving them to a superb dinner and a glorious autumn evening and each other, all night long, and almost every night after that until this would-be god took her life by snapping her neck —

The agony was crippling. Suffocating. There was no power in it, nothing he could use the way he'd used anger and hate. It gave him no strength; it bled him of strength. He could not allow himself to feel it.

"— so the definition I like most is that *Homo sapiens* is the animal that makes things, and not just creates but embellishes, and needs beauty in the creating —"

A quick sweeping glance located Denise and Noel, still within his shrunken Circle. There were bowls and candles and implements on the floor, and sixteen impatiently fluttering ravens. Lachlan sat on a stone bench, looking peevish. And Holly was *still* talking.

"— when we respond to beauty, it's the same way we respond to the whole of Creation. With joy. Simple, honest, inevitable. And we glimpse what Yahweh felt when looking at Creation, and seeing that it was good. What makes us human is our compulsion to create, and to create beauty, and to look on it with joy —"

Susannah's voice again echoed in his head: *"Whatever happened to joy?"*

This was no time to feel anything but rage. Not sorrow, or loss, or any of the weakening emotions that were of no use to him. He silenced Susannah's voice in his mind, and deliberately forgot what joy meant. He would not have the purity of his anger and his hatred blighted. He would not allow the power it gave him to sieve away. The thundercloud inside him billowed blacker and thicker, a promise of sacred lightning.

It was how the Towers fell, in billowing clouds and fire like lightning.

"Evenin', Your Honor," Evan Lachlan said loudly and firmly. "Not to be pushy or anything, but d'you think you can get me the hell out of this?"

Bradshaw concentrated on Noel, glimpsing in the shadows around him avid faces and seeking hands and greedy, glowing eyes.

"Hey! Bradshaw!"

He had no time for this. Anger and hate reseeded within him, spreading, stronger.

"Or maybe you haven't got the chops?" called Lachlan's sneering voice. "Aren't you supposed to be Mr. Big Kahuna Magistrate? Prove it!"

"C'mon, Elias!" Holly held up one finger, squeezing a plump drop of blood. "Prove it!"

Noel sucked in a breath, naked avarice on his face.

*That's* my *Spellbinder, you obnoxious asshole. Mine!*

Prove it?

Facing Lachlan, he began to murmur. The phrases flowed across his lips, smooth as kisses. Oh, yes—this was power, sharply satisfying, enhanced by the secret trembling of the gemstones in his pocket. How did anyone live without this? Elias wrapped his fingers around the rocks, his mind giving him colors and shapes and the scent of Holly's blood.

Lachlan pushed himself up from the bench. Wobbly for a moment, he stumbled, righted himself by locking his knees, shook out his fingers, and blew out a long relieved breath. Then he unholstered his Glock and instantly looked much more relaxed. "*Thank* you." He eyed Noel, who stood perfectly still before the altar, riveted to the welling of Holly's blood. "Can I just shoot him now? Please?"

Holly gave a choking sound that was half laughter, half sob. "Later, *a chuisle*, later."

"Okay, but only if you promise," he replied grudgingly. "I'd cuff him if I'd brought mine along. Anybody got some rope?"

Bradshaw reached into another pocket of his robe and drew out a length of golden cord. Denise moaned at the sight of it, and clasped her arms even more tightly around herself. As Bradshaw started forward to tie up Noel's wrists, Lachlan grabbed the Measure.

"Amateur," he muttered. He tried to sort out the cord one-handed, puzzled when he found no ends and no knot tying it closed. "Gimme that knife thing from over there—"

Denise gave a strangled shriek. But it wasn't the threat to her Measure that brought her up off the floor, wobbling on shivering knees. With one finger Noel directed her, a smirk twisting his face. She bent over the plinth and spread her legs and arms wide, offering her perfect white ass. His robe swirled as he turned, and his voice echoed like something from a primeval sepulcher: *"The act of worship!"*

*THE WOMAN WAS BLONDE, BEAUTIFUL. The man in the glistening purple-black robe clasped her by the waist, bent her over the black altar, plunged into her. His fingers moved to her throat, buried themselves in her tumble of golden hair, preparing to snap her neck.*

Bradshaw gasped and stumbled back. Gemstones ground against the bones of his fingers as revulsion seized his muscles. Susannah, it was Susannah—

The rocks stung like a handful of cinders gone almost cold. The blue of the turquoise and the red specks of the bloodstone skittered at the edges of his vision, but what his mind seemed to taste was the reddish-brown carnelian: the gem that was a talisman against mental invasion, that healed grief, that granted joy.

The joy that Susannah had been for him filled the gaping emptiness he'd thought she'd left inside him. She would never have been that selfish, to take with her that which allowed him to love. Hatred did no honor to what she had given him. Anger did her no justice. It was for him to remember joy: *"She who is remembered, lives."*

He shut his eyes, shamed and oddly grateful. The pain lingered; it would always be there. The joy was stronger. And it protected him.

*TENDRILS OF GREEN STEMS SNAKED up, sprouting purple flowers that became summery skirts that swirled around her legs as the man in the black cassock grasped handfuls of purple hyacinths and pushed up, up, and her blonde hair straggled down as she turned her head to look at him with those gray-green eyes—*

*No!* It hadn't happened this way, he'd never seen her face, only her flowered dress and the cassock hitched up around powerful thighs—she was dead, long dead, the priest was rotting in jail as he deserved, she wasn't here and neither was he but oh God it looked just like them—

*—hair darkened to deep gold-threaded russet, writhed around eyes of clear Irish blue and when the man turned his head and grinned, her blood was on his lips.*

SHE DIVIDED HER STARE AMONG the three men, not understanding Noel's glee or Elias's fury or Evan's anguish. All she really understood, as they froze into a *tableau vivant* of power she couldn't feel, was that she had damned well had enough of this.

Striding to Elias, she grabbed the pistol at his waistband. "I knew this thing would come in handy sooner or later," she muttered, and pointed it at Noel. It had been quite a while since Cousin Jesse had taken her out for target practice, but Noel didn't have to know that. "Whatever it is you're doing, knock it off," she snapped, "or I'll make you a castrato. So much for your 'act of worship' then."

Noel's arms remained outstretched, but his gaze met hers—a glitter in his eyes, something of vehemence and fire that matched the sonorous rumble of his voice. *"Put it down."*

"Back off!" Holly cocked the little gun, her fingers slippery with blood. "At this range I can't hardly miss!"

"I am a god!"

She heard a difference in his voice, an abrupt hollowness in his claim, and saw something like fear cross his face. "And so you're immortal? Want to test your theory?"

The lustrous power flickered erratically in his eyes. Sammael, Abraxas, Belial, Set, Abbadon—they were not creator deities but bringers of death, destroyers of souls. As long as they anticipated worship, they would linger. But if they weren't going to get what they wanted, they might abandon Noel as useless.

"If I don't hit you," she taunted, "I'll probably hit Denise—you or her, I don't really give a shit! If she's dead, there goes your act of worship!"

His eyes smoldered and his lips curved, and she knew she'd said exactly the wrong thing. There was more than one woman here, more than one opportunity for the ritual.

*"Death and God—one and the same."*

The gods within him laughed in his eyes. She knew a quiver of temptation to speak directly to them. Well, why not? "You others—yes, all of you skulking around—what if I shoot him? What good will he be to you if he's maimed? That's not what brought you here!" The luminescence flared and wavered like a guttering candle flame and she knew she was finally on the right track. "What if I kill him? What god would inhabit something dead?"

There was a flutter of black wings and an outraged tumult of *kawing*. Noel swayed backward toward the altar, all the substance gone out of him. His cry of despair became a howl of agony as Denise's fisted hands lashed up and clouted him right in the balls. He collapsed, moaning.

Denise crawled away from him, green eyes glaring feebly at Holly as she groped for her velvet cloak. "Him or me, you don't give a shit?"

Holly knew exactly one really filthy phrase in Hungarian. She used it now. *"Baszóд meg*, lamb chop. You got us into this mess."

"Holly," said Elias, startling her so much, she nearly dropped the gun. "Give me that before you shoot yourself in the foot. And take care of Lachlan. He doesn't look so good."

"Abbadon!"

This time she did drop the gun. Noel's voice held no Power but that of his craving.

"Abraxas! Baalberith!"

He had risen to his knees, arms flung wide.

"Abbadon!" he called again. "Abraxas! *Baalberith!*"

Holly flung a wild glance at Bradshaw. He had heard it, too.

*"Shiva and Set! Eblis, Thoth, Eurynome! Malphas! We are come! We are here!"*

Elias chanted frantic counterspells to Noel's Summonings. Ravens shrieked and candle flames shuddered and all the Powers gathered in this place hovered excitedly, more substantial with every passing moment.

Noel's hands lifted, writing in the air, fingers tracing sigils of flame. From the darkness prowled a man-shape with the head of a lion, and serpents for legs, and at the end of those legs, scorpions. In his right hand he held a pharaoh's gold-and-lapis flail; in his left, an oval shield.

*"Abraxas! He who speaks the hallowed and accursed word which is life and death at once and together!"*

Another fiery symbol, and another shape coalescing, and yet another, Summoned to reality—bizarre fever-dream figures with the bodies and heads and limbs of snakes and horses, eagles and hunting cats. She recognized the ibis-head of Thoth, and many-armed Shiva. The rest were unknown to her. Noel's voice named them, louder and louder until she could not longer hear Bradshaw's frantic words, until at last the cellar stones trembled with a final elated shout: *"Sammael the Accuser! Sammael the Seducer! Sammael the Destroyer!"*

From the outer shadows, where the other grotesqueries lurked and lingered, came a tall, elegantly made youth, perfect in every human attribute. Long white hair cascaded below his black-robed shoulders in shining waves; eyes of pure, soft blue glistened in a face of surpassing beauty. Both hands gripped the pommel of a darkly glowing sword held high. A black droplet glittered at its tip.

The apparition paused to regard Bradshaw with an inquisitive smile, as if wondering who this strangely chanting person might be. With a dismissive shrug, he moved a few paces forward, then stopped and stared down at the floor. An expression of delight intensified his beauty as he bent to pluck up the wand—made of the wood of the holly tree, symbolic of immortality, used in spells to ease the passage of the living into death. He examined it, nodding, long white hair drifting about his shoulders.

When he looked up again, he saw Holly. He dropped the wand, no longer interested. An eloquent smile curved his lips. And he glided slowly forward, the sword uplifted, his steps timed to Noel's ceaseless call of his name.

He walked toward her.

No. Toward Evan—crumpled on his knees, the golden Measure in one hand, the Glock in the other. She knelt beside him, whispering, *"Éimhín?"*

He stared up at her, his dragon's eyes quite mad.

"Whore," he said coldly.

This was a different anger from his drunken rage of their parting. That had been brutal. This was lethal. And if she had been frightened of that other fury, this one paralyzed her.

The Measure slithered to the floor. The Glock was gripped in both large, strong hands. Holly watched, numb with terror, as the gaping black hole of the barrel moved closer and closer to her chest.

Cold steel rested in the hollow between her collarbones. She looked past the dark barrel and his hands to the silver oval resting at his heart. She had thought him invulnerable. She had believed the spelled medal was enough to protect him. *Flesh and blood, skin and bone—*

# Thirty-one

*NOT REAL! NOT REAL!*

He tried to believe it. The words throbbed through his aching skull with every beat of his heart. But he knew what he'd seen, the black cassock and the dress with purple flowers and the obscene "act of worship"—

That phrase snagged in his mind, cried out in Noel's voice. Noel—Denise—not *her* at all, and not Holly—*not real!*

Sound thudded into his brain, sound that was someone who spoke without words, commanding him to stand. He could scarcely see; everyone and everything he knew to be in this cellar was made of shadows.

Except for Holly, kneeling before him, pale face framed in tangled russet hair and a black sweater. *Her* face, *her* hair, *her* eyes. He felt faint quivering heat in the center of his breastbone, next to his heart. In this unholy muddle of shadows and shapes and birds flapping their feathers and light that hurt his eyes, she was the one reality. In his whole life, in all the world, only she was real.

And so was he. Gleeful, he sensed his own height and strength and the breath filling his lungs, and the sword in his hand felt more innately right than his Glock. He looked at Holly, and wanted her.


*FLESH AND BLOOD, breath and bone*— The pitiable little rhyme nattered mockingly as the angel called "blind to God" stole what she had sought to protect. Her mistake had been that of the rank magical amateur—and a Greek goddess. Eos, in asking eternal life for her lover Tithonos, had forgotten to include eternal youth. In protecting Lachlan's body, Holly had forgotten to set a matching guard over his mind. Sammael was about to take both.

Yet he seemed to be having a hard time doing it, not quite able to stay in sync; the two images blurred and twinned and merged and parted again, one dark and hazel-eyed, one with long white hair twisting about his beautiful blue-eyed face. Both of them gazed at her, as if only she had meaning, as if only she was real. Both of them wanted her.

"No!" screamed Noel. "It's supposed to be *me!* The Summoning was *mine!* Sammael!"

Sammael didn't seem to care. All Holly cared about was that the resonance was gone from Noel's voice, and he was inhabited by nothing more than what was human.

So was she. Just human. And this thing that was inhuman was thieving what did not belong to it. Evan's hazel eyes were shading to blue, the two forms occupying the same space. Soon they would share the same body. Conscious as she had never been before of the blood pulsing through her, Spellbinder's blood gleaming on the tip of her pricked finger as she squeezed the wound yet again, she reached toward the small silver medal. She touched it, looking up into his eyes.

The etched image of St. Michael began to glow, fiery outline of a tall, fierce man bearing a sword. Evan cried out and dropped his pistol, scrabbling with both hands at the medal, trying to claw it from blistering skin. Holly struggled to her feet and threw her arms around him. She felt heat against her breast but only held him closer. "*A chuisle,*" she murmured, her voice shaking. "*A chuisle mo chroí—*"


NICK WAS THE FIRST DOWN into the cellar, and stopped at the bottom step, all too aware of the Circle that fluxed nearby. He looked around, mystified by the ravens, the implements, the bowls, the candles. Neither did he understand the people: Holly and Evan clutching each other, Denise on the floor in a welter of bare limbs, Elias standing with his hands fisted and his eyes squeezed shut, gasping for breath. And Noel: doubled over, rocking slowly back and forth as if silently weeping.

What Nicholas understood all too well was the taint in the room. His Romany grandmother's word for it, *mahrimé*, had occurred to him earlier and now it seemed even more appropriate. There was something defiled here, something contaminated by evil. When he felt Alec at his back on the stairs, instinct made him stop his partner with an outstretched arm, blocking his way.

"I'm aware that it's perfectly foul in here, Nick. We need to do something about it. Come on." He pushed past and went to Holly and Evan.

Nick swore under his breath and hurried to help pry them gently loose from each other. While Alec calmed her down, Nick searched Evan's face.

Hazel eyes, smudged beneath as if he hadn't slept in a week, focused blearily. "W-wasn't her," he whispered—not quite a question.

"No. It wasn't her," Nick affirmed, having no idea what he was talking about but knowing a need for reassurance when he saw it.

"That goddamned dress . . . the flowers. . . ." His eyes sharpened. "I never knew what they were. Fucking hyacinths." He raked his hair from his brow and sucked in a deep breath. "Where the hell have you *been?*"

Nick ignored the question. "Can you move? We have to get you and Holly out of here."

"Yeah, I can move." His lips twisted. "Which wasn't the case earlier—and you don't wanna know. Just don't go anywhere near that bench."

Nick regarded Noel where he rocked and shivered on the floor, pathetic would-be god in a heavy black robe. A few ravens skittered over to pluck petulantly at him. Nick shooed them carefully away and picked up the gold cording. It would serve to tie the man up for the time being. It was only when he could not find an end that he realized it was Denise's Measure.

Well, it would do anyhow. Expertly looping it doubled around Noel's lanky arms, he tied and tightened a few knots and settled back on his heels to evaluate his work. Hands bound behind him, cord passing around his neck, Noel would be unable to move without throttling himself.

"Nice," Evan said. "I've seen cattle tied up worse for gelding." His hand lifted to his chest, shied back. Nick saw then an oval burn. "Shit, this hurts. Can we get the hell out of here now?"

He was talking to reconfirm his own reality, Nick surmised; he hadn't looked at Holly once. "You, yes. The rest of us have Work to do yet."

"Tell me a new one," he replied wryly. "What's with His Honor?"

Elias was breathing normally again, but looking spell-shocked. Nick went to him, touched his arm, and said, "Are you all right?"

"Stupid question," the Magistrate muttered. "Time to shut down this Circle. It's giving me a headache."

Nick followed his gaze: the restive ravens, the black candles, the remains of Noel's instrumentation. A travesty of Samhain. Tonight was meant to be a remembrance of the dead at the turning of the year. The summer's Oak Lord gave way to the Holly Lord of winter; the slowly shortening days led to Yule, when the god was reborn with the sun. The Christ story followed the pattern: birth at the Winter Solstice, death at the Vernal Equinox to sanctify the Earth with blood and make fruitful the land. But this Circle was a thing of shadows, ravens, and death, and Nick had no idea how Elias would nullify it without the cooperation of its maker.

Nick stared down at the trussed and helpless architect of this Circle. Silver-blue eyes met his. They neither beseeched nor defied; they merely seized and held his gaze with surprising strength. As Nick instinctively fought him off, Noel's bloodless lips moved. Without sound he said, "Kill me."

Nick shook his head. Still the pale eyes demanded his awareness. He moved back a little, awkwardly. "Stop it." The attempt to spell him faded away.

"What does he want?" Bradshaw's voice was raspy.

"He says he wants to die."

"*No!*" Noel exclaimed, and coughed. "*Kill* me!"

Lachlan said softly, "Yeah, there *is* a difference, isn't there?"

IT REALLY WAS TOO PERFECT. An hour ago Bradshaw could have given Noel exactly what he wanted and savored the experience. It was his right as Magistrate to judge and pass sentence; he'd met few who deserved death more than this man.

He couldn't do it. Neither could he order it done. Between his anger and this quietude of soul had come the truest memory of Susannah. Vengeance was dead in him.

He was peripherally aware of the others in the cellar: when they had arrived and what they had witnessed interested him not at all. Kate and Simon, Lydia and Martin and Ian, Leah Towsley and the Reverend Fleming—they clustered in the doorway, curious or worried or anxiously alert. They must all be protected from whatever remained here, and to do that he must negate this Circle.

Gathering himself, he said, "Take the places you occupied the night Lydia read Susannah's music."

The Reverend had other ideas. "I will have no truck with Satanism," he warned, "or the worship of demons—I know what you people do on Hallowe'en, a celebration of death and all that is evil. 'And the soul that turneth after such as have familiar spirits, and after wizards, to go whoring after them, I will even set my face against that soul, and will cut him off from among his people.'"

"Leviticus, Chapter Twenty," Elias said tiredly. "Forgive me for not remembering the verse numbers. Can we at least agree, Reverend, that Noel is the one whoring after spirits tonight? And that you haven't the slightest notion of how to deal with him?"

Fleming drew breath as if to argue further, then swept his gaze around the room, resting at last on Noel. His brow pinched and he shied back. But his voice was fiercely defiant as he said, "I am strong in the Lord."

"Elias," Lydia said as the others took their positions, "you don't need me, so why don't I look after the Reverend?" Gently she took Fleming's arm and coaxed him aside to stand with Holly and Marshal Towsley. Farcically enough, Holly introduced herself and he shook her hand. When all else failed, Bradshaw told himself, take refuge in civilities; how very Jane Austen of her.

"Miss McClure, you're bleeding," said the Reverend.

"Oh — sorry." She pressed thumb and forefinger together. "I'd say 'occupational hazard' but it would take too long to explain, and His Honor needs silence right now."

Bradshaw surveyed the Circle: the implements he hadn't used and the ravens he hadn't brought into being and the candle flames he hadn't kindled. If his fifty years had taught him nothing else, they had taught him to improvise. The configuration wasn't quite right; he considered, then said, "Simon, you're our Death Lord. Kate — "

"I know, I know — The Crone." She sighed and stood beside Ian in the North. "Why is it always me? I'm forty-six, not a hundred and twelve."

Elias was about to begin when another voice whined, "Wh-what about me?"

"You?" He stared at Denise where she crouched on the floor. "You'll stay put and shut up."

For a second she looked as if she might resist him — but then her green eyes flickered to the golden Measure tethering Noel, and whatever fight had been left in her wilted.

He called the Guardians. Raphael, Ariel, Gabriel, Michael; East, North, West, South; Air, Earth, Water, Fire. Unexpectedly, with each invocation the name and nature of a goddess came into his mind also: brilliant Athena in the East; nurturing Demeter in the North; Selene, Keeper of the Silver Wheel of Stars, in the West; to the South, Brighid of the Sacred Fire. In each was something of Susannah's beauty: her green eyes, her wheaten hair, her wry smile, her welcoming arms. The associations surprised him, but there was a pleasure and a promise, too.

"This is a time which is not a time, a place which is not a place, a day which is not a day. On Samhain we pass into darkness with the turning of the wheel, on the night when the veil between the worlds is thin. On this night, the Lord of the Sun passes from us, the Lord of the Day becomes the Lord of Shadows. Let goodness — let *joy* — be harvested as wheat in the fields, and let hurt be cast aside, winnowed away as chaff."

The Crone's turn came, and Kate chanted, "Though the Sun Lord leaves us on this Samhain night, fear not Death. Death is the Comforter and the Consoler, Death is Heart's Ease and Sorrow's End. Remember those who have died, for they who are remembered, live."

Simon, the Death Lord, spoke next. "The circle is ever turning. The days are growing shorter. The Sun Lord leaves us now to the long nights of winter, but shall return with the spring, when the days lengthen and the nights are warm and sweet. That which dies is reborn. They who are remembered, live."

"All that is born shall live and die," Elias murmured, "and all that dies shall be born and live again. This is the Trinity," he went on with a certain relish, fully aware of Reverend Fleming's scowling disapproval, "the Three-in-One that defines the universe. Thought, word, and deed. Morning, noon, and night. Seed, fruit, and wine. Birth, life, and death."

"That which dies is reborn," Simon repeated. "They who are remembered, live."


SHE WHO IS REMEMBERED, LIVES. Holly silently promised it to Susannah, grateful to concentrate on the traditional reason for Samhain instead of worrying about Evan. He hadn't so much as looked at her since—well, since. She supposed that sooner or later she'd be able to convince herself it had been a hallucination brought on by delayed reaction to the incense—until the next time Evan took off a shirt and she saw the scar.

She could feel him standing next to her, tall and solid, warm and alive. She was just beginning to believe it, as Elias continued his tranquil recitation, when Noel's sudden movement snagged her gaze.

"*Bayemon!*"

Noel's voice, resonant with power, echoed from the flagstones to the vaulted ceiling. He was on his knees, his arms and throat helplessly knotted in Denise's golden Measure. He turned his head as far as the cord would allow, glaring at Nicky, who stood in the West, domain of Gabriel.

"*Bayemon!*"

Nicky's eyes, the color of a summer sea, flickered with darkness like rain clouds. Opposite him, Alec swayed slightly and moaned.

"*Amayon!*"

This to the South, where both Elias and Martin stood, the latter like a Crusader knight carved of ebony—and the Sword in his hands flowed orange and crimson with flame. Martin gave a blurt of surprise but held on to the Sword.

"*Amayon!*"

In the North, Ian grimaced in sudden pain.

"*Lucifer!*" screamed Noel. Alec, in Raphael's realm, already reeling from Nicky's anguish, shuddered and gasped for air.

"By the Lord Jehovah, *no!*" roared Reverend Fleming. And before Noel could complete his second calling of Lucifer, the servant of God surged forward, away from the Jewish girl who stood stricken by shadows and the two stunned marshals and Holly, and grasped Alec Singleton by the shoulders. "Begone from this man! In the name of Jesus Christ the Son of God I cast thee out!" Alec struggled for breath, his head lolling as Fleming shook him. "Hear me, Angels, Prophets, Apostles! Drive out from these men the evil spirits that possess them! Now, I say! Help me, Father Abraham, Moses the Lawgiver, Mary the Gentle and Merciful Mother of Christ—"

The four men standing the cardinal points of the compass cried out and collapsed to their knees. Reverend Fleming staggered and fell, tangling with Alec; Simon and Kate sagged to the stone floor. Bradshaw stayed upright a little longer, fighting frantically, but now Noel focused on him alone and whatever the Magistrate's hands and lips were conjuring did him no good. Lydia gave a single sob of horrified vision and covered her face with her hands when Elias slumped to the flagstones.

Holly groped desperately for Evan's hand—but he, too, was down, curled on his knees, arms wrapped around himself. She was about to bend over him, to touch him and damn the consequences, when a gentle hand clasped her arm and a soft voice whispered, "No. They are none of them harmed. Watch."

A cloud of shadows gathered around Noel, black shadows subtly iridescent and trailing sparks as a sudden wind wailed through shattered glass. The ravens gathered, chittering excitedly, feathers blurring into a swirl that became a garment. Within it a figure coalesced, ancient and withered and smiling.

Holly knew who this must be: the Morrigan. Guised as a woman, on the night before battle she washed the bloodstained clothing of those who would die on the morrow. In her shape of the great Raven, she soared over clashing armies, *kaw*'ing her eagerness to feed on the corpses. For an instant it was indeed an Irish face above the raven-wing cloak: broad-browed, green-eyed, white-skinned amid a wild tangle of curls.

The features changed. Cheekbones widened, angled; eyes darkened to rich earth-brown; skin glossed to coppery bronze; thick hair straightened, became long and lustrous and inky black.

"*Kâ'lanû Ahkyeli'skï,*" murmured the unknown woman at Holly's side. "Raven Mocker. The Cherokee witch who seeks out the dying to rob them of the last of life."

With a chuckle like a raven's, and with arms spreading like wings, black feather-woven material fell back from her hands. Her fingers trailed sparks. Noel slid down, curled now on the floor, gasping. Glittering embers fell on his rictus of a face, smoldering on his robe and the golden cord. The would-be god writhed, struggling against Raven Mocker, fighting for his life. Or perhaps for the death he had envisioned. The death, Holly finally understood, that would make him a god. But not this. Not this. There was now no deep resonance in his hoarse cries; his gods and parts of gods had deserted him.

Denise screamed without cease, her Measure singed by fire dancing from Raven Mocker's hands. Holly heard her agony from a great distance, for her head was filled with the rasps of Raven Mocker's voice. She understood every word.

"*Sgë! Nâ'gwa tsûdantâ'gï tegû'nyatawâ'ilateli'ga!*" Listen! Now I have come to step over your soul!

Raven Mocker bent over Noel, a swirl of rainbow black.

"*Ä 'nûwa'gï gû'nnage' gûnyû'tlûntani'ga! Sûn'talu'ga gû'nnage degû'nyanu'galû'n-tani'ga, tsû'nanugâ'istï nige'sûnna!*" I have come to cover you over with the black cloth! I have come to cover you with the black slabs, never to reappear!

She reached for his chest, where the Measure crossed his breastbone, and clawed the golden cording aside. Where sharp nails raked his skin there opened up a gaping bloody hollow braced by white ribs. Her fingers burrowed deep, and from between bones Raven Mocker dug out a heart.

"*Tsûdantâ'gï ûska'lûntsi'ga!*" Now your soul has faded away!

The heart beat frenziedly in her palm, starved for blood to pulse through the body it had served. With the last air in his lungs Noel groaned hopelessly. Raven Mocker nodded.

"*Tsûtû'neli'ga!*" So shall it be for you. "*Sgë!*"

But there was nothing to hear. The heart lay still and silent in her hand.

She tucked it away beneath her cloak of feathers and mist, became a cloud of shadows once more, and was gone.

A soft sigh. "And so he knows Death."

Holly's own heart was thudding, thick with blood, her Spellbinder's blood that still smeared Noel's dead fingers.

"How could it be your fault?" the quiet voice asked. "He summoned Death, and so Death came—but not as he expected."

"And—and he was alone." She heard the words; she had not spoken aloud.

"Yes. Alone. Do you understand?"

She wrestled with it, the aloneness and the reasons for that aloneness. In pursuit of godhood, he had severed connection to his own kind. A rift such as this from humanity's intrinsic magic bestowed the power to kill other humans without thought or qualm. To murder Scott Fleming and snap Susannah's graceful neck with no regard for the lives he was ending. To be aloof, distant, separated—was this what it meant to be a god?

No. Never. Deity was everywhere, in all Creation. To turn one's back on Creation was Death.

"Look within. Discover what you are at this moment creating." Her confusion brought a snort of impatience. "Your blood, so important to others—listen to what it tells *you!*"

Blood—cells—nuclei—the elegant double helix where all that she was curled in a code of chemicals that were as old as the Universe. "*We are stardust—*"

And there was the soft rhythm of the drums, and of voices murmuring in the star-strewn night. The laughter of water over river rocks, the whisper of the wind. The crackle of flames in the sacred circle of stones, and the heartbeats—billions of them—the shift of soil under her bare feet as she approached the place where the slight, delicate woman crouched, swaying lightly back and forth, hands extended to the warmth of an ancient fire.

Dark eyes luminous in a small dark face, she looked up and smiled welcome. They had not met before, but they were as familiar to each other as water and skin and recurring dreams. The modern brain that knew modern science identified the linkage of mitochondrial DNA, the unique pattern of mother to daughter to daughters uncounted throughout the millennia; the ancient blood that knew timeless things made her bend her head in reverence to the woman rocking beside the fire.

In the vast singing silence of the grasslands, magic had been created. And then had come the flow of humankind across the Earth, out of Africa and across Asia, the Americas, Europe, to every gigantic continent and tiny island, until the planet was connected by ever-seeking, ever-curious, ever-creating humankind. Always bringing with them the first magic, connecting it to the magic in new places that wasn't really new magic at all, only waiting for humans to come and listen.

If humans could only listen to each other—listen without prejudice or intolerance—listen with opened minds and compassionate hearts—the connections could be something so splendid, so powerful, so perfect—

"It begins with one," the woman murmured. "And from that one, others. Now you begin to understand."

# Thirty-two

THE FIRELIGHT WAS ONLY CANDLELIGHT now; the circle of stones a Circle of fading power. She looked at no one as she spoke aloud the words, easily recalled from a hundred rituals, that would thank and disperse the Guardians, and when that was finished she gathered up the leavings: wood, glass bowls, incense pots cold with ash, and little black carvings of ravens. These she placed on the black marble altar, and to them she called flames enough to burn and melt and char.

The women were the first to stir. Lydia, blinking at Holly with wide, speculative eyes; Kate, searching instinctively with long fingers in the pockets of her robe to find a restorative herb; Leah Towsley, rocking lightly back and forth for a moment on her knees before the dazed expression left her dark eyes. Holly smiled at her, and very nearly bowed her head once more. But that would only confuse her. Denise did not move at all.

"I'm not going to ask what happened," Kate began slowly.

"Wise choice," Holly told her. Any explanation she might attempt would, in honor, be authentic—but not the truth, the way the sparkle wasn't really the diamond.

"That's what I was afraid of." She sorted among the little colored silk bags of herbs before her on the floor, selected one, and breathed deep of its scent. "*That's* better." Pushing herself to her feet, she moved to Alec, Ian, Nicky, and Martin, pressing the sachet to each nose in turn. Holly was amused to note that Kate automatically moved sunwise around the Circle; Elias had trained them all very well.

He was recovering, too, gaze sharpening as it probed the Four Quarters and found them quiet. The diminishing fire on the altar made him arch a brow. He frowned at Holly. "You?"

"Yes."

"All of it?"

"All."

He grunted with effort as he got to his feet. "Good." He stared down at Noel. "Dead?"

"Very."

Kate was ministering to Simon now. The old man drew back from the herbs, wrinkling his nose. "Get that away from me—you'll have me sneezing my sinuses raw, like Holly."

She watched them all—the Reverend sitting on the cold stones, whispering a prayer; the Witches, alert now and tending to each other; the young black deputy marshal who might or might not remember who she had for a little while been—all but Evan. She could not go to him. He must come to her.

"Oh, no!" Kate dropped to her knees beside Denise, feeling frantically at her throat for a pulse. "Simon—"

The Healer and the Apothecary huddled over her, straightening out her limbs twisted all awry, exclaiming angrily at the bleeding scratches. They hadn't a clue, and Holly knew it. She said, "It was her Measure."

Both looked at Noel's corpse and saw the small frayings of the doubled cord crossing his chest.

"Can we stitch it together?" Simon wondered. "Elias, you're the expert—"

The Magistrate shook his head. "I don't know. I only saw a Measure used once." He visibly shook off a memory. "The man died."

Holly delved in a pocket and came up with her needle. "If you're going to try, you'll need this."

"But what will we use for thread?" Kate fretted as she accepted the needle.

"It's not magicked or anything," said Evan from behind Holly, "but it's available." He stepped around her, not touching her, and tugged at a loose bit of cashmere, unraveling a good length before nipping it loose with his teeth. "I'll untie him."

He seemed most intent on watching Kate and Simon at work. Holly refused to let it hurt her. She had to give him time.

"It's over?" the Reverend asked suddenly.

Holly nodded. "It is."

He exhaled a long sigh. "Thank the good Lord God."

"Would you take it amiss if I said 'Amen to that'?" She smiled at him. "I know what you saw tonight wasn't exactly Sunday service, Reverend Fleming."

"Not quite," he replied. He gazed for a moment at the corpse, freed of the Measure that was now in Kate's busy hands. "I can't understand what this man wanted. Deeply as I abhor such an act, if death was his goal, why didn't he commit suicide?"

"He wanted to die, but to die as a god."

"And thereby find eternal life?" Fleming shook his silvery head. "Those he called upon were evil, and thus a threat to the life given us by the Almighty—"

"Who looked upon Creation," Holly murmured, "and saw that it was good."

"Precisely," said the Reverend. "Association with wickedness rejects God's Holy Work. Had Noel called out to Christ Jesus, he would have been saved."

"To defeat death, he had to *become* Death." She spread her hands helplessly. "There may be some sort of logic in that, but damned if I understand what it is."

"Belief is belief because you *believe* it, not because you can prove it."

"Reverend," she said, "as different as our beliefs are, we do agree about that. But can there be only one path? Life is a journey toward knowledge—of self, of the world, of Deity—and if we don't challenge ourselves to seek and to know, doesn't that betray what we're meant to be? Isn't the journey the important thing?"

"It could be argued that this was what this man was doing," he pointed out. "He made Death into a divinity, and sought after it. I would say that the striving does count, if it is toward the Light."

"Yes, I see what you mean, and you're right." She chuckled. "Did you ever think you'd hear a Witch tell you that?"

There was a twinkle in his eyes as he replied, "There's hope for you yet."

"Oh, but that's exactly it!" Holly exclaimed. "That's what Noel didn't have! It isn't 'Where there's life, there's hope,' it's exactly the other way around!"

" 'Where there is hope, there is life.' I must admit that *you* are right—and I may steal that for my next sermon." He gave her a smile. "Nevertheless, I know that the way shown to me *is* the true path. I pray that you will find enlightenment."

"Enlighten *me* about something, Holly," Elias said smoothly, coming up in time to hear the Reverend's last few words. "Why is Noel dead?"

"That's an excellent question," she said, using a phrase beloved of all those who need time to think up an answer. The Magistrate's sarcastic eyebrows let her know that he knew she was stalling, so she stalled some more by looking around the cellar. Lydia, Simon, and Kate had departed. Leah Towsley stood by the stairs, arms folded across her chest, unsympathetic gaze fixed on Judge Bradshaw. Alec and Nicky walked the Circle, extinguishing candles, and soon the only light left was the dying smolder of Holly's fire on the altar. Evan was over in the shadows by the table. Ian lifted Denise to carry her upstairs; she was wrapped in her coat, barely conscious, her eyes dull greenish slits in her white face. Martin followed them, cradling his Sword.

"Will she be all right?" asked Reverend Fleming.

"I haven't the slightest idea," Elias said frankly. "We'll do what we can, of course. Holly, I'm waiting."

Inspiration had not made its face to shine upon her.

She freshened the fire a little with a casual gesture, and Fleming's eyes narrowed with an expression that hinted that had he been Catholic, he would have crossed himself. "You might want to head back upstairs now," she told him. "We're finished here, or almost, anyway." There was still that bench to deal with—she wasn't sure if Noel's death had broken its spell.

Fleming took a last look at Noel, shook his head once more, and started for the stairs. Elias eyed her again.

"If I didn't know better, I'd say you reinforced that suggestion a little."

"Maybe he just likes redheads."

"Holly?" Alec touched her elbow. "Are you all right?"

"Fine. Tired."

"Aren't we all? Elias, what do you want to do about Noel's body?"

Before she could stop herself, Holly said, "There can't be an autopsy."

"Why not?" He was looking at her again, and she gulped.

"Well, the thing of it is—"

Holding up a stone raven, Nick approached and asked, "Anybody want a souvenir?"

"Holly—," Elias warned.

"Take one," she invited. "After all, you're named for the Prophet Elias, and ravens fed him in the desert."

"If I have to ask one more time—"

"All right, all right! It was heart failure." Which had the virtue of being true. Sort of.

Alec looked her in the eyes. "Oh, really?" He never let her get away with anything.

"He hasn't *got* a heart anymore," she said bluntly. "It's gone. It was—taken. I know there's no hole in his chest and no blood and no visible reason why he's dead. But he is, and that's why—and there can't be an autopsy or they'd ask all kinds of questions we can't answer."

"'We'?" Bradshaw asked.

"We," Evan confirmed, and Holly nearly jumped out of her skin. "You may have noticed, Your Honor, that technically we're all accessories—and anyone who wants to sort out who's before the fact and who's after, be my guest. Alec, you want to help me with this?"

Alec took Noel's shoulders and Evan, his feet. "The bench," he directed. "But don't touch it unless you want to get stuck to it. I don't know if it still works, but let's not chance it. When I say 'Drop him,' let go completely. Okay?" A few moments later Noel hung suspended over the stone bench. "Now!" Evan said, and they dumped him onto it with a thud of flesh. Holly shivered. He looked just like that painting of Marat, dead in the bathtub. Evan dug into a pocket of his jeans and brought out a small plastic evidence bag.

"What the hell is that?" Alec asked.

"Once a cop, always a cop—even when being a cop is useless. This is wood from that table over in the corner. Forensics would almost certainly ID it as the splinters in Susannah's knee. Are we all eye to eye about who's guilty?"

"Case closed," said Elias. "Court adjourned."

"Good. Nick, gimme that goddamned bird." This and the plastic bag he let fall onto Noel's chest. "And if you quote Edgar Allan Poe at me, I'll shoot you where you stand."

"Actually, I was considering it—but not the one you have in mind."

" 'Dream within a dream'?" Evan suggested.

Nick shook his head. " 'Thank Heaven! the crisis—/ The danger is past, / And the lingering illness / Is over at last—/ And the fever called "Living" / Is conquered at last.' "

"There's another one," Alec murmured. "Not Poe, just as appropriate, but perhaps more than he deserves. 'Death makes angels of us all, and gives us wings where we had shoulders smooth as raven's claws.' " He glanced around as if waiting for someone to place the quote. "Jim Morrison."

Elias walked slowly around the bench. "I'll do the honors," he said, kindling new fire to the black candles. They blazed up like flamethrowers, circling the corpse, plucking at it, soon to ignite it and burn the evidence to ashes.

"Can we get out of here now?" Alec asked. "Cremation tends to smell a bit."

They climbed the stairs to the foyer, where the others waited. The sky had lightened to pearl gray through the high windows. Soon sunlight would refract off the hundreds of crystals in the chandelier, casting rainbows over the walls and floor.

"Finally!" Martin exclaimed. "We were about to send a search party."

"You were right, Elias," Nick said suddenly. "This place does have a weird feel to it. Like something's waiting. Alec, are you sensing anything?"

"I think I'm still glutted from what went on down there. Not to mention I feel a migraine coming on—"

"Where's Denise?" Elias asked.

Martin gestured to the open door. "Kate and Simon took her outside—she seems to be coming around. No telling if there's any permanent impairment."

"We can only hope," Ian muttered, then had the grace to look abashed. "Umm — Lydia went with them. Are we finished?"

"We can only hope," said Marshal Towsley. "Your Honor, if this kind of thing goes on a lot, I hope you won't mind if I ask for hardship duty pay."

"No, Marshal," the Magistrate told her. "This night was . . . unique."

Alec arched a brow. "We can only, et cetera."

"'The night is far spent,'" Reverend Fleming said suddenly, "'the day is at hand: let us therefore cast off the works of darkness, and let us put on the armor of light. Let us walk honestly, as in the day. . . .'" He smiled slightly, and before Elias or Alec could pull their usual tricks, said, "Romans. And I'm ashamed to say I'm not certain of the chapter or verse."

"*Ego te absolvo,*" Holly responded, winking at him. Maybe he really did like redheads; he winked back.

Evan led the way toward the front door and breathed in a huge gulp of un-sullied sea-scented dawn air. As Holly lengthened her stride to catch up with him, a bit of uneven paving snared her toe and she fell flat on her face.

"Oh, for — !" Evan strode back to where she sprawled, gathered her up and stood, wobbling a bit.

"My hero." She rubbed her knees, already sore from crawling across the cellar.

"Hero with an incipient hernia." He carried her toward the door. "You weigh a ton."

"Yeah, that's my gallant knight in tarnished armor," she retorted, and wrapped her arms around his shoulders. He chuckled, then bent to kiss her. When he drew back, she asked, "What was that for?"

"Just makin' sure."

"Of what?"

"That I'd rather kiss you than breathe."

"Oh," she replied in a very small voice. A moment later: "Evan? Can we go home now?"

He angled his head to look at her. "You mean Virginia, don't you?"

"Just for a little while. Would it be all right?"

"We can spend the next fifty years there if you want. I think we should raise the kids on the ancestral acreage."

She gaped at him. "How did you — ?"

The old stones of the house began to rumble. Evan swore and tightened his grip on her, running for the threshold. Splinters of wood, shards of window glass, chips of plaster, fragments of stone rained down. Holly choked on clouds of dust and dirt, her attention drawn upward as the chandelier chimed and rattled, swinging in erratic arcs. Metal whined as the anchoring plate wrenched from its bolts.

Evan was constantly and creatively cursing. She heard Nicky's voice shout a frenzy of what had to be Rom spellchants, and Alec's roar of their names. The sun had cleared the surrounding treetops, its thin November light angling through the wide-open door.

*"This place does have a weird feel to it. Like something's waiting—"*

Waiting for them, or waiting for the sunlight to prompt it? She would never know—and if they weren't through that door in the next five seconds, neither she nor Evan would ever know anything again. He stumbled, breathing hard, his arms locked around her. And she realized she wasn't really frightened at all. He was here; she was safe.

The ringing crash of the chandelier was a faint clamor compared to the tumult of stone and glass and metal and wood that instantly followed. Deafened by the noise and blinded by swirls of powdered debris, Holly's senses contracted to three: the warm smell of Evan, the dry taste of dust, and the secure feel of his arms around her—and the chunk of something hard and heavy that smashed into her left arm.

He staggered to his knees, not letting her go, and wet grass tangled in her fingers. They were outside. She coughed and sneezed, blinked teary eyes, and hid her face in the warm hollow of Evan's throat. Her ears stopped ringing in time for her to hear Nicky's voice, his accent thick with relief.

"Not a scratch on either of them," he said, and Holly didn't see any use in correcting him; it was just a bruise.

"Thanks, Nick," Evan said shakily.

"I had nothing to do with it. It was Holly. Your St. Michael medal."

He sighed, a long descending note, then joggled her a bit in his arms. She looked up at him. "Told ya you're magic," he teased, and his dragon's eyes danced.

Nick left them to each other, and Holly shifted in Evan's embrace.

"Stay put," he ordered.

"Okay. It's your chiropractor's bill."

"Speaking of magic," he said as he rose to his feet again and carried her toward Alec's Mercedes, "are you going to tell the Rev why you shook his hand?"

"Why I—?" She blinked. "I guess I did, didn't I?"

"Uh-huh."

"I didn't do it on purpose."

"Uh-huh."

"Evan, I didn't!" She wrapped her arms more securely around his shoulders. "I really didn't. I think it's like when I'm writing, and I'll put in some detail that seems like a throwaway, just local color or whatever, but then twenty chapters later I realize I was subconsciously setting myself up for something important and didn't realize it while I was doing it, and—"

"Holly."

"Yes, *Éimhín?*"

"Lady love."

"What, my lord?"

"Shut the fuck up."

# Epilogue

"COME ON," HOLLY SAID, taking Elias's arm. "Let's go for a walk."

They left by the kitchen door, hurrying past the chicken coop to escape the suffocating smell of hot feathers, and headed for the paddocks. The August heat had been ferocious all afternoon, but as shadows lengthened the air began to cool.

"So how d'you like Woodhush Farm?" asked Holly.

"I wasn't sure what to expect," he admitted. "Ramshackle Rustic, Colonial Overkill—and you could've been wearing anything from overalls held together with twine to jodhpurs and a hacking jacket."

She laughed. "It's just an old Southern homestead. Couple dozen horses, a few cows, chickens, cats—and Evan's big old mutt burying hot dogs in the irises."

"I'm surprised you got Lachlan to agree to live here. I would've thought 'You Belong to the City' was his theme song."

"Scratch an Irishman, find a peasant underneath. This spring he actually volunteered to help Aunt Lulah with the vegetable garden."

"How's he like country life?"

"He's getting used to it."

"You know what I meant, Holly. Has he recovered from last Samhain?"

"Well, he'll always have the scar on his chest. I think I finally figured out why. Breath, blood, flesh, bone—I forgot 'skin.' And the medal doesn't protect him from accidents, either. He broke a toe out in the barn this May, and you should've seen the bruises the first time he fell off a horse. I spelled against enemies, you see. Not mishaps."

"But aside from the toe and the bruises—?"

She climbed over a split-rail fence and waited for him to follow. "He had trouble sleeping at first. Dreams, of course—we both had nightmares for months—but he kept saying it was so *quiet* here. He was used to traffic, sirens, people yelling, and here there's nothing but owls and the wind, maybe a horse whickering in the paddocks. . . ."

They passed a group of mares with their yearlings, then climbed a rise where a small graveyard spread within a white picket fence. There were about fifty marble headstones, a little fleet of white sails on an eternal voyage through snowstorms and sunshine . . . never going anywhere.

"That was the first of us to live at Woodhush," Holly said, leaning on the fence, pointing to the nearest headstone. "Thomas Flynn. His great-granddaughter married a McClure."

Bradshaw read names aloud. "Sarah Amaryllis, Elizabeth Sage—Petunia Pearl?"

"Over there's the one I pity most—Clarissa Tulip Bellew, who was called Lippy all her life. Probably accurate, too," she mused. "All the Bellews could talk the hind leg off a donkey and still have breath to cuss out the parlor maid for setting the silver wrong."

"I'll refrain from the obvious remark about familial characteristics," he told her. "What made you decide on Rowan?"

"Evan went through all the family names and liked that one best. The rowan is a very magical tree, you know—sacred to Brighid, used for runes and divining rods, and the berries even have a tiny pentagram on them."

"The Witch Wood," Elias murmured. "Susannah Rowan Lachlan—it's a good name."

She glanced sidelong at him. "I can't believe you actually thought she and Kirby might be yours."

"Until you sent the pictures, I wasn't sure. You have to admit the timing was a little dicey."

"Nonsense. They were early. Twins often are. And a good thing, too, or I wouldn't have any back left. Six-and-a-half pounds each!"

"Oh, they're Evan's all right," Elias said. "Susannah's got his hairline, Kirby has his nose."

"I know. Poor little guy."

He grinned at her. "There's always rhinoplasty."

She opened the iron gate and started picking weeds off the graves. He crouched down to help.

After a while Holly asked, "Did Marshal Towsley ever remember anything?"

"Not that I can tell. We've never really talked much about it. I'm not sure what there is to remember."

"How very unsubtle a hint. What do *you* remember about that night?"

"It's the feelings that have stayed with me, and the shame of feeling some of them. The rage, mostly. Hating Noel. Wanting to kill him. It was rather a shock to find I couldn't give him exactly what he wanted."

Holly nodded. "I find myself agreeing with Reverend Fleming—it seems an unnecessarily complicated way to commit suicide. But I guess Noel just didn't like being human. That's the only way I can explain it to myself. Being human and therefore mortal, he saw Death as his enemy. And it terrified him."

"He asked the crucial question all of us ask eventually: What happens when I die? And look at his answer, Holly. To become a god, to be immortal and powerful and free of the fear—"

"How could anyone live like that? He couldn't endure being human, knowing one day Death would come for him and he'd have no power against it—I can't imagine what it must have been like, to exist in such appalling fear, to be so completely devoid of joy."

"Susannah told me once that it doesn't matter what your faith is, as long as it provides comfort and keeps you in touch with the better part of yourself. As long as it helps you to celebrate what it is to be human. To find the joy in living, to create something meaningful of your life."

"I miss her."

"Me, too."

She gathered up an armful of weeds and threw them out into the field. "Let's go down to the springhouse."

She led the way downhill to a bend in the creek, and they were silent until Elias observed, "You've been incommunicada since Christmas. Any chance you'll rejoin the real world anytime soon?"

"Oh, Elias," she smiled, "this *is* the real world!"

"A century ago, maybe." He kicked at a rock.

"And a century from now, if we're all lucky," she retorted. "My kids will make their mud pies with dirt their ancestors farmed. So will my grandchildren and their grandchildren, I hope. What could be more real than that?"

"You're hiding," he accused.

"I did my hiding in New York." She opened the door of the springhouse and went to a cupboard for a quart Mason jar of clear liquid. "You couldn't make it to the wedding, so you didn't get your party favor," she teased. "This is some of the very last batch of the late Widow Farnsworth's 'shine. Uncle Nicky says that in Hungarian, this stuff is called *keri'te'sszaggato'*—literally, 'fence-ripper.'"

He accepted the jar warily. "No smoking for twenty-four hours after imbibing?"

Holly nodded. "And no imbibing anywhere near an open flame."

"Must've been a hell of a wedding."

"It was. We should probably be getting back. Lulah likes to begin just before sunset."

"What made you choose Lugnasadh for the—what shall we call it? Not a christening."

"Just a blessing, Elias. Nothing more complicated than that. I chose tonight because the twins are two months old as of this morning. And also because I can almost get into some decent clothes again!"

THE GUESTS WERE FEW AND, with the exception of Evan and possibly the twins, all Witches. A baptism would occur when the Lachlans went to visit his relations at Thanksgiving, but tonight's was a gathering upon which any church would frown.

Then again, it *was* Lammas, Holly reflected as she gathered Kirby from his crib. Cousin Clary called it that, rather than Lugnasadh, with a wink. "Loaf Mass" in the Catholic calendar, celebrating the harvest; another co-opting of a much more ancient holiday. It was the most popular date for the movable feast of St. Catherine, when in some villages the burning Catherine Wheel of her martyrdom would be rolled down a hill—remnant of a rite in which the flaming disk representing the sun-god in his decline.

Evan cuddled Susannah in the crook of his elbow, tickling her cheek with one finger. Daddy's Little Girl, Holly thought with fond amusement. She couldn't wait to watch him go completely apeshit once boys started hanging around. *"I'm the sheriff in these parts, I carry a gun, and I know how to use it. Have her home by ten or else."*

She'd been apprehensive, but he was honestly enjoying his new job. Cousin Jesse was a year from retirement, and had taken to Evan like pen to paper. After the Lachlans moved here permanently in January, the men had spent two days a week driving every road in the county, checking in on all the residents, getting them familiar with Evan as their new deputy sheriff. By now he was finished handing off his case files (Wyatt, Dillon, and McCloud were now administered by others) to the Marshals Service in Richmond, so he didn't have to commute a couple of times a month anymore. This was his third law enforcement agency, and, he swore, his last.

He was, contrary to all her apprehensions, happy here. He was satisfied with his work, and he loved the house, which they had to themselves. Lulah had moved into the old overseer's cottage by the creek with every evidence of relief. *"Kickin' me out of my own home? Don't be more dim-witted than Nature made you, boy. You think at my age I want to be cleanin' and tidyin' that big old barracks? No, this'll do me just perfect. I'll be close enough to spoil the children, and a far enough walk so you won't get on my nerves."*

As for the noise and excitement and adventure of New York City—who needed it? Holly didn't. Neither, it seemed, did Evan. She gazed at him now, tall and sun-browned, cuddling his daughter. Yes, this was *real.*

He was wearing his wedding present, an antique gold stickpin set with a blue-green raindrop emerald. It had first been worn by William Alexander Mc-Clure at his marriage to Delilah Rose Mayfield in 1866. Evan had positioned it at a rakish angle in the lapel of his tuxedo jacket. He wasn't wearing a tie— indeed, he had on jeans and a white cotton shirt, and the inevitable ostrich-hide cowboy boots.

Her own wedding gift was on the little finger of her right hand: a gold signet ring engraved with the Lachlan crest. Around the shank was carved her name in Irish Gaelic: Cuilenn Eilís MacLeòire Lochlainn. She hadn't been kidding when she'd told Elias she could finally get back into some of her clothes, though the DKNYs and Armanis were not only still out of the question, they were packed away. Levi's and shorts, summer dresses, workshirts, T-shirts: these were all she needed. This evening it was a yellow blouse, black trousers, and her mother's pearls. She hadn't bought a stitch of clothing in months—except for nursing bras.

The table, covered by a linen cloth embroidered in yellow and orange, was decorated with wheat sheaves, lavender wands, a vase of full-blown white roses, and a corn dolly. Pitchers were full of lemonade, various teas, and Cousin Clary's applejack and elderberry-flavored mead; brass serving plates held five kinds of bread; earthenware bowls contained fruit salad, three-bean salad, and Evan's experiment with the tomatoes, green peas, and onions he had grown himself.

Alec and Nicky, Clarissa and Jesse, Lulah and Elias: these were the sponsors, or patrons, or godparents, or whatever term one wanted to use. They had come bearing gifts and magic to celebrate the Sabbat and welcome the twins. Holly swayed lightly back and forth with her son in her arms, ostensibly to soothe him, fully aware that Kirby Nicholas Alexander Lachlan was a child who never required soothing. His sister might be screaming at the top of her lungs, and all he ever did was cast an annoyed glance in her direction and go back to sleep. He was sleeping now, black hair curling around his cheeks and forehead, missing the honor of having his very first Circle called by a Magistrate around the dining room table that tonight served as altar.

East, North, West, South. Guardians invited; candles lit. Smudge sticks of lavender and sage and rosemary, sent by Kate, wafted sweet smoke through the air.

Elias said, "To the Shining God we offer thanks. To the Goddess of Plenty we give homage. For the harvest they have nurtured, the beauty they have provided, and the children who join us in their first celebration, we honor them on this night of Lugnasadh."

Alec smiled at Holly and Evan, saying, "We've all gone Irish for this, so here's my contribution." Placing two silver-banded amulets on the table—one moonstone, one malachite—he went on, "May you have the hindsight to know where you've been, the foresight to know where you're going, and the insight to know when you're going too far."

"*You* can pretend to be as Irish as you like," Nick said. "Me, I'm Rom—and as everyone knows, *tshatshimo Romano*: 'truth is expressed in Romany.' So, to go along with these—" He set two small leather drawstring bags on the table. "—*Kon del tut o nai shai dela tut wi o vast*, or, 'He who willingly gives you a finger will also give you the whole hand.' Watch your fingers, little ones."

"Sound reasoning," said Clarissa as she took her place. "But I'll stick with the Irish. Leprechauns, castles, good luck, and laughter, lullabies, dreams, and love ever after." Her gifts of small pillows stuffed with herbs were laid on the table.

Lulah's turn came next. "These were some of my brother's favorites, the man who was these children's grandfather. May you never forget what is worth remembering, or remember what is best forgotten. May you get all your wishes but one, so you always have something to strive for. May the saddest day of your future be no worse than the happiest day of your past." She tucked two folded child-size quilts among the other gifts.

"My cousin Margaret," said Jesse, "who was these children's grandmother, learned this one from our grandmother. It goes, 'A sunbeam to warm you, a moonbeam to charm you, and a sly Irish angel so nothing can harm you.'" Two bottles of Irish whiskey were his gift. "Not until you're twenty-one," he said, shaking a finger at the children. "By which time this should be smooth as a barbershop shave."

At last Elias came forward and said, "A Magistrate is supposed to take the part of baptizing priest at this point, and outline the basics of the faith. Thing is, there's no one right way, no single correct path. Whatever you choose to create of your lives, you have worthy examples in your parents. If you live with integrity and honor, and keep getting back up if you stumble and fall, you'll do just fine." He rested long, gentle fingers on each child's head. "May the strength of Three be in your journey: the strength of your mother, and of your father, and of your own soul. So mote it be."


LATE THAT NIGHT, WHEN CLARISSA and Jesse had gone home and everyone else had gone to bed, Holly and Evan went upstairs to check on the twins.

"Sleeping like the sweet darling little angels they aren't," she observed.

"Look at all this," Evan muttered. "A whole zoo of stuffed animals and enough clothes to stock an outlet mall."

"Your pardon, sir, but who came back from D.C. last month with two fuzzy little baby-panda toys? This isn't to forget the two pairs of pint-sized cowboy boots. And are you *ever* going to tell me the truth about where you got those awful things?"

"Nope." He grinned; she growled; the rocking chair purred.

"Brigand, you stay out of here or I'll tie your tail in a knot." Holly marched in, snared the cat, and tossed her toward the door. She landed nimbly, twitched her luxuriant white tail as if daring a follow-through on the threat, and stalked off. After making sure the baby monitors were switched on, Holly kissed both children and returned to the doorway. "You're wearing that silly look again."

"I've earned it." Circling her shoulders with one arm, he guided her next door to their bedroom. "How bad a hangover do you think His Honor's gonna have tomorrow?"

"Epic." She snorted. "His own fault. He's the one who opened the jar and spiked the lemonade."

"I was expecting he'd give the kids something a little less normal. A gift certificate for a swingset and wading pool isn't exactly Witchy."

"I thought it was sweet." She watched as he unbuttoned his shirt and rubbed reflexively at the scar on his chest. It had become a habit, and it reminded her of something Bradshaw had said earlier. "By the way, he thinks you must be going crazy here." When Evan arched an inquisitive brow, she explained, "City boy all discombobulated in the country. No Starbucks within seventy-five miles."

"No locks on my doors, either. No smog, no mob hits to clean up, no whack-job taxi drivers, no gridlock, no wondering what's in the water this week, no neighbors hollering at two in the morning—" He grinned. "Are we sensing a trend?"

"I did worry about it, you know."

"So did I."

"You never said—"

"I didn't want you to fuss." He sat on the bed to haul off his boots. "It's slower here, yeah, but there's a rhythm to the place, like New York has a rhythm. I just had to keep listening until I heard it."

Holly rested her hands on his shoulders. "And what do you hear, *a chuisle?*"

He smiled. "People who don't live as fast, because they're not afraid of not living enough."

"So you're okay with staying here? Really okay, I mean?"

"Lady love," he said in a tone of infinite patience, "have I ever said anything to make you think I'm not? Am I the type of guy who'd keep his mouth shut about something like that? And are we ever gonna get to bed tonight?"

"In order: No, no, and whenever you're up for it, Sheriff darlin'."

# Author's Note

TO THOSE WHO ARE DISAPPOINTED that this isn't another book—*The Captal's Tower* or an offering in the Golden Key or Dragon Prince universes—well, what can I tell you? Life happens. So does clinical depression. If it happens to you, and I earnestly hope it doesn't, *get help*. When I was able to write again, I wanted—needed—to do something entirely different from anything I'd done before. This book certainly is that. *Spellbinder* is a considerable accomplishment for me: it wouldn't exist if I hadn't sought therapy.

My Aunt Gena once complained that the names in my novels were weird. I asked if she'd believe in a world that had dragons or Mage Globes and guys called George. I never expected it to be so difficult to name people in my own world and time. When choosing contemporary names, one runs into the problem of "If I call this guy George, then every George I've ever met will think I'm writing about him." (Although one ought never to overlook the Author's Unique Revenge aspect, which is when you casually mention that if so-and-so isn't nice to you, you'll put him in your next book and make him the palace eunuch.) No one in this novel is anyone I know. What I ended up doing was stealing names from my ancestors, with several exceptions—one of which is "Scott Fleming" (not his real name), winner of a convention charity auction. I hope he thinks the money he paid was worth it!

In case you were wondering: the subtitle of this novel was cribbed from Dorothy L. Sayers's *Busman's Honeymoon: A Love Story with Detective Interruptions* (pretty cheeky of me, huh?); the tale of the fur-lined tent is true (my father *really* hated the cold!); *Laranja* is performed with Grand Marnier and coffee at Armand's Restaurant in New Orleans; and finally, for anyone interested in my line of descent from Mary Bliss:

Mary Bliss m. Joseph Parsons
Joseph Parsons m. Elizabeth Strong
Noah Parsons m. Mindwell Edwards
Thankful Parsons m. John Deane
Rhoda Deane m. Willam Powers
William Powers m. Elizabeth Cutter
Benjamin Powers m. Martha Stevens

Elizabeth Rebecca Powers m. Philetus Leroy Fisk
Claude Ernest Fisk m. Stella Alderson
Alma Lucile Fisk m. Robert Dawson Rawn

Many thanks to: Russell Galen and Danny Baror; Beth Meacham; Mary Anne Ford, world's bestest best-friend; Laurie Rawn, my one and only Sister Unit; Caislin Weathers; Gena and John Lang (on the occasion of their sixty-fifth wedding anniversary) for being my Aunt Gena and Uncle John; Jane Endries and Beverly Haskin for reading early drafts; the denizens of the bulletin board (http://www.MelanieRawn.com); the good folks at Jitters on Route 66 for triple-shot mochas and endless iced tea; and all the various Busbys, Browns, and Johnsons for being such wonderful neighbors to the Crazy Writer Next Door.

Most of all, *always*, Mom and Daddy. I miss them more than I can ever say.

Melanie Rawn
Flagstaff, Arizona